GW00771730

A FLOWER IN WINTER

David James

Copyright © David James 2024
Published: 2024 by The Book Reality Experience
Leschenault, Western Australia

ISBN: 9781923020894 - Paperback Edition
ISBN: 9781923020924 - E-Book Edition

All rights reserved.

The right of David James to be identified as author of this Work has been asserted by him in accordance with sections 77 and 78 of the Copyright, Designs and Patents Act 1988.

This book is a work of fiction based upon historical events. Except for Captain Mallory and Sim Gokkes, any resemblance to actual people, living or dead, is purely coincidental. Parts of Rotterdam and Chatham Dockyard have been altered for the sake of the story.

No part of this publication may be reproduced, stored in retrieval system, copied in any form or by any means, electronic, mechanical, photocopying, recording or otherwise transmitted without written permission from the publisher. You must not circulate this book in any format.

Cover Design by Brittany Wilson | Brittwilsonart.com

The love of an old man is like a flower in winter
Portuguese proverb

This book is dedicated to the memory of
David Gokkes
murdered in Auschwitz, February 1943

Prologue

My father, Jimmy Gale, died on Christmas Eve 1990.

It was a peaceful death. For the staff of Lymington Cottage Hospital, he was just another old man slipping away. For me, the hours before he died brought an unexpected intimacy.

Arriving at my father's bedside soon after lunch, he asked me to clean his false teeth as bits of parsley were stuck behind them. Teeth back in place, I wiped his face with a damp flannel and sat down.

Clean, comfortable and lucid, he gazed at me, his eyes the bluest and clearest I had ever seen. He seemed to be looking deep inside me, a feeling I only had once before, when my son first opened his eyes and stared at me.

My father stretched out his hand, took hold of mine and began to talk. His voice was weak and he stopped often to sip water and compose himself.

Those moments are engrained in my memory, along with a deep regret that he had never shared his story with me before, and I had never thought to ask.

We remained hand-in-hand as the hours went by, his voice growing quieter and quieter.

There was a long silence when he finished. I thought he had gone to sleep until he squeezed my hand and told me a story about a boy. He then told me what he wanted me to do. I promised I would do as he asked and he closed his eyes for the last time.

Two months later my wife died. Her death was a great shock and it swept that promise from my mind but in 2020 a random act of kindness unlocked my memory.

It was after a concert near my home. I was talking to one of the young players, when her mother joined us. I remarked how well the girl had played, whereupon the woman put her arms round my neck and hugged me. It was a spontaneous and open-hearted gesture. I must have looked startled because she hurried away.

Curious, I asked the conductor who she was, thinking we may have met before.

"Ah," he said, "that's Martha Da Souza."

Da Souza.

It was the name of the boy my father had told me about.

Memories of the afternoon he died flooded back.

Next day I asked my old friend, the local doctor, if he knew Martha Da Souza. What he told me was intriguing. Apparently, Martha was the granddaughter of a sailor whose name, Da Souza, was on a gravestone in the local church. He understood she had kept her maiden name to honour him.

I went to the churchyard and found a small stone inscribed "Samuel Da Souza" together with the name of his ship, *HMS Persephone*, and the date he died.

This was the boy who saved my father's life and whose family my father made me promise to find. I was to tell them what had happened and give them a small package from his desk.

Subsumed by grief after my wife's death, I had forgotten all about it but now remembered putting it in a trunk with his other belongings. It had remained closed since his funeral. Now it lay in my hands.

Feeling my father's eyes upon me, his words began to return.

PART ONE

1.

Rotterdam - 1940

Samuel looked at the clock and leapt to his feet. "Must go Papa. Bye." He dropped his schoolbook and ran out.

Simon gazed out of the window as the boy raced down the narrow road, dodging between slow moving trucks, cars and carts to avoid pavements crowded with people.

Simon knew where his son was heading, unlike the growing crowds of refugees. He would be in time to take the lines of the paddle steamer *De Ruyter*. She was not due in until 1605.

Steamboat Captains prided themselves on their punctuality. Of them all, Kapitein De Groot, or Paul to Sam's family, was the most punctilious. It went badly for the deckhand who fumbled a mooring line, or the boy on the quay if they were slow dropping it over a bollard.

Only when the Kapitein was ashore were passengers permitted to leave and embark.

Simon smiled. He had been a wharf-rat himself, head filled with tales of the sea by his father. It had been stoomboten he had loved best, the endless beat of their paddles, the quiet power of their single engine, the smell of burning coal, hot oil and steam. He loved the way they traded up and down the River Lek, carrying people, cattle and cargo between towns and the great seaport of Rotterdam. He loved the unfussy ways of their Kapiteins and crew, the swiftness of each turn-around, the gleaming copper and brass on the bridge and in the engine room, and the workaday cleanliness on deck and below.

He sighed. His dear son Sam was just the same; he might be only thirteen but he was already a veteran of the quayside, a nimble handler of ropes and keen carrier of bags for overladen passengers. He knew the cheapest and cleanest hotels and rooms; where meneer could get his shoes repaired or mevrouw find a doctor. He could answer most enquiries a stranger to this teeming city might make, especially the thousands of Jews pouring into Rotterdam from towns upriver and beyond.

What he could not tell them was when the next ship was sailing for America.

*

A few days later Paul de Groot, the steamboat captain, came into *Da Souza's* café. Simon beckoned him over, delighted to see him. They sat in the quiet of the family back room, savouring their coffee and, for Simon, his first cigar of the day. Paul broke the silence. "How is Rachel?"

Simon shrugged. "She is mending. Solomon is pleased with her progress but she may need another operation. He won't know until he takes the plaster off." He smiled. "If she doesn't, she'll be ready to come home on the 10th of May."

Paul smiled back. "And Samuel?" Simon took a sip of the rich black coffee. "Sam blames himself for his sister's accident. Left the front door open and she followed her big brother. She got hit by that cart and broke her leg. Sam can't forgive himself even though he wasn't really to blame."

Paul nodded. "He's a good lad so takes it hard." He glanced at Paul. "I have been thinking about you and your family and have a proposition."

Simon looked up. "We're not in trouble, Paul. Rachel's leg is mending and business is good." He studied the glowing end of his cigar. "Judith is worried but what can we do? The world is full of worries."

He glanced again at Paul who was frowning. "What is it?"

"It is the war, Simon. The bloody war." Paul rarely swore. "It's a matter of days before the Germans come. This man Hitler is different from the Kaiser. This is not 1914. They will invade and we will surrender."

"G-d, Paul, that bad?"

"That bad," Paul replied quietly, "Probably worse. Especially for you Dutch Jews." He gazed fondly at his friend. "There are many of my countrymen who hate Jews. Do you think you will be safe when the Germans come?"

Simon shook his head slowly.

"We will fight," Paul continued, "but we can't stop them." He gestured to the full café beyond the door. "How many of your customers are locals these days? How many of these people do you know?"

Simon shrugged. "A few. Most are strangers…"

"Refugees," Paul interrupted.

"Yes." Simon looked down at the old scrubbed table. "Refugees, and not all can pay."

"So you take them in and give them coffee, cakes, and keep them warm. Do you think they feel safe?"

Simon looked into the Dutchman's eyes. "Why are you here?"

Paul put his large brown hand on Simon's arm. "If you stay, Simon, the Germans will close you down. They will take your business. Then they will take you. You know that."

He felt Simon tense and tightened his grip. "You must pack up your home now, while you can." His voice dropped to a whisper. "You must come and live with Christina and me until I can get you all away. We have no immediate neighbours and no family of our own. No-one will know."

Simon stared at the older man. "What does Christina say?"

Paul smiled. "It is Christina's idea!" He laughed, "You don't think I want a scruffy landsman in my house." Simon was about to reply but Paul squeezed his arm. "You and I know what those bastards do to Jews." Simon nodded. "And you know how jealous many Dutchmen are of Jews in our country, what they say about you behind your back?" Simon nodded again. "Those same people who smile at you today will look the other way when the Germans take you away." He paused, his face fierce. "Some will betray you, betray their friends, their countrymen."

It was difficult for Simon to hear what he knew to be true.

Paul went on, "I wasn't just ferrying those German Jews down river. I was listening to what they said. Talking to them, asking questions. The answers were always the same. They are German people. They're Jewish as well but they are Germans. Their families lived there for generations. Now they are running for their lives, betrayed by their own country… and it will happen here." Paul shook his head. "But never to my friends. Not to you, Judith and the children."

"But…"

"No buts. Just tell me this. Have I said anything to surprise you, other than you coming to live with us?"

"Nothing, Paul. Nothing at all." The two men sat in silence as voices murmured in the café. At last Simon spoke, his eyes fixed upon his hands.

"What do we do about Samuel?" He glanced up at his friend. "He will never settle in the countryside. He's a wharf-rat." He paused, "Perhaps he should go far away, go to sea."

"I agree," replied Paul, "which is why I will take him onboard *De Ruyter*. Now. Get him working, used to being part of the crew. My hands all think like me. I wouldn't have anyone onboard who didn't. They're an independent, bloody-minded lot, but very much my crew."

Simon spoke quietly. "And if anything happens here...?"

"Samuel will be somewhere else."

Simon's eyes were hollow.

"He will be another refugee, Paul, just not with a label round his neck."

Paul shook his head. "No Simon. He will be a seaman, working onboard my ship." He gazed at Samuel's troubled father. "Get him a South African passport and make sure he brings nothing onboard that identifies him as a Jew."

Simon refilled their glasses. It gave him time to think.

Paul continued, "If I believe there's going to be trouble, I'll put him onboard a neutral ship and get him away."

Simon put his glass down, untouched.

"You have been thinking about this for a long time, Paul." He took a deep breath, "Whatever happens, we have much to thank you for."

He sat down, facing his friend across the table and took Paul's large, strong hands in his. Turning them so the palms faced upwards, he whispered, "Our lives are in these hands."

Paul shook his head. "Our lives, Simon, are in our hands." He picked up his glass. "To the future. One day at a time."

Simon's hand was shaking as he raised his glass, "One day at a time," he repeated. "It is enough. But how do I tell Judith?"

"She will understand," Paul replied. "You will tell Samuel what is necessary." He paused. "I am glad Judith's parents are dead. We don't have to worry about them." He took a sip of brandy before saying, "You said Rachel could leave hospital on the 10th of May. We collect her and I will put you all onboard a ship to England or America."

Simon put his head in his hands. The only sound was the muted chatter from the café, the bells of passing trams and, once, the faint whistle of a tug on the river.

Paul was silent, waiting for his friend to come back from the dark corners of his mind. He looked at the rigid set of his shoulders, sensing within the bowed head a turmoil of racing thoughts, then the gradual acceptance of an uncertain future without an end in sight. He saw the lift of Simon's head before the man himself was conscious he had reached a conclusion.

*

The following day, Simon sat in the café, watching Samuel over the rim of his coffee cup when the thought entered his mind that his son would make a formidable foe. Although skinny, the years he had spent swimming, fishing and latterly working on the quayside had broadened his shoulders, deepened his chest and given him an air of quiet strength.

They drank their coffee in silence, enjoying the moment. There won't be many more, thought Simon, nor any peace in our lives when the Germans come. Putting his cup down, he cleared his throat.

"Samuel, you must not tell anyone what I'm about to tell you." He sharpened his voice. "Do you understand?"

"Yes Papa."

"Not even your mother. Not yet." Simon paused for Samuel to answer.

His "Yes Papa" was a faint whisper. "Come and sit here," Simon dragged another chair over and patted it. Sam scrambled out of his seat and sat close to his father.

"Do you remember the story of Moses? When he was a baby and his mother hid him in a basket and put him in the bull-rushes?"

"Of course I do." Samuel was indignant.

"Well, tell me why his mother hid him?"

"Oh Papa, what is this, a lesson?" Samuel started brightly, "His mother hid him because the Pharaoh was going to…"

His voice tailed off.

He stared as his father finished for him. "Because the Pharaoh had ordered all Hebrew babies to be drowned."

5

Simon pulled his son to him and swung him onto the table. Still holding him, he said softly, "That is what you have to do, Samuel, hide in the bull-rushes."

Samuel was still for a long moment. Finally, he asked, "Is this because there will be war?"

"Yes, my son, there will be war. Oom Paul had said so. He has told us what he has heard and seen. The Germans are coming."

Samuel sighed and leaned against his father. "What will happen, Papa?"

"If we stay here, they will close our shop and throw us out. Maybe not straight away, but it will happen. Then they will take us to their camps." Simon looked at his son and was saddened to see he was not surprised.

Taking a deeper breath, he went on, "Your mother and I are going to the countryside until Rachel leaves hospital." He hugged Samuel tighter when he felt him flinch.

Samuel stared at his father. "What about me? Why can't I come with you?"

Simon smiled. "What have you been wanting to do for as long as you could walk?"

Samuel stared at his father, eyes wide. "Oom Paul. Oom Paul's *De Ruyter*. Oh Papa." He stopped abruptly. "Do you mean that? I can sail with Oom Paul?"

"That is up to Oom Paul. He asked if he could interview you about joining his crew. But not a word to anyone, my son, not one word."

"I promise, Papa. I promise."

Samuel jumped down as Simon stood up. "We have an agreement, my son. We must shake hands on that. And then you must go to school."

They clasped hands and Simon watched the boy leave. Young as he was, Samuel's childhood was behind him.

*

Simon saw Judith walking towards him and stepped into the middle of the pavement. To her surprise, he took her by both hands and drew her close. Ignoring hisses of disapproval from passers-by, he put his hands on her cheeks and kissed her. For a moment he was at peace, lost in the warmth of their years together.

Then Oom Paul's words came crashing back.

Taking her hand, he led her to the bridge. They often talked there, leaning against the parapet and gazing at the busy Niewe Maas. It was a place that connected them to their history, for their ancestors had arrived here by sea centuries ago. Like many seafaring families, it was to the sea they looked for hope and salvation.

Simon chose his spot with care. Judith smiled as he said, "This will do." It was where he stopped every time they came here. She tucked her arm under his and said quietly, "What troubles you?"

Simon took a deep breath and turned slightly to look at her.

"It is what Paul has told me. It is what we fear." His eyes searched hers.

"There will be war." He saw her flinch. "The Germans will come, soon, within a week or two." Judith paled. He put his arm around her shoulders and said, "We must leave home."

Judith stared at him, shaking. "But where do we go, Sim? How can we just leave?"

Simon held both her arms, buried his face in her hair and said, "We tell everyone we are going to England on the next ship. Then we pay off our girls and close the café."

Judith stared at him. "That is ridiculous," she burst out. "What are you talking about?"

Simon looked around carefully and lowered his voice. She came closer. "We are not going away. We are going to stay here. Paul will take us to his home and we will live there, hiding until Rachel comes out of hospital."

"Hiding?" Judith was incredulous. Her voice rose.

Simon pulled her to him. "Shush, my love. Shush. You must not raise your voice"

She shook herself free and stared at him. "But who are we hiding from?" she hissed, "And why now?"

"Look," he said, pointing to the crowds milling about below them on De Boompjes. "Look at them. Tell me who they are."

Judith's eyes followed his outstretched arm. "They've come off the boats. Down river. They are Jews."

Simon continued, his voice softer, sadder. "They are Jews. Like us. Driven from their homes." He sighed. "By their friends, their neighbours, their countrymen."

They stood in silence, holding each other tightly. Simon could see the pulse beating in her neck, feel her heart, her life.

"And what about Sammi?" she said at last. "You can't keep him in hiding. What will happen to him?"

"Listen, my heart, Paul and I have thought about Sammi. About our dear, restless child. Paul will take him onboard *De Ruyter*. He will work with Old Jannie."

Judith smiled. Jannie was their favourite.

"Sammi will work in the engine room as a fireman. Jannie will teach him and look after him. Paul says there is a place he can hide onboard if he has to. He'll have a berth and will have to keep out of sight. But he will be safe."

Judith was silent for a long time, staring at the brown water swirling below them.

Eventually she raised her head and gazed at Simon, tears running down her cheeks. "Will we be able to see him?"

She knew the answer before Simon spoke. It was written in his eyes.

"Only if it's safe. For him and us."

He paused. Judith knew there was more to come.

"If it becomes dangerous for Sammi on the boat, Paul will get him onboard a neutral ship sailing for America."

"America? So far? Why, Sim, why so far?"

Simon held her tight, his voice hoarse with strain.

"Because it is so far. England is too close. The Germans will come here. France will be next, and then England."

"Why can't we go with Sammi?" Judith was desperate.

Simon stared at her. "We will, if the Germans give us time. But we cannot go until Rachel leaves hospital."

Judith was crying quietly as she gazed hopelessly at her man before pulling away and staring at him, shaking her head as she wiped away her tears.

"Oh Sim," she whispered, "Fate is so cruel."

Rage filled Simon, a fire that would burn to the end of his days. He drew himself up. He would not be crushed; his family would be safe. "Judith, listen to me." Shaking his head, he drew her gently to his chest, put his arms around her, held her as if he would never let go.

His mouth to her ear, he whispered, "This is not our fate. It is not written. This is madness. It is not just Hitler. It is Germany. And here, everywhere. Give people an excuse. Give them someone to blame, to hate, and they will. This time it is Jews. Next time it will be blacks. Or Turks… or anyone. Pick a country." He stopped. His eyes bleak as he stared over her head at the crowds aimlessly meandering up and down.

"We could fight," he whispered so quietly Judith could only just hear, "but what with? Who would lead us? Nee." She felt him shake his head, "We must hide. It's not just the Germans. It is our neighbours," He snorted, "Our countrymen."

Lifting his head and easing her away, he said. "Paul is a man we can trust. We will be safe with him. Sammi will be safe onboard his ship." He looked at her for a long moment, "We must go with Paul."

Judith nodded. "Come," she whispered. "We go home. Now. We have much to do."

∗

Simon stared at the tulips Judith had brought in the market that morning, thinking how beautiful they were, deep gold in a sea-blue vase in the middle of their worn old table. "How many times have I scrubbed that over the years, Opa before me? Who will scrub it when we go?"

He shook himself, focusing on his wife and first-born.

"Sammi." His voice was low. Samuel had never before heard it so serious.

"Yes Papa."

"I have told your mother about our talk this morning. She is happy for you to sign on with Oom Paul, if he will have you."

"Oh Mutti." Sammi moved as if to go to his mother but Simon stopped him with a grunt.

"Listen, Oom Paul will be here soon. You must go upstairs with Mutti and pack your suitcase and your sea-bag."

One of Samuel's prize possessions was Simon's old kit-bag, the one his father had given him when he first went to sea. He had embroidered "S Da S" on it during a dog-watch in the trade winds.

"Leave room in your suitcase for the papers I'll give you. Mutti will help you choose your clothes, working clothes mostly, but pack a clean shirt."

Simon looked at Judith. They had not talked about what Sammi would need. As she was close to tears he stood up.

"Go." He gave Sammi a gentle nudge. "Get your bags out. Mutti will be up in a minute."

Samuel raced upstairs. His adventure was just beginning. He was going to be a sailor.

Simon went to the bottom of the stairs to make sure he had gone into his room. Taking Judith by one hand he drew her back to her chair and sat close to her. He put his other hand on her shoulder and leaned his head against hers. Whispering, he told her what he and Paul had discussed.

"When Sammi goes onboard *De Ruyter* he goes as a South African." He paused. "He will not be a Jew."

Judith gasped.

He quickly went on. "He cannot be a Jew." Holding her tightly he murmured, "He has to leave his faith, his identity here, with us. Do not pack anything that could betray him. It is the only way he will be safe."

Loosening his grip, he turned her chin gently so they could look into each other's eyes. "You understand what I'm saying?"

She nodded, tears trickling down her pale cheeks. Simon wiped them away. "When he goes onboard we say goodbye to him until the war is over." He saw her wince, felt her sag against his chest.

"We will be leaving here very soon. I'll tell Samuel tonight." Judith nodded. "I'll tell him we are closing the café and going to the country. I'll tell him we don't know where yet." He took her hand. "Or would it be easier coming from you?"

Judith sighed deeply, "Nee, my love. You tell him." She shook her head. "I would break down. He needs us to be strong."

He kissed her softly on her brow. "I will tell him."

He looked at his wife. In her eyes he saw their world falling apart. "We have to pack when Samuel has gone and be ready to move when Paul fetches us."

He pushed Judith gently away. "You had better go."

Judith climbed the stairs slowly. Sammi was waiting for her.

"Look," he said, eyes sparkling with excitement. "Here is what I will take."

His clothes were scattered across the bed, among them his suit, a white shirt and best shoes. Judith sifted through them, knowing he would not need much. Paul would give him a set of working clothes, his uniform and an oilskin. She sorted out underclothes, shirts, socks and his favourite Guernsey sweater. He would leave wearing the clothes he always wore on the quayside, his battered tweed cap set aslant, pilot coat unbuttoned and leather boots shining.

She had noticed the scarves many of the crew wore so she packed two of his father's neckerchiefs and a soft, dark blue woollen scarf of her own.

"Roll these up and pack them away in your kit-bag," she said, pointing to the clothes she had selected.

She went out, telling him "I'm going to put together a hussif and your wash-things."

Sammi looked at her quizzically, "What's a hussif?"

Judith smiled, glad he was listening. "Needles, thread, darning wool, a mushroom, spare buttons, a thimble." She stopped. "Have you got a knife?"

"Nee, Mama, you know Papa won't let me have one."

Judith grunted. She had forgotten. "I'll get some scissors and put everything in an old cigar box, with some pencils and paper. It can go in your suitcase."

When Simon called from the room below, Sammi came bouncing out of his room and clattered downstairs. "We're ready, Papa. Mama's made me a hussif." He beamed at his father. "Did you have one when you went to sea?"

"Yes, my son. My mother made mine, just like Mutti's made yours." He turned back to the family room, "Come. I have something for you," he said and looked long and hard at his son. "This, Sammi, is your passport, it is who you are when you leave this house. You will always be Samuel da Souza. All you have to remember is you are now fifteen and you are South African, a Calvinist, but you don't go to church. This is your address. You live in that boarding house in the Schiedam. You have taken people to stay there often enough for you to be familiar with it."

Simon smiled at his round-eyed son. He sat down and pulled him onto his knee. "It's a game, Sammi, a great game. Only you, Oom Paul and Jannie know who you really are and they are playing this game too. You also have to tell people your parents are dead."

Samuel's wail ripped into Simon and Judith.

"Stop that," he said fiercely. "You must listen to me."

Samuel closed his eyes tightly, took a juddering breath and looked at the stern face of his father.

"That's better." Simon's voice softened. "You have to remember this. You must never say we are alive."

He hugged his son to his chest.

"We are all going to play hide and seek. You will be on board and we won't be here."

He pushed Sammi away so he could look at him properly. Taking a deep breath, he went on, "The prize is our lives."

Simon felt Samuel go rigid, heard Judith gasp and hated himself for what he was doing.

"You will be safe with Oom Paul. But only if you do exactly as he says. You will be part of his crew, a fireman. You must never go on deck unless he says you can. You must never go ashore in Rotterdam. Never try to find us."

Tears filled Samuel's eyes.

Simon went on, his voice softer, gentler. "Sammi, you may go to England. If Oom Paul puts you on a ship for England you must go. If that happens, you must go to London, to my Tante Miriam. She lives at this address and will make you welcome."

Simon gave him a piece of paper. "You have to remember this. You must never carry anything that shows you are Jewish, not even the address of an old lady." He took the paper off Sam and smiled fondly at his confused little boy.

"It really is a game, Sammi. We are going to fool the Germans because we are clever and brave and because we have friends like Oom Paul. The Germans have friends here who want to hurt us because we are Jews. So we hide, and wait, and use our brains to keep safe and our courage to keep going."

He picked Sammi up and kissed his forehead. "You, young man, travel as a goy. Your heart is Jewish but your head is not."

"Now, tell me who you are, how old you are and where you live?"

Samuel studied his passport carefully, put it down and repeated slowly what was written there.

"Again, Sammi. With conviction."

Sammi looked at his father and spoke faster and more clearly.

Simon nodded, kissed him again and lowered him to the floor.

"Good boy, Sammi." He paused and suddenly barked, "Are you a Jew?" Samuel recoiled, looking at his father as if he was a stranger. "Nee, meneer, Zuid-Afrikaan."

Simon smiled at his son. "Very good. Now what's that address in London?"

Samuel rattled it off. He always had been a quick learner, words and languages, numbers too.

"Oom Paul will be here soon."

Simon stood. Putting his arms around his wife and son he drew them to his side.

Closing his eyes and bowing his head, he recited the prayer his father had said with him when he went to sea.

"May it be Your will that You will lead us in peace… and cause us to reach our destination in life, joy and peace."

Holding his family tighter, he whispered, "Save us from every enemy and ambush, from robbers and wild beasts, and from all kinds of punishments that rage and come to the world."

Simon raised his head. "May You confer Your blessing upon the work of our hands and grant us grace, kindness and mercy in Your eyes."

His precious family stood for one last time within the strong, safe certainty of his arms. He took a deep breath, steadying himself before stepping away. "I will go outside to wait for Paul."

*

Judith and Samuel walked slowly upstairs, unshed tears in their eyes. Samuel picked up his kit bag and hefted it into his shoulder. He looked around the only room he had ever known and left. His mother stood there, tears now flowing as she watched him go down the stairs. Scolding herself, she picked up one of his neatly ironed kerchiefs and pressed it to her lips. Putting it back in the suitcase, she closed the lid, picked it up and followed him downstairs just as Jannie drew up at the side of *Da Souza's*.

The captain entered the family kitchen, a smile spreading across his face as he saw young Samuel coming towards him.

"So, Samuel Da Souza, you want to join my ship?"

"Oh yes, Oom Paul, I…"

He stopped.

"Yes sir." Crisp and assured, as he had practiced with his father, and standing to attention.

Kapitein De Groot responded to the change in the boy. He put his hands in his reefer jacket and looked closely at him, a stern sea captain looking at a lad with sea fever, wondering how the child would cope with the demands about to be made of him. At the back of his mind was the only question that mattered. Would Samuel betray them?

Samuel stood before him, thirteen years old but looking fifteen. He is a good-looking kid, thought Paul. You saw boys like him every day on any of the hundreds of craft working on the waterways that criss-crossed the Netherlands. They were a breed apart, nimble, sure-footed, quick-witted and old beyond their years. They had proved time and again their loyalty and their worth, at sea and in harbour.

"Tell me, young man, why should I sign you on?"

That was not a question Samuel had been expecting.

He looked down at his shoes, thinking fast.

His parents were standing to one side of the room, watching the tableau play itself out. They knew that Paul would not risk their lives by hiring Samuel if he thought there was the slightest chance he would fold under pressure.

"He is so young," Judith whispered in Simon's ear. "Such a boy to be asked that."

Samuel took his time. His future depended on his answer.

"Sir, I work hard, I'm honest and I do what I'm told."

He looked the captain in the eyes and continued. "I need to be onboard, sir, to save the lives of my family."

He drew a deep breath. "If I had closed the door behind me when I went out, my sister would not be in hospital. We would be going to England together. Sir," Samuel continued, "my father has told me the Germans are coming."

He looks so serious, the old captain thought, so resolute.

He asked. "Why should you be onboard my ship? Why aren't you staying with your family?"

Samuel paused before replying. "Sir. I have a friend, Piet. Piet's father is a Fascist. He hates Jews. If I stay with my family and Piet sees me, his father will know. Piet tells him everything. He will find my family." He took a deep breath. "If I work onboard, Piet will never find me. The Germans will only see a boy. My papers are in order."

Paul looked at Simon and Judith. "Your son has grown up fast. All the children will grow up fast." He turned to the boy. "I will take you onboard, Samuel. You will work with Jannie in the engine room and do exactly what he tells you. You must never come on deck in daylight or in harbour. Is that understood?

"Yes sir," Samuel answered.

"One more question, Sam, if there is a neutral ship sailing for England or America, will you go onboard if I arrange it?"

Samuel paled. His mouth tightened as his eyes flicked over to look at his father and then his mother. Neither moved.

He looked at the captain, a man he had known all his life and replied.

"Yes sir. I will go."

Paul nodded. "You will come onboard now. Say goodbye to your parents. I will wait outside." He looked across at Simon and Judith. "Five minutes," he mouthed as he left.

Simon and Judith looked at the kitchen clock as the door closed. Samuel moved slowly towards them. Pulling out his chair, Simon indicated they should sit. "This," he said, taking a knife from his pocket, "was given to me by my father when I went to sea. It is yours now, Sammi. Keep it sharp."

Simon stood and pressed it into his son's hand. "Opa also gave me some advice which I've never forgotten." He looked at Samuel and smiled, "You know it?"

Sammi nodded and they said together, "One hand for the ship and one for yourself."

Simon picked up Samuel's bags. "I'll take these out while you say goodbye to your mother."

Judith moved swiftly to fold Samuel in her arms. She pressed his head against her neck and closed her eyes as she uttered a silent prayer.

Samuel held her tightly, trembling.

"I haven't said goodbye to Rachel, Mutti. I haven't said goodbye." His voice was tremulous.

"There, Sammi, there," she whispered, soothing, calming, as she had done since he was born, rocking him slightly in her arms. "We haven't told her you're going away, darling, she's too little to understand."

She held him more tightly. "It is for the best." Shaking him very gently, she sighed and said quietly, "You will have much to tell her when you see her." Taking a breath, "Much to tell us."

The door opened behind them. They both stiffened, clung to each other for a brief, final moment, then stood apart.

Simon looked at his wife, face ashen and lips trembling and at his son, his first-born, staring beyond him into the darkness outside.

"Is it time, Papa?" A faint whisper in the quiet of the room.

"It is time," replied his father.

Samuel turned to his mother, kissed her once, kissed her again and walked swiftly to the door. Simon held his arms out wide, gathered his son to his chest and kissed him on both cheeks.

"Go." He pushed Samuel through the door where Oom Paul was waiting.

Judith ran towards the door as Simon was closing it. He held her, stopped her going through, looked at the tears streaming down her cheeks and kissed her.

"Samuel is safe, my love. We will see him soon. We must stay strong for him and for Rachel."

The sudden noise of the engine starting shocked them. Gears clashed, the engine revved a little, then the noise faded as the truck drove down the narrow lane and into the road.

They looked at each other. Their lives had changed forever.

2.

De Ruyter

"Welcome aboard, Samuel." The captain smiled. "It's not how I imagined you would be joining."

Samuel smiled back hesitantly, "No sir. Thank you. I'll work hard."

Paul ruffled his hair. "I know you will. Listen. I have to go ashore. Jannie lives onboard now. He will look after you."

He paused and said in a sterner voice, "Remember, you must keep out of sight."

Samuel replied in a small voice, "Yes sir." And watched his Kapitein walk slowly over the gangway to the lorry and drive away.

Jannie sighed at the sight of the child sitting there, shoulders slumped, close to tears.

"Hey, Sam," he rasped, "Let's go below. I'll show you your bunk and where to stow your kit."

Jannie ushered Samuel to the after companionway. He was looking forward to having company onboard, and especially to having a full-time fireman.

There were no lights as the generator ran off steam. Jannie went swiftly down the steep ladder, kit-bag in one hand. At the bottom he turned, "Pass me your case," he said, "then take your time coming down."

Samuel entered the cabin and stopped in amazement. Jannie gently moved him on and closed the door. "We keep doors shut all the time, deadlights too. We don't want any light showing outside."

Samuel gazed around him in wonder. He had never seen such a beautiful room. It was built into the curve of the stern, with four rectangular windows facing him. Each had a white metal shutter screwed shut by two big polished

17

bronze lugs. Padded red leather seats ran underneath the windows either side of a mahogany table. It was fastened to the back wall and stuck out into the room with its sides folded down. The walls of the room were covered in mahogany panels, gleaming in the soft light of an oil lamp swinging gently from its hook above the table. A small potbellied cast iron stove was bolted to the floor in the middle of the front wall with a bucket of coal beside it.

Jannie watched delight push the shadows from Sam's face. He liked the way he was taking in the neat, well-ordered comfort of the cabin, the growing wonder at how it was put together.

He stood and asked, "Well, what do you think of it?"

"Oh Jannie," Sam whispered, "I never expected anything like this."

"Let me show you where you sleep," said Jannie. Facing the port side of the ship, he pressed his hand against one of the panels above the bench, lifted it slightly and slid it open.

To Samuel's amazement there was a full-length bunk behind it, complete with pillow, sheets and blankets.

"This is your bunk, Sam. Stow your kit in here." Jannie lifted the lid of the bench below the bunk to reveal a large locker. "Don't leave anything lying around. There is a candle in that sconce." He made Sam lean in to look. "You light that when you go to bed, but only if you want to read. We never leave candles alight if we're not there. The matches are kept in this cupboard. When you use one, blow it out and put the dead match in this tin."

Jannie was pointing out where things were kept as he talked.

He looked at Sam to make sure he understood what he was saying. Then, scowling slightly, he asked, "What are sailors most afraid of?"

Sam thought for a minute and replied, "Storms. No! Icebergs!"

Jannie laughed. "Nee Sam. It's fire. Fire is what terrifies us." He looked intently at the boy. "Never forget that."

Contrite, Sam replied, "Yes sir. I mean no sir. I'll never forget."

Satisfied, Jannie said, "One more thing to show you." It was the heads, the other side of the ladder. Samuel peered into the small, clean, white tiled room with a W.C. and wash-basin. Jannie told him, "The heads outlet is above the waterline. It only flushes when the engine's running and we have pressure on the fire-main. We flush it with a bucket of river water when the

18

engine's shut down. You can do that if it's dark and the tides running. Not by day and not at slack water. Use the bucket then and don't kick it over!"

Samuel gulped. There was much to learn.

Going back into the saloon, Jannie said, "It's late and you've had a long day. Save your questions for the morning." He smiled at Samuel. "Get ready for bed while I get a bucket of water for the heads. Clean your teeth, wash your face and hands and get turned in."

Samuel nodded. "What about a candle?"

"Not tonight, jonge. I'll leave the lamp alight, turned down low."

By the time Jannie came back with a bucket of river water for the heads, Samuel was asleep.

Jannie peered in to make sure he was comfortable and noticed Samuel's left arm lying outside the blankets. Clasped tightly in his hand was an old bone-handled seaman's clasp knife.

Jannie stood back with a lump in his throat. 'That must have been his grandfather's,' he thought. He turned the lamp down and walked quietly to the door. As he left he whispered, "Good night, Samuel."

From the bunk came a drowsy, "Good night, Jannie, thank you."

*

Sam woke to the sound of water lapping against the hull. He stretched and wriggled his toes in excitement. It was warm, dark and very different from his room at home. Sticking his head out of his berth, he saw the lamp swaying above the table, still alight. He was mesmerised by the shadows dancing around the room. No, *saloon*. He must remember the names. Swinging his legs out, he jumped down, quickly grabbing the edge of the table to stop himself falling. The floor of his new home was moving. Only a little but it tilted slowly one way and then the other. It also seemed to rise and fall gently.

"Of course it does," he chided himself. "We're afloat and there is lots of traffic on the river."

Creeping out of the saloon, Sam relieved himself in the heads and tipped in some river water to flush it. He was itching to go exploring but knew he must not go anywhere without permission. He noticed oilskins swaying on their hooks and wondered if there was one for him.

Sam's heart bumped and his stomach tightened on hearing footsteps on the deck above. Quiet as a mouse, he crept back into the saloon, closed the door silently and climbed back into his bunk. The shutter scraped slightly as he closed it.

Sam sat, knees drawn up to his chest and felt around for his knife. Opening it, he held it in his right hand, ready to strike. The saloon door swung open with a bang. Sam jumped, tense and trembling as footsteps approached.

"Wake up sleepy head!" Jannie's cheerful growl was followed by a knock on the shutter before it was drawn back. Sam let out a huge sigh and jumped out, stumbling as he landed.

"What's this?" asked Jannie as he caught the boy and held up his right arm.

He looked at the open knife. "That's quite a weapon you've got there."

"Sorry, Jannie," Sam stuttered, "I was scared."

Jannie smiled at the lad as he let him go. "I'll whistle next time, then you won't stab me!" He paused before asking, "Did your father give it to you?"

"Oh yes," replied Sam. "It was his father's too. Opa gave it to Papa when he went to sea and now Papa's given it to me."

He held the knife out for Jannie, who took it and ran his thumb cautiously across the blade. "That is sharp." He looked at Sam. "D'you know how to sharpen it?"

Sam shook his head.

"Nee?" said Jannie, "I'll show you later. We'll make a lanyard for it too. Now, let's light the fires and have breakfast."

When Sam opened his locker to get his clothes, Jannie stopped him. "I forgot," he said, turning to a hitherto unnoticed cupboard. "The Kapitein left these for you. He said they should fit." Reaching inside he pulled out a pair of faded blue cotton trousers, closely followed by the jacket and trousers of the Company uniform. Handing them to Sam, he stretched inside again, then handed the delighted boy his uniform cap, navy blue with a leather peak and the Company cap badge sewn neatly on.

"Now," he said, "Put the jacket and trousers on a hanger in that locker," pointing to another unnoticed door. "You won't need them in the engine room." He looked at the cap. "Keep this for best. You won't get another. Wear your own like me. And a singlet and those blue trousers."

As Sam hurried to stow his clothes, Jannie said, "I'm going ashore for some provisions. Get dressed and tidy up. I won't be long – and wear your boots to work in."

When Jannie left, Sam picked up his new cap and tried it on. It fitted perfectly. He pulled the peak down over his eyes; he tilted it to one side and then the other. He pushed it to the back of his head and spun around. There was no mirror in the saloon but that did not stop Sam slipping on his blue serge bum-freezer jacket and fastening its shiny brass company buttons. "Oh my word," he breathed. "Oh thank you, Oom Paul." He slipped his fingers into the jacket pockets and pushed them down, leaving his thumbs outside, just as he had seen his Kapitein do.

Hearing the gangway clang, Sam whipped off his jacket, picked up the trousers and hung them in the locker. He climbed into his work clothes and was putting his boots on when Jannie returned. The old man looked at his new fireman sitting on a bench with one knee drawn up, his brand-new Company cap on the back of his head as he tightened the laces on his boot. Paul was inspired to have kitted the boy out like this. Sam was so preoccupied by dressing up that he had forgotten why he was onboard.

Dumping a canvas bag on the table, Jannie went out again, saying, "Come on, we have work to do."

The sun was sparkling off the river, its bright light dazzling after the darkened saloon. Sam was seeing the old ship with new eyes. He had never really bothered about anything but taking in or letting go the mooring warps on the quay. He had been on the bridge with Oom Paul on a few short voyages last spring and even had a short trick at the helm on one of the straight reaches. Now he was to be introduced to the mysteries of fire and steam, and how they drove the pistons that turned those great paddles.

Sam hurried after Jannie who had opened a heavy hatch and was climbing down a vertical steel ladder. Sam followed when he was clear.

The combined engine and boiler room smelt of oil, grease and burnt coal. Jannie went to a steel locker, took out and lit a small oil lamp. "Hang this there," he ordered, pointing to a bracket in front of the great round drum of the boiler.

The lamp gave Jannie enough light to work by. He knew his domain so well he could have fired up the boiler blindfold. Now he took his time, so that Sam could see how it was done.

"Right, Sam. This is a two fire Scotch boiler." He patted the front, swung open the door to the port fire and told the boy to look inside. Sam saw a pile of ash and knobbly bits of burnt coal. "That's how we leave the fire. We rake the coal into a heap and let it burn out. The water cools down slowly." He smiled. "And in a minute we will heat it up slowly."

He picked up two large iron buckets and put them close to the nearest fire door. "First we clean out both fires, put the ash in these and dump it in bins ashore." He gave Sam a shovel and a long rake and moved back to the ladder. "Keep the deck-plates clean, Sam. We don't want ash in the bilge, and don't fill the buckets too full or you'll never move them." Pointing aloft he said, "I'll haul them up and the deck hands will empty them." With a reassuring smile he scurried up the ladder.

By the time Sam had half-filled the first bucket he was covered in powdery ash and streaked with sweat. Dragging the bucket to the bottom of the ladder, he hooked it on and looked up. Jannie took hold of the tackle and the bucket vanished.

The first part of his morning passed in a blur of sweat, dust and aching muscles. Sam quickly learnt to pace himself. He knew he was being tested and was determined not to falter.

"That's the last one, Jannie," he called as he hooked the bucket on.

When Jannie returned, he lowered the bucket and followed it down. "Here," he said, offering Sam a bottle filled with brown liquid. "Drink this."

Gratefully Sam took a mouthful, and promptly spat it out. "Ugh, what's this?"

Jannie laughed, "It's cold tea. You need it down here."

Sam looked at him suspiciously.

"Nee lad, it's good." Jannie took a great mouthful. "I learnt this when I was working with Lascars on the East Indies run." He leant a grimy arm on a valve. "They know how to keep cool and what's best to drink, and it's tea. Now drink up. We have much to do."

Jannie swallowed the rest of his bottle and tucked it into the locker. Sam drank his more slowly. He had no choice.

"Now we light the fires and watch the temperature and pressure gauges and we'll soon have steam up."

This was Sam's introduction to oily waste and kindling, how to shovel coal and how to make sure it lay flat, the importance of air, and all the other skills needed by a fireman. In between shovelling and trimming and adjusting and watching gauges, always watching gauges, Jannie took Sam round the engine, telling him, "This is a two cylinder, 500 horse power compound engine." He smiled at Sam and said, "You don't need to know what that means," before showing him the grease points on the two great pistons and on the shafts of the paddles, and where to oil and what to avoid and where to hold on and what not to touch. He turned a valve on a pipe coming from the boiler and a small, beautifully painted machine hissed and sighed as its piston started to go up and down and its flywheel span at one end and a wheel drove a belt faster and faster at the other end.

"This is the generator Sam," Jannie explained. "That belt drives a dynamo. You know what that does?"

Sam nodded, his eyes shining as he studied the machine, taking in oil caps and grease points and noting how dangerous the belt was. "Are these meters?" he asked, pointing at three flickering gauges on a varnished teak board.

"Ja. Now stand here." Jannie pointed to the front of the control board. "This is the revolutions counter. When the revs are steady, this one," pointing at another meter, "should be here, and that one there." Jannie tapped the glass on a different gauge. "That's when you pull down that lever and make sure it clicks home."

Jannie indicated a large black handle on a hinged brass U. Below it two brass lugs stuck out of the board. "This," tapping the handle," is the circuit breaker. You pull it down to complete the circuit." He looked at Sam. "Any questions?"

Sam shook his head.

Jannie stood back and let Sam take his place. "One more thing. The dynamo starts working when you close the circuit. That makes the generator slow down so it needs more steam."

Sam nodded.

"I'll be busy so you must open that valve until the revs come back up." Jannie tapped the steam valve. "Don't forget, open it slowly." He looked at Sam again. "Can you manage that?"

"Yes sir."

Satisfied, Jannie began to make their breakfast.

Sam watched in fascination as Jannie put a shovel into the fire and lifted out a thin layer of glowing embers. Placing the shovel on the deck plates, he took a frying pan from under a bench and put it on the coals. The layer of white fat soon melted. Jannie tossed Sam a loaf of fresh white bread. "Cut four thick slices." He pointed to the bench, "Get two tin plates and the butter."

Four slices of bacon sizzling in the hot fat filled the engine room with a mouth-watering smell. He lifted them out when their rinds were crisp and cracked a couple of eggs into the pan. They cooked quickly, their bottoms soon crinkly and brown.

"Here you are, Sam, your first engine room breakfast." He smiled at the boy, handed him a thick sandwich and sat on the deck plate.

Sam had never tasted anything so delicious. Butter, bacon fat and egg yolk dribbled down his chin. He had not realized how hungry he was, nor that a simple meal smelling of coal smoke could taste so good.

Wiping his chin with the back of his hand, and his hand on his trousers, he sat back and sighed with pleasure.

"That better?" Jannie asked him, throwing a handful of tea leaves into the kettle as it began to boil.

Sam nodded, staring in amazement at Jannie's tea making.

'Why do we drink tea, Jannie? Don't you like coffee?"

"Ja. But I like tea down here. I told you, I served my time with a crew from Calcutta who always drank tea, hot or cold. I got used to it. Paul calls me a heathen." He laughed as he put three heaped spoonsful of sugar into two metal mugs. "Mind you, don't burn yourself," he said, passing one over.

While Sam sipped cautiously at his sweet black tea, Jannie cleared away their makeshift kitchen. He threw the embers back in the fire, wiped the plates with cotton waste and put them beneath the bench.

The temperature in the engine room was rising steadily. "Look at these," Jannie said, pointing to three gauges mounted on a piece of varnished teak bolted to a steel bracket.

"Water temperature. Vacuum. Steam pressure." He moved to the port side, and put his hand on a clear vertical glass tube held between two valves.

"We never take our eyes off this." He tapped it with his forefinger for emphasis. "It is the sight glass." He looked down at Sam. "Do you know what it's for?"

Sam shook his head.

"It tells us if we have enough water in the boiler. Do you see where the water is?"

Sam looked and saw the sight glass was half full. "Yes sir."

"Good," Jannie nodded. "If you ever see the water level dropping tell me straight away." He looked carefully at Sam. "If it drops what does that mean?

"There's not enough water in the boiler, sir."

Jannie nodded, "Nearly right, it means we let more in to bring the level back up. But," he paused so he could make sure the boy understood, "if it drops suddenly, or if it is empty, what does that mean?"

"I don't know sir."

"It means I have to shut down the boiler straight away. Why do you think that is?

Sam shook his head.

'If I don't, the boiler will explode!"

Sam's mouth fell open. He looked at Jannie with scared eyes.

Jannie tousled his hair and smiled reassuringly at him. "Don't look so worried. I've been at sea over forty years and haven't blown up a boiler yet!"

Shovelling in more coal, he said, "I need you to know these things so I live another forty years."

The rest of the morning passed in a haze of work; building up the fires, raking them level with long iron rakes, watching the gauges and keeping the plates swept. As the steam pressure increased, Jannie began to warm up the engine, opening valves and pulling levers to let steam through pipes and cylinders. Sam watched, fascinated, as huge cold pieces of metal, gleaming with oil or grease, slid and slithered and huffed steam here and there and gradually ran smoother; all the time he was busy shovelling and raking and sweeping.

They paused for a "Smoke-oh" as Jannie called it, settling down with the kettle on and their mugs ready for a brew. Sam was amused that Jannie simply added more tea leaves to those already in the kettle. It tasted just as good, of tannin and coal. Jannie passed him two thick sweet biscuits while he filled his pipe. "Eat up."

Sam stared as Jannie thumbed tobacco into his big, curved pipe, lit it, tamped the glowing tobacco with his calloused thumb and leant back to enjoy his first smoke of the day. Sam leant back beside him, legs stretched out, one ankle crossed over the other. Jannie saw the way the boy was copying him. 'Poor kid,' he thought. It was easy to forget why he was onboard.

'Christ!' A sudden thought hit him 'He's a Jew! I just gave him a bacon sandwich!' He chuckled, disguising it as a cough as Sam turned an enquiring face towards him. 'And the boy ate it.' He closed his eyes again. 'He'll have plenty more before we're done.'

Sensing his Kapitein's presence, Jannie opened his eyes, looked up and gave him a cheerful wink. Paul smiled, nodded and moved away.

Jannie nudged Sam awake, stretched and stood up. He checked the sight gauge, temperature and steam pressure before picking up a shovel and moving to the port bunker. Sam jumped up, yawned and copied his master's actions.

While the engineer and his trainee fireman were busy below, Paul began his "Captain's Rounds". He finished his inspection by going up to the promenade deck and onto his bridge. All was well onboard *De Ruyter*, if not with the world beyond her iron hull.

The old captain walked slowly towards the enclosed wheelhouse. His helmsman and friend, Henri, had finished cleaning the brass and opened the door with a cheery, "Good morning, sir."

"Good morning, Henri," he replied, "We have fair weather and a steady glass. It should be a good run today."

Henri grinned. "Aye aye sir. I'll fetch our coffee."

The coffee steamed up the windows on either side of the wheel as they lit their cigars, *Da Souza's* finest. 'We'll miss these' thought Paul, 'and they'll be missing their boy.'

Shaking away the thought, he finished his coffee and blew down the voice pipe to the engine room.

The sharp whistle startled Sam. He looked at Jannie as he walked unhurriedly to a shining brass spout at the end of a copper pipe, took out a plug and called, "Engine Room."

Sam could not hear what Jannie was told, just his "Aye aye Kapitein," before he replaced what Sam saw was a brass whistle on a chain.

Jannie glanced at the clock. "We sail at 1100."

∗

Kapitein De Groot pulled the black handle all the way down on the gleaming brass engine telegraph. Without a pause he brought it back to stop against the white letters, bright against the black background. "Stand By."

The jangle of the telegraph bell was loud against the hum of machinery. Jannie moved his telegraph to "Stand By" in reply. The bell rang on the bridge and the small arrow of the repeater moved to line up with the larger bridge command.

The deck-hands needed few orders. The tide was still flooding so they cast off all the lines. Standing on the starboard bridge wing, Kapitein Paul watched the last warp come inboard, looked ahead and astern to make sure he was clear of traffic on the river and rang down "Slow Ahead".

Henri did not need any orders about steering *De Ruyter* out of her berth and soon had her moving seawards along the starboard side of the Niew Maas. Kapitein Paul walked unhurriedly through the wheelhouse to the port wing to get a clearer view of river traffic before ringing "Half Ahead." He saw they had a couple of heaving lines secured to the guard rails at each end and grunted with approval. They would be collecting soldiers from a military quay and there would be no handy nippers to take the lines.

Below, Sam felt his stomach clench with excitement when Kapitein Paul rang down "Slow Astern". He watched, wide-eyed, as steam hissed, the engine groaned and its two mighty pistons started to move. Jannie let in more steam then turned to Sam and ordered, "More coal. Three shovels each."

Sam started at the port fire, falling into the rhythm of the fireman, shovelling, raking, sweeping, before standing with one hand on his shovel watching the gauges.

Another flurry of engine manoeuvres as *De Ruyter* berthed at the Military Quay kept them busy until the telegraph rang "Stop." After a couple of minutes, the voice-pipe whistle blew.

"Engine room," replied Jannie. "Two hours notice. OK."

He put the whistle back and told Sam. "The Old Man wants us up top. We're steaming again in two hours so we'll bank up the fires before we go." They were busy for the next ten minutes, topping up the fires, closing down the air supply, checking the steam pressure was steady. Jannie told Sam to check the sight glass and when that was done, led the way up the ladder. He handed him some clean cotton waste. "Wipe your hands and arms with that, Sam, and grab your coat. We'll be cold up there."

Blinking in the bright sunlight that greeted them on the Panorama Deck, Sam looked around curiously, then stared at the guns and limbers drawn up on the quay There were piles of boxes too, but no sign of any soldiers. He swiftly sat on a wooden bench when Jannie tugged his arm, and looked around at the rest of the crew.

Sam had not seen Oom Paul that day and wondered at his solemn expression as he began to speak. "We are here for two hours while the army embarks. It's the 21st Infantry Battalion and they are going to reinforce the garrison at the Hoek. We all know what to do so I don't need to say any more about that." Pausing to gather his thoughts, he put his hands in his jacket pocket and took a couple of steps forward before continuing. "Listen to me carefully. The Germans will invade." He looked at each man, woman and the boy. "Today, tomorrow. Very soon."

His words fell like stones. No-one moved. "You know what that means?" A murmur of assent broke the silence.

"Those boys," indicating the soldiers assembling on the Parade Ground, "they will fight, and many will die, and the Germans will win." He sighed and looked across at the red, white and blue flag flying at the mast on the quay. "They are brave enough, foolhardy perhaps, but they will fight. And once the Germans have beaten them, they will be here to stay. And Sam," he said looking at the boy, "forgive me for not introducing you." Sam smiled, blushing as every head turned towards him. "Sam is our new fireman."

The crew looked to their captain for an explanation. "Karl is ill. Appendicitis they think. I took Sam on because he wants to go to sea." A brief smile crossed the Kapitein's tired face, "I thought he should start as a fireman." The deck crew laughed. It was the toughest job onboard. The Kapitein laughed with them. "Fortunately for Sam, we don't have long days ahead. We don't know what our duties will be when the fighting starts. The

Company has been told to keep us at four hours notice on return to Rotterdam. I want the ship ready to sail so top up with fresh water at the Hoek. I imagine we'll be needed for trooping and resupply." He took a breath. "And the Germans will want to stop us."

There was a stillness about the crew. The steward and his wife held hands. Sam moved closer to Jannie and leaned against him.

The Kapitein continued, "We won't sail with a full crew. Just enough to steam her and berth and unberth. I will only sail with single men. Volunteers," pausing, "If there are any."

Jannie growled, "I'll sail, so will the boy." Sam nodded. Henri looked at his captain and said, "I'll sail." The four deckhands put their heads together, a low rumble of voices emanated from them before the oldest said, "If three's enough, Kapitein, I'd like to go ashore. The others will sail with you."

Kapitein Paul moved towards them, "Three is enough. Your family need you ashore. You too," he said to Joop and his wife. He was interrupted by a red-faced sergeant major who addressed him from the quay. "Ready to embark, sir," he called. "Permission to come onboard?"

Kapitein Paul nodded, turned to his crew and said, "Back to work."

As they went to their stations, Jannie moved over to the Kapitein, Sam following. Paul was talking to the helmsman, Henri. Jannie pushed Sam in front of him, "You haven't met my new fireman."

"Nee, but I know our Kapitein. If you're good enough for him, you're good enough for me." He winked at Jannie and went back into the wheelhouse.

Paul turned to Jannie, "How's your new fireman?"

"He'll do."

That was high praise from his engineer. Paul looked at the boy and said more gently, "Have you settled in?"

Sam smiled shyly. He was not used to talking to the Kapitein. Being onboard his ship was very different from meeting him in the café. "Yes sir."

"Carry on, Chief."

"Aye aye sir."

Jannie turned and went down to the main deck. He and Sam watched for a moment as columns of soldiers marched from the parade ground to the quay. "They don't look very old, do they?" Sam said. Jannie shook his head. He looked at their uniforms, the old rifles and webbing. They were so young and ill-equipped. He had heard stories about how unprepared the Netherlands was for war. Now he was seeing it for himself.

They went below where, after engineer's tea topped off with fruitcake, Sam fell asleep while Jannie smoked contentedly, one eye on the clock, the other on the gauges. They had another half hour before they need stir.

∗

There was a knock on the wheel-house door.

"Come in."

It opened to reveal a tall, thin young army officer. "Lieutenant Alenson, sir." He saluted the stern, grey haired captain facing him.

Kapitein Paul returned the salute casually and said, "Relax. How can I help you?"

"We have four guns, limbers, ammunition and men to take to the Hoek, sir. Is there room for us?" He stopped, then added, "The horses are already there."

Paul grunted, "That's a relief!" He smiled at the young man. "We can take you if they're not too heavy."

"They are 7 Veldt's, sir. Not heavy."

Paul looked at him, surprised. "Those old guns? From the…"

The lieutenant interrupted, "Yes sir. They're old and they were in storage but they are what we have."

Paul saw the slight tic beneath Alenson's right eye and realised how tense he was. He turned to Henri. "Take the lieutenant down to the foredeck and see what he needs to secure the guns. And tell the hands to get the gangway back out." Turning to Alenson, he said, "See if it's wide enough."

The lieutenant nodded and followed the old sailor down to the foredeck as Paul called the engine room. "Half an hour, Jannie. We're also taking a battery of guns." He listened for a moment. "Nee, no horses. Just the battery and gun crews."

It did not take long to ready the ship for their cargo and to make sure there was enough soup and coffee for the infantry and gunners. Paul lit a cigar and watched them lining up on the quay. They were a mixed bag, a few regulars buttressing reservists. They looked keen enough but clearly lacked experience.

Hearing boots on the deck behind him, Paul turned to see Sam coming smartly to attention and knuckling his forehead. He smiled at him, "At ease. I wanted you to see what's going on. We haven't carried guns before."

Moving to the bridge wing they leaned over to watch the first limber being wheeled onboard and taken to its spot on the fo'c'stle.

"Four of those, Sam. One for each gun. They carry the ammunition. That's why they're well forward."

Sam nodded, his eyes bright with excitement. Each of the limbers was securely lashed to eyebolts sunk in the deck. Once they were secure the guns were wheeled onboard. They had been freshly painted; breeches glistened beneath a thin film of oil and the polished brass-work shone. Jannie joined them and muttered, "They look as if they're going on parade, not to war!"

"True enough," agreed Paul. "But at least they fire."

After a few minutes, Paul ordered Sam back to the engine room and the two men smiled as he doubled away. Paul asked, "Has he missed his family?"

"Not at all," Jannie replied, "Too busy to think. He's a quick learner, that boy, and strong too."

"Just as well," said Paul, "Your regular man won't be back until Monday." He looked over the side as the last of the guns trundled across the gangway. "It looks like war, any day now." He looked down into the oily water for a while before turning to Jannie, "When we get back, I'll bring his parents onboard. We'll have a meal together. All of us."

Paul looked at the guns, neatly lashed down, the men filing onboard, and sighed again. "I hope we can get the Da Souzas away in *Malines*" he said, referring to the British ferry berthed near the bridges.

Jannie studied his captain, seeing sorrow weighing him down, the tiredness in his eyes. "I'll be sorry to see Sam go. He works hard and could make a good engineer in time. Talking of which," he glanced up at the funnel, then at Paul, "I'd better make sure he hasn't let the fires go out."

Paul laughed, "He's more likely to be wondering why you're still on deck." He looked over the side to see if the tide had changed. "We'll get underway once all the soldiers are onboard."

The lieutenant was still on the quayside, talking to a senior officer as Jannie went below. He saw him salute the older man, embrace him then hurry onboard. Jannie watched the colonel, now alone on the quay. He looked sad and worried. "Thank God I don't have kids," he muttered. "He must know what's coming."

*

It was a short run to The Hoek and Paul was soon berthing *De Ruyter* with his usual unfussy skill. He called up the engine room when he'd rung off main engine. "We sail at 1800. Tell the boy to get some sleep."

He stood for a moment, watching his crew unlash the guns and limbers and help the soldiers get them ashore, then bent to the voice-pipe again. "Come up when you've finished. Bring some coffee. Three mugs." He looked across at Henri. "Join us my friend. There is much to talk about."

Henri gazed after Paul as he walked slowly off the bridge, chose a chair facing the sun and sank into it with a sigh. Like the rest of the crew, Henri had studied the young soldiers and asked himself how their country could be defended by such an ill-equipped army and what he would do when the Germans came. Neither he nor Jannie was married. *De Ruyter* was all they had. He thought about the boy and what sort of future he would have. Moving to the starboard bridge wing, Henri pulled out a cigar and lit it. He took a deep breath, held the smoke for a moment and exhaled slowly. At least Sam would have a future in England.

Gazing across at the riverbank, he wondered what the Germans would do with the ship, who would man her, what the Old Man would do. It was hard to contemplate a dark, uncertain future on such a beautiful day.

"You're very thoughtful, Henri." He turned to see Paul smiling at him. Henri looked at his Kapitein. "Have you got berths for Simon's family?"

Nodding, Paul stood and walked to Henri's side. He put his hand on his shoulder and tugged him towards him. "Yes," he replied quietly. "Onboard *Malines*. She's sailing on Saturday evening. Sam will go with them." He looked at Henri. "Her captain has been ordered to take British citizens only so not a whisper to anyone. He's a good man and will take our friends because I asked him." He smiled at Henri. "I told him they're South African."

They both turned as Jannie clattered up the companion-way, three mugs in one grimy hand and a jug of coffee in the other.

"Thanks," Paul said. "Has Sam turned in?'

Jannie laughed, "Only after I said I'd get a new fireman if he didn't do what he was told!"

He poured three cups of coffee and pulled a flask out of his pocket. "Cognac?"

"Ah, Jannie, you spoil us!" Henri and Paul held out their mugs.

"Cherbourg on a cold, dark February morning after a rough passage from New York," Henri had his eyes closed. "We'd just cleared customs and the bosun went below. We were down that gangway in a flash, three of us, straight into the nearest café. Zinc bar, glowing stove, sawdust on the floor, couldn't see across the room for smoke. Coffee, cognac and a Gauloise." He smiled as he opened his eyes. "Takes me back every time."

He offered his friends a cigar and took one himself. "We should go there when this nonsense is over. Just for a coffee and cognac."

Jannie laughed, "Too old for the ladies?"

Paul chuckled, "I'm a respectable married man. I'm happy with a coffee You can chase the girls, Jannie. If you can run fast enough."

He looked at Jannie and Henri lying back in their chairs, eyes closed, faces held up to the sun. In that instant, they could have been on holiday but the moment passed when Henri spoke, his eyes still closed. "What do you think will happen? And when?"

Paul took his cigar out of his mouth and looked at the glowing end for a moment before replying, "I think the Germans will invade. Today, tomorrow, any day now. We know what they did in Poland and Norway. This won't be like last time. They want our ports and our airfields and they'll take them. Neutral?" He gave a short, bitter laugh. "If we were strong enough, like Switzerland, they might keep out. But we're not, and we're between them and the sea so they will stamp all over us. 'He spat a bit of tobacco out, "And there are people here who will help them." He stood up abruptly and walked to the guard-rail. Turning his back to the river he stared down at his friends. "We've served a long time together in this old girl. We know and trust our crew and they know and trust us." He paused for a while, then continued quietly, "But none of us know how we'll behave until we're tested."

Jannie stretched his wiry frame and stood up slowly. "Did I hear you say Simon and Judith are coming onboard tonight?"

Paul nodded, "Yes, For a meal. The last time we'll see them for a while. The family sail on Saturday night, so I'm afraid you'll be losing your fireman, Jannie, and just as he's getting to know the ropes."

Jannie sighed. "That's a shame. He's a good lad. But he'll be better off in England."

Henri nodded. "D'you want the rest of us onboard tonight?"

"Yes," Paul said, "until we know what's happening. We might have to shift her in a hurry."

He walked slowly up to the bridge and called back,

"Rotterdam will be no place for married men. Bakker can go home after supper. The boys can stay onboard. I'll take Simon and Judith home with me and we'll collect Rachel on Saturday. Once I've taken them to *Malines*, I'll come back for Sam." He turned to Henri. "I shan't be here tomorrow so you'll have the ship. There are no planned movements. Water up when we get back. We don't need any coal do we, Jannie?"

Jannie shook his head, "Nee, the bunkers are full."

Footsteps clattered up the companion-way. Lieutenant Alenson approached Kapitein De Groot and saluted. "All ashore, sir. Thank you for your help. The men particularly asked me to thank you for the meal."

"It's the least we can do for you." Paul shook the young soldier's hand. "Look after your men and they will look after you."

He stood back and saluted Alenson. The boy was standing straight and seemed taller. He saluted, turned and marched away.

The three shipmates moved to the port wing of the bridge to watch the soldiers move off.

Paul reached for the cord and blew a prolonged blast on the ship's steam whistle.

*

Sam woke with a start, the unexpected sound of the steam whistle rousing him quicker than any alarm clock.

He turned out, put his boots on and hurried to the engine room. To his surprise, Jannie was not there. Sam looked at the sight glass, checked the vacuum and pressure gauges and opened one and then the other fire door. Taking the rake from its stowage he riddled both fires before putting more coal on.

34

Jannie noticed the slight increase in smoke from the funnel and turned to Paul, laughing. "You woke Sam. Look," he said, pointing.

Paul and Henri looked up. "He's keen, that boy," said Henri.

"Yes," agreed Paul. "It's a shame he can't stay." He looked at Jannie. "We have to get him away safely. It's all we can do. Holland will be no place for Jews once the Germans are here."

He moved towards the bridge, "Come on Henri, time to go home."

"Who's this?" said Henri sharply as a fast-moving ship approached the mouth of the Nieuw Maas, smoke pouring from her two funnels, her bow throwing white water across the green-brown sea. Jannie paused at the top of the companion way. Paul walked quickly to the bridge and blew down the engine room voice-pipe. When Sam answered he said, "Come to the bridge, quick as you can."

As the ship slowed to pick up a pilot and the boarding party from the launch that had hurried out to meet her, Dirk came to the bridge with a brown envelope in his hand. Approaching Paul he said, "Message from the Harbour Master."

Paul opened it, saw his orders to return to Rotterdam and said, "Single up, Dirk. Tell the others we'll be getting underway in," he looked at his watch, "Fifteen minutes."

Sam came scampering up the ladder as Dirk turned to leave. He nipped onto the bridge and saluted his Kapitein. "Sir?"

Paul gestured Sam to follow him. Pointing to the ship now stopped in the river mouth, he said, "That ship and the *Malines* are sailing on the 10th of May They will probably be the last English ships we will see and they are your best chance of getting away." He looked closely at Sam. "Do you understand?"

"Yessir," the boy muttered tightly.

"I'm going to pick up your parents and Rachel on the tenth. I'll put them onboard *Malines* then come back for you."

Sam was about to speak but Paul hurried on, "If I don't, it will mean something has gone wrong and you must stay onboard."

Sam nodded.

"Make sure you travel in uniform and don't forget your papers. I'll pay you off before you go."

"Aye aye sir," the boy replied in a whisper.

"Cheer up, Sam," his Kapitein's face creased in a smile, "we're having a party tonight. Now off you go. Jannie is waiting for you"

Paul rang down "Stand By" and clapped Henri on the shoulder as Sam raced below.

Henri did not move. He was studying the *Deben* through the bridge binoculars. "Look at this, Kapitein," he said, "She has extra crew onboard." He stared at the ship again before handing the glasses over. "I'll bet those are Navy men," he said softly.

Paul nodded as he scrutinised the ship. "Yes," he said eventually. "I wonder what they're up to."

The captain of *Deben* and a young, fair-haired officer were inspecting *De Ruyter* through their binoculars as they drew abreast. They waved and turned away. Paul and Henri waved back.

*

By the time *De Ruyter* was secured alongside in Rotterdam, the first-class saloon had been transformed. The deck-hands had been sweeping, dusting, scrubbing and polishing. Bunting hung in gay loops above gleaming scuttles, white table clothes were covered in crockery, cutlery, glasses and candlesticks. The bars were stocked and ice-buckets filled. The room smelt of beeswax, Brasso, paraffin and flowers, and of steam and coal. Embracing these rich smells was the richer smell of their dinner cooking.

Brushing himself down and straightening his cap, Paul made his way to the gangway to greet his guests.

"Shalom, Simon. Shalom Judith," he said, then hurried them onboard. "We'll have a drink in the cuddy while they finish off below."

Judith was looking around for Sam. Paul turned to her and said gently, "He's still working with Jannie. They'll wash and change before they join us." Smiling at her, he confessed, "I haven't told him you'll be here. We have others who are leaving the ship tonight. The married men. This is their party. Yours too."

Paul took Judith's arm as they went into his little cabin beneath the bridge. "It is a time to be thankful for our friends and for our families." She smiled uncertainly at him. He said gently, "We must love and look after what we have; our lives, our families, our trusted friends. That is all we can do; all we need to do."

Henri was there in his best uniform, a bottle of champagne in his hands. He eased out the cork and filled four glasses.

"Judith, Simon, Kapitein." Lifting his own glass, Henri said "*De Ruyter*". They drank to the ship before sitting. The scuttle was open, letting in the soft May air. Sunlight danced on the river, shimmered on the deckhead and lit up their faces.

Paul glanced at Simon. "What news of Rachel?"

Simon smiled, his eyes lighting up. "She is fine. They take her stitches out tomorrow and we pick her up at midday. Solomon says her leg will be as good as new after a summer of fresh air and exercise."

Judith smiled. "Yes," she agreed. "He said swimming is best."

Henri leaned forward and stretched out a hand to her. She took it and stroked the callouses on his palms and fingers. Softly, in a voice Paul had never heard before, he said, "Listen to the water and the wind, dear child. Today the breeze is gentle and the river is calm. Tonight, tomorrow, in a week, it will change. A storm will sweep in, turning the river into a wild beast. It will pass. The water will calm. Children will play at its edge once again."

He took her other hand and looked at Simon and Paul. "We three have been to sea. We know this to be true. Sometimes it is a squall, fierce, wild, tearing canvas, beating us senseless. Sometimes a storm builds over days and weeks. We are better prepared then. When it breaks, we are in for a long, hard fight. With a stout ship and a good captain, we come through the storm."

Henri looked into Judith's eyes, "You have heard the stories many times?" She nodded. "You know sailors always exaggerate?" Judith nodded again. "Well, the storm that is building now is like none we have ever seen. But we have stout hearts and we have a good captain and we will come through."

Henri let go of her hands to cross himself, "God willing."

He stood up abruptly. "I talk too much." Picking up the bottle he poured more champagne. "To life. L'Chaim."

Simon rose to his feet with the others and lifted his glass in reply, "L'Chaim V'l'vracha!" He translated before they drank, "To life and blessing."

The door flew open and Sam raced in with Jannie a step behind.

The cuddy was instantly filled with noise and laughter as Sam apologised to his Kapitein and Paul scowled his most ferocious scowl, betrayed by Jannie's laughter.

Simon gazed at his son in amazement. He had only been away a dog-watch and yet he looked different. He reached out and took Sam's right hand in his. He ran his thumb over the blisters, across his broken nails, noticing the ingrained coal dust and small burns on the back of his hand. He looked at his face as he talked to his mother. Paul took Simon's arm.

"I need a cigar before we eat."

Simon nodded.

As the ship was starboard side to the quay, they walked up and down the port side. After Simon lit their cigars, he remained standing at the guard-rail, gazing across the river at the island and, on its other side, the cranes and the masts and funnels of cargo ships. This was one of the busiest ports in the world, and one which he would soon be leaving, possibly never to return. Even this late in the day the river was full of life, with streams of barges behind bustling tugs, cranes bowing and rising as they filled or emptied ships' holds, steam whistles blowing and the air full of the muddy smell of the river, overlaid with coal-smoke, fish, spices, coffee and tobacco.

Simon turned to Paul. "Well, my friend, we won't be doing this again for a year or two."

"Nee, Simon, or maybe longer. But we will do it again, one day."

Paul rested his hand on his friend's shoulder. "Sam is a good boy." He thought for a moment before continuing, "I would like to have him at my side in a storm." He shook Simon lightly. "You can be very proud of him. Judith too. You have raised a fine son."

Simon breathed deeply, taking time to control his voice before replying. "He has changed much in a short time. Seeing him in his uniform…" He paused to clear his throat, "seeing him in uniform…" He stopped, shaking his head.

Paul tugged Simon lightly, "I know, Simon." He looked at the bowed head of his friend. "He will be safe in England. You all will. You can stay there or go on to America." He shook Simon again, "Can't you?"

Simon raised his head to look Paul in the eye. "Yes, my friend. Yes. We will be safe; my family will be safe."

He took a deep, unsteady breath. "And my friends, my dear friends will be here." He gazed at Paul. "I wish you would come too. My girls from the café – all of you."

Paul stopped him. "You must only think of your family." He took a long drag of his cigar. "They, and only they depend on you. You will sail onboard *Malines* and I will wait here for your return."

He took a pace up the deck. "We must join the party. Let us have an evening to remember with joy in the dark days ahead."

Simon shook himself, as if to throw off a burden. "You are right. Damn it." He laughed, "You usually are." Linking arms, they went back to the cuddy.

Laughter greeted their return. Jannie was in the middle of telling Judith one of his more outlandish stories of a run ashore and Henri was adding details that were so remarkable they could easily have been true.

There was a knock on the door and Dirk, scrubbed and gleaming in a clean blue shirt and his best trousers, invited them to come below.

The first-class saloon was always elegant, retaining its charm and décor over the years. Brass oil-lamps, converted to take electric light bulbs, gleamed, cream and Delft-blue curtains rippled and swayed in the breeze coming through open bronze scuttles. The tables would not have looked out of place in the finest hotel in Rotterdam. Polished silverware glinted on brilliant white tablecloths, glasses shone and every place was graced with a starched napkin and a hand-written menu.

Paul led Simon and Judith to their places either side of him. His crew found their names on the menus placed with care by Betje, the ship's cook after she'd spoken to the Kapitein.

It was a sumptuous feast. Paul knew that once the Germans invaded, food would become scarce, especially anything imported and he wanted his crew to have a meal to remember, as well as to say farewell to the married men and woman with whom he had served for so long.

Paul turned to Betje, "You always know where the best food is to be found."

She smiled back, "I have a good nose."

Paul looked at her, serious for a moment, "You're going to need it when the Germans come. They'll take what they want and leave us the scraps." He looked at his crew and continued, "We'll all need good noses soon."

Betje was silent, not wanting to think about the future. Then she asked, "And you, Paul, what will you do when they come? Will you be here or at home with Christina?"

Paul smiled, "At home, Betje. I'm too old to change my ways and I've never liked taking orders from strangers. Besides, Christina will need me more than the river."

Judith heard what Paul said and laid her hand on his arm. "I am so glad, Paul," She smiled at him. "We will think of you digging your garden."

Paul smiled back, knowing he was being teased. "I'm more likely to be fishing than gardening."

Sam, seated between his father and Jannie, leaned forward to gaze at his mother. Her face was full of merriment, eyes sparkling and lips smiling. The soft light made her hair look golden and highlighted the colour in her cheeks. He had not seen her so relaxed and animated since Rachel's accident.

Simon was talking to Jannie over Sam's head. He looked down at his son and pushed his chair back. "Sit here, Sam, next to your Kapitein. Your mother would like that."

Sam changed places and sat a little taller. He felt very grown up tonight.

Course followed course, wine flowed, ties were loosened, the noise rose and then it was time for coffee.

Paul tapped his glass with a knife and the saloon quietened. He stood, straightened his jacket and leant forward to fill and then raise his glass.

"Ladies and Gentlemen," The only sound was the rippling of small waves against the hull and a distant steam whistle, "my dear friends, I have only a few words to say tonight," The boys cheered. Paul smiled at them, "It is true." He paused before continuing, "Tonight we say farewell to our married friends and their wives. We have talked about this over the past few weeks. Now it is time. The Germans will be here any day and our lives will change. I have spoken to the unmarried men and they have agreed to stay onboard for the time being." He paused again. "No-one will think any the worse of you if you sign on again once the Germans have taken over the Company. There'll be fuel shortages and all the chaos of occupation. These old stoomboten will be needed, as they always were before lorries and busses came along."

40

Looking at his friends, Paul said, "I am leaving *De Ruyter* as well." He paused for a long while. "Let us stand and drink to the old girl."

Chairs scraped and glasses were raised as they growled, "*De Ruyter.*"

"One more toast." He raised his glass, first to his crew and then to the Da Souza family. "To you and to our country. To the Netherlands. Keep Courage."

His crew and friends stood still for a moment, then cheered as they lifted their glasses and shouted, "Nederland. Houdt Moed."

In the silence that followed, Simon raised his glass and said quietly, "Chazak, chazak v'nitchazek."

They all heard Sam's piping voice tell Paul, "That means 'Be strong, be strong and let us strengthen one another'." and roared, "Chazak."

*

The clang of the gangway broke the silence. Someone had come onboard.

Henri was already moving towards the saloon door when it burst open and a breathless hospital orderly entered.

Recognising him immediately, Judith sprang to her feet before he could speak. "Is it Rachel?" she asked, her voice harsh with tension.

"Ja, mevrouw. But nothing bad."

"What's happened?" Simon stood beside Judith and took her arm.

"I didn't mean to alarm you, mevrouw," apologetic, the orderly explained, "We have been told to clear the wards tonight. Doctor Solomon sent me to tell you to collect Rachel." He looked at Simon. "He has taken out her stitches and she is ready to be moved."

"Thank you," said Paul to the orderly, getting to his feet. "Wait while we get our coats, I will take you back to the hospital with us."

Paul ushered Simon and Judith out of the saloon and up on deck so he could talk without being overheard. "Listen," he said, "there's nothing to worry about. This is just a precaution the government's taking. We'll pick Rachel up now and go back to the farm."

Simon squeezed Judith's hand. "It will be good to have her with us."

"Yes," she whispered, "It will be very good."

"Right," said Paul, "We'll say goodnight, thank Betje and get underway." He turned to Judith, "Sam must stay here. He has work to do." He smiled at her. "Don't look so worried. **You will** see him tomorrow."

*

The single men were sitting round the table after the party broke up. Sam wondered why Henk was still there as he thought he was married. He was much older than the other deck hands and had shown him how to tie up *De Ruyter* when he was a new wharf-rat. Dirk and Willem were the 'lads' according to Jannie. Sam thought they were proper sailormen and copied the way they walked and talked and carried out their duties, but only when no-one was watching.

They stopped talking when Henri said, "Listen boys, you know Paul's left me in charge?" He paused. "If the Germans invade, he's told me to take the old girl to England."

The men were silent.

Henri continued, "If I can't get her away, I have been ordered to sink her."

He heard their sharp intakes of breath. Sam felt his stomach clench.

"If any of you want to leave now, let me know."

He spoke more slowly and emphatically, "Whatever you decide, you must not tell anyone what I've just said. If you do, you will be putting all our lives at risk." He stood up. "I'll give you a few minutes to think," he said and went on deck.

Leaning against the rail and smoking, he watched people still promenading up and down the quay on this beautiful May night. He wondered if any of the Jewish refugees in the synagogue had taken passage in *De Ruyter*.

Henk came up to relieve him.

"A guilder for them," he said as he joined him at the rail.

"Ach, Henk, I'm getting old. I was wondering what those Jews must be feeling. What drove them from their homes?"

Henk was silent for a long time before he answered.

"We have sailed together a long time, Henri, and never seen anything like it." He cleared his throat and spat into the river. "It leaves a bad taste to say this, but I never knew some of my friends were so full of..." He waved his hands, searching for the right words.

"Hatred?" asked Henri.

Henk shook his head. "Worse." He looked at Henri, his pale blue eyes troubled, "I think it is jealousy, a jealousy that's been festering for years, eating away at them like maggots in apples."

"What are they jealous of?"

Henk shrugged. "Success. Family. Ability. I don't know." He stared across at the synagogue. "Most of those families have been here for generations, some working hard, some not, some rich, some poor, just like the rest of us."

The **two** men were silent for a while. Then Henri brought his hand down on the rail. "Right," he said. "time to go below and see if the rest of the boys are ready to take this old girl to England."

As expected, the reply was swift and unanimous.

∗

Simon heard them first. The uneven, pulsing throb of hundreds of aircraft approaching from the east.

He slipped out of bed, drew back the curtains and gazed at the fast-paling sky. Judith woke with a start at the noise. Rachel slept on, oblivious. They had collected her from the hospital the previous night and brought her to the sanctuary of Paul and Christina's farmhouse. And now the sky above it was alive. Husband and wife stood at the open window, his arm around her. She was trembling. Their world was trembling.

They heard Paul and Christina go downstairs, the kitchen door opening, footsteps crossing the yard below their window. They saw Christina enter the stable to quiet the restless horse and Paul go round the yard, checking the pigs and hens before stopping to stare at the endless stream of aircraft.

Judith slipped out from under Simon's arm to put on her dressing gown. She knelt beside Rachel, drawing comfort from her peaceful sleep. As the noise of the aircraft faded, Simon moved to his wife's side. He bent down to whisper, "I'll see if Paul wants a hand."

Judith nodded and squeezed his hand. "Don't be long, my love. I'm scared."

"I won't be," he assured her, kissing her hair.

Christina was in the kitchen when Simon went downstairs. She stared at him with wide, worried eyes. "Did the little one wake?"

"Nee, she can sleep through anything." Simon said with a lightness he did not feel.

"Oh, thank God," Christina relaxed a little. "I've put the kettle on."

Paul came in as she spoke. Simon looked at him and smiled, "Here comes the man who can smell coffee five miles up wind in a typhoon."

Paul pulled out a chair as Christina made the coffee. Simon remained standing. "I'll take a cup up to Judith."

She was still kneeling beside Rachel when he returned, her left arm resting on the pillow by the child's head. Simon put the tray on the dresser and passed her a coffee. He went to the window, cup in both hands, gazing at the empty sky, the air filled with sweet music as birds greeted the dawn.

"Listen," he whispered to Judith, "Even the hens are joining in."

A distant rumble came from the west

"What is that?"

Simon listened carefully. "I don't know," he said. "I don't think it's thunder." He looked at Judith, "Stay here. I'll ask Paul."

Paul was already on his way upstairs. He met Simon on the landing. "You hear it?"

Simon nodded. "Never heard anything like it, Paul." He looked at the old man, "Have you?"

Paul led Simon away from his bedroom door before answering. "That is the sound of high explosives." He looked hard at Simon. "I think they are bombing Rotterdam."

"Schijt, Paul. Are you sure?"

"Ja, Simon, I am sure."

Simon gripped Paul's arm. "What about Sam?" He whispered fiercely. "I must get him out of there." His grip tightened. "I can't leave him."

"What are you saying?" Judith's voice came sharp and clear. She stood in the door, looking from Simon to Paul.

"Mama. Papa." Rachel's sleepy voice called out. Judith spun round and ran to her bed as Rachel asked, "What's that noise?"

Simon was close behind Judith and answered softly, "It is a storm, honey, just a storm." He held her hand and stroked it, "Go back to sleep, there's a good girl."

He looked at Judith, saw the fear in her eyes and reached across to her with his other hand. He mouthed "Wait until she is asleep."

Comforted by her parents, it wasn't long before Rachel's eyes closed and they could move quietly downstairs to join Paul and Christina.

"What is happening?" Judith was close to tears.

"It is the war, my love. It has come." Simon gathered his wife into his arms, holding her tightly as her tears began.

"We must get Sam," she cried, "We must get him."

Simon closed his eyes and held her closer still. He took a deep breath, exhaled with a long sigh and whispered, "We must wait, dear heart, we must wait." He kissed her wet cheek, "It is all we can do."

"Why?" demanded Judith, pushing herself back to look into Simon's face. "Why must we wait?"

"Because of those aircraft," he said, "We cannot move until it is dark."

Paul spoke quietly from the window where he had been listening to the sounds of the distant air-raid. "The army will have blocked the road by now. Even if they let us through, we would be spotted from the air."

He let his words sink in. "Simon is right. We can only move by night and only then if it's safe and if the army lets us."

Judith clung to Simon, shaking her head and crying quietly.

The kettle began to sing on the hob. Christina shook herself and took the big tea-pot down from the shelf.

Turning to Judith, she said, "I promised Rachel she could help me milk Daisy. Wake her up and tell her to get dressed while I'll make a pot of tea."

Judith smiled at Christina though her tears. "Thank you."

She stretched up, kissed Simon lightly before wiping her eyes and going upstairs.

Christina glanced at Simon before asking Paul, "Do you think you will be able to fetch Sam?"

Simon straightened up and answered before Paul could speak, "Nee, I do not. Henri and Jannie will keep Sam safe. If they can't get *De Ruyter* away they will bring him here." He looked at his two dearest friends. "May we live here with you?"

Christina replied without hesitation. "Of course. Where else would you go? We shall have to keep the little one busy. And her mother." She took Simon's arm, "You too, my dear."

Paul nodded. "And also make a place where you won't be seen in the day." He looked across at Simon, "Shall we start that after breakfast?"

"Ja. It is important." To Christina he asked, "How will we keep Rachel inside?"

"Today will be easy," she answered, "We worry about tomorrow later."

She heard Judith and Rachel coming downstairs and said, "This is Rachel's first day on the farm. We will make it an unforgettable day for her."

It was an unforgettable day for them all.

3.

HMS Pembroke, Chatham, Kent. April 1940

"Ask Lieutenant Gale to come to my office."

The Commodore put down the 'phone and read again the signal from the Commander-in-Chief. Gale was the right man to lead the young sailors he had been training for the past month. Commodore Higham snorted. Not that Gale would agree. He wanted a ship.

There was a knock on his door. "Come in"

Gale walked into his office and came smartly to attention, his cap beneath his left arm.

"Good morning, Gale. Have a seat." He indicated the chair by a round table. "Cigarette?" He slid a silver box across and watched Gale light up, liking again what he saw in this quietly assured young officer.

"I have a job for you, Jimmy." The use of his nickname made Gale look more closely at his commanding officer.

"Yes sir."

No pause, no question. Gale had been long enough in the Service for there to be few surprises. He was a 'Temporary Lieutenant', an officer who started his career as a Boy Seaman and had "come up through the hawsepipe".

He wondered what the Old Man had in store for him.

He studied him through his cigarette smoke, seeing a grey-haired, elderly Commodore who was unlikely to go to sea again, unless he was lucky enough to be given command of a convoy. Jimmy almost laughed. Lucky? Not from what he had heard.

The Commodore cleared his throat.

"It's quite simple. I want you to select two hundred of the fittest young seamen, get them on the range and teach them to shoot straight." He studied Gale before continuing, "I've got hold of enough rifles, Lewis Guns, ammunition and equipment. I want you to start right away. You can choose your own Senior Rates. Scratch will give you a list of the Subs."

"Aye aye sir." Gale hid his disappointment. "May I ask what our role will be, sir?"

The Commodore smiled. "Of course, Jimmy. Nothing unusual. We're going to have a cadre of trained men ready to go anywhere at short notice. Here if the Hun decides to invade, or France if needed there. I've got hundreds of sailors waiting for ships. Instead of sitting on their arses they can learn to shoot straight."

He studied Gale before adding, "You remember what happened in Spain when you landed the survivors from *Baleares*?"

"Yes sir."

"Teach them about controlling panicking people, getting them safely onboard, patrolling streets, that sort of thing. Just in case."

He looked hard at the young officer. "You are the right man to get this underway." He paused. "And to set the standard for your successor."

"Thank you sir." Jimmy Gale knew a sweetener when he saw one.

"I'll take Petty Officer Ward and Leading Seaman Spencer." He looked at the Commodore. "And the Chief G.I. and Mr Smith."

The Commodore interrupted, "They're the best in the barracks."

"Yes sir," He straightened in his seat, "We do have standards to set."

"Carry on, Jimmy." The Commodore stood up to mask his amusement at being outmanoeuvred.

Closing the door quietly, Jimmy turned to the Commodore's secretary, a lean, grey-haired Lieutenant Commander sitting at a desk piled high with papers. "Do you have my orders, Peter?"

A swift glance, educated by years of experience, told Peter De Villiers that Jimmy was unhappy about his new command.

"Your thoughts?"

Jimmy opened his arms wide and smiled. "I think he is right. There's no point in having hundreds of sailors sitting around while the balloon's going up over there. God knows what'll happen in Norway but it doesn't look good. The Germans are bound to have a go at the French soon. They have

48

a score to settle with them – and us." Peter nodded as Jimmy continued. "We'll take about a month to get them shooting in the right direction. I don't know anything about street fighting and hope it doesn't come to that. If it does, I hope you can handle a rifle. Two hundred boys won't stop the German Army."

Peter nodded. "I've got you three Subs. They've finished their training with good reports and appear to be steady." He fished out a brown cardboard folder and handed it over. "Take this and let me know what you think. You'll find another three names at the back. If any aren't up to the mark, get rid of him and pick another."

"Thanks, Peter." Jimmy took the file and stood up. "Do you have a back-up for me, in case I'm not up to the mark?"

Peter rose to see him out of his office, "Of course, but only if you break a leg."

"Who is it?"

"Lieutenant Bell, Nick Bell."

'He's senior to me, Peter. Why isn't he in charge?" Jimmy had stopped in the doorway, puzzled.

"As the Commodore said, he wants you to set the standard."

As Jimmy made his way to his cabin, he wondered why Bell had not been chosen. He knew him slightly, a tall, distinguished looking Admiral's son, ambitious and well-connected. He hoped Bell would not make trouble for him.

*

Mr Smith was in his early forties, a short man, whippet thin and owner of one of the loudest voices Jimmy had heard. Jimmy caught him as he was marching off the Parade Ground. Salutes given and returned, he asked "May I walk with you, Mr Smith?"

"Aye aye sir."

Jimmy steered him towards the river. "I'd like your opinion, Mr Smith. It's a sensitive matter."

Bill Smith had served onboard *HMS Duke of York* when Jimmy was a Boy and had admired the way he learnt the ropes. That admiration grew into respect as he heard about Jimmy's steady advancement. The exploits of *HMS Kempenfelt* in the Spanish Civil War had been discussed in great

49

detail in Gunners' Messes throughout the Fleet, cementing Bill's high regard for this young officer.

Jimmy took his cap off and leaned against the rails. "Cigarette, Mr Smith?"

"Thank you sir." He looked at Jimmy and smiled, "Call me Bill. Everyone does."

Jimmy relaxed. "Thank you. It's Jimmy." He struck a match, cupping it in his hands with practiced ease. "I've been given a job to do, Bill and I'd like your help." He took a deep pull at his cigarette and exhaled slowly. "However, you're a family man and I'll quite understand if you want nothing to do with what I'm about to say."

Bill waited for Jimmy to continue. "I have to choose two hundred men, train them to shoot straight, teach them the basics of fighting and stand by to defend the shores of Kent." He gave a short laugh. "More likely to be sent to some French port to keep order. I really don't know. The Commodore is certain that life will soon get sticky. He wants trained men. All we have here is boys."

Bill remained impassive. "Where do I fit in?"

"I need a sound man to run the Headquarters Platoon, someone who won't flap; who the boys will trust. I need someone to organize the stores and the routines – and steady the ship if anything happens to me." He paused for a long while, watching Bill's eyes. "I'd like you to be that man."

Bill looked across the river. He thought of his wife, their daughter working in the bank, his small house with its neat garden. He thought of going off to some French port with a bunch of kids with guns. Then he thought of this newly promoted officer. Bright, keen and steady and he thought it was true, Jimmy would need someone like him, someone who would not panic if it all went wrong.

He took a deep breath, "My father told me never to volunteer, Jimmy. Hope I won't regret this."

Jimmy stretched out his hand.

"I hope you won't either."

*

Three weeks later Jimmy was once again in the Commodore's office.

"Right, Jimmy, d'you understand your orders?"

50

The Commodore was staring at a map of Rotterdam. It was lying on top of a pile of charts covering Dutch ports and the southern North Sea. He raised his eyes to study the young man leaning over the map.

"Yes sir," Jimmy straightened up and smiled. "It's a shame the boys haven't had longer on the range but they'll be alright. Sub Lieutenant Coombes is my second-in-command."

The Commodore nodded.

"Chief Petty Officer Miller, Petty Officer Ward, Leading Seaman Spencer and Able Seaman Webb are my key personnel. Miller will watch my back. Webb is in charge of stores. Ward and Spencer have a section of ten men each." Jimmy laughed. "Ten boys, that is. Ordinary Seamen, none older than nineteen, but they are the fittest and the best shots." He paused. "I hope we won't have to use our guns. Not on the civilians. Nor on anyone else."

The Old Man's lips tightened. "I'll put Bell in charge of the others while you're away. Do him good. He needs to be kept busy, and he is the senior gunnery lieutenant." He went on before Jimmy could say anything, "Don't worry, he won't have a chance to alter the training programme. Mr Smith will see to that."

"Thank you sir," Jimmy picked up and folded the street map. "Mind if I take this with me? I don't want to get lost."

"Help yourself." The Commodore indicated the charts on the table. "Do you want any of these?"

"I shouldn't need them sir. They'll have charts on *Deben* and I'm not planning on going boating." He patted his map, "This will get us to the Hook if we do have to borrow a boat." He smiled at the Commodore's worried expression. "We'll never be far from the *Deben*, sir. She won't sail without us." Jimmy looked at his watch. "If that's all, sir, we'd better push off."

"Carry on, Jimmy," The Commodore extended his hand, "Good luck."

The two men shook hands. Jimmy stood back, picked up his cap and gas mask and came to attention.

"Thank you sir," he paused, searching the old man's face, "We'll be back before you've had time to miss us."

Jimmy walked slowly to his cabin. The Old Man had looked apprehensive and he was right to. This jaunt to Holland could easily be a one-way ticket.

*

"Stand the men at ease, Mr Coombes."

"Aye aye sir."

Jimmy took a breath and pitched up his voice. "We embus as soon as we've drawn weapons and ammunition. If any of you are missing any kit, if your water-bottles are empty, tell your Section Commander when we dismiss."

Telling them they would be drawing weapons and ammunition made several of the boys look uneasy. He hardened his voice.

"This is an exercise in guarding a ship. She's berthed in Harwich. We're drawing arms and ammunition because this is war-time. We'll be away two or three days."

He paused. "Any questions?"

Half a beat, no time for awkward questions.

"Carry on Mr Coombes."

Jimmy shook his head as he walked away. Misleading his platoon was not the start he would have liked but he could not see what else they could have been told. They had to cross London and get on the Harwich train without anyone knowing why and that only took a slip of one tongue.

The train journey from Chatham to London Bridge passed in a buzz of cheerful conversation. A bus was waiting to take them across London. Crossing the Thames, they stared down at ships discharging cargo, and smoky tugs towing lighters beneath Tower Bridge. The City was new to most of the youngsters. They gazed in awe at the closely packed buildings, crowded pavements and barrage balloons swaying overhead.

Pulling up at Liverpool Street Station, the platoon fell in while Able Seaman Webb checked that nothing had been left onboard. He was a tough and reliable Seaman Gunner with no interest in promotion and Jimmy knew his boys would follow Webb to the ends of the earth.

Jimmy watched the old gunner report to Sub Lieutenant Coombes. It was incongruous to see the boy being saluted by a seaman old enough to be his father but Coombes had been an early volunteer when war seemed inevitable and Jimmy knew he was lucky to have him.

"Mr Coombes"

"Sir"

"Take the men to the front of the train. The guard has a coach for us. Get the Senior Rates in first and tell the men to hand them their rifles and bayonets. They're travelling first class." He laughed at Pip's expression. "Chop chop. Don't keep the train waiting."

As Jimmy moved away, his Chief, 'Dusty' Miller, fell in beside him, "We're off to Holland, aren't we, sir?"

Jimmy nodded.

"Only Sharky and me know, though the other two Seniors probably will by now." He looked at Jimmy, "You know how it works."

Jimmy nodded again. "I hope the buzz isn't going round the pubs."

"Don't worry sir, it's just us. No-one else is interested."

"Thank you Mr Miller. I'll break the happy news to the boys once we're moving."

∗

Jimmy and Miller joined Coombes and the Section Commanders in their compartment as the train moved off.

Jimmy remained standing once out of his webbing.

'I'll start with an apology, gentlemen. I couldn't give you our orders until we were on this train. We're off to Holland. I'll tell the boys in a moment."

Webb piped up, "They'll be alright, sir."

"Thank you, Webb. I'm sure they will." He looked at the rows of sun-lit houses they were passing.

"We are sailing in *Deben*, a regular Harwich to Hook of Holland ferry. She'll leave as soon we're onboard to evacuate British civilians from Rotterdam. Our job is to ensure there's no nonsense on the quayside, get 'em onboard safely and come back."

He stopped. "Any questions?"

"Does anyone know how many there'll be?" That was the Sub.

"No idea."

"How will we know they're British?" Leading Seaman Spencer asked.

53

"I'll talk to the Captain and Purser. They'll have a system."

While Ward and Spencer moved the sailors into the Dining Car, Jimmy told Pip and Dusty what he was about to say to the platoon. "Have I missed anything?" They shook their heads.

"Right," he said "let's see how they take it."

*

The young sailors presented an incongruous sight seated at the elegant tables of the First-Class Dining Car. Jimmy turned to his Chief, "Mr Miller, keep that door shut." Miller walked to the rear of the car and leaned his broad back against it.

"Sub."

Pip nodded and raised his voice, "Silence."

The excited murmur stilled as the boys shifted to see their officers.

Jimmy stepped forward and pitched up his voice. "Can you hear me at the back?" Miller nodded.

"I told you earlier we were going on an exercise, I could not tell you what we are really doing for reasons of security." He paused. "I regret misleading you, but secrecy is important." Looking at the expectant young faces, he continued, "As you know, Germany invaded Norway and it seems that Holland may be next, so the Admiralty has commissioned two ferries to embark British civilians and bring them home." He paused. "*Malines* is already in Rotterdam. We are sailing in *Deben* to assist with the evacuation." Jimmy looked at his platoon. "This is what we have been training for."

There was a low murmur.

"We'll have a quick passage across the North Sea and up river to the city. Once there, we'll liaise with the ships' officers to make sure the civilians embark in an orderly fashion. Women and children first. If they get restless, we'll steady them, as we have practised. Any questions?"

"Yes sir. Smithers, sir." Jimmy looked at the anxious expression on the boy's face. "Sir, why have we got ammunition and them bayonets?"

An apprehensive buzz went round the compartment.

Jimmy waited until they were quiet.

"That is a reasonable question, Smithers. I don't know what we will face on arrival. No-one does. Rifles will be loaded when we reach Holland. They will be inspected to ensure the breech is empty and safety catch is on. Carry

54

your spare ammunition at the top of your pouches. We will only fix bayonets if the situation demands it."

Pausing, he looked around at the sombre faces. "Is that clear?"

"Yes sir."

"Right, unless you have any further questions, I think we should see if the stewards have wet the tea."

*

"Lieutenant Gale?"

Jimmy nodded and saluted. "Yes."

Sketching a salute, the officer said, "I'm Lucas, Chief Officer. Get your men onboard."

Jimmy's "Aye aye sir" was addressed to the officer's swiftly retreating back.

Jimmy ordered, "Mr Coombes, get them onboard, quick as you can."

A working party dragged the gangway onto Parkstone Quay as the last man stepped aboard. Engine telegraphs clanged, the deck started vibrating, fenders creaked and ropes splashed into the muddy water.

'Christ,' he thought, 'they really are in a hurry.'

Pip had the platoon fallen in and standing easy. Jimmy glanced at the boys. "This will be the first time most of them have been to sea. Good job it's calm."

Pip smiled. "It's my first ship, sir."

Jimmy looked at him, "So it is. I'd forgotten. You'll be fine."

The Purser came on deck, "Lieutenant Gale?" Jimmy nodded. "Captain Wilson's expecting you. I'll look after your boys."

Deben was picking up speed as she approached the harbour mouth, heeling slightly as she turned to starboard. There was an old V & W class destroyer ahead which, he assumed, was their escort.

Jimmy went onto the bridge wing and stopped, not wanting to be in the way while the ship was in confined waters. The door to the enclosed bridge opened and a surprisingly quiet voice said, "Come in. The Navy's always welcome." The captain's handshake was firm but Jimmy noticed his eyes were unsteady. Jimmy knew *Deben* had been on the run from Tilbury and Folkestone to Boulogne for months, and supposed the constant threat of mines and submarines had worn her skipper down.

"The Old Man's got the wind up," was his verdict when he returned to Pip and Miller. "I don't know why but he is twitchy about us being onboard. We'll keep our heads down and wait until we're asked to help. It's a millpond out there and we'll make good speed. When we get there, the boys must stay here. They can use the heads next door but must not go wandering off."

He finished his coffee, stubbed out his cigarette and stood up. "I'm going back to the bridge." He smiled wryly, "I think the captain might show me the sights, and I'd like to be there when the Boarding Officer comes onboard. If there are any questions about our lot, I'll answer them."

Neither he nor Captain Wilson need have worried. On their arrival, the Dutch naval officer asked for the gun's breech block, confirmed there was a berth for *Deben* astern of *Malines* and departed.

Jimmy smiled at the captain. "I hope the rest of our mission goes as smoothly" at which the Old Man touched the arm of his wooden bridge chair and replied "So do I, Jimmy, so do I. Your men can come on deck. They may as well see the sights."

None of the boys had been out of England. They ran up the companion way to the promenade deck astern of the bridge, leaving their hats below; "No point in advertising," Jimmy said, though an experienced observer would recognise their blue jean collars.

A cloud of black smoke issuing from the funnel of an old paddle-boat alongside the quay caught his eye. She reminded him of summers past, the *Medway Queen* and Isle of Wight ferries, capable, unfussy, popular with holiday-makers and day-trippers as they waddled along, their paddles beating a wide wake astern. He thought her captain would give the stoker an earful for all that smoke.

The passage upriver was uneventful. There were few craft about, apart from the paddle-boat following them. His sailors were like those day trippers, excitedly pointing to windmills, farm houses and the peaceful, bucolic landscape. They chattered happily amongst themselves, the war and why they were here far from their minds.

As *Deben* approached Rotterdam, Captain Wilson again ordered them below, telling Jimmy to keep them out of sight.

Once below, Jimmy told Pip, "See if you can find out why the captain's so windy."

Pip nodded. "I'll have a word with the Chief Steward. He's served with him a long time."

"Thanks. I don't want to put my foot in it. But nor do I want us to be dropped in the cart."

Pip went to find the steward while Jimmy joined the men in the saloon. Miller had organised the release of their small arms and had them cleaning rifles, filling magazines and checking their packs. The compartment was alive with conversation, interspersed with the rattle of rifle bolts and click of bullets being loaded.

"Just like home," Dusty muttered. "They could be off for a day on the range."

They looked up as Pip approached with the Chief Steward.

"Thanks Chief," Jimmy said to the elderly man. "Mr Walden, isn't it? You've been with Captain Wilson a long time?"

"Yes sir. Since '23 when we commissioned *Deben*. He's a good captain, looks after us like his family."

"But he's worried, yes?"

Walden glanced at Jimmy and nodded. "He was a prisoner of war in the last lot. Three years. Torpedoed and picked up by the Hun." He glanced at the busy young seamen before continuing. "He had a very bad time. Not enough food, beatings, solitary confinement." He raised his head and looked again at the carefree lads. "That was the captain twenty-five years ago. Not a care in the world." He looked around the table. "We've had a couple of very close shaves. Mines. We set one off a couple of weeks ago. Made my teeth rattle." He gave a grim smile. "But it's not being shot at or sunk that worries him. It's being taken prisoner again."

Jimmy nodded. "Our job is simple. Make sure the embarkation goes smoothly and return with them. No heroics. We're sailing tomorrow for a fast night passage home. We appreciate your captain's concerns. I share them."

Jimmy stood up, straightened his uniform and leaned across the table to shake the Chief Steward 's hand. "Thank you for talking to us, Mr Walden."

As he let his hand go, Jimmy said quietly, "Your captain is a brave man. Look after him."

*

"Right lads, this is where we earn our pay."

57

Dusty Miller looked hard at each boy before continuing. "You will not go on deck unless you are ordered. You will stay on the port side of the saloon. As you already know, our job is to ensure the orderly embarkation of British citizen onboard *Maline* and *Deben*. This will to take place tomorrow.'

The Chief G.I. looked again at the boys. "Holland is a neutral country which means the Dutch would have every right to intern these ships if they thought we were playing silly buggers." He nodded to himself. "They have invited us to embark our citizens because they are friendly neutrals. But what they absolutely won't tolerate is us doing anything to give the Germans an excuse to invade so no larking about, no shore leave and do exactly what you are told.' He drew a deep breath. "Do I make myself clear?"

"Yes Chief" echoed through the saloon.

"Very good."

Miller took the section leaders to the other side of the saloon. "Get your lads sorted out. There's a meal at 1900. One section on duty at all times, four hours on. They'll keep watch in the upper deck saloon, next to the gangway. Curtains drawn and no noise." He looked at his colleagues. "Sort that out. Another section on standby. They can turn in all standing. Off watch sections are to get their heads down. The stewards will look after them." He relaxed and smiled. "Sharky, you've got the First Watch. Spider, take the Middle. I'll do the Morning." When they nodded, he stood up, "Right. I'll brief the Boss."

Miller joined Jimmy and Coombes in the bar, whistling up more coffee as he sat. "Right, all sorted. There'll be a meal at 1900."

Jimmy smiled. "Thanks. I'm going ashore to get my bearings. Sub, Chief, come with me. We can't wander round in uniform. Chief, see the Purser and draw three seamen's jerseys. Loan if possible, otherwise sign a chit." Dusty nodded.

"ID cards only. If asked for papers, we are British seamen from *Deben*. Only produce your ID cards if we get picked up by the police."

"Are we looking for anything in particular, sir?" asked Pip.

"We've got two ships' gangways to cover," replied Jimmy. "We want to be clear how we can control a crowd and ensure they embark safely." He glanced at the Chief, "We've seen what happens when people start trying to rush gangways. It gets ugly very quickly." Jimmy looked at Pip, "We are under strict orders to embark British citizens only. That is why the Dutch

58

have allowed these ships into Rotterdam. We have to make sure no-one else gets onboard. The Dutch police will be manning a cordon and checking papers. We are here solely to guard the gangways in case they lose control."

Pip and Miller nodded.

Jimmy offered his cigarettes around.

"One thing I am interested in is that old paddle-boat. We've got our return tickets, in *Deben* and *Malines*, but there's no harm in having a spare, just in case."

Miller looked at Jimmy with interest. "Care to expand, sir?"

"If there is a bit of a scrum and any of us get left behind, we'll need a ship to get home. That's all." He grinned at the Chief. "If that old girl has full bunkers, I reckon she'd make it back, as long as the sea stays calm."

Pip looked carefully at his cigarette. "Isn't that piracy, sir?"

Jimmy smiled, but his eyes were as blue and cold as the Arctic Ocean. "Possibly, Pip. Quite possibly."

He stood up, stubbed out his cigarette and said, "I'll tell the captain we're going ashore. Chief, brief Ward and Spider. He can look after our kit."

Captain Wilson was still on the bridge. He frowned when he saw Jimmy. "Don't worry, sir, I came up on the port side and made sure I wasn't seen."

The captain relaxed, "How may I help?"

"I need to go ashore to get my bearings and make sure of positioning my men tomorrow. I'll call on the captain of *Malines* to brief him." He smiled a little and said, "I'm taking Coombes and Miller with me. We'll be indistinguishable from your seamen, sir, and won't be ashore for long."

There was a heavy silence. Captain Wilson walked over to the starboard bridge wing and looked up and down the bustling quay. People were strolling about or sitting at tables outside cafés and bars; bicycles, cars, lorries and horse-drawn carts flowed past and over the road bridge.

"Don't go far," he said eventually. "I don't want to have to bail you out."

"Thank you sir." Jimmy hurried below.

Dusty had a handful of seamen's jerseys with him. "The Pusser's as good as gold. He gave me a few extra so we get ones that fit."

Jimmy loosened his tie, ruffled his hair, stuck his hands in his pockets and took a few paces, slouching as he walked. Dusty nodded, "Right sir, got the picture."

Jimmy grinned at him, "Cut out the 'sir', Dusty. We're three seamen stretching our legs. That's all. And remember." This to Pip, "Don't be too obvious when you're looking around."

With that, they went ashore.

*

The captain of *Malines* understood the need for brevity and his meeting with Jimmy was short. As Jimmy turned to leave, the captain stopped him. "I've been here for ten days. The Dutch are expecting the invasion any day now. Their army's been stood to along the border for a while and they seem to be ready to put up a fight, but it's not much of an army." He shrugged. "We should be alright to embark the British contingent in the morning. We sail in the evening whether they're here or not. My orders are very clear about that, so are Captain Wilson's."

Jimmy nodded. "Thank you, sir. Let us hope we have an orderly embarkation." He shook the older man's hand. "I'll see you in the morning."

He rejoined Dusty and Pip as they approached the paddle steamer. 'She's a beauty,' he thought, broad in the beam, with clear decks forrard and a handsome deck saloon aft. There was an elderly sailor leaning on the guard-rail by the gangway. Jimmy hailed him, "Permission to come onboard?"

The sailor stood up and gazed at them for a long time.

"English?"

"Yes. English, from *Deben*," replied Jimmy. The Dutchman nodded and beckoned them over.

Jimmy held out his hand, "Jimmy, Dusty and Pip. We saw you when we came in."

"Henri. Steersman. Come."

He turned and led the way to the cuddy. "We can't stay long," Jimmy said. Henri shrugged and carried on, opening the door and announcing, "Englishmen."

Paul put down his glass and cigar and stood, smiling broadly during the introductions. Without asking, he poured three glasses of clear liquid and handed one to each of them. "Welcome onboard." He raised his glass, said "Proost" and tossed the contents down his throat.

"Proost" they replied and followed suit. Dusty and Jimmy survived the impact of neat Geneva. Pip was left gasping for air.

Jimmy casually asked Kapitein Paul about his work on the river and was intrigued to hear how many people could be carried onboard, amused to learn that several of the crew could milk the cows they often carried, and very curious about how far they could sail without refuelling. It came as no surprise to the Kapitein when Jimmy idly wondered if Paul had ever taken *De Ruyter* out to sea.

When they left, Paul and Henri watched the sailors wander along the quay and pass out of sight behind the synagogue.

"Tell me, Paul," said Henri, "Why did they come onboard?"

Paul laughed, "I think we have just been sized up by a pirate."

∗

Henri and Jannie were leaning on the bridge wing, watching people moving about on the quay in the evening sun.

"How's the boy?" Henri asked.

"Quiet," Jannie shook his head, "The poor kid's happy here. He won't want to leave."

"I don't suppose Simon and Judith want to either." Henri nodded at the synagogue. "Unlike those poor souls over there."

The old friends were silent. Henri stirred after a while and looked at Jannie.

"If the Germans come, Paul wants me to take this old girl to England."

"You're joking?"

"And if I can't take her, I must sink her."

Jannie stared at his friend. "What will you do?"

"I can only take her across the North Sea if you will help me."

Henri passed Jannie a cigar and lit it. Turning back to the rail he flicked the match into the water. They watched it float away.

"That will be us, Henri," Jannie said softly, "Flotsam."

"Nee, Jannie, if it stays calm, we will be there in a day. Harwich is closest."

"And if it gets rough?"

Henri laughed. "Well, Jannie, we sink." He looked at the old engineer. "Or we swim, but if the glass is steady and the gods smile on us, *De Ruyter* will get us across. And anyway, if we don't take her, those English pirates will."

Jannie straightened up and looked at Henri. "What will you do in England?"

"I will look for a kindly widow who is lonely. What about you?"

Jannie smiled. "There had better be two kindly widows or you will be lonely."

They shook hands solemnly.

∗

The three seamen had reached the side of the great synagogue at the end of the quay before they became aware of the hubbub within. Jimmy paused, trying to make out if a service was taking place.

"Go and see what's going on, Pip. Try not to be too obvious." He pointed to a bridge over the adjacent canal. "We'll wait there. Five minutes, no more."

Dusty gave Jimmy a cigarette and lit up. "They don't sound too happy," he muttered.

Jimmy gazed at the building. "It sounds full." He looked across the bridge at the small park beyond and murmured, "It must be lovely here in the summer." He looked up the canal, "We'll go back through the city. I'd like to see what's behind the old buildings on the quay."

Pip looked shaken and almost saluted when he returned.

"It's packed, sir. Hundreds, men, women, kids, all ages. They look as if they're waiting for a meeting to start."

"Did they have any baggage with them?"

Pip shook his head. "Not much, Chief. They're dead worried about something. A lot of the women were crying."

"It's nothing to do with us," Jimmy said curtly, and moved off. "We're going back through the city, Pip. Keep together."

They walked along the narrow road beside the canal, the evening sun casting its golden light over tall, red brick buildings and glinting on the still, black water. There were a few sea-going sailing barges moored alongside, smoke from their coal fires mingling with the scent of Stockholm tar, fish and water. They turned to walk parallel to the river, strolling along a street full of people darting in and out of shops or sitting outside noisy bars.

"I don't think the streets would be this crowded if they were expecting trouble."

"I agree," replied Dusty, "They'd empty quick enough at the first sign. It's just another lovely Spring evening."

"Except for those poor sods in the synagogue," muttered Pip.

∗

"It's just another lovely Spring evening." Jimmy told Captain Wilson. "Nothing unusual. We didn't see any police or soldiers around. Just a big crowd in that synagogue, for a meeting we think."

The captain grunted. "I've seen the agent and he's confirmed we embark only British citizens. They'll be here tomorrow afternoon. We sail at dusk." He looked at Jimmy. "I'd be grateful if one of your hands could keep watch with my watch-keepers tonight. We're all a bit jumpy."

"Of course."

As he stood to leave, the Old Man said quietly, "I don't like the Germans, Jimmy. I spent three years in their company in the last war and that was quite long enough. They're going to invade soon and I really do not want to meet them again." He paused for a long time, gazing at the young officer before him. "I am Jewish."

There was a lengthy silence before he continued.

"We talked on the way over about what was happening to Jews. I didn't tell you we took thousands of Jewish children to Harwich before the balloon went up." He paused again. "There won't be anyone coming to fetch us if we get stuck here, will there?"

Jimmy looked at the tired and worried captain and resisted the instinct to put his hand on his arm. "Then I suppose we'll have to make sure that doesn't happen, sir," he said.

∗

The First Watch passed quickly, with nothing of any significance to enter in the log.

The Middle Watch was different.

"What the hell is that?" The captain's voice was barely audible above the roar of hundreds of aircraft engines.

"German aircraft, sir, at about 10,000 feet, heading west," replied Jimmy.

"How d'you know they're German?"

"Heard them off Spain, sir. Unmistakable. The question is, what are they doing overflying Holland? That's a clear breach of neutrality." The aircraft

63

flew on and were soon out of sight, leaving tension and unease in their wake as dawn brightened the clear sky. A light breeze occasionally riffled the water. Jimmy thought of his father on the edge of blacked-out London, barrage balloons swaying at their cables over the city, smoke from thousands of chimneys lying across the roof tops, sandbags piled against buildings and monuments, windows covered in brown sticky paper, and people waking and hurrying to work on the early shifts, gas masks slung over their shoulders.

He turned to the captain, "Well sir, there's not much we can do up here. If there's nothing else, I'll turn in." He smiled. "We'll be busy later on."

Captain Wilson nodded. "Carry on."

Then the aircraft returned. Lower, faster, sweeping over the city. Jimmy checked the time on the bridge clock. 0330 on Friday 10th May.

The invasion of Holland had begun.

*

"Get below and call the hands. Marching order. Muster in the saloon and keep off the upper deck. Stand by to issue arms and ammunition." Jimmy turned to the ship's watchman. "Call the hands. The captain is on the bridge. I'll stay here."

Jimmy watched them go and turned to survey the quayside. He was amazed by the number of people standing around, staring at the aircraft. Then bombs began to fall on the other side of the river. The crowd flinched at the explosions but no-one took cover.

Miller joined Jimmy. He had put on his boots and gaiters and was carrying a rifle. "They're getting dressed, sir. Mr Coombes is taking charge. Spider's ready to issue arms and ammunition."

"Thanks" said Jimmy. "Stay here. Don't let anyone on or off the ship. I'll see what the captain intends doing."

Captain Wilson had not moved, a look of horror on his face as he watched wave after wave of bombers attacking the airfield at Waalhaven on the other side of the river. He started when Jimmy tapped his arm. "Sir, you must get under cover. Please."

The Old Man shook himself. "Thank you." He was turning away from the flames and smoke rising from the other side of the river when the sky filled with parachutes.

"Christ," whispered the captain, "There are hundreds of them."

Jimmy suddenly pointed. "Look, seaplanes. They're landing here."

"They're going for the bridges." The captain looked anguished. "We're stuck in the middle of their bloody invasion."

Jimmy wondered how many men the seaplanes had landed.

"Come on sir, I need to get my men organized. I suggest you keep your men below decks, sir. There are bullets flying all over the place."

Captain Wilson nodded. "We've kept steam up. I hope we can get her away when it's dark."

Jimmy looked at him. "With your permission, I'll post sentries around the ship. They can keep an eye on the Germans and warn us if they're getting closer."

"Tell them to keep their heads down, Jimmy," the captain replied, "I'll muster my crew forrard and tell them to give you a hand."

"Thank you." Jimmy headed to the saloon.

The sailors were dressed and putting their webbing in order when Jimmy entered. Coombes called them to attention and reported, "All present and correct, sir. Webb is in the weapons store and the Chief is on the gangway."

"Very good.," replied Jimmy. "We'll have a briefing in the bar as soon as Miller returns. Tell Webb to join us, and to lock the store. I'll tell Ward." Pip nodded and left.

Jimmy walked over to the tables where the boys were getting ready. He caught Ward's eye and indicated he should join him. Sharky finished helping one young sailor sort out his webbing before coming over.

"How are they?" Jimmy asked.

"A bit jumpy," he replied, "but they're a good bunch and should keep their heads.'

Jimmy nodded. "It's up to us to see they do."

Miller entered the saloon, followed by Pip and Webb.

Jimmy's voice cut through the chatter and the sounds of battle across the river.

"Stop what you're doing and pay attention."

All eyes turned towards him.

"Germany is invading Holland." There was a rustle of movement.

"Stay still" barked Miller.

"Thank you Chief," Jimmy continued. "Our job remains unchanged; to ensure the safe embarkation of British citizens. To do that means that each one of us must do exactly what he is told to do."

"Excuse me sir," It was Ordinary Seaman Buckland. "Yes, Buckland."

"What do we do if we see a German trying to get onboard?"

"Shoot him." Jimmy paused. "And don't miss."

The saloon went very quiet, but for the distant crackle of musketry.

Jimmy continued. "We are here until it gets dark. Before then, we'll get those British civvies safely onboard and keep the Germans off. Any more questions?" None came. "Are you all clear about what we have to do?"

A rumble of assent filled the saloon. "Right then. Carry on getting your kit sorted. Fill your water bottles. And," he said in a loud clear voice, "do not leave the saloon. And don't go sticking your head out of a scuttle. It might get shot off."

"I'm now going to brief the senior hands and Mr Coombes. Buckland. You are in charge here. Understood?"

Buckland stood straight and replied, "Aye aye sir."

Jimmy pulled out a chair when they were in the privacy of the bar. Once settled, he looked around the table.

"Right gentlemen," Jimmy looked up at a louder burst of gunfire. "This is the situation as far as I can tell. The Germans are bombing the area around the airfield at Waalhaven to the south and have dropped hundreds of parachutists there. You saw the seaplanes. They dropped men off in rubber boats to seize the bridges. The Dutch are fighting back at the airfield and bridges. The *Deben* is very exposed in this berth. She is too close to the bridges and has already come under fire." Glancing around to make sure they were alone, he went on more quietly. "I do not agree with Captain Wilson's plan to move her after dark. It is already unsafe to embark civilians. I will suggest he transfers his crew to *Malines* and scuttles his ship."

There was silence.

"I'm going to see the captain of *Malines*. If he doesn't want us, I'll arrange transport back to the Hook where, I am sure, the Navy will be up to something." Jimmy stood up. "I'll brief the Old Man when I get back. Sub, you are in charge. See me over the side please."

There was a lull in the fighting and the upper deck was quiet. Jimmy drew Coombes away from the gangway and said, "Listen, Pip, in case I don't get back, you must carry out my orders. I'm not expecting trouble but you never know."

Coombes nodded. "Yes, sir."

Captain Wilson looked up when Jimmy knocked on the open door, "Come in. Have a seat." His voice was calm. "I was just writing to my wife. She does like a letter when I'm away."

Jimmy smiled, "I write to my father, sir. He keeps all my letters." He paused. "I have spoken to Captain Mallory, sir. He has agreed to take my men onboard *Malines*." The old man remained silent. "It's a shame they berthed us so close to the bridges, sir."

"Aye," The old man lowered both hands palm down onto his desk. "I love this ship," he said at last and patted the desk. "I've been very happy with her." He spoke quietly. "I'll not let them have her, Jimmy."

Jimmy nodded.

The old captain glanced at him. "Saved you having to tell me, eh Jimmy?"

"Yes sir." He looked squarely at Captain Wilson. "No-one could get her away from here, not right under their guns, even at night." He took a breath, "I recommend you scuttle her where she is."

There was a long silence.

"Thank you, Jimmy." The old man smiled, "I doubt if either of us will forget this voyage."

Jimmy stood, "I am sure we won't."

The two men shared a moment of silence before the captain spoke, "You'd better get your men over to *Malines*, Jimmy. I'll make arrangements to scuttle this old girl and join you later."

"Good luck sir." Jimmy held out his hand. Captain Wilson shook it firmly and turned away.

4.

0330 10th May

"All hands on deck!"

Sam swung his legs off the bunk and felt his way up the ladder and onto the poop deck. In the misty pre-dawn light Sam could see the other members of the crew gazing skywards.

"The bastards are bombing us!" shouted Willem, "They're fucking bombing us. Look." He pointed at a small seaplane as it skimmed just above the surface of the Nieuw Maas. It was followed by eleven others flying in close formation straight towards the bridges. The engine noise dropped when the pilots of the first six cut their speed, descended a few metres and landed smoothly on the river. As soon as they were down, they blipped their engines and motored towards the Boomjies and the northern end of the two bridges.

The crew of *De Ruyter* watched as the other six hopped over the bridges before landing.

Henri looked at his crew, "We knew this was coming. Dirk, take the deck." Dirk nodded as Henri ordered the others below. Once there, Henri turned to his crew. "Do any of you want to leave *De Ruyter*?"

"Nee, Henri," came back as one from the crew.

"Good."

Ignoring the crackle of rifle and machine-gun fire nearby, and the more distant howl of diving aircraft and thudding explosions, Henri glanced around the table.

"We can't sail until tonight." There was a murmur of assent. Henri held up his hand for quiet. "Our first task is to find out if the men and women in that synagogue want to come with us."

68

The old engineer looked across at the boy. He gave him a gentle nudge, "Eh, lad, there's nothing to be gained by fretting about things we can't change." He put his hand on the boy's shoulder and gave it a squeeze. Sam looked at him, his eyes full, "My family…"

" Your family are nowhere near the fighting and Paul will keep them safe. It is a time of chaos ashore. Now is the time for order onboard, order and discipline."

Sam looked up at the old man. He saw concern in his eyes and resolution in his kindly face.

"Ja, now is the time for order," He gave Jannie a hesitant smile. "Tell me what we must do."

"We have to get the old girl ready for her first sea voyage." Smiling, he slapped the front of the boiler. "We have enough coal to last at least a week." Turning to the main engine he said, "She'll keep going as long as we oil and grease her, and nothing works loose. We know the generator and sea-water pump are working. We'll check them again to make sure but first I need to talk to Henri."

The boy nodded as Jannie headed up the ladder.

Finding Henri in the cuddy, Jannie said, "I'd better get ashore now. There'll be chaos in the streets later." He looked at the clock on the after bulkhead. "0430. I'll get bread, milk, bacon, butter, onions and rice. I think we've got everything else."

"Take Dirk, and the handcart," replied Henri. "Better take this too," he added, passing over a short truncheon. His voice softened. "Jannie, I would like you with me when I speak to the Rabbi."

Jannie nodded.

They paused, gazing across the water to the fighting on the bridge. Jannie looked at Henri, "Sam's worried sick about his parents."

"I'm not surprised," said Henri gently, "Paul's aiming to get them onboard *Malines* tonight. That might be difficult. We'll take them if they can get here before we sail. That's 2330 at the latest." He looked grim. "If they are not here, we take Sam to England."

Henri banged on the front door. It was opened a crack by a young man gripping an iron bar. "What do you want?" he demanded.

"To see Rabbi Wietzer. Please tell him it's Henri and Jannie from *De Ruyter*."

"Ja," The man looked closely at them and said, "Wait here," before slamming and locking the door.

"Friendly so-and-so," Jannie muttered before the door opened wide to reveal a smiling Rabbi who showed them into a side room. Jannie cleared his throat. "I'm Jannie, the engineer of *De Ruyter*. Henri is now the Kapitein. Your friend Paul has given him the ship."

"Is he ill?"

"Nee, Rabbi, not ill. But sick of what is happening to our country."

Leaning forward, Henri asked quietly. "Rabbi, what will happen to the people you are sheltering here?"

Rabbi Wietzer shrugged and raised both hands towards the ceiling. "Only He knows."

Henri looked the Rabbi in the eye. "We are sailing for England at 2330, sir."

"And?" The Rabbi's eyes were steady on him.

"We were wondering…" Henri glanced at Jannie, who nodded. "…whether your people might like to come with us?"

Rabbi Wietzer stared from one old Dutchman to the other, wondering 'Is this how Moses felt?'

"Father, we can only take your people, the ones who are here now," Henri said quietly. "If word gets out…" His voice trailed off. Janne continued, "If word gets out, we will be swamped. We will not be able to sail."

Still the Rabbi could not speak. "What can I say…" he began.

"Say yes."

The Rabbi sat forward , "This can happen? You really can take my people to England?" He looked from one to the other. "It is a river boat. How will it get to England?

"The sea is calm, Father," said Henri, "It is expected to stay calm for several days, more than enough for us to sail to England." He smiled at the Rabbi, "It is only a day away."

"And it can go that far?" asked the Rabbi.

"Of course," Jannie replied. "We sail for a week or more without taking on more coal."

"What about food and water? We are many people, over 700."

Henri leaned forward. "Listen, Father, it is very important we know exactly how many men, women and children, how many babies, how many are families. Also, do they have papers, identity cards, passports? We have enough drinking water for a day at most for that many people. We have some food, enough to make soup, some bread. Your people must bring water with them, and food for three days."

"Three days?" the Rabbi interjected, "I thought you said it was one day?"

"Yes Father, but it may be longer. We may have to anchor, or go a port further away." He looked at the worried man sitting opposite him. "This won't be a summer cruise."

"Of course," Rabbi Wietzer was silent for a moment. "I understand the need for secrecy, of course I do, but I have to talk to the Committee."

"Committee?"

"They are good people, Jannie, we trust them with our lives." He looked at each sailor. "They organize everything. This is a time for order, for stability in the chaos around us. They bring order to our lives."

"We had better meet them, Father," Henri said, "if we are to put our lives in their hands as well."

The Rabbi smiled. "As they will want to meet you before they agree to put all our lives in your hands."

They shook hands and hustled through the half-open door and back onboard, the sound of fighting loud in their ears after the quiet of the synagogue.

*

Jimmy straightened up and looked around the small group. "I'm going ashore to check tram times." He turned to Miller. "Chief, come with me."

They were soon moving towards the buildings on the other side of the quay. The fighting around the bridges flared and died away sporadically. From what he had seen earlier, Jimmy thought the Germans would find it hard to break out. The Dutch army was well sited in a solid building commanding both bridges. It would take more than small-arms fire to dislodge them. As long as the Dutch held on, the bridges were impassable. A few spent rounds whipped through the leaves on the trees. The

71

occasional "whang" of a ricochet kept them moving carefully from cover to cover.

When Jimmy was certain they were out of sight of *Malines*, he took Dusty by the arm and steered him down an alley that led to the west.

"I'm just going to have a word with that paddle-boat, Dusty." Jimmy felt his Chief's eyes on him.

"And why would that be, sir?"

Jimmy pulled out his cigarette case. "Because, Dusty, we are going home in her."

"I see." Dusty lit up and blew smoke into the evening. "May I enquire why, sir?"

Jimmy looked at his friend. "I was invited by her coxswain to take command and sail her to England."

"I take it you accepted."

"I didn't have any choice."

"Why, sir?"

"Because he asked me to take the refugees from that synagogue."

"Bloody 'ell."

"Indeed."

"Jimmy, that is a big ask."

Jimmy nodded. "He pretty much ambushed me on the quay."

"Why you sir?"

"He thinks the Navy ought to be able to find England." He gave a short laugh. "He certainly can't. He's never been off the river." He stamped out his cigarette. "We'll go onboard now to make sure he hasn't changed his mind" He looked at Dusty. "I'd like you with me, but only if you're happy to give it a go. It will take a while to reach England, and the Germans might have something to say about that."

Dusty looked at his officer. "And you think we should do it?"

"Of course. They can't stay here."

"Right, sir." He flicked away his cigarette. "I've often fancied a trip in a paddle-boat. Promised the missus we'd give it a go once, but it was raining."

Jimmy smiled. "Thanks, Dusty." He punched him lightly on the shoulder. "Let's find out if they still want us."

*

"How many?"

"Seven hundred and fifty six."

Jimmy glanced at Henri, who shrugged. "Yes, it's a lot. And some are very young."

"And some are very old," said Dusty. "Getting them onboard will be slow."

Jimmy thought for a moment. "Is the Rabbi with them?" Henri nodded. "Good. You must speak to him when Dusty and I leave. Tell him we will take him and the people in the synagogue to England. You must make him understand we cannot take any more people than are already in the building." Henri nodded. "If the word gets out we're sailing for England, *De Ruyter* will be swamped. If any attempt is made to rush the ship, I will not take her to sea."

"I understand, Kapitein," said Henri, "And the Rabbi will understand. I will instruct him to tell only the most trusted members of the Committee and to keep the synagogue doors locked until we are ready."

"Thank you." Jimmy checked his watch. "Start embarking the oldest at 2030. Take them in small groups – no more than twenty. Next, families with babies, and then the rest. Keep them moving. Keep them quiet and don't show any lights. No-one must run off to tell their friends or we'll have a catastrophe on our hands." He stood up. "We'd better be getting back. I'll send some men over at 2030. Please set all clocks to Greenwich Mean Time now. And make sure all watches are altered as well. We don't want any cock-ups."

"Cocks-ups?"

"Mistakes. Petty Officer Ward and his men will return onboard *Malines* by 2245. No further passengers must be allowed onboard once they leave. Is that clear?"

"Yes sir," replied Henri.

"My party will embark once *Malines* is underway. Leave a gangway out for us."

"Yes sir"

"We sail at 2330. You will take her down river, Henri. Tell Jannie we require steam for full power at 2300. Tell the Committee that no-one is allowed on deck. The ship must be darkened from now on. We do not want to draw any attention to her. There must be no noise from the passengers, especially the babies, while we're making our way down river. Please make sure the Committee know and that they pass this on."

Jimmy looked at Dusty and Henri. "What have I forgotten?"

"Heads, sir."

"Ah," Henri smiled, "The crew will show them. And the drinking water tanks." He looked at Jimmy, "I will tell the Committee to post sentries on the water tanks."

"Good."

"How much drinking water do we have," Dusty asked Henri.

"Enough for two or three days if it's rationed."

"Anything else?" asked Jimmy.

"Yes. I will be happy when we are at sea." Henri smiled at the Chief Petty Officer. "We will have a warm English beer when we arrive."

"More than one," laughed Dusty as he shook the old man's hand and followed his officer.

"The situation is fluid," Jimmy remarked to Dusty as they headed back along the quay.

Dusty smiled at the classic description used by officers when they had no idea what was going on.

"I don't know what you find so funny, Dusty. We'll be in the lap of the gods once this caper starts."

"Aye aye sir." Dusty returned Jimmy's quizzical gaze with the bland mask of a seasoned matelot.

He could sense his young friend's anxiety and his doubts about the wisdom of their chosen course of action. He waited patiently while Jimmy stopped to study the fighting on the nearest bridge and the action on the far side of the river. Air activity seemed to have tailed off, though there were still enough aircraft around to be a worry.

"We might just get away with it, sir." He looked at the young Lieutenant. "But you will have some explaining to do the other end."

Jimmy shrugged and felt for his cigarettes.

"One thing at a time, Dusty," he said. "One thing at a time."

∗

"My family?" The boy's voice cracked with pain, "What about my family?"

Jannie tightened his grip on the boy's hand. "They can't get through before we sail but they are safe, Sam. You know that. You know they will come when they can."

The boy gazed helplessly at the implacable old engineer. Jannie waited, watching Sam carefully. He saw his chest fill as he took a breath, saw resolve cross that frightened young face, the shoulders pulled back, and nodded.

"Good lad."

*

Dusty and Henri moved quickly across the empty quay. The door of the synagogue opened as they approached and was locked and bolted behind them and they went into the side room.

It was full. Henri was surprised to see six tough-looking young men and four young women seated or leaning against the walls. So, this was the Committee. He had been expecting grey-bearded Elders.

Their leader came forward and held out his hand. "Henri, welcome. I am Gideon." He smiled. "We are not what you expected."

"That is very true," Henri said. "Has the Rabbi explained…"

Gideon stopped him. "He has, Henri. We are overwhelmed. What can we say?" He shrugged, "Some of us stopped believing in G-d many months ago, some have been praying for deliverance." He looked hard at the two seamen. "Now you turn up. Why?"

"Because it is the righteous thing to do," said a young woman. "I am Sarah. I have not met many righteous people on my way here."

Henri spoke clearly and slowly, "Not righteous at all. But we have our ship and she can sail to England; it will be a long, strange voyage for us all so ask them to bring their instruments, if they have them. We may need music to lift our spirits."

Sarah looked more closely at this teak-hard sailor. He was a man of surprises. She listened carefully as he spoke.

"Lieutenant Gale has asked me to introduce Chief Petty Officer Miller. He will be sailing with us. He has much to tell you."

Miller stepped forward. In a quiet, relaxed voice he told them what Jimmy had decided and the need for swift movement across the quay.

When he had finished, Sarah asked, "Why will they be armed?"

"To protect us all, Miss." Dusty looked around, "To stop the ship being rushed by other people." He sighed, "In case we have trouble with Fifth Columnists."

He went on, "They are eight young men with rifles, here to help us get away." Smiling at the earnest expressions of the young people, he said, "They will be very gentle."

Sarah smiled back. "Thank you."

Dusty nodded. "Will you be ready by 2025?"

"Yes," replied Gideon.

Dusty went through his short check-list.

Number of passengers. Papers. How many groups.

How many babies. Any orphans or unaccompanied children.

One small bag per person. Water. Mug, plate and spoon.

Warm coat and hats. Any sickness. Medicines and first aid.

Musical instruments.

He checked his watch again. "We have two and a half hours to move 756 people across the quay. They must stay in their groups. If they move quickly everyone will get onboard by 2300. We need half an hour before we sail to brief them and go through the safety drills. We sail no later than 2330."

Henri took over. "I need six on deck, two on the steps and four below." He looked at Gideon and Sarah. "They should be young, strong and kind." He smiled at their surprise. "Don't forget, most of your people will never have been on a boat. They'll be anxious about the voyage, sad about leaving home and terrified of the sea. They'll need help to move across the deck without tripping, and to get safely down the stairs. Once down there it will be dark. It will get stuffy until we sail. It will all be very confusing."

Gideon laughed. "It will be very confusing for us all."

"And terrifying," said Sarah.

"Have you twelve people I could take with me now?" Henri asked.

Gideon nodded, "In thirty minutes. You go. Sarah will come soon."

"Right," said Dusty. "I'll see you onboard."

He went up to the Rabbi and took him out of the room, followed by Henri. At the door he asked him quietly, "Father, can we persuade you to change your mind?"

The Rabbi shook his head, "Nee, Dusty. I have my duty, just as you have yours."

"You can always change your mind, Father, right up to the moment we let go of the last rope."

The Rabbi nodded. "I know. Thank you, my friend."

Back on the quay, Dusty looked at Henri, "He'll stay, won't he?"

"Ja, he will."

*

"Engine room. Sam here."

"Henri here. Your report please."

"Engine room ready for sea, sir. Engines turned over. Pressure on the fire-main. Generator running. Power to all circuits. Bilges pumped out, sir."

"Thank you, Sam. Supper at 1930. Eat in relays, Jannie first."

"Aye aye, sir."

Sam turned to Jannie and told him, "Supper at 1930. Henri wants you to go first."

While Sam was surprised, Jannie was not. There would be no time for Sam to brood while he was responsible for keeping the ship at immediate notice for sea.

From the bridge, Henri saw Sarah leave the synagogue and run across the quay. He called down.

"Sarah, up here."

"Have you been on a ship before?" he asked when she arrived.

"Nee. Not until now." She smiled nervously. "I don't know anything about them, or the sea."

"Are your parents coming with us," he asked gently.

Sarah shook her head. "Nee. My father will not leave my mother. She is not well enough to travel. They've lived all their lives in the same place and have many friends there. He believes their friends will look after them."

Henri looked at the girl, "Why are you here?"

She shrugged. "I want to live."

Henri went down the after ladder ahead of the girl and opened the door to the after cabin. "Here we will put mothers with babies."

Sarah gasped with delight. She had never seen an old-fashioned ship's cabin with its gleaming mahogany panelling, a big brass oil lamp glowing as it swung slowly from side to side over the table and four box bunks open and inviting.

"Oh my," she breathed. "They will love this."

77

He led the way forward to the first-class saloon. "We'll fill this room with the elders." Sarah could not believe her eyes. "Such a beautiful place."

They went along the passage to the forward saloon. A blast of hot air hit them as they passed a hatch. "What's that?" said Sarah, recoiling from the smell of burning coal and hot oil.

"The engine room."

The forward saloon was spartan compared to the other room. Sarah wondered how long they would have to stay below decks when they sailed.

"When the after saloon is full, we'll bring everyone down that," Henri said, pointing to a ladder at the back of the room. "We'll fill the saloon from the front so we don't block the ladders." He looked at Sarah. "Once they're all aboard, we'll get them to move as close to this wall as possible before they sit down." He tapped the after bulkhead.

"Why?"

"We don't want too much weight up front," Henri said. "Once we're out at sea, we will move people up into the deck saloon. That makes more space down below."

"Is that everything?" Sarah looked suddenly overwhelmed by the prospect of what was to come.

"Hey," Henri smiled at her, "people pay hundreds of guilders for a cruise like this."

He guided the girl to the after saloon where Willem and Dirk were laying places for supper. Henk was busy at the galley stove. They stopped to stare at Sarah as she walked in.

"Where are your manners?" shouted Henri.

Sarah laughed and walked up to Henk, "What are you cooking?"

Henk, forty years old, staid and steady, blushed to the roots of his deep red hair just as Jannie and Sam burst through the door.

"Sarah," called Henri, delighted at their timing. "Come and meet the crew."

Sarah turned, unaware of the confusion she had caused in the galley. Her eyes widened when she saw the solemn, grubby little boy in oily, faded blue trousers and a grimy singlet standing next to a similarly dressed old man. "Jannie and Sam," explained Henri, "are responsible for making sure the paddles keep turning."

"He means we are the only ones who do any work," Jannie said, "Welcome aboard."

The boy did not say a word.

"Sarah is from the synagogue," Henri continued. "She's a Council member and will be bringing help to get our passengers safely onboard."

"We'll need that," grunted Henk before turning to the girl, "Would you like some soup, mevrouw? There's plenty here."

"You are very kind," she replied, "I'd love some."

Henk placed a steaming bowl of soup in front of her. "Pass the bread, Willem."

Sarah ate, grateful for the warmth of their welcome and their quiet, undemonstrative kindness.

Sam and Jannie ate quickly, stood up, excused themselves and vanished. "We are at immediate notice for sea," Willem explained, seeing the question in Sarah's eyes.

"What does that boy do?" she asked, "He is far too young to be working."

"Sam is the fireman. He is older than he looks."

No-one lingered over supper. They cleared the tables and went on deck. As she approached the gangway, Sarah touched Henk lightly on the arm. "That was delicious. Thank you."

Henri watched the exchange and smiled before picking up the engine-room telephone.

"How is the boy?"

"Steady enough," Jannie replied quietly. "He'll be busy as soon as we get underway, and then too tired to think."

"Come up when you've done your checks, Jannie. Sam can keep steam up on his own."

Henri turned and gazed across the quay at the old synagogue. He straightened as Jannie approached.

"I think we should share this moment, my friend," he said sadly. "My home is burning over there and we're certainly burning our bridges here."

Jannie nudged his shoulder, "Why do you say that?"

Henri looked at the synagogue and saw the door open.

"When the first of those Jewish families set foot onboard, I will have signed death warrants for us all. Do you suppose those Germans will pat us on our heads and tell us we've been naughty boys if we don't get away?"

Jannie shrugged. "What else can we do?" He stared at his oldest friend. "Are you worried this old girl won't make it?" he said, stroking the engine telegraph in the corner.

"Nee, Jannie, not that." He sighed. "There are mines in the river and aeroplanes in the sky. If we get out to sea…"

"We will get out to sea, Henri, and we will get to England." Jannie put both hands on Henri's shoulders and gripped them hard. "Look over there." He pointed to the synagogue where a small crowd of elderly people were shuffling through the gates. "There are seven hundred and fifty-six reasons why we will sail on time." He gave Henri a little shake. "And one very important reason onboard." He stopped talking to look into Henri's troubled eyes. "We promised Paul we'd take Sam to England, didn't we?"

Henri shook himself, as if waking from a dream. "We did, Jannie. We did just that."

He smiled at the old engineer. "And don't forget the kindly widows."

"Never," said Jannie, "Kindly and comfortable. They will welcome us with open arms."

*

The embarkation began. Jannie went along the deck to see how it was going. The guides kept everyone moving quietly and competently. There was not much of a delay at the ladder into the saloon because the young men and women had positioned themselves so they could keep everyone moving safely without getting separated from their bags.

Jannie joined the hesitant old folk as they descended cautiously, clinging tightly to the handrail. In the saloon there was a quiet mutter of conversation and prayer. Jannie noticed they all held onto the handles of their bags. Once the elders were safely onboard, mothers and babies appeared. Groups of refugees flowed across the quay as the sky darkened. Down below, people sat quietly, keeping their thoughts to themselves. Most were tired and anxious. Elderly couples sat close, holding hands, saying little. Those who had left their families behind created a small space around themselves in which they sat with eyes either closed or staring, unseeing, their thoughts turned inwards.

*

It was Henk who found the little girl. She was standing on the port side near the stern, gazing across the river at the smoke and flames rising into the night sky.

He noticed tears on her grubby cheeks and took in her shabby clothes and the small, scuffed suitcase at her feet. He thought she might be about three years old.

Coughing softly to attract her attentional, Henk stopped a couple of metres away. "Hello,' he rumbled softly, "My name is Henk. What is yours?"

The child turned slowly to gaze up at him. She stared at him for several seconds before answering, "Ruth."

"Hello, Ruth," Henk's teeth gleamed in his beard as he smiled at her. "Where are your mummy and daddy?"

Henk had to bend down to hear Ruth's whispered reply. "Gone home." Henk knelt on the deck beside her and asked, "Are they coming back?" Ruth shook her head. "I stay here."

"Come," whispered Henk, holding out his arm. The girl moved towards him. Very gently, he placed his hand on her back and drew her close to him. She was shaking.

Reaching into his trouser pocket, Henk took out his handkerchief to wipe away her tears. Before he could do that, the girl buried her head in his jacket.

Henk gazed around. He dared not move and yet there were still many people flowing onboard who needed his help to find places to sit in the darkness below.

By now he was holding the girl and patting her back, much as he had seen his sister hold and comfort her children when they were upset. He pulled back a little so he could look at the girl and said, "I must stand now."

The girl nodded and tightened her grip as Henk rose to his feet. He lifted her up, wondering what on earth he should do.

Sarah saw him when she brought another group to the top of the companion-way. She moved to his side, "Who is this?"

"Ruth," replied Henk, relieved at the thought of handing the little girl to Sarah. The girl's head remained firmly buried in his shoulder. She had stopped sobbing.

"Ruth," whispered Henk into her ear. "Sarah has come to say hallo." He lifted her up slightly so she could see over his shoulder. "Here she is."

Two solemn brown eyes peered over the top of Henk's jacket. Ruth stared at Sarah before lifting her head to say "Hallo."

Henk whispered, his head facing away from Ruth, "Her parents have gone home and left her here."

He saw Sarah's eyes widen as he continued, "They told her to stay here," and pointed at the deck where she had been standing.

Sarah shook her head and sighed. She knew them and would tell Henk why they had gone once Ruth was asleep.

"Come here, Ruth, come to Sarah." She held out her arms and gently took the child from Henk. "Let's go downstairs and find somewhere to sit. Henk will come too, as soon as he's finished working." She smiled brightly at the little girl. "He won't be long."

Ruth stared as Henk pulled out of his jacket pocket a large gleaming turnip of a watch. He held it to her ear so she could hear it ticking before showing her the hands, black and bold against the white enamelled face. Placing the watch carefully in her right hand, he said "I'll come and find you when the big hand is pointing to six." He put his forefinger on the number then bent forward to whisper in her ear, "Will you look after it for me?" Ruth nodded and clasped the watch firmly with both hands.

Henk picked up Ruth's suitcase and told Sarah, "I'll look after this. You'd better get below." He looked at the steady stream of people still moving across the deck and going down the companion way. "There can't be many more. We sail at 2330."

As Henk hurried forward along the port side, Sarah joined the people at the head of the companion-way. "It's very cosy down there," she said, "and dark. We'll have to be careful we don't tread on anyone's toes."

Ruth nodded, her eyes fixed on the face of the watch.

The after saloon was alive with the whispers of many people. It reminded Sarah of the hum of one of her aunt's bee hives. She made her way through the crowded room by the dim light coming though the skylight. It smelt of unwashed bodies and smoke from the fighting on the bridge.

A large round English sailor rolled towards them, a cheery smile showing through his beard.

"Hallo, ladies, seats for two this way," he said and turned to lead them into a passage. Sarah realised he hadn't recognised her as she was holding Ruth. Hurrying after him she called, "Spider."

Webb turned and looked closely at her. "Oh, sorry, Sarah, I didn't know you had a little girl. This way," he said, continuing along the passage.

A wall of heat hit them as they approached the brightly lit hatch leading down to the engine room. Spider stopped abreast it to shield Sarah and Ruth as they hurried past.

The forward saloon was refreshingly cool. There was ample room against the after bulkhead as people coming down the forward companion way were ushered towards the bows.

"Over here, Sarah." Spider had collected one of the hammocks used by *De Ruyter*'s crew and made a seat of it in the port after corner.

"You sit there with the little girl." Gesturing at the increasing number of people in the bows, he said, "We'll shift them aft once everyone's onboard." Moving a couple of chairs to form a barrier, Spider went on, "You'll be out of the way and comfy here."

Sarah sank gratefully onto the tightly rolled canvas. "Thank you, Spider. She's heavier than she looks." She saw that Ruth was fast asleep, Henk's watch held tight in her hands. She said quietly "Could you let Henk know where we are? He's got her suitcase." She smiled. "If you see Gideon tell him I've picked up a stray."

*

On the bridge, Henri checked the time. *Malines* was due to sail in twenty minutes. He slid down the ladder to the deck below. Making his way to the cuddy he met Petty Officer Ward checking that nothing had been left behind.

"I wish we were coming with you, Henri," he said.

"So do I," replied the old sailor. "Your boys have been good. We'd never have managed without them."

Sharky came to attention. "That is very kind of you to say, sir. They'll be pleased to know that."

They shook hands. Sharky saluted Henri and ran ashore. He rounded up his boys, checked their kit and doubled them back to *Malines*.

Jimmy was waiting for them at the foot of the gangway.

"All present and correct, sir," reported Ward.

"Well done. Get onboard now, Sub Lieutenant Coombes is waiting for you and the stewards have a meal ready." He looked at his petty officer and held out his hand, "Good luck, Sharky."

"Good luck, sir. See you in Chatham."

Jimmy watched them go onboard.

The Old Man hailed Jimmy from the wing of the bridge, almost invisible in the smoke, "Good luck, and thank you."

"Good luck, sir," Jimmy called back as smoke poured from *Malines'* two tall funnels and rolled slowly along the quay.

A voice called "Cheerio" as *Malines* slowly gathered headway and disappeared into the evening.

Jimmy stared after her. His hand shook slightly as he lit a cigarette.

*

Footstep rang out on the quay. "All set sir?" asked Miller quietly.

"Yes. That went well."

"Aye sir."

They made their way to *De Ruyter* where Henri was waiting for them. He shook Jimmy's hand, "Welcome, Kapitein."

Jimmy patted the old man on the shoulder. "Thank you, Henri." He looked over towards the paddle-boat. "Is all well?"

"All is very well, meneer, now that you are here." Jimmy could sense the relief in Henri's voice. "We have embarked all who were in the synagogue, seven hundred and fifty-six people. Some are very small." Jimmy smiled as Henri continued, "Your Sharky Ward was a God-send. He was like the Good Shepherd. Those boys of his, they were so kind, so gentle." Henri shook his head in wonder. "I did not expect that." He paused. "Nor did the Jewish families." Henri cleared his throat. "They do not have good experience of men in uniform. Even of some Dutchmen, I am ashamed to say."

A man approached from the ship. Henri turned to him, "Here is the English Royal Navy, Rabbi."

The Rabbi moved towards Jimmy and, to his surprise, embraced him warmly.

Jimmy had not been kissed by a man since he was a child, and never by one with a full beard.

A rumbling laugh spilled out of Rabbi Wietzer's broad chest. "You are surprised? So am I? I did not believe such a miracle could happen."

Jimmy smiled, "The miracle is yet to happen, Rabbi. We have a long way to go. We need all the help God can give us on this journey."

"I will pray for you, my son. That I will do. Perhaps He will be listening."

"I hope so," said Jimmy. "And I hope you will be with us to remind Him from time to time."

"Ach. Nee, meneer." The Rabbi shook his head. "My place is here, in my synagogue. I will pray for you and for my people who cannot leave with you."

Jimmy looked at Henri, "Did you know this?"

"Nee, Kapitein, I thought he would sail with us."

Rabbi Wietzer interrupted. "Enough talking. You must go. I will let your ropes go, but I will never let go of you."

Jimmy put both his hands on the Rabbi's shoulders. "You are a brave man, sir. We will pray for you." He kissed the priest lightly on one cheek and went onboard.

5.

De Ruyter sails

Jimmy waited at the head of the gangway. "Where are the passengers, Henri?" He was looking around the empty decks with some surprise.

"All below, Kaptitein, as ordered." Henri glanced at the Englishman. "I have darkened ship. We will check before we sail, yes?"

"Yes," answered Jimmy, before asking, "Did you get the flag?"

Henri laughed with joy. "Ja. That was, how do you say?" he paused, searching for words. "Inspired." Still laughing, he continued, "And the boards and paint."

"Well done," Jimmy interrupted, leaving Dusty, Webb and the seamen none the wiser.

He turned to Miller, "Stow our kit in the captain's cuddy and pair the hands with Henri's deck-hands. Two forrard, two aft and two on the gangway. We'll get it in before slipping." Taking Dusty aside he said, "Check no lights are showing."

"Aye aye sir."

"You're in charge of the deck and passengers. They'll stay below until we're well clear of the Hook." Dusty nodded as Jimmy concluded, "I'm going below with Henri to talk to our passengers."

He looked at Henri. It was difficult to read his expression in the darkness. Jimmy leant over the guard-rail and called to the Rabbi.

"Five minutes, Father. If you go to the front, we'll tell you when to let that rope go. Then make your way to the back end and let us go when we say so." He waited a moment before adding. "If you change your mind, sir, come onboard after you've let the front go."

As Jimmy turned away, he said to Dusty, "Try to persuade him. He doesn't stand a chance when the Germans find out what he's done." To Henri he said, "Let's go below."

"Aye aye sir," Dusty replied to Jimmy's back.

Henri stopped at the bottom of the ladder. It was very dark and very hot. "It will be cooler when we get underway. We have good ventilation." He switched on a small pocket torch with his fingers held over the glass. "We have a saloon forward and another aft. I have told people to sit and stay quiet."

"Let's start at the front."

Henri led the way into the crowded second-class saloon. Jimmy could make out figures sitting very still, as if holding their breath. "Translate for me please," he muttered, before raising his voice.

Speaking slowly and clearly, he said. "Welcome onboard. My name is Lieutenant Gale. I am an officer in the British Royal Navy. I have requisitioned this ship in order to sail to England." Several men started to talk. He could hear they were asking questions and raised his hand to silence them. "You are all onboard because you want to escape before the Germans get here. So do I." Sighs and quiet prayers rippled through the crowd.

"We have about one hour before we are in the North Sea. You must stay quiet and you must stay below." He paused. "Is that understood?"

There was a murmur of assent. In the silence that followed he said, even more slowly and clearly. "Our safety depends on everyone doing exactly what I have told you." He waited until Henri had finished his translation before adding, "No lights, no smoking. We sail in darkness."

He nodded to Henri and went aft to repeat his instructions. On the way, Henri stopped at the hatch to the engine room and gave a sharp whistle. Jannie had obviously been waiting a call for he shot up the ladder. "Here is our engineer, Kapitein. His name is Jannie. The fireman is very young. His name is Sam." A grubby face peered up at the naval officer, eyes white against his soot-streaked face.

Jimmy shook Jannie's hand, noticing him quickly wiping the oil off on his trousers. "All set, Chief?" he asked.

"Yes Kapitein, all set," replied Jannie. "And full bunkers."

"Good," said Jimmy. "While we're on the river I'll pass all engine orders by phone. There is no point in advertising our position." Jannie looked at him and asked, "Could you give me a seaman, Kapitein? For the phone?"

Jimmy nodded, "Yes. I'll send one of mine. You OK with orders in English?"

"Yes Kapitein."

"Right," said Jimmy, "We'd better get on," adding quietly, so as not to give offence, "Not too much smoke, Jannie, there's a good man."

Jannie looked into Jimmy's eyes and saw the strain behind his calm expression.

"Not too much smoke, Kapitein."

Jimmy nodded at him and carried on to brief the people in the after saloon.

Back on deck, Jimmy took a quick glance around, noting a sudden upsurge in small-arms fire at the bridge-head. Many fires were burning to the south, on the far side of the island. He was glad to see smoke drifting across the river, blurring the outline of buildings and cranes.

"Time to go," he told Henri as they went up to the bridge.

Dusty had taken charge there so Jimmy told him to send Buckland down to the engine room to act as communications number.

"Take her out when ready, Henri," he ordered. "Dead slow until I tell you we're out of sight of the bridges. In gangway, Chief." Henri called "Slip head rope" to the fo'c'stle hands and the splash of the rope hitting the water coincided with the rumble of the gangway coming inboard.

"Slow Astern".

The great paddles wheezed and splashed. Jimmy thought they would wake the dead as they slowly beat the water.

Once the bows swung clear, Henri ordered "Stop." There was a moment of silence as the bows continued to swing out, then he picked up the telephone to the afterdeck and ordered, "Slip stern rope."

He waited for confirmation before ordering, "Slow Ahead".

There was a brief puff of smoke as Jannie engaged the clutch and the paddles bit the water. *De Ruyter* slowly drew clear of the quay, empty save for the stocky figure of the Rabbi, one arm raised in farewell, or was it a benediction?

Jimmy wrote in the log,

"2330. Slipped and proceeded to sea."

*

Sarah awoke as *De Ruyter* got underway, confused and alarmed by the strange noises. Ruth did not stir when she slipped her arms from under her and stood up. The saloon was full of people sitting on chairs or on the floor. There were many couples and fewer people on their own. It was hard to tell their ages in the dim light coming from the companion way.

She was wondering when Spider would come back when Henk appeared. He smiled as she saw him and held out an enamel mug. "Spider told me to bring this."

He gazed round the saloon and then down at Ruth. "Her parents didn't come back?"

"Nee, Henk." Sarah laid her hand on his arm. "They couldn't." She felt him tense and quickly went on. "They both have elderly parents who wouldn't leave." Sarah's eyes filled with tears. "I was standing by the gangway when they pushed through the people coming onboard." She wiped her eyes. "I don't even know their names. Just what her father told me before he said, 'We have to go'. He had his arm round his wife's shoulders. I could see she was crying."

Henk looked at the little girl, fast asleep on the hammock, still holding his watch. He looked at Sarah. "Who is going to look after her?"

Sarah looked at him but said nothing.

∗

With the last of the ebb tide and at full power, *De Ruyter* splashed her way down river towards the sea. The land either side of them slid by in darkness, broken by vivid flashes of gunfire to the north.

They passed burning buildings a few miles inland, marking the site of fighting. The men on the bridge grew silent as they approached and then passed them, knowing the chances of being seen increased while they remained silhouetted against those fires.

"We should carry the tide to the Hoek, Kapitein," Henri said quietly.

"Thank you, Henri," Jimmy replied. He looked at his watch, "About an hour?"

"Ja. She's making about sixteen knots over the ground."

Jimmy moved to the engine room telephone. "Jannie, how's that lad of yours, Sam?"

Henri was impressed the Englishman had remembered the boy's name.

"No need to worry about the boy, sir," he said, with a quick glance at the lieutenant. "Jannie takes good care of him."

Jimmy nodded in the darkness as he replied. "He certainly does. Sam is driving the ship while Jannie is teaching Buckland to be a stoker." He was silent for a while. "We'll have to sort the watches out. There's a long day ahead of us."

He looked all round as they passed another burning building about three miles away.

Jimmy took Dusty into the wheelhouse so he could talk to him and Henri at the same time.

"Someone's bound to ask us what we're up to when we get to the Hook. Henri, if they're Dutch, you tell them you're sailing for Vlissingen. If they ask, tell them we have refugees onboard. Whatever you do, don't stop. If it's the Royal Navy, we'll keep out of the way. Reply in Dutch and tell them you don't understand."

Henri smiled at Jimmy, "You ever seen an angry Dutchman?"

Jimmy shook his head.

"Maybe you will tonight." He nodded to himself as he concentrated on steering his ship down the dark river.

There was a loud cry from the bow lookout. "Aircraft approaching. Starboard bow."

Jimmy and Dusty moved out to the starboard wing as an aircraft flew past. They could not see it but it was low and close.

They listened intently to its engines.

As Jimmy feared, the aircraft began to turn. He presumed it was going to have another look at them and picked up the engine room telephone.

"Stop engines."

"Stop engines ," repeated Buckland.

"Give me Jannie. Quick as you can."

"Jannie, there's an aircraft nosing about. I've stopped engines so our wake doesn't give us away." Jimmy's ears were tuned as much to the aircraft engines as to the engine room.

"Stand by for rapid manoeuvring," he paused, "and to make smoke."

Turning to Dusty, he said, "Go below, warn the hands. Tell them to keep our passengers calm. Henri, bring her as close as you can to the port bank. It's darker there."

"Aircraft closing, starboard side," called the starboard lookout. Jimmy moved to his side and listened. It seemed to be flying from east to west along the north bank. There was a short burst of anti-aircraft fire from further inland, enough to make the aircraft increase speed and climb away.

"Slow Ahead".

The paddles splashed back into life. Jimmy called up the engine room. "All clear Jannie. Bring her back up to full power. That was a smart bit of manoeuvring. Well done."

Jannie's heartbeat returned to normal. "That, Kapitein," he replied "was a close call. We were a few seconds away from blowing the safety valve."

"I think we have a guardian angel, Jannie."

*

Dusty came back to the bridge with Gideon and Sarah. Jimmy turned to the two Committee members, "How are the passengers?"

Sarah spoke first. "All is well. The children are being good, those not asleep. The elders are finding it hard. It's hot and dark and noisy and very confusing for them. They hold hands as if they are newly married…"

"…and pray," continued Gideon. He was silent for a moment before he said quietly, "Come, Sarah. We will tell the people we can smell the sea."

The bridge was silent as the young Jews went down below.

After a while Henri looked across at Jimmy, "That's the Hoek to starboard," pointing to wharves on the north bank. "I'd better be ready to talk to anyone curious enough to ask what we're doing."

"We'll hoist the Swedish flag about ten miles out." Jimmy gazed through his binoculars at the shipping alongside the Hook. "But first we have to fend off the Dutch Port Authority. Over there, Henri." He pointed to a launch leaving a wharf.

Henri walked slowly over to the starboard bridge wing where he lit a cigar before leaning nonchalantly against the rail.

The sleek dark hull of the launch made a brave sight as her bows thrust purposefully towards them. She slowed when close alongside the bridge.

"Good evening, *De Ruyter,*" came the breezy hail through a megaphone, "What are you doing here?"

"He sounds friendly enough," muttered Jimmy.

"Aye," replied Dusty, "They must all know each other."

There was a short conversation between the Harbour Master and Henri before the launch increased speed and sheered off.

Henri turned to Jimmy. "He wanted to know where we were bound so I told him. Harwich. He didn't believe me so I said we were really going down to Vlissingen as Rotterdam was getting too hot." He shook his head. "He's my cousin. He said even an old fool like me wouldn't be stupid enough to take this bucket out to sea." He grinned. "I'll send him a post card from London."

"Well," said Jimmy, laughing, "It's a good job the Agent didn't tell him you'd cleared Customs and been given a clean bill of health."

"He can be quite forgetful," replied Henri. "If you speak to him nicely." He winked at Jimmy and Dusty. "He'll tell them in the morning."

"How much did that cost you?" asked Dusty.

"Nothing," Henri looked serious for a moment. "He is a good Dutchman."

"There's the Navy," Jimmy said, without lowering his binoculars. He studied the destroyer secured alongside. "She's at Action Stations." He saw an officer looking through binoculars at the bizarre sight of a paddle steamer setting out to sea and waved. It was a relief to get a friendly wave back.

Then they swept between the moles and out into the dark waters of the North Sea.

"Alter course to port please. Course North, quarter West."

"North, quarter West it is," replied Henri as Jimmy moved to the engine room phone once more.

"Clear of the Maas, Jannie." He listened for a moment before saying, "Full speed while it's dark. About four more hours." He was about to put the phone down but paused and added, "Orders by engine telegraph."

Turning to the Chief, he said, "Change the look outs and ask Jannie if he needs any reliefs."

"Aye aye sir."

It was a clear dark starlit night. *De Ruyter*'s broad wake was bright with phosphorescence on the calm, black sea. "We'll just have to hope our luck holds," muttered Jimmy to himself as he gazed astern. "You'd have to be blind to miss that."

Henri looked across at the English officer. He wondered if he believed a Swedish flag would protect them.

∗

"Thank God it's calm." Dusty Miller said as he came into the wheel-box. "It would be hell if it wasn't."

Jimmy grunted. "We wouldn't be out here, Dusty." He looked at the Chief and asked, "What's it like below?"

"Hot, dark and terrifying, sir." He shook his head. "Talk about trust. We told them we'd get them away and they believe us. We asked them to be silent and they're silent. Just sitting patiently. They smiled at me when I walked through. Never said a word. Occasionally someone would reach out to touch me, as if to make sure I was real." He took a deep breath. "By Christ, Jimmy, I do hope we make it, I really do."

"So do I, Dusty," Jimmy said. "We have a long way to go." He stood back from the wheel. "Take the helm, please, I need to check the chart. And keep an eye on the glass, Dusty. We don't want any surprises."

The oil lamp in the cuddy had been turned right down. Jimmy closed the door quickly and turned the wick up so he could study the chart.

He pencilled a cross one cable north west of the eastern mole and circled it before adding the time. Picking up the parallel ruler, he drew on the course they had steered for the first twelve minutes, pricked off 3.2 miles with the dividers and made another mark, added the time they altered course and drew their new course, 335 True, across the chart.

"That'll do for now," he muttered. "I'll sort the tides out later." Jimmy did not like being away from the bridge but he was the only one who could navigate.

Running quickly back to the bridge, he ordered, "Steer North nor'west."

He kicked himself for not getting those Swedish flags painted on the boards.

∗

Jimmy looked at his watch. 0130. Three more hours of darkness. He wondered what the day would bring.

"All well, Dusty?"

"All well, sir." replied the Chief. "Permission to send Evans down below to organise a brew, sir?"

"Good idea. I'll tell him and keep watch."

It was Gideon who came up with a handful of tin mugs and a fanny of hot sweet coffee. As he dished it out, he asked, "Will it be possible for some of the people to come up, maybe to the deck saloon? They would keep out of the way."

"Yes," replied Jimmy, adding, "I don't want anyone wandering around the deck while its dark. If someone went overboard, we'd never find them."

"Thank you." Gideon gazed around the bridge for a moment and then shook himself. "I'll take coffee to the bow and stern look-outs first."

When Gideon returned below, he encountered a smiling Spider.

"You got family onboard?"

"Ja, Spider," Gideon answered "My grandparents. My father told me to take them to England. They are too old to go by themselves." He gave a short laugh. "We had no idea there weren't any boats. The Rabbi took us in. Just like all the others."

Gideon gazed at Spider. "My father is a doctor and he will not leave. I went home to help him in 1938. In November that was. Thousands of Germans were escaping into Holland and a lot ended up in our town."

"I read about that in the papers," said Spider.

"Did you also read what happened to them?" The bitterness in Gideon's voice made Spider look at him closely as he continued. "Most of them were Jews and they were not made welcome."

"Why not?"

"We did not want to upset Germany. That is why not." Gideon spat the words out. "You have your Chamberlain. We have our neutrals. All they wanted was peace. Not to anger those bastards. Not to give them any excuse to invade. So they would not give them papers. No work permits. Nothing. Just hoped they would go away. When they did not go away, they built a camp. Westerhoek. In the north, near the border. My father was told to send the Jews, the German ones, to Westerhoek. Told by the Jewish Council in Amsterdam. It was Government policy, enforced by our mayor and police."

Gideon was silent, remembering hope turning to helplessness, the ever-present fear of the refugees he accompanied on the trains; how other passengers waiting on the platform moved away before staring at them.

"Living close to the border, my family saw the Dutch army mobilise and then stand down a few times. We noticed their antiquated weapons and felt sorry for the boys in uniform. The Netherlands had been neutral a long time and meant to stay that way." Gideon thought for a moment before continuing. "It was after Yom Kippur," Gideon saw the confusion in Spider's face. "Sorry, October last year."

Spider smiled at him. "I don't know much, do I?"

"No-one does. But you will learn." He paused. "Yes, October last year. My father and mother told me I had to take his parents to England. Of course, they had not told them."

"No? Why not?"

"Because they were as stubborn as their son. And when he told them about camps in Germany, they did not believe him."

"What made them change their mind?"

Gideon's face hardened. "Papa took them to the station. Stood with them on the platform to watch me lead another group of Jews onto the train." He winced at the memory. "One of their neighbours, someone they had known all their lives, spat at those Jews. When Opa said something, this bastard told him 'You'll be next'."

"Christ, Gideon," Spider whispered, "and your mother's family? What happened to them?"

"They died in 1919. She's an only child."

"Why didn't your parents come?"

"He's the doctor. She runs the surgery. He will not leave his patients, any of them, and she will not leave him. My sister is a nurse in Amsterdam. She would not leave. That is why they have sent me." He glanced at the old sailor. "It is my duty. And when my grandparents are safe, I will go home."

For a while the two men sat in a silence broken only by the murmur of others and the steady beat of the paddles beyond the hull.

*

"We'd better get our flag and boards sorted out." Jimmy slapped the side of the wheel-box. "Transform ourselves into a Swedish pleasure boat caught out by an accident of war."

"They'll have the boards painted the Swedish colours soon. Shouldn't take long to dry." Dusty looked at Jimmy, "Where shall I hang them?"

"On the bridge wings." Jimmy lowered his voice, "The higher they are the more likely it is an aircraft will see them."

"Unless we meet one who shoots first."

Jimmy shook his head. "I'm hoping they'll be so surprised to see us puffing away out here that they'll have a look and go away."

Dusty smiled at the young officer. "Do you really think that'll work, sir?"

Jimmy shrugged. "Who knows? But at least people will have something to do, painting the boards and making the change. Better than sitting around with time to think. The flag is enormous. That and the boards might stop a nosy pilot shooting at us."

"What are we going to do with the passengers?"

"They'll have to come up on deck, those who want to. Once the sun is up it shouldn't be too chilly and it'll be better than being below."

Dusty nodded. "I'll let Gideon and Sarah know when they're awake. You'll tell Henri won't you?"

"Tell me what?" Neither had noticed Henri open the door.

"Morning Henri," replied Jimmy, "We're talking about getting the passengers on deck when it's light enough."

"And changing into a Swedish ship," added Dusty. "The Morning Watch will be busy."

"Ja," Henri looked at the two English sailors then tapped the side of the barometer. "The glass is steady and the sky is clear." He smiled. "It should be a lovely day."

*

"Have a look, Spider. About five degrees off the port quarter."

Spider took the glasses from Jimmy and scanned the horizon carefully. "Ship, sir, closing. About five miles away."

"Thanks Spider. Take the wheel and tell the lad to nip aft and tell Henri to come to the bridge. And tell the stern look-out to report by messenger."

"Aye aye sir."

Dusty and Gideon headed for the bridge as soon as they became aware of the increased activity. They arrived just as the starboard look-out shouted, "Ship, right astern, sir, closing fast."

96

"Very good," replied Jimmy calmly. "Continue your all-round sweep," he wanted eyes looking everywhere, "and keep your ears open for aircraft."

"Aye aye sir."

"Looks like a destroyer," said Dusty, still studying the ship. "Could be one of ours."

Jimmy said quietly, "I hope so," before turning to Gideon, "Tell any passengers on deck there is a ship coming to have a look at us. Ask them to wave cheerfully. But don't shout out."

As Gideon headed down the ladder, Jimmy called after him, "Keep the rest of the passengers below, please."

Gideon raised a hand in acknowledgement.

It was getting lighter rapidly. Jimmy saw with relief it was a British destroyer, one of the old V & W's. He had served in several as a Gunner and wondered if this was one of them.

"Take the helm, Spider. Course 335. And tell the engine room to stand by."

"Aye aye sir, course 335."

The destroyer approached, smoke streaming astern from her two funnels, a brilliant white wave either side of her bows as she sliced through the calm sea.

Henri tumbled up to the bridge as a light flickered from the destroyer. "What ship?"

"Do we have a signal lamp, Henri?"

The Dutchman thought for a moment, "I'll get the torch from the cuddy. That should do."

The Naval signalman was continuing to interrogate them as the destroyer slowed down. It was light enough now for Jimmy to see that her forward guns were trained on *De Ruyter*.

Henri handed Jimmy the torch and he slowly spelt out. "Swedish ship *De Agathe*."

The destroyer slowed down about a cable off their port beam, turrets swinging round with silent menace, white ensign streaming from her masthead.

"Wave," Jimmy whispered urgently, "Wave at them."

"We are Swedish ship. Who are you?" Jimmy's torch stuttered, hesitant and wavering around. Few merchant ships had trained signalmen onboard.

"This is British warship *Wanderer*." A harsh, metallic voice boomed across the sea. Their captain had switched on his loud-hailer. "What was your last port of call and where are you bound?"

"From Malmo to Dover." Jimmy replied by light, slowly and deliberately. He ignored Dusty's suppressed laugh.

"Anchor at the Downs. Await inspection."

"Yes please," Jimmy spelt out.

Wanderer's telegraph clanged, water boiled at her stern and she sped off to the west. Once she was hull down, Spider headed to the cuddy to rustle up the sandwiches they'd brought with them from *Malines* while Henri conjured up another fanny of coffee.

*

Jimmy leaned on the rail, watching passengers stream up on deck. "Just like the *Southsea Castle*," murmured Dusty, joining his officer and giving him a cigarette.

"Would you mind taking over from Dusty?" Jimmy asked Henri who stepped forward and took the wheel. "Stay here, Dusty while I plot our Estimated Position. I'll be about ten minutes. I want to check the tides."

Henri and Dusty nodded and Henri said, "I'll stamp twice on the deck if you're needed."

Jimmy started with the Reed's Nautical Almanack he'd taken from *Deben*, checking the accuracy of the lifeboat compass they had jury-rigged against the bearing he had taken of the sun. Satisfied, he worked out the course to steer, allowing for the ebb and flow of the tidal stream before stretching and lighting a cigarette.

*

The old Dutchman and younger English Chief stood in companionable silence for several minutes, eyes constantly searching for any sign of a ship or aircraft. Dusty had observed the way Henri went about his duties with the casual expertise of a deep-sea sailor and eventually asked the question that had been bothering him all night.

"Why did you ask us to take over *De Ruyter*, Henri? You've been a seaman all your life. You could have found your way." He looked at Henri and saw him smile.

"You are right. We could have found our way to England. But then what?" He shrugged. "In the last war your Examination Officers gave us a bad time, stopping our ships here and in the Channel, searching them sometimes. The same thing is happening now, since last September. Jimmy knows that." He punched the Englishman lightly on his arm. "So, Dusty, we ask you to take our ship." Smiling broadly, he said, "I did not expect your Lieutenant to make us a Swedish ship."

"Nor did I," Dusty replied with a short laugh.

"I will change her again when we get closer." Jimmy had been standing outside the wheel-box for a while, intrigued by the conversation he overheard.

The two seamen turned to ask simultaneously, "What to?"

"My first command," Jimmy replied, "*HMS De Ruyter.* We'll go home under the White Ensign. Spider brought one. Just in case."

Laughter rang out, startling the look-outs, the sound rolling across the empty sea. "*HMS De Ruyter!*" said Henri, grinning. "The Dutch admiral who swept your Navy from the sea?" He slapped the wheel in delight.

"Yes," said Dusty, "And he'll take her up the Medway. We'd better tie a broom to our masthead."

Jimmy watched them laughing. It took a few moments before he joined them.

*

"I'm going to get my head down," he told Henri. "Thanks for the deck-chair."

He closed his eyes but they flicked open again at the distant hum of an aircraft engine. He listened intently, relaxing slightly when he realised it wasn't closing. Easing out of his chair he walked onto the bridge.

"There's a German aircraft around, high and some distance away. Eyes and ears open, lads."

Jimmy went into the wheel-box, checked the course, tapped the glass and went back to his chair. He was asleep in minutes.

Down on the fo'c'stle, Spider and Henk were playing games with the children to give their tired parents a chance to rest. Each sailor had a tail of small people following their leader up to the bows and back, carefully copying every exaggerated move they made.

99

Dusty watched as Henri gently ushered the watching adults aft, helped by Gideon. They went willingly when they understood the need to keep their weight behind the paddles.

He saw a little girl leave her mother's side and dart forward. She was carrying something that glinted as she handed it to Henk. Was it a watch? Henk stood still, as did the children following him, and put that shiny object into his trouser pocket. They copied his movements. When he took the little girl by the hand, there was a great deal of shuffling about before the column settled down, each child holding another's hand.

Henk set off once again, every step, twist and turn faithfully copied by the children.

Spider took the hand of one of the children following him, to cheers from Henk's crew and applause from the bridge as his children copied him.

Henk and Spider stopped and sat the children down in a circle when Sarah and some of the mothers appeared with jugs and mugs and trays of cut up oranges.

"Well," said Jimmy as he leant on the rail beside Dusty. "This is turning out to be quite a party."

They smoked in silence, listening the piping voices of the children and the rumbles of Henk and Spider's replies, the steady slap-slap of the paddles and the pulsing engine.

"It would be easy to forget there's a war on," Jimmy said quietly. 'It must seem unreal to those people."

Dusty studied his officer for a while before replying. "I hope for their sakes it stays like this." He sighed. "It's not much to ask."

Neither of them had noticed Gideon come onto the bridge and turned in surprise when he said, "Whatever happens in the future, none of us will forget today."

He made a gesture that embraced the whole ship. "It is enough that we are here, free, sailing to England with you." He looked at Jimmy, then at Dusty before adding, "You did not have to take us." He paused to draw a deep breath. "But you did."

They were interrupted by the sound of cheering from the fo'c'stle.

The children were crowding round Spider, cheering because he had produced his squeeze-box.

"He never ceases to surprise me," Jimmy said, laughing, as Dusty joined him. "I wonder what else he's got in his pack."

"Best we never know."

Henk shooed the children away from Spider and made them sit in a circle around him. After bowing to his left and right, Spider struck up a tune.

Without a word, Henk took off his boots and socks and stepped forward, arms folded and feet tapping. Waiting a moment, he started to dance. It was a hornpipe, up and sideways, forwards and back, never more than a pace in any direction, left foot crossing, then his right, each delicate step perfectly executed. Henk's head and upper body rose and fell, his legs and feet moving rapidly in the early morning sun.

The children started clapping in time, their feet beginning to tap. Ruth was the first to stand, trying hard to copy Henk. Sarah stepped forward, took her hand and danced with her, immediately followed by the other children.

"Christ," whispered Jimmy in amazement.

Dusty slapped him on the back and said, "You can dance as well as Henk. You should join them."

"Thank you, Dusty," Jimmy replied dryly. "Maybe another day."

A violin picked up the tune. Then another. A cello joined in, then more violins and violas.

Spider slowed and stopped, his little dancers happily panting around him. Applause rippled from forrard to aft. Henk went up to the nearest violinist and asked, "Will you play for the children, for us all?"

Henri leaned over the bridge rail to suggest "Perhaps you could play from the top deck, that way everyone will hear you."

*

And so it was that *De Ruyter*'s concert party started. It continued for the rest of that strange, bucolic day as the sun moved from east to west in a cloudless sky above the calm, deep blue sea. The war seemed far away.

Children danced and laughed and slept; fear left the eyes of their watching parents; old men and women told stories, held hands and dozed in the sun.

Watches changed every three hours, look-outs every thirty minutes. Jimmy stayed on the bridge or dozed in his chair while Dusty and Henri alternated between the helm and moving among the passengers. Off-watch British, Dutch and Jewish watch-keepers slept, ate and listened to the music.

101

Only down below in the engine room did nothing change. Jannie watched his boys with care, never taxing their strength for long as he switched them between stoking the boiler, greasing pistons, standing at the controls and then sleeping, each for twenty minutes at a time He moved effortlessly from task to task, untiring, alert and cheerful.

The engine never faltered. Years of meticulous care and maintenance drove *De Ruyter* across the sea, just as it had driven her up and down the river Lek.

Up top, Henk moved to the galley to start organising soup and bread for everyone. He pulled out the big pans they had prepared yesterday and put them on the stove, muttering, "thank heavens it is calm".

"Would you like a hand?" asked Sarah. Ruth peeped shyly from behind her legs.

"Ja, please," Henk looked flustered. He looked around for something Sarah could do with Ruth. "Perhaps cut up some bread?" He indicated the sacks of loaves. "The little one could fill those baskets."

Three women came into the galley, drawn by the activity. One spoke rapidly to Sarah who translated for Henk. "She says they would like to help. Please let them make the food." Sarah looked fondly at this tough bearded sailor who kept surprising her with his gentleness.

Henk nodded. "Ja, please. Let me show them where everything is."

The eldest woman pushed Henk gently out of the galley, talking all the time to Sarah in what Henk supposed was Yiddish.

"She says they will find it."

Henk grinned at the ladies, bowed politely, dug his watch out of his pocket and gave it to Ruth before giving Sarah a shy smile as he left.

Sarah blushed bright red as Mrs Abrahams nudged her friends and said loudly, "She has an admirer."

*

Gideon and Dusty came up to Jimmy. "Muster complete, Kapitein." He raised a large exercise book, "Everyone is listed here."

'It didn't take long, sir," added Dusty. "It was just a question of checking the people onboard against the names in the register they'd taken in the synagogue."

"And adding their passport numbers." finished Gideon. "The two who left before we sailed have been noted, Baas. The little girl, Ruth, does not have any papers."

"Well done," said Jimmy." He paused. "Are they all Dutch?"

"All Dutch," Gideon replied.

"Except Sam," called Henri from the wheel-box. "He's South African."

Seeing Jimmy frown, he quickly said, "His father died when he was a baby. His mother came home. She's Dutch." Henri shrugged, "Sam's Dutch enough."

Gideon and Dusty looked at Jimmy. He nodded and said, "Leave him Dutch. He's ship's company anyway."

Dusty took the register from Gideon, "We have an interesting mix of people onboard, sir. Musicians, doctors, nurses, businessmen, skilled craftsmen and women, students," he looked at the pages, "All sorts, mostly couples, several with children." He paused, "And Ruth."

"If you don't mind me saying, sir, I think you are wise to insist on going to Chatham." Dusty chose his words carefully. "I took a few soundings when we were onboard *Deben* and gather that some Immigration Officers have been refusing Jews entry to England. Government policy apparently, unless they've got sponsors or a lot of money."

Jimmy nodded, "I'd heard much the same, though the reason we're going to Chatham is because it is our home port."

He looked steadily at his old friend. "I would rather deal with people we know than get caught up in a row with someone trying to make a name for himself." He smiled. "Admiral Teagle is a hard man but he makes up his own mind." He paused. "And our people on board? Well educated, professional. Quite affluent I imagine. Is this the case?"

"Ja, Baas," Gideon said. "These are people who read the papers, talk to people, who've heard what's happening in Poland, what happened in Germany." He indicated the book in Dusty's hand. "They don't bury their heads in the sand."

"And the people who do?" asked Jimmy.

Gideon's voice was quiet. "We tried to tell them, begged people we know to leave. Gave out pamphlets, put up posters." His eyes filled. "It was hopeless. The fascists tore them down. People would not listen. We tried, Baas, we really tried."

"Gideon," Jimmy moved to his side and gripped his arm. "I'm not blaming you. I'm just trying to understand."

"So are we, Jimmy." Gideon shook his head. "So are we."

*

"What will happen to Ruth?" Sarah had taken Gideon to one side while Henk played with the child. "None of the families know her."

"Or want to know her," said Gideon sadly. "If she doesn't have anyone to look after her, I suppose the English will put her in an orphanage."

Sarah felt sick. She looked at Gideon and saw only compassion in his eyes. "What can we do?" he asked her quietly. "None of us knows what will happen when we arrive."

"I was listening to Henri talking to the Kapitein," Sarah replied. "I didn't mean to." She smiled. "But I'm glad I did."

"What did they say?"

"Henri said he has been talking to the English sailors from the ferries. He told the Kapitein it would be better to let the Navy look after us."

"Better than who?"

"Better than the Immigration Officers." Sarah went on. "Apparently they don't like Jews very much."

Gideon looked at Sarah intently. "Why does Henri think the Navy will be better?"

Sarah shook her head, "I don't know, But the Kapitein agreed with him. He said it will make life easier if everyone has Dutch passports."

"The crafty so and so." Gideon smiled and took Sarah's hands in his. "He knows who we are."

"I told you I was glad I listened." Sarah went on happily. "We must tell everyone to say the truth. We are all Dutch. And you must tell them not to admit they are Jewish. Even if they are asked."

"We will do that now," Gideon started to move away when Sarah caught his arm. "And Ruth?"

"I don't know, Sarah. What can we do?"

"I will think of something," Sarah said slowly, "We have time to think of something."

Gideon nodded and left to talk to the Committee and start briefing the passengers.

Sarah moved down the stairs to find Ruth and Henk. She had an idea.

"Port look-out. Ship bearing Red 20. Closing."

A few minutes later, *Viking* was slowing down alongside as unlikely a ship as ever to be flying a White Ensign in the North Sea.

"What ship?" The loud-speaker crackled across the water,

Jimmy buttoned up his jacket and put his cap on before stepping out of the wheel-box and over to the port wing. Cupping his hands, he called out, "His Majesty's Ship *De Ruyter*, Lieutenant James in command. Under orders for Chatham."

"That should put the cat amongst the pigeons," he said to Dusty who had come up as soon as he was properly dressed.

Jimmy saw the consternation on the face of *Viking*'s captain as he turned to talk to another officer. "They'll be looking in Jane's." he said, referring to the annual publication giving details of warships the world over. "I'll save them the trouble."

Hailing *Viking*, he explained, "Requisitioned into Naval service in Rotterdam when the Germans attacked."

"That you Jimmy?" It sounded as if the captain was trying not to laugh. And when Jimmy raised his hat and waved it, he responded, "David here. Good to see you again."

"David Cooper," Jimmy explained. "We served together in the Med."

The Navy was a tight-knit family. It was no surprise to Dusty that the officers knew each other; it was a bonus they were friends.

"Slow down please. Captain coming onboard."

"Slow Ahead, Henri, and tell Jannie what's happening."

Jimmy turned to Dusty, "Brief Gideon and the others and stand-by to receive 'tenant Commander Cooper."

There was a bustle about the ship as passengers crowded to the port side to stare at the British warship. *De Ruyter* listed alarmingly. Henri was unconcerned though Jimmy did ask if this was usual.

"Ja, Baas. Nothing to worry about. Not with this ship. Should we worry about her?" he asked, jerking his thumb at *Viking*.

"They shouldn't be a problem," Jimmy replied, "We're a private ship and our orders are clear."

"What orders are those?" asked Henri. This was the first he had heard of them.

"My orders," said Jimmy, "From the Commodore."

Henri was not convinced. "What are these orders?" he persisted.

"Return to Chatham." Jimmy smiled. "Clear enough?"

They were clear enough for David Cooper, though he was surprised by the large number of passengers onboard.

"All Dutch nationals," Jimmy explained. "We've mustered them and checked their papers. Could you let the Commodore know, and ask him if he could arrange for them to be looked after on arrival?"

After a pause he added, "Seven hundred-and-fifty-six men women and children. Plus a crew of six Dutch and six Naval personnel." He looked at David, "Seven hundred and sixty-eight souls onboard."

David whistled. "That many?"

"If there had been more waiting, we could have brought out another thousand."

*

"Goede God," breathed Henri as he looked at the busy waters of the Thames Estuary. "So many ships."

He followed *Viking* as she altered course to starboard to give more room in the narrow channel to an outward-bound destroyer. She was signalling their escort, her morse too fast for Jimmy to read. He ordered Webb to sound the "Still" as she swept past, answering their salute formally. She replied with a cheerful "Whoop, whoop' with her siren and a wave from the bridge.

Viking left when they reached the Medway channel buoy, steaming close by in a flurry of smoke and spray as the passengers onboard *De Ruyter* waved and cheered the men who had welcomed and guided them to safety.

*

Jimmy slapped Dusty on his back. "Here we are, Dusty. Pass the log."

Taking his pen out of his pocket, he wrote neatly, '1715 Saturday 11 May 1940. Secured alongside *Thunderbolt*. Finished with main engine.' He looked at his Chief and back to the log-book before adding,

"HMS *Pembroke* Naval Party returned to Chatham as ordered."

Jimmy added his signature, printed his name beneath it and put his pen away.

"And now," said Dusty, watching a Lieutenant Commander hastening towards them, "the fun begins."

"I think you'll find he's a friendly face," replied Jimmy. "I asked *Viking* to let the Commodore know our ETA and to arrange accommodation for our passengers."

He turned as Jannie appeared, closely followed by a weary, filthy Sam. Moving to meet them, Jimmy held his arm out to the grimy, sweat streaked old man and took his blackened paw in his hand.

Holding it firmly, he looked at Jannie and then, putting both his hands on Jannie's shoulders, drew him forwards and hugged him. He then shook the boy's hand. He spoke with quiet intensity to Jannie, drawing the boy closer with a gesture. "You brought us home. You both did that. It is something to remember. Thank you. Thank you, Jannie, thank you, Sam."

Before they could speak, Jimmy turned and went swiftly down the companionway to the deck below.

*

The First Lieutenant was aware of being watched by hundreds of pairs of eyes as he picked his way across the hulk of the old warship. He was slightly unnerved by the silence and stillness of the watchers.

"Evening Jimmy," he said, returning Gale's salute.

"Evening Bob. It's good to see you again."

Lieutenant Commander Bob Young had been a Midshipman when he met Jimmy for the first time, one of the many Boy Seamen onboard their first ship, *York*.

"Glad you got home safely," Bob looked around. "You made good time."

"We were lucky." Jimmy looked at Bob carefully. "Will you be able to accommodate my passengers?"

Bob looked at the crowded decks, seeing the anxiety in all those weary faces. He did not see the little girl until he felt a tugging at the bottom of his jacket.

"Hello," he knelt down, "Who are you?"

"I am Ruth," she replied. "Who are you?"

Before Bob could reply he was approached by a worried looking Dutch seaman. "I am sorry, Kapitein," Henk said, reaching out to take the girl off him. Turning back to Jimmy, Bob smiled, "Accommodate them? Of course we can." His smile became a grin. "As you knew very well before you set off." He could not help laughing as he said, "Fancy pinching a paddle-boat! And filling her with day-trippers."

The pure notes of a single violin cut through the noise of the Dockyard and silenced the excited hubbub onboard *De Ruyter*. People stood still to listen to the unknown, haunting tune that swelled as others players joined in. Gideon reached Bob and Jimmy as the last notes died away. "That was 'Out of the depths I cry to you, O Lord.' Psalm 130. It's by Sim Gokkes." He wiped his eyes. Jimmy looked around him as his passengers stirred. "It was magnificent." Then they were surrounded by laughing, clapping people, reaching out to shake their hands or pat them on the back. So too were Dusty and the other five members of the Naval Party.

Bob shook his head in wonder at the state of one young sailor until Jimmy shouted, "He's been stoking the boiler. Since we left."

Jimmy led the way to the bridge. "Do you have any news from Rotterdam?"

Bob shook his head. "It is very confusing over there. The Dutch army is falling back in places and holding out elsewhere. As far as I know, the Germans have not taken Rotterdam." He paused. "You and *Malines* are the only ships to have escaped."

He looked around at the suddenly serious Dutchmen close by. "I'm sorry. We'll let you know as soon as we have more news."

*

He turned back to Jimmy, "How many passengers are there and do you have their details.?"

"756, sir, all Dutch nationals," Jimmy replied. "I'll fetch their representatives."

Gideon and Sarah had been waiting at the foot of the companion-way. Sarah was now carrying Ruth.

Once they had been introduced, Bob was handed the muster book. He flicked through it, noting how carefully the names and details had been recorded.

"First things first," said Bob, "I imagine you'd prefer to come ashore?"

"Yes please, meneer," replied Gideon, "If that is possible."

"Possible, and highly desirable," smiled Bob. "It's not the Ritz but we have accommodation for you with your own bath rooms. We don't have room to accommodate you all together. Families and single women are in one block and single men in another. Now," he went on, "I suggest you walk. It's not far and I imagine you would welcome the chance to stretch your legs." He smiled encouragingly. "I've arranged transport for your bags and anyone who's unable to walk."

"Excuse me sir," It was Sarah who spoke, "We only have what we can carry." She paused, "And the musical instruments." She looked at the serious man in his smart uniform and wondered if he would understand. "Everything we own is in them. We carry them."

Bob nodded. "Of course you must carry your bags." He spoke gently. "We have sailors to show you where to go and if anyone needs help all they have to do is ask. Also, we have a sick-bay here. Our doctors and nurses will come to your barracks when you've settled in to see if anyone needs medicines or treatment." He smiled at Sarah, "Don't be afraid to ask. There are a lot of people here who would like to help."

The Chief G.I. stepped forward. "Sir?"

"Yes Chief."

"I imagine most people would like a bath, sir. Perhaps some towels could be provided. And maybe somewhere to dhoby their clothes?"

"Thank you Chief." He looked around apologetically, "We did not know what to expect." Adding with a cheerful smile, "But we'll manage."

He clapped his hands, "Right, Jimmy, please invite your passengers to come ashore and bring them over to the Drill Shed?"

"Aye aye sir." Jimmy saluted. Bob turned to go, then paused, "Come with me, Chief. I could do with a hand" He looked round to find Gideon and Sarah. "Perhaps you could come with me as well? Help sort out the accommodation? And bring that book with you. We mustn't lose that."

He went over to Ruth and asked, "Would you like to come with your mummy?"

"She's not my mummy," replied Ruth, matter of factly, clinging tightly to Sarah.

Smiling, Sarah told him, "Ruth would love to come, wouldn't you, honey?"

When Ruth nodded, she whispered to Bob, "I'll explain later."

"Say bye bye to Henk." Ruth stretched out an arm to the blushing Dutchman and leaned precariously across to give him a kiss when he came close enough.

"Will you read me a story?"

"Ja, one day." Henk stuttered before stepping away.

"Sir," It was Gideon. "I must tell our people before I go."

"Quick as you can, there's a good man. We'll wait for you on the jetty."

About a dozen of the older passengers took advantage of the lorry to ride to the barracks. The others streamed ashore, relieved to be standing on land again, even if it did sway alarmingly with each step they took.

*

Jimmy Gale leaned on the port bridge wing, watching the flow of passengers going ashore.

"Just think how many more would like to come," murmured Henri when he joined him.

Jimmy nodded and then asked, "Why is that lad standing at the gangway?" pointing to Sam, who was now staring across the hulk at the crowd gathering on the quay.

Henri offered Jimmy a cigar. "His family should have been in *Malines*. She sailed without them. Sam hoped they would be onboard. He didn't want to believe Jannie when he said they had not made it."

He looked down at the boy and then told Jimmy what had happened and why they had missed the boat, sighing as he ended, "I don't think there will be many who escape from Holland. Not unless there is a miracle."

Jimmy looked at the boy again. "What will happen to him?"

At that Henri smiled. "He has an aunt. She lives in London. She will take him."

He looked closely at Jimmy before telling him, "He has South African papers. His father insisted. His papers do not say he is a Jew."

"Why should that matter?"

"If the Germans come here, he will be safe."

"They have our army to deal with first," Jimmy replied quietly, "And yours, and the Belgians and French." He looked at Henri. "And if all else fails, there's the Channel to cross. And to do that they have to defeat the Navy."

Jimmy's sudden smile surprised the Dutchman. "In the morning I have to face a far more daunting prospect than the Germans."

Henri shook his head. "I don't understand."

Jimmy pointed ashore with his cigar. "I have been ordered to report to the Commander-in-Chief."

∗

The passengers were walking slowly through the dockyard, guided by Leading Seaman Spencer and Able Seaman Webb. They met the sailors sent by the First Lieutenant of *HMS Pembroke* and soon sped up as suitcases and bags were passed over by the older people.

The other members of the Naval Party, Faulkner, Evans and Steve Buckland were bringing up the rear, each laden with cases and bags.

'Guess wot?" Steve asked. His oppos shook their heads. "That kid, Sam, you know, the Dutch nipper." They nodded. "Well, when Jannie went up to the bridge I asked 'im if he knew we was carrying all them Yids and the kid sparked right up. Crikey. I fort 'e was gunna 'ave a real go at me. 'Oi, can it,' I says , an' 'e does. Then I asked 'im wot 'e was all 'et up abaht. Yew could of knocked me dahn wiv a fevver when 'e said, 'Cos I'm a fockin Yid' and 'e told me what 'ad 'appened. 'is best mate told by 'is old man not to play with 'im 'cos 'e was a dirty Jew. And 'ow 'is mum and dad got all upset and got 'im on the boat to keep 'im safe and how they was supposed to be onboard too but the Germans screwed that up so 'e come by 'imself and all because he 'adn't closed a door." Steve drew breath. " I didn't understand that bit but 'is kid sister got knocked down by a car so it's 'is fault she's in 'ospital and 'is mum and dad are stuck there. 'e said they've been livin' in 'olland, for 'undreds of years and they're as Dutch as anyone else but 'cos they're Jews they'll all get carted off by the Nazis and stuck in them camps. And 'e said some of them Nazis is Dutch. Like 'is mate's dad."

Steve stopped abruptly.

The others stared at him. Geordy whispered, "Christ! It must have been like that for all of them."

Gary looked at him and then Steve before saying, "That's what'll happen if those bastards get here."

"The last thing that kid said, 'e said 'your officer got us 'ere. You look after 'im'. All in that funny accent of theirs, with steam escaping and the fire flickering and us all covered in coal and oil." He laughed and shook his head, "And 'ere we are and 'ere they are."

And Geordy said, "An' we'll all be in the rattle if we don't get a wriggle on."

Which is roughly what Spider Webb said when they caught up with the passengers in the Drill Hall.

*

Lady Emma Teagle looked more like the Admiral's house-keeper than wife. Short, plump with a cheerful, round red face and a mop of unruly brown hair, she had born his temper with the same equanimity she had born him two sons and a daughter, whom she had raised largely single-handed while he was away at sea.

Apart from her serene good nature and quiet, if somewhat chaotic organisation of his home, she was also a remarkably good shot with pistol and rifle.

"I know you are worried about those poor people," she said when he had sat down. Ignoring his "harrumph" she carried on. "You don't have to be. We'll soon find homes for them if they want to stay round here, in London too."

She poured William a cup of tea and passed it to him.

He looked up and asked quietly, "You do know they are Jews, don't you? The whole ruddy lot of them."

"William." She placed her cup carefully in its saucer. "I really do not see what their religion has to do with anyone but God."

Emma stood and moved round the polished mahogany table to his side. She put her hand on his cheek and drew his head to her bosom. The tension flowed out of him as she stroked his face and hair. She kissed the top of his head and murmured, "Drink your tea before it gets cold."

Sitting down again, Emma gazed at him. He was tired. "Don't worry about them, William. We'll sort everything out between us."

Wiping his fingers on the crisp, double damask napkin, he reached for Emma's hand and held it for a while. Strength flowed both ways.

Their steward entered unnoticed, as he often did. Osborne had been with Sir William a long time and knew him well. When he thought they had been holding hands long enough, Osborne cleared his throat noisily. "More tea, my lady?"

Emma laughed. "You are a spoilsport, Osborne. No more tea, thank you."

The Admiral stood and stretched. "I'd better get back to the bunker." He looked at his steward and said, "Keep an eye on her, Osborne, she's off to see those refugees. Make sure she doesn't fill the house with them."

Osborne opened the door for his Admiral, handing him his cap as he walked out.

*

It was a warm, still May evening, far too pleasant to be below decks. Dirk and Willem fetched chairs from the cuddy and arranged them on the foredeck. Henk brought a table and then the boys went below to make coffee and see if there was any cake left.

Jannie had seen Sam's shoulders slump as the last passengers crossed the hulk and gave him a few minutes to compose himself before telling him, "Time for a quick wash before we join the others."

Jimmy went to the cuddy, checked the rifles were empty, unloaded his revolver and put the firearms in a locker until they and their kit could be taken ashore. "I'd better not forget those," he said to himself, "Or I really will be for the high-jump."

Henri saw Jimmy grimace as he came on deck but did not hear him say, "As if I'm not already."

"Kaffie en taart?" asked Dirk. "It is a tradition at the end of each voyage." He handed Jimmy a mug of coffee and a slice of apple sponge cake. "With compliments of Oom Paul."

"Oom Paul." They raised their mugs to the old Kapitein, silent for a moment until Jimmy stood.

He looked slowly round the table, gazing at each of them before raising his mug and saying, "To you, all of you." He paused and glanced around the ship, "And to *De Ruyter*."

They all stood. "*De Ruyter*."

As they were sitting, a clear English voice asked from the gangway, "May I join you?"

There was a moment of confusion, chairs scraping as they stood and turned to stare at the dumpy, cheerful, red-faced woman standing there in a light-green tweed skirt and jacket, sensible polished brown shoes and a jaunty green beret on her unruly hair.

Jimmy was the first to recover. He took a pace towards her and said shyly, "Er, ma'am, er, good evening, may I ask who you are?"

"How silly of me," she laughed, "Of course. You must." She patted her pockets and looked momentarily put out. "How silly. I've left my pass at home." She smiled at the weary, unshaven lieutenant and held out her hand, "Emma. I live here."

"Lieutenant James, ma'am." He indicated his chair, "Please. Have a seat."

As she sat, Henri got back to his feet, bowed, and introduced himself. "Henri van der Leiden, mevrouw." He smiled at her, "Senior Dutch man." Before she could speak, he went round the table, introducing his crew and telling her what they did.

"Here is Henk, steersman. Dirk and Willem, deck hands, They cook sometimes. Here is Jannie, engineer and Sam, fireman." Henri bowed again. "Our ship is now in the Royal Navy." Henri smiled at Lady Teagle. "We like very much that *HMS De Ruyter* is here in the River Medway." He pointed to the mast head. "Flying the White Ensign."

Lady Teagle clapped her hands in delight. "How perfectly splendid." Then said, "You must tell me how that happened."

So they did. Jimmy never said a word but watched the elderly woman, wondering why she was sitting amongst them.

*

The coffee was good. The cake was finished and still they talked.

The sudden noise of boots on the deck of the hulk was ignored by all except the weary, confused officer. Chief Gunnery Instructor Miller never batted an eyelid at the remarkable sight of the Commander-in-Chief's wife sitting in a chair on the deck of their paddle-boat, deep in conversation with five animated Dutchmen while a grubby little boy leaned sleepily against her shoulder.

It was not until Jimmy got to his feet that the Dutchmen fell silent. Looking up and seeing her favourite G.I. brought fresh joy to Lady Teagle. Holding out a hand, she cried gaily, "Dusty! How lovely to see you. What are you doing here?"

Dusty saluted her formally before taking her hand. "Ma'am. I've come to collect our things and fetch my officer."

Looking over his shoulder, Lady Teagle noticed two scruffy sailors carrying rifles ashore. There was a Bedford truck on the quayside and she watched them stack the guns in the back and return for the rest.

"Oh," she said quietly. "Did you go too?"

"Yes ma'am." He nodded towards Jimmy. "He asked me to. Been a bit of a show, ma'am, what with one thing then another." He smiled at her. "Still, he got us home safely." He paused, "And thanks to Henri and him we got over 700 refugees out too. All Dutch, ma'am."

"All Jewish, Chief," said Jimmy, still no wiser as to who she was. "We had no choice."

Emma Teagle stood, waking Sam as she did.

She moved closer to the strained young officer, "You did have a choice, young man. And you made the right one."

She pushed Jimmy towards the gangway, "Now go. Get a bath and go to sleep." Lady Teagle turned to Dusty, "The poor man is out on his feet. Off you go. I'll see to your crew."

At which Jannie asked Henri in rapid Dutch, "Is she your kindly widow?"

Emma caught their swiftly suppressed smiles and guessed what the old stoker had said. She laughed. She had been around sailors a long time.

*

"Ah, there you are, Jimmy." The cheery hail of Bob Young rose above the soft babble of many voices at the west end of the Drill Hall.

Ten canteen tables were spread across the width of the hall. Two Writers were sitting behind each, with a couple of Petty Officer Writers roving and advising as required. There was an equal and orderly queue of passengers in front of each table, each attended by a member of the Committee to act as translator if required.

Once they had been checked in, the passengers were ushered across the Parade Ground to the Canteen.

"Talk about 'Good order and Naval Discipline', Dusty," Jimmy said quietly. "Well done."

"Not me, sir," Dusty murmured. "The First Lieutenant thought this out. All I did was introduce him to Gideon, Sarah and the others."

Jimmy stood with Bob for a while, watching the Writers enter the details of each passenger into *HMS Pembroke*'s books. He moved closer to read what they were writing.

Names, age, previous address, occupation. Any medical conditions. Address in Great Britain if known. Passport number. Nationality.

Jimmy's eyebrows went up slightly when he saw "Dutch" entered against each name. He did not comment.

"What happens next?" he asked.

"We've got a meal for them in the canteen," replied the First Lieutenant. "Nothing fancy but Gideon told me they'd welcome it when I offered." He looked at Jimmy, "Don't worry about the diet. Dusty told me."

Jimmy smiled. "Fussy Dutchmen," he said quizzically.

"Very," replied Bob, pausing, "We took their nationality from your signal. The Commodore sees no reason to change it. Do you?"

"No sir." Jimmy's emphatic reply sealed the matter.

"Good. And by the way," Bob added, "Lady Teagle's brother in the Home Office is coming down on Sunday to oversee the issue of visas."

"Lady Teagle?" Jimmy turned to Dusty, his face pale. "Christ Almighty."

"Not quite, sir," Dusty was smiling. "More like the Angel Gabriel."

"What on earth are you two jabbering about," called Bob, intrigued.

"Nothing sir, Lady Teagle called on *De Ruyter* as we were leaving." said Dusty. "I believe she was planning to invite the crew to use their bathrooms and then feed them."

Bob laughed at Jimmy's discomfort. "Don't tell me you didn't recognise her?"

Jimmy shook his head. "I had absolutely no idea."

"Never mind." Bob patted his back. "She's saved me a job; and will give them a better meal."

"But what about the Admiral, Bob?" Jimmy was worried.

Bob smiled. "Look at it this way. *Malines* is stuck in the Downs waiting on the Immigration Service. You brought your party here, avoiding all that nonsense. We've gained another ship for the Navy. Those Dutch sailors are welcome and so are the passengers."

He laughed happily at Jimmy's deepening gloom. "There's a fucking disaster in Holland, another unfolding in Belgium. Thousands of German parachutists scattered over the Netherlands, seaplanes landing alongside you, ships sunk - and you swan off in that paddle-boat with a hold full of people, and waddle unscathed across the North Sea like a fat old Pompey Hooker."

Jimmy did not say anything. He was watching the tables filling up as more and more people came in from the Drill Hall. Naval cooks were standing behind their gleaming counter, talking to a number of laughing

116

women. Passengers, Jimmy realised. More women joined them until the counter was almost obscured.

When the last passenger sat down, Gideon appeared and clapped his hands. The room fell silent. He paused, then raised his hands to give a short blessing.

"A-men" rang loud. The cooks sprang into action, loading plates held out by the women who whirled away to place the food in front of those seated. Jimmy noticed the children were fed first, then the oldest people and then everyone else.

"We'd better grab a seat," said Bob, leading the way to two empty spaces on a bench.

Plates of bread and butter, jugs of water, glasses, and salt, pepper and mustard had been put in the middle of each table. Bob was thinking about getting the families with young children over to their barracks when a violin started to play.

The first note stilled the room. Not a knife, plate or pan moved. It was a song of loss and longing that hung in the air long after Jacob stopped playing.

Tears flowed, quiet sobs were muffled as wives buried their heads in husbands' shoulders and individuals sat with their heads bowed, eyes staring, unfocussed.

Their spirits were lifted by the laughter that greeted the first slow notes of the Portsmouth Hornpipe. Feet stamped, hands slapped the table. The other musicians found and tuned their instruments. The joyful tune floated out of the canteen, across the Parade Ground, into barrack blocks, the Warrant Officers' Mess and the Wardroom itself.

For that brief moment, music held their world in the palm of its hand.

As the crowded canteen became quiet once more, Bob rose to his feet. He tapped his glass with a fork to get their attention before saying.

"Thank you for that music. It was magnificent." He held up his hands to quell the applause. "We must get you to your bedrooms now" He looked around the room and carried on, "We call them barracks. I'm sorry we don't have enough rooms for you to have your own, but we have found some screens so most families and couples can be private. Everyone has a bed. Your towels are on the end of it. There's plenty of hot water so you can all have showers." Opening his arms wide, he said, "Welcome to our home. I hope you will feel safe, warm and comfortable here."

Looking down at his weary friend, he rested his hand on Jimmy's shoulder, "and we can all thank this young man for bringing you here."

*

Henri had just fetched his special bottle of Jenever when the Admiral's steward came onboard.

Osborne coughed discreetly and said, "Excuse me."

"Oh, Osborne," Emma waved her hand, gesturing to the crew, "I'm so glad you're here."

Osborne sucked his teeth and looked at her.

Lady Teagle frowned at him. "Don't sulk, Osborne, these sailors have come all the way from Rotterdam."

"Yes, milady." said Osborne, "I had heard."

Lady Teagle was unconcerned. She knew Osborne had only come to see if the bottle was out. His sense of timing was rarely wrong.

She stood. "They need baths and feeding." She looked at Henri. "I suppose you have to leave a watch-keeper onboard."

He bowed, "Yes lady. Two. One for the deck and one for the fire."

"Right," She looked at Sam, "This boy needs a bath, food and bed."

Henri looked across at Jannie and nodded. "He does." Then he asked, "Please, could he go with you now? Maybe Jannie comes too? They work together."

Lady Teagle nodded. "I'll take them over? The lad is nearly asleep."

She looked at Osborne and smiled. "Bring the others in half an hour."

"Yes milady." Osborne face had not altered but Lady Teagle saw how pleased he was.

'You owe me,' she thought. 'That is worth half-a-tot in your currency.'

Henri walked with Lady Teagle, Jannie and Sam to the gangway and saw her safely across the hulk,

"I won't give him too much, lady," Henri said with a smile, having watched the unspoken exchange between the Admiral's wife and their steward.

She laid a well-manicured hand on his sleeve and said, "Thank you. Henri. Just enough to keep him sweet."

*

Emma's housekeeper, Queenie Hawkins, was a loud, warm-hearted woman who took one look at the grubby little boy and whisked him off to one of the guest bathrooms. She sat him on the cork top of the dirty clothes box and chattered away as she drew his bath.

Sam looked on with exhausted bemusement, understanding about one word in three.

When the water was deep enough, Queenie said, "Right, Sam. Take off those dirty clothes and drop them on the floor. Then hop in the tub."

When Sam had been splashing about for a while, she returned to make sure he was scrubbing himself thoroughly and to collect his filthy singlet, trousers and underwear. She picked up the soap, rescued the nail brush from the water and, kneeling beside the tub, carefully scrubbed the fingers, nails, palms, backs and wrists of each hand.

"There," she said, "That's better, isn't it?"

"Ja, mevrouw, danke," Sam mumbled, "Better."

Queenie levered herself off the floor and left Sam to finish his bath in peace.

Lady Teagle was sitting in her drawing room when Osborne came in and announced. "Jannie and Sam, Milady."

"Thank you, Osborne, show them in please."

Emma had to look twice to make sure these were the same people who had walked off the ship with her.

Jannie, lean, clean, freshly shaven and elegant in his tailored uniform, bowed as he entered. Sam, pink, shy and hesitant in his serge bum-freezer, brass buttons gleaming, and pressed trousers, followed suite. Where Jannie was relaxed and comfortable, Sam looked lost.

"Come in, please, and have a seat." She patted the sofa beside her for Sam and pointed Jannie to the red and white striped arm-chair opposite.

When they were seated, she said, "Cook is just getting supper ready. You'll be eating with Henri and Dirk." She turned to Sam. "What do you do onboard?"

'Fireman, Milady," Sam sat up proudly. "I am the fireman." He waved his hand towards Jannie, "He is the engineer."

Seeing Lady Teagle's surprise, Jannie sat forward, "Ja, mevrouw, Sam is the fireman," He paused and thought for a moment, "For two weeks now."

"Ja Milady," Sam nodded enthusiastically. "And I keep watch on the engine when Jannie is not there."

"Was it very difficult?"

Sam, smiled, "Ja, very difficult." He paused, "To begin with." He gave a nonchalant shrug, "So much to learn. So much to do." He looked serious. "I have much lessons from Jannie, the Chief." He looked at the Old Man and said, "He is a good teacher."

They ate their meal in the dining room but Sam was asleep where he sat by the time the table was cleared for pudding, slowly tipping forward until his head was resting on the polished mahogany, one hand still holding a spoon.

Lady Teagle sent for Queenie and asked her to take Sam to the bedroom overlooking the river.

Jannie stood up. "I will carry him, mevrouw." To Queenie he said, "If you could show me the way?" He smiled at her. "I am used to carrying sacks of coal."

As good as his word, Jannie lifted Sam out of his chair without effort. "Perhaps not over my shoulder," he said to Lady Teagle, and carried the boy out in his arms as Quennie followed. She did not notice Jannie close his eyes and say a brief prayer over the boy as he tucked the top sheet in and adjusted the blankets.

"He can stay up there till the crew go back onboard," Emma told Henri while they waited for Queenie to come downstairs.

Osborne served plates of stewed rhubarb, freshly picked that afternoon. He made sure there was enough left for his admiral. China jugs of custard were passed around, sniffed at tentatively and enjoyed.

When Jannie had finished, he stood up and came to the head of the table. "Danke, mevrouw."

He bowed. to Lady Teagle.

"You are very kind. Now I must go to the ship. The others must bathe and eat." He looked across at Henri as he said, "It would be a kindness if Sam could sleep here this night." Henri nodded as Jannie continued. "He is young and has worked very hard."

Lady Teagle took his hand in hers, "Of course he may." She hesitated, "Won't he be worried if he wakes up in the night and you are not here?"

Jannie smiled, "I do not think he will wake for a long time."

Henri added, "If he can see the ship in the morning, he should be happy." He looked at Lady Teagle, "We have watchman on deck all night. He can come quickly if you need him."

"Thank you, Henri. I expect we will all sleep very well."

*

There was just enough light for Henk and Willem to find their way across the darkened dockyard and back onboard after they too had bathed and eaten.

"All well?" Dirk hailed them softly from the bridge wing.

"Ja, very well, danke," rumbled Henk. "They are very kind to us here."

"Ja," laughed Willem, "I have eaten too much."

Dirk leaned over the wing and said, "They are in the after saloon."

They made their way below and joined the others. It was very hot and the air was thick with cigar smoke.

"I'm sleeping up top." Henk grabbed his hammock and bag, and bedded down in the deck saloon. Jannie joined him when he had completed his engine room rounds and banked up the fire.

The night afloat passed peacefully.

*

"Business as usual."

Sir William hung his jacket, loosened his tie, undid his collar and kicked off his shoes before sitting on Emma's side of the bed.

It had been a long night. A ship had been despatched to bring the Queen of the Netherlands to England. Others had been sent to collect her government and gold. Demolition parties had been sent to Dutch ports to deny facilities to the enemy, but Dutch soldiers and officials did not want them destroyed. Magnetic mines had been dropped in the Thames Estuary and the Downs. The battle for Norway was a disaster. Casualties were heading back to be patched up and sent out again. A northbound convoy had been attacked by E-boats. The number of sunk and damaged was unknown.

Sir William stood up, stretched - and suddenly stood stock still. He padded across the carpet, opened the door quietly and paused, listening carefully.

There it was again. A child was crying. He looked back at Emma, saw she was fast asleep and went out onto the landing. There was definitely a child crying, upstairs, in his house.

"That's all I bloody need," he muttered as he started up the staircase. "What's Emma been up to now?"

There was a sob from behind the door at the top of the stairs. "Best bloody room in the house," he muttered, quietly opening the door. He stopped. "Well I'm damned."

Sam turned, his eyes wide with terror. Staring, tears pouring down his cheeks, he shrank into the bed before the Admiral's gaze.

"Hello," said Sir William gently. "Who are you?"

Sam gulped but said nothing.

"May I come in?" asked Sir William, "You see, I live here."

He walked further into the room and saw Sam's uniform hanging neatly over a chair.

"I say. That is a smart uniform." He looked at Sam, "Is it yours?"

"Ja, meneer," Sam stuttered. He thought the old man looked tired.

"My jacket isn't nearly as smart as yours," said the Admiral. "Are you a captain?"

"Nee, meneer, don't be silly, I am fireman." Sam stopped crying and sat up straight in the bed.

"Stoker, eh. That's hard work."

"Hard work, meneer. Ja." He smiled to himself. "But good."

Sir William looked at the boy. It dawned on him he must be off that damned paddle-boat.

"What is your name?"

"Sam, meneer. Samuel Da Souza."

His shoulders began to shake. A thin wail escaped his tightly clamped lips. He stared unblinking at the old Admiral, for a long moment; then flung himself face down on the pillow, sobbing freely.

Sir William sat and pulled the sobbing boy into his shoulder. "There, there, Sam, there there."

Sir William felt a thin, wiry arm reach round and hold onto him as Sam laid his head on Sir William's shoulder.

Not knowing what else to say, Sir William asked "Would you like me to make you a cup of tea?"

Sam thought for a second then sat up, turned and smiled joyfully at the old man. "Nee, danke meneer. I will make you tea." He smiled again, his whole being transformed. "I will make you boiler room breakfast," and leapt out of bed to pull his uniform on. When dressed, he took the Admiral by the hand and led him downstairs to the front door where Sir William managed to disentangle himself long enough to grab his old tweed overcoat while Sam slipped on his boots.

As they approached *De Ruyter*, Sam could see Jannie dozing comfortably in a deck-chair in the wheel-box towards the end of his watch. It had been a peaceful May night, stars bright in the sky, the occasional fish jumping in the stream. Not a light could be seen anywhere.

The clatter of feet woke Jannie just before Sam appeared in the doorway, towing a lean, white haired elderly man.

"Jannie, Jannie, this is my friend." Sam was gabbling, over-excited. Jannie could see he had been crying. He stood as the old man came forward.

"William Teagle." He held out his hand. Jannie shook it automatically, "Jannie, engineer."

Sir William went on, "I'm so sorry to bother you, but Sam insisted I come with him." He smiled at the boy. "He wants to make me breakfast."

"Ah" sighed Jannie, beginning to understand, "You live over there?" pointing at Admiralty House.

"That's right," said Sir William. "Quite a few of us do."

Sam had let go of his hand to approach Jannie, "First I will make the tea. Then you will make the breakfast? Ja!"

"Ja, Sam. You make the tea."

Sam approached the old man and asked, "Would you like to come with me while I make the tea?"

The Admiral allowed himself to be led below. He drew back slightly at the engine room hatch. Sam let go of his hand and said, "Don't worry. I go first and show you how it's done."

By the time Sir William got down the ladder, Sam had the kettle filled and in hand and the tea caddy, sugar tin and three stained mugs lined up on the bench. He handed the kettle to the Admiral, opened a fire door and loaded a shovel with a flat layer of glowing coals. Carefully lowering the shovel to rest on the deck, he pointed to the kettle and then the shovel. The Admiral did as he was shown and stood back.

While waiting for the kettle to boil, Sir William studied the engine and boiler, noting how well the machinery was kept, the neat stowage of tools, spares and equipment and the cleanliness of the compartment. "Wouldn't be out of place in a warship." he muttered, unaware that he had spoken aloud.

"Please," said Jannie, who had observed the shrewd gaze of the old man and was beginning to realise who he might be. "Did you say something?"

"Yes, er, Jannie. I was just saying what a smart engine room you have."

"You have seen many, meneer?" asked Jannie, conversationally.

"A few," said Sir William.

"Kettle's boiling. Put the tea in Jannie." The Admiral watched, appalled, as Jannie put three handfuls of tea-leaves into the kettle and gave them a vigorous stir. Sam let it boil for a few more minutes before picking up an oily rag and lifting the kettle onto the boiler plates.

"I move this then we have tea," he told Sir William, his young face a picture of concentration. The Admiral watched the care with which Sam threw the coals back into the fire and looked in after them before hanging up his shovel. He was impressed to see him pick up a rake, level the coals and close the fire door.

"You have trained him well," he said to Jannie, noticing that Sam had checked the steam pressure gauge and sight glass before bending down to pick up the kettle.

Sam handed it to Jannie. "You pour." He did not want the old man to see he was not strong enough to pour the tea without spilling it and busied himself at the workbench, ladling three heaped spoons full of sugar into each mug. He chose the cleanest and handed it to Sir William with a bow. "Engineer's tea, meneer. Very strong, very good."

They leaned against the bench, sipping the hot sweet brew while Sam sucked his down noisily.

Jannie laughed at Sir William's hesitation. "It keeps us going. Strong makes us awake, sweet is for energy." He nodded at Sam, "That is what kept the boy going. Eighteen hours or more from Rotterdam until we finish with engine."

Sam looked up from his mug of tea. "And now, what about breakfast."

Jannie looked aghast. "What," he asked Sam in Dutch, "Have you promised this man?"

"Boiler room breakfast, Jannie, like we always have."

Jannie turned to Sir William. "Meneer, we have eggs, we have bacon and we have butter. But we have no bread."

He was about to ask if that was enough when Sir William cut in. "Send a hand to my house and ask Cook for a couple of loaves. Better ask her for more eggs, bacon and butter too. She can send a basket over."

Henri was coming down the ladder as Sir William was speaking. When he got to the bottom he bowed and introduced himself, "Henri, meneer, steerman."

"William Teagle." The Admiral held out his hand. It was catching. "I live over the road."

"Ah," said Henri, "We have met your wife. A very kind lady." He smiled. "Very gracious."

Sir William wondered what exactly Emma had got up to last night. He looked forward to hearing about it, but first there was the matter of breakfast, and of salvaging Sam's honour.

Henri looked at Sam and said, "Find Dirk or Willem and tell him to come here."

He picked up Sam's empty cup, filled it with tea and added three heaped spoons full of sugar.

After a couple of mouths full he stood straighter than usual and asked, rather formally, "Are you **milady's** husband?"

Straight-faced and gently, Sir William replied, "I am indeed, and very pleased to meet you." He looked at Henri and then at Jannie and asked quietly, "Could either of you tell me why I found Sam crying his eyes out just now?"

Henri was glad of that question. He had sent Sam up top so he could have a word with the Admiral about him.

"Jannie, you tell him."

Thus Jannie told Sir William how Sam came to be onboard and how his family had missed the boat and why he had worked him so hard that he would be too tired to think.

He took a breath. "He must have been thinking about his family when he woke up, poor kid."

Jannie looked at Sir William for a long time, his grey eyes steady and searching, before saying. "You are a good man, meneer. You fight the war all night and then you fight a Dutch boy's demons this morning."

There was a cheerful whistle from the hatch before a full basket was lowered down, closely followed by a grinning Sam.

"We had better leave them to it, meneer," Henri said with a laugh, "Unless you would like to watch."

Taking the hint, Sir William followed Henri swiftly up the ladder. Pausing at the top, he asked, "Could you show me round?"

"Ja, of course, Admiral. She is your ship now."

The Admiral laughed. "So she is, by Jove, so she is."

∗

"It was extraordinary, my dear," reported the Admiral to his wife, heedless of Osborne standing at the side-board waiting to serve the coffee.

"A ruddy great wad of your bread, stuffed full of bacon, topped with a fried egg, all cooked on a shovel-full of coals in the boiler room."

"Sounds like a banjo," murmured Emma.

"Yes, but I'll wager no banjo ever tasted so good."

"Must be the coal," said Emma and Osborne together.

"And the company," laughed Sir William. "Nothing to eat, thank you Osborne. Just coffee please."

When Osborne had finished pouring, the Admiral said to him, "I had the most remarkable mug of tea I've ever tasted." He shuddered a little. "Even fouler than the foulest middle-watch brew." He shook his head. "But, by God, it does the trick."

"Time you were off, William." Emma stretched up to kiss him, as she did every time he went on duty. He held her for a moment, eyes closed and resting his chin on her head.

"Car's at the door, sir." said Osborne, watching as his admiral kissed his wife, closed his eyes, then stepped back, smiled at her, patted his pockets and turned to leave. He was looking forward to hearing Lieutenant Gale's version of the remarkable story the Dutchmen had told him.

∗

Regardless of the remarkable story the Dutchmen had told him, Sir William was livid with Gale for the flak he was getting from Whitehall and was determined to make an example of him. Initiative was admirable but not when it created such confusion that he had to waste time sorting out the mess on his doorstep. He had a war to fight.

The Admiral stood in the window looking at the white ensign flying from *De Ruyter*'s mast. He was a tall, lean man with a shock of white hair above piercing blue eyes set in a lined and weather-beaten face. He turned from the window and regarded Gale without expression.

"Close the door behind you." His voice was clipped.

The room was silent as each man took stock of the other. Sir William walked over and sat behind his desk. He gestured to a chair in front of it. "Sit down."

Jimmy sat, placing his cap on the floor, before looking up and meeting those fierce eyes.

"Right, Gale, you better have a bloody good reason for bringing those Jews here?" He paused, and seemed to have difficulty with the next question, "In that bloody paddle-boat?"

Jimmy sat very still. He did not think this was going to end well. He hoped he could smooth a path for his men, and, more importantly, for his passengers.

He took a deep breath and gave Sir William an only slightly adorned version of the truth.

The admiral listened in impassive silence. Knowing no details of the invasion, his eyes lit up when Jimmy described the attack on Rotterdam. "It was most impressive, sir, especially the seaplane assault on the bridges."

He leant forward, 'like an old war horse,' thought Jimmy, 'nostril flaring at the first whiff of gunpowder.' He was careful not to smile.

Not careful enough. Sir William noticed Jimmy relaxing but said nothing.

"There's not much more to tell you, sir, once we'd got out to sea," Jimmy concluded. He was longing for a cigarette.

"Not much more?" Sir William barked. "What in hell's name made you come here?" He stood abruptly and started pacing about. His voice rose, "I've had half of Whitehall wanting to know that." He snorted, "The other half just want you to go away."

Jimmy waited until the admiral sat down.

"May I ask a question, sir?" he said quietly.

"What?"

Jimmy took another deep breath. "What would you have done, sir, if you were in my shoes?"

And with that Jimmy bade farewell to his career.

There was a long silence as Sir William stared at the young officer.

Suddenly the granite face of the old admiral split into a smile, followed by a bellow of laughter. Recovering, Sir William sat back, stared at Jimmy, shook his head and told him, "That is exactly what my wife asked me."

He stood. "I hope, young man, that I would have had the courage to do the same."

*

Divisions, the formal Sunday morning parade when the Commodore inspected the ship's company of *HMS Pembroke*, had taken place at 1000. It was followed by a brief drum-head service taken by the Chaplain before they dispersed. Many went back to their barracks to write letters, read or sleep. Some of the youngsters went ashore.

"It's a good job we're between intakes," Bob said to the Commander as they retired to the Wardroom.

"Yes, though I expect we'd have managed." The Commander had great faith in the Navy's ability to deal with anything that came its way. However, he was thinking about how soon before their unexpected guests would leave.

"If the clerks turn up later on with their visas, we should be able start getting them away tomorrow."

The Commander did not want to chase their guests out. He had heard too many disturbing accounts of how Germans were treating their own Jews to have any confidence that life would be different for Jews in Holland - and elsewhere.

"I wonder if we'll get any more, sir." Bob was looking pensive. "Jimmy said his passengers were all in one place, right on the quayside. There must be hundreds of others trying to escape."

"I hope they get away, Bob, I really hope so." The Commander shook his head. "But I don't suppose they'll end up here. Not unless there's another Jimmy Gale out there."

He looked at his watch, finished off his coffee and stood up. "We'd better find the Commodore."

It was an inspection like none other the Commodore had experienced in his long and illustrious career.

The audience was close, familiar and vocal. And musical. When he was about half-way along the first rank, what became known as the Rotterdam Ensemble struck up with a rousing dance tune.

He had not met the crew off *De Ruyter* until this morning and so was unaware of the vast difference in age between the Master and stoker.

Nor had he expected to see one of his young seamen standing smartly to attention with oil, grease and coal-dust ingrained in his face and hands.

The music stopped as he finished inspecting the Dutch crew.

The Commodore stood before the Naval Party, in which he now included the Dutchmen. He thanked them and welcomed his guests before returning Lieutenant Gale's salute and starting to walk away.

"Please wait, Admiral."

Gideon's shout echoed from the Drill Hall roof, startling them all.

He ran towards the Commodore and stopped in front of him. "Please, Admiral." he asked, "A few words."

"Of course," replied the Commodore.

Gideon took a deep breath.

"We must thank Lieutenant Gale for bringing us here. For our freedom, our lives, he…" Gideon's voice was drowned out by the wild cheering of his fellow Jews. Cheering that swelled and echoed in a storm of emotion and relief quite unlike anything heard before by anyone present.

Highly embarrassed, Jimmy snapped "Get me something to stand on,"

Two of the Naval Party swiftly fetched a stout wooden box from the side of the Hall.

Jumping up onto it, Jimmy held up his hand for silence. When the cheering died down, Jimmy turned to the Commodore. "Permission to speak, sir?"

The Commodore nodded, studying the stern features of this young man and wondering what on earth he had to say.

Jimmy stared at the crowd; the faces of the elders filled with relief; the young ones still with cheers on their lips. Wide-eyed children looked up at him. He looked at the Dutch crew, noting concern in Henri and Jannie's eyes, the same concern that was on Dusty's face. His boys looked puzzled, his senior hands unreadable.

The Drill Hall was still as he started to speak, addressing his remarks to Gideon. As he spoke slowly, his words were translated, creating a soft murmur like wavelets breaking on shingle.

"Thank you for your kindness but it is not me you should be thanking but Henri and the crew of *De Ruyter*. It was Henri who asked me to bring his ship to England and who persuaded me to bring you. He asked me because he said he could not navigate. He said he had never been to sea."

129

There was a gasp when Jimmy told them, "He lied to me." He looked at Henri. "I knew that and chose to believe him. We both knew that coming here, to this particular Royal Naval port, would be easier for you than going to Harwich or London."

The Commodore cleared his throat loudly.

He turned to include him, "The other people to be thanked are the Commander-in-Chief and the Commodore for making you welcome." He paused, choosing his words carefully. "They could have ordered me to go to London. Or Harwich." He paused again, "Or to anchor and wait until the Home Office decided what to do."

Jimmy saw the Commodore nodding.

He continued, "Instead, they welcomed you. They welcomed us all."

His voice became quieter.

"Your escape was not a miracle. You were in that synagogue because you had been listening to the wireless, reading newspapers and talking to people. You were wise enough to know Germany was going to invade and fortunate enough to be able to leave your homes and make your way to Rotterdam. Now you are free and can use that freedom to help your families and friends in the Netherlands and to offer your skills, your training, your knowledge and your hearts to help this country defeat Germany."

He paused, taking in the faces before him. "You are welcome, here, in hospitals, schools, factories and shipyards." He smiled. "Some might even join the Navy." Jimmy held out his hands, "The musicians here, play for your country, play for my country. Make yourselves heard."

And, as he jumped off the box, music once again filled the hall.

∗

"I am worried about Sam," Jannie told Henri that morning as they walked through the Dockyard. "He's gone very quiet." He was silent, remembering Sam's expression as he stood at the gangway yesterday, scrutinising every passenger as they disembarked. "He has too much time to think."

"Ja,' Henri agreed, "And we will not be busy. Not now we are here."

"We must go to London soon. To find his aunt." Jannie looked at his old friend. "She might have news."

Henri nodded slowly while he thought. He did not want Jannie to leave. Nor Sam. But they could not stay here.

"You must take him to his aunt, Jannie. This afternoon. As soon as you get your visas." Henri was crisp and clear. "Sam has her address?"

"Ja, Henri, Sam has her address." Jannie knew he had memorised it. "He will not want to leave *De Ruyter*. She has become his home."

"I know," Henri replied, "But he has to go. We all do." He held Jannie's shoulder. "They take the ship today."

"Schijt!" Jannie knew she was in the Navy now. But they had sailed *De Ruyter* for so long he could not imagine leaving her.

They didn't speak again until after they had been inspected. Henri took Jannie outside. "I've been thinking. I will ask Jimmy if we can travel together, you, Sam and me. I promised Paul I would look after him, and Simon. It's best if we go together."

"It makes sense," said Jannie. "She might not want him."

He looked at Henri, "Then what do we do?"

Henri laughed, "Then we find rooms and sleep on it." He smiled at Jannie's long face, "But first we tell Sam, and then send a telegram to Aunt Miriam."

As they went back into the Drill Hall, Jannie asked, "What did you think of Jimmy's speech?"

"He made me wonder about leaving the ship. You too, I imagine but our first duty is to Sam."

Jannie nodded. "I wonder what Henk and the boys will do."

"Henk," Henri laughed again, "I think he has already a new purpose. Only he does not yet know it."

"What d'you mean?"

"You heard about the little girl who was left onboard?" Henri's voice was quiet and serious.

"Ja, a sad business," replied Jannie.

"It was Henk who found her."

Jannie's old eyes widened and his mouth twitched with the beginnings of a smile. "Go on," he murmured.

"Her name is Ruth. Henk was marooned, with her." Henri shrugged. "He's forty, a bachelor. What does he know about children?"

They both answered together, "Nothing!"

"No, and he knows nothing about women either." Henri looked at Jannie, a wicked glint in his eye, "I think our fisherman has been hooked.

After all these years sitting beside a muddy polder trying to catch his tea, I think he has been hooked."

Jannie was amazed. "Who is she?"

"Me."

Sarah laughed with delight at the way they stopped and spun round, their faces covered with confusion.

"Mevrouw," Henri stuttered as Jannie struggled to speak.

There were tears of laughter in Sarah's eyes. Ruth, in her arms, was staring at the two old men as they fumbled for words. Then she too started laughing.

"Please," said Henri. "You must forgive us."

"Ja, mevrouw," Jannie added hastily. "What must you think of us? Two old women gossiping away."

"Nee, nee, you are Henk's friends." Sarah was still laughing. "And I should not have come up so quietly behind you."

"What can we say?" asked Henri. "Is it true? You will look after Henk?"

"Ja. If he will allow me." She glanced at Ruth, "This little one needs us both. I think, perhaps Henk will look after Ruth very well." She smiled happily. "I think, perhaps, I will look after Henk very well."

"You will have to find somewhere to go," said Jannie. "I do not think that will be easy." He paused, "You do not know each other."

Sarah gazed at him fondly, "Nee, Jannie, we do not know each other. Not yet. But we have somewhere that will take us."

She laughed at their surprise. "It is true. Milady Teagle found a position for Henk and for me, and Ruth can come too."

Delight flooded Henri's face, surprise on Jannie's.

"Henk told her he was a fisherman last night. I think he talked too much." Seeing their expressions she laughed again, "It is true. She asked him many questions. He was happy to talk."

Sarah cuddled Ruth, "He talked about her." She lowered her eyes and went a little pink. "He must also have talked about me."

Talking very quietly to the floor, she whispered, "I do not know what he said. Nor why he said it," she looked up, almost defiantly, eyes sparkling, cheeks going red, "But milady said she has found a place where we may both live and work, and where Ruth will grow up. She said she hopes we will like it there."

Jannie was amazed by their good fortune "Where is this place?"

Sarah shook her head. "I do not know England. It is a big house with a river. Henk is to work on the river. I am to work in the house. This little one will live with me and play with their children."

Henri noticed the way Sarah came alive, how she glowed with happiness, and hoped such good fortune would extend to their other passengers.

*

Sam leant against the wall, shoulders slumped, his hands in pockets, eyes on the Drill Shed and the happy throng within it. He straightened when he saw Jannie, took a couple of paces towards him and then waited. Jannie stopped nearby and took a cigar from his pocket.

"Got a match?"

Sam patted his pockets and shook his head, "Nee, Jannie, sorry."

"Just as well I have," Jannie tossed a box of Vespas over. "Light one for me, will you?"

Jannie studied Sam while he was holding the lighted match to his cigar, noting the traces of tears on his cheeks. He blew the smoke away from the boy, who shook the match out and tucked it in-between the tray and the bottom of the box.

"Who taught you to do that?"

"My Papa." Sam started to say more but could not finish. His eyes filled again.

"Your Papa? Of course." He leant towards Sam and lowered his voice, as if imparting a secret, "Your Papa gave you an address, Tante Miriam. Yes?"

Sam nodded.

"We must send her a telegram. Ja?"

Sam nodded again.

"Ja, Sam. We send her a telegram saying we are coming to London." Leaning even closer to Sam, he whispered, "Today."

Sam whispered back, "Today? What about…"

"Our ship? The Admiral is so happy with her, he wants to keep her." Jannie smiled. "But he cannot keep us." He tapped an oil-stained finger on his nose. "Can you keep a secret?"

"Yes," whispered Sam, eyes round.

"He is buying us our tickets." Jannie looked into the boy's troubled eyes. "Don't tell anyone else, Sam." He looked up and saw Lady Teagle approaching. "Not even her."

"I won't," Sam whispered.

Lady Teagle joined them and turned to Sam. "I have you to thank for introducing my husband to that disgusting tea you drink." She shuddered so dramatically that Sam burst out laughing.

"I came to say good-bye," Lady Teagle went on. "I have to go home, and you have to go to London."

Sam gasped. "Who told you?"

"I am the Admiral's wife, Sam" Lady Teagle replied kindly, "He can't keep secrets from me." Which, she acknowledged to herself, was simply not true.

"You must not tell anyone else," Sam told her, looking very serious.

"I won't," Lady Teagle promised, looking at Jannie with interest, seeing again the love this old man had for the boy. "If you ever need help you can always write to me." She opened her handbag to find a pencil and paper, thought a minute and wrote carefully: 'Lady Teagle, c/o Admiral Sir William Teagle, The Admiralty, London.'

"That should find me anywhere in the world." She handed the address to Jannie, adding, "Just put a tuppenny-ha'penny stamp on the envelope."

She kissed Sam on the cheek, to his embarrassment and secret delight, shook Jannie by the hand and bustled out of the Drill Shed onto the Parade Ground where Esther was waiting for her. Together, the two women walked away without speaking.

*

"I hate saying goodbye," remarked Jannie to no-one in particular.

"They always drag on," agreed Henri.

"I never said goodbye to milady," said Sam, aghast.

"Ah," sighed the two old men, "That's because you were too busy talking to those pretty girls."

Sam went pink. Then he laughed. "Ruth and Sarah?"

"Yes," said Jannie, "Especially Ruth."

Sam looked down at his hands, "I gave her Tante Miriam's address." He paused, "Well, I gave it to Sarah and asked her to write when they have

134

somewhere to live." He looked anxiously at his two friends. "I hope you don't mind."

"Nee, lad, of course we don't." Henri tapped Sam on the knee. "We all have to keep in touch with each other. In fact, I also gave them Tante Miriam's address. And I gave it to milady."

Henri did not add that he had also given her address to Dirk and Willem as well as to Gideon, Jacob, the Navy and several others. If she objected, she could always forward letters to their Embassy.

Not many people were going to London that afternoon. Henri found an empty compartment into which they settled. Comfortable seats, the clickety-click of the wheels and warm air blowing in through the half-open window soon had Sam nodding. Jannie made him take his boots off and lie down on the bench seat while he and Henri settled in the corners opposite. Henri's eyes soon closed , leaving Jannie to gaze out of the window on his own. Behind them, all they had known was receding. Ahead of them lay London and an uncertain future.

Jannie closed his eyes and folded his arms across his chest. Ten minutes later, he too was asleep.

PART TWO

6.

17 Wilkes Street, London

"Oh my," breathed Sam, waking and gazing out of the window at rows of little houses with smoking chimneys and blackened brickwork. The evening sun shone through the haze, glinting off hundreds of silver-grey balloons swaying above the city. He woke Jannie and Henri as the train was slowing down. The guard slid the door open and said, "London Bridge next stop."

"Please, where will we find a taxi?" asked Henri.

"Over the footbridge and down to the street on that side." he replied, pointing to the north. "You shouldn't have no difficulty getting one." He smiled at them, "Where are you going?"

"Spitalfields," answered Henri swiftly, suddenly cautious. He did not want Jannie or Sam to give the address to this man.

"That's alright then. It's not far." The guard paused, then asked, "You're Dutch, ain't yer?"

When Henri nodded, he said, "Thought so. Been to London before?"

"Nee, meneer. This is the first time."

"Well, if I was you gents, seeing as you haven't got much luggage, I'd walk across London Bridge and get a taxi the other side." He smiled at their puzzled faces and added, "It ain't far and you'll get ever such a nice view of the river, Tower Bridge and all."

Ashamed of his suspicions, Henri thanked the guard before asking, "How did you know we are Dutch?"

Tipping his cap back, the guard laughed. "Well, you ain't French, and my brother works in the Dockyard. He told us a load of Dutchies had arrived." He laughed again, "In an old paddle-boat, he said, like day-trippers from Southend."

As the train jerked to a standstill, he said, "Good luck, mates," and moved on.

Jannie stood up, pulled from its stud the thick leather strap below the window and lowered the heavy glass. He reached outside and turned the brass handle to open the door. The grimy, soot-blackened station was full of noise; doors slamming, voices shouting, whistles blowing amidst clouds of steam from the engine. A louder whistle was followed by a cry of, "Mind the doors," more slamming and the heady noise of the engine straining to get the carriages rolling.

They watched it disappear before making their way through the bustling station, down the steps and onto the streets of London.

A large policeman approached while they were getting their bearings on the pavement. He looked them up and down, taking in their strange uniforms and evident unfamiliarity, before saying, "Evening all. Mind if I ask a few questions?"

Sam instinctively moved closer to Jannie, a movement not unnoticed, nor was the way Henri moved slightly forward before replying. "Not at all, meneer."

Henri saw the policeman's surprise at the accent and went on, "We are from Holland. We have papers."

Their passports and visas having been inspected and passed muster, the constable asked them a few more questions before pointing to the road for London Bridge with a cheery, "Welcome to London."

As he was moving off, Henri asked, "Where are all those people going, meneer?"

"They're off to church. Evensong, innit? In the cathedral." The constable jerked a thumb at Southwark Cathedral rising above the surrounding buildings.

"No bells?" asked Jannie, used to the sound of church bells echoing through the narrow streets and along the canals of Rotterdam on Sundays.

"No, mate," replied the policeman, "Took them down at the beginning of the war." He smiled, "Streuth, that was some effort, lowering all them ruddy great bells." He looked at his wondering audience and went on, "We've been getting ready for this war for years now." He shrugged sympathetically, "Shame your lot didn't do that and all, ain't it?"

Jannie and Henri looked at each other with a wry smile.

140

"Have a look around you, all them white lines on the kerbs, white paint everywhere." He paused, "You'll be glad of that at night. Black as Hades, it is. Don't go out less you've got a pocket torch." He looked around before continuing, "Parks dug up with trenches and shelters, them bloomin' balloons; schools evacuated to the countryside, teachers, kids an' all."

He pointed to a sandbagged railway arch with a large white **S** outside its entrance. "Make sure you know where these are. Public shelters, that's what. Get inside one if you hear them sirens go."

Sam nudged Jannie who said, "Danke, meneer. We had better go. Tante Miriam is waiting." He laughed, "We mustn't be late for our first meeting."

The constable touched his helmet as they set off for London Bridge.

"High water" muttered Henri when he glimpsed the green-brown waters of the Thames. He pulled out his watch, "1800. We had better get a move on."

The river was busy. Ships were getting underway, their cargoes unloaded onto quays or into barges and lighters. Others, newly arrived on the tide were moving into vacated berths or onto moorings in the stream. The river was churned by tugs and launches fussing over vessels from ports around the world.

The sun was lowering behind the barrage balloons bobbing at their tethers. The air was rich with the smell of coal smoke, steam, tar, oil and the muddy, salty smell of the river. To this was added the warm, fruity smell of malt, hops and barley from a nearby brewery, overlaid with wafts of the sharp acetic smell of a vinegar factory.

The bridge was surprisingly busy with people, some moving purposefully, others, mostly families or couples, strolling across, stopping to gaze at their river and its traffic. The two Dutch men dawdled, chatting about ships and cargoes. Sam was even slower, gazing with wonder at the cranes, dipping like herons over a fish pond as they unloaded bales, crates and sacks, swinging their loads onto lorries waiting on the quay below. He tugged Jannie's jacket to draw his attention to Tower Bridge, its bascules starting to rise as an outward-bound freighter was lined up by its tug for the passage downstream.

"We must get a taxi." Henri looked left and right. "First we must cross the road."

"Without getting squashed," added Sam, helpfully.

"Without getting squashed," confirmed Henri. Seeing a gap in the traffic, he hurried them across, then flagged down a taxi and told the cabbie the address.

They did not know that another refugee had arrived in London's Liverpool Street Station at approximately the same time and even then was travelling to Buckingham Palace with King George.

*

"You knock, Sam," Henri told him. "We'll wait here."

"Tante Miriam?" Sam asked, tremulously when she opened the door.

"Who?" asked the slim, elegant woman standing there with a bemused expression on her face.

"Oh," stuttered Sam, "I mean Mevrouw Cohen." He looked up at her, "It's me. Samuel Da Souza. We sent you a telegram."

All the pent-up fear and anxiety of the past three days burst out of Sam's young heart, just as it had at the Admiral's house.

Tante Miriam was momentarily overwhelmed when Samuel collapsed into her arms, sobbing noisily. Instinctively she held him tightly, one hand stroking his hair. She whispered "Samuel, Samuel. There, there," as she rocked him gently from side to side.

Pushing Samuel gently away from her, she said, "Let me look at you."

Taking a deep breath, he wiped his eyes with the backs of his hands and took a pace away from her before raising his face. As he tipped his head back, Miriam gazed at the tousled mop of wavy dark brown hair above brown eyes bright with tears. She noticed the bridge of freckles across his slightly upturned nose, his wide, generous mouth and the dimple in his chin and thought, "You will break a few hearts when you get older."

She also noticed his hands. Wondering why his long fingers were so stained, she took his left hand in hers and turned it over.

"It's oil, mevrouw," Sam whispered, "And coal." Seeing how puzzled she was, he stood a little straighter and said, "I am a fireman." He looked for and found Jannie and Henri. "In their ship."

Miriam saw the pride in the boy's bearing, heard it in his voice.

"They must think me very rude," she told Sam. Still holding his hand, she called, "Forgive me, I was forgetting my manners. Come in, please. Bring your bags."

She led Sam into her home, followed by Jannie and Henri. "Put your bags in the office," she told them, pointing to an open door on their right, "And come into the kitchen. I'll put the kettle on."

Evening sunlight poured through the open window above the butler's sink. Miriam filled an electric kettle while telling Sam where he would find the teapot, cups, saucers, plates and cutlery.

"Sit down," she told the two men, "We can introduce ourselves over a cup of tea."

Henri noticed that Jannie could not take his eyes off the woman as she bustled around her kitchen. He kicked him gently under the table and muttered very quietly, in Dutch, "It is rude to stare."

He nearly laughed aloud as Jannie started, went quite pink and looked anywhere but at Miriam.

Miriam turned her snort of laughter into a discreet cough and told Sam to set the table. She decided not tell them she was bilingual. Sam decided to show Tante Miriam how to make tea another time. The three sailors were treated to their first of many meals round that scrubbed kitchen table.

Miriam sat at the foot of the table, her back to the window, the low sunlight making it hard to see her expression. She put Sam on her right-hand side and Jannie to her left, leaving Henri to sit at the head.

As she poured their tea, she starting talking. "My name is Mrs Miriam Cohen and this has been my home for many years. You know me as Tante Miriam, though I am not Samuel's aunt. I am one of Simon's distant cousins and have lived in England all my life. Our families vaguely kept in touch which, I suppose, is why Samuel is here. You are very welcome." She paused, the teapot in her hand, and looked around the table before adding, "But," there was a long silence, "Who are you and why have you come?"

Henri cleared his throat as the others looked at him. "Mevrouw Cohen, we are sailors, refugees. Our Kapitein is a friend of Simon and Judith. Simon asked him to take Samuel onboard our ship three weeks ago when there was trouble. Fascists. We had to sail when the Germans came. Simon and his family did not sail with us. We had promised Simon we would take Samuel to England." He shrugged. "So we did."

Sam bowed his head as Henri spoke. The brief, bleak account laid bare the nightmare of the past few weeks.

Jannie reached across the table and took one of his hands in his, squeezing it firmly, before adding, "Samuel could not go on deck in case he

143

was seen. There are many fascists in the Netherlands and they make trouble. He worked with me in the engine room." He smiled at the boy, "He is now a Fireman, First Class."

Samuel nodded, his head still bowed. "This is true, Tante Miriam. I am a Fireman, First Class." His voice was soft and strained.

Miriam was silent. She sensed there was much more to be told, and that these men would tell her. But not while Sam was there.

She looked at the three of them, recognising their weariness and sense of loss, wondering what on earth they would do, so far from their homes and families.

She decided questions could wait and that practical matters must be settled.

Addressing the two men she said, "I thank you for bringing Samuel safely to my home. He may stay here as long as he likes."

"Danke, mevrouw," Henri and Jannie replied together.

"What about you two? What are your plans?"

Henri shrugged, "Find a hotel. Go to the embassy. See if they have work. We don't know."

Jannie added, "We have money. Enough for a few weeks." He laughed. "Perhaps the Germans come here too. We won't need money then."

"You don't mean that?" Sam gasped.

"Nee lad, of course I don't." Jannie looked at Mevrouw Cohen, "They won't get over the sea." He gave Sam's hand a reassuring shake. "The English Navy will stop them."

"More tea anyone?" Miriam said gaily in the silence that followed.

"Danke," Henri passed his cup and gave Jannie a nudge to pass his.

*

"Early night for you, Samuel," Tante Miriam told him after another prodigious yawn. She led the way upstairs to his bedroom where he had already unpacked and stowed his few clothes and possessions. "Don't forget to clean your teeth and wash your face..."

"Tante Miriam," Sam's sleepy protest stopped her.

"I'm sorry Sam, it's been such a long time since there were any children in my life." She held her hand up to quell any protest. "I know you're not a child, but you'll have to indulge me."

144

She gave Sam a hug and went on, "I sleep in the next room. Call out if you need me. Now, get undressed and get into bed. I'll be up again soon."

Miriam checked the blackout curtains were properly closed and went downstairs, leaving the landing light on.

Jannie and Henri had washed the supper things and left them neatly on the table for Miriam to put away. She watched them leaning against the wall of her small synagogue at the end of the garden, talking while they smoked their cigars. It was nearly nine o'clock. She switched the wireless on to warm up before calling Jannie and Henri. Like people all over the country, the BBC's nine o'clock news had become an almost unmissable feature of wartime life.

They listened in silence, heads bowed, eyes unfocussed, each lost in thought. Miriam broke their reverie when she turned it off.

"Not so good." was all Henri said.

"Not good at all," agreed Jannie.

Miriam stood, went to a cupboard and returned with a bottle of brandy and three glasses. "Drink, gentlemen?" she asked.

"Danke, mevrouw. Yes. Please." She put an ashtray on the table, took a packet of Du Maurier from her handbag and passed them round.

They sat with the door open, listening to the hum of London as they smoked and drank in silence. When Miriam had finished her brandy, she stubbed out her cigarette and asked Henri, "What happened to Samuel's family?"

She listened intently to his reply, her eyes never leaving his face. All she said when he stopped was, "G-d have mercy," to which both Henri and Jannie replied "Amen."

Eventually Jannie broke the silence, "It is possible they will escape. Paul de Groot has many contacts, as does Simon."

"And if that is not possible, they will be safe with Paul on his farm," Henri said. "It is 35 kilometres from Rotterdam, out in the country. It is a good place for Rachel to grow up."

"Do you really believe that?" asked Miriam. "They are Jews."

"They are Jews," agreed Henri, "But the Kapitein is not, nor is his wife. They will be careful."

"Very careful," agreed Jannie. "But first the Germans must defeat our army and they have not done so."

"Not yet," whispered Henri.

Miriam broke the silence by pouring another brandy for the men and asking, "What about you, Henri, and you Jannie? Where are your families?"

"Henri's wife died a few years ago," Jannie answered, "He has no children." He looked at Miriam. "The Kapitein sent all the married men home a few days ago. None of us have any ties to keep us there."

"That is so sad," said Miriam quietly, before asking Jannie, "You have no one at all?"

Jannie's smile lit up his creased and work-worn face, "Nee, mevrouw, I was never home long enough to get married when I was young. And…"

"And," Henri butted in gaily, "Who would want an old man like him anyway?"

Henri noticed Miriam's eyes widen in surprise when Jannie muttered "Neuk je," in response.

He raised his glass and gave a toast, "To you, mevrouw, thank you for making us welcome."

"And thank you for welcoming Sam," said Jannie. He looked at Henri and said, "We had better leave before it gets dark."

Both men pushed back their chairs and stood up.

"Where are you going?" asked Miriam, a puzzled look on her face.

"We have to find lodgings, mevrouw. We will come back tomorrow to see Sam and talk about his future," Jannie replied, moving into the passage.

"But you must stay here," said Miriam, springing up and putting a hand on Jannie's arm. "You can't leave the boy. He needs you. Both of you."

Jannie looked at Miriam. "It is not proper, mevrouw. What will your husband say?"

He saw a flicker of pain in Miriam's eyes, swiftly followed by a warm smile that lit up her face.

"You are a dear," she said, gripping his arm, "My husband died in 1936. If he had lived, he would have told you to stay here."

She turned to Henri and said, "You do see, don't you, you must stay? For the sake of the boy. And," she added with a mischievous smile, "who would take in two old Dutch sailors at this time of night?"

"You are most kind, mevrouw." Jannie lifted her hand from his sleeve and raised it to his lips as he gave a courtly bow. "Dankuwel."

To her surprise, Miriam curtsied in response to Jannie's old-fashioned formality, thinking as she did, 'He might swear like a trooper but he has such elegant manners'.

"That is settled," Miriam said briskly. "Fetch your bags and I'll show you to your room," adding, "You don't mind sharing, do you?"

Reassured, she continued upstairs, pointing out Sam's bedroom and the bathroom next to it. "You are on the top floor. Wait while I fix the blackout curtains."

Jannie and Henri were surprised how long that took until she called them to come up and they saw the large sloping windows in the front wall.

"You must not open them," Miriam explained, "The blackout has to be complete so I use sticky paper to stop any light escaping."

"We can sleep anywhere, mevrouw and we won't smoke up here," Henri reassured her.

Seeing them looking around the large white-painted room, Miriam explained, "This was a lace-maker's house. They worked up here because the light is good. Now it is my guest room. I hope you will be comfortable."

"Most comfortable, mevrouw," said Henri, echoed by Jannie's "A lovely room."

"Good." Miriam moved back to the stairs. "I'm going to make a pot of coffee and smoke a cigarette. I would welcome your company in the drawing room in a minute."

Henri and Jannie quickly settled into their new room and were downstairs in time to take the tray off Miriam and put it onto the low round table beside her armchair.

With cups of coffee to hand and cigarettes drawing, the three of them relaxed into the easy conversation of people who are comfortable with themselves. The simple elegance of their surroundings helped. Four armchairs, a sofa, bookcases, a crowded desk, photographs on the mantle-piece, an empty flower-pot in the grate, rugs scattered on the wide, polished floor-boards, paintings on the walls; it was a lived-in, welcoming room, reflecting the charm and taste of their hostess.

"Forgive me for asking, mevrouw," Jannie said gently, "but do you know why Simon was so insistent Sam must come here,"

"I have been asking myself the same question," Miriam answered. "Simon was a cousin of my husband, not a very close one. They hadn't seen each other since they were children."

She sighed. "You know what Jewish families are like. I had a letter from Simon when Isaac died." She shrugged, "Condolences for his distant cousin, hoping to see me one day, asking after the children." Miriam stopped. Her eyes filled with tears. She took a lace handkerchief from the sleeve of her cardigan and wiped them away.

Neither man moved.

Sitting very straight in her chair, knees pressed together, head lowered, Miriam sighed.

She raised her head and gazed at Jannie. "Perhaps you were wise not to marry. Henri will understand." She turned to the old sailor and saw him nod. Turning back to Jannie, she continued, "Nothing can prepare you for the joy children bring. Ours were born in the War, Reuben in 1915, just after Ike went to France, and Gabrielle at the end of 1917." She suddenly lifted her head, an expression of tender love filling her eyes. "Ike had been wounded, a Blighty one he called it, so Reuben had a little sister." She smiled to herself. "They were so beautiful, just like their father."

"Ike's leg took a such long time to mend he was sent home to get his strength back. Those were happy times."

Miriam fell silent, her head bowed and shoulders slumped. She took a deep breath and continued. "We did not have a house in those uncertain days so I lived with Ike's parents. They had a lovely home on the edge of London with a big garden and fields close by. They adored their grandchildren." She shook her head as if to clear her thoughts, "Ike went back to war in July 1918. He was wounded again in October. Maybe that saved his life."

Miriam stood up and moved across the room to the mantle-shelf. She picked up a photograph and stared at it for a while before carrying it back and handing it to Jannie. He gazed at the two children looking back at him.

He was only half conscious of Miriam standing next to him. "They both died in 1919," she said quietly, "They were so little."

Standing, Jannie put his hand on Miriam's arm as Henri took the picture from him.

"It was the Spanish 'flu," she said.

Jannie caught Henri's eye but neither said anything.

"Come, sit," Henri said at last and drew Miriam away from Jannie and led her to her chair.

Jannie poured a little brandy into a glass and passed it to her before pouring a large tot for Henri and a larger one for himself.

Miriam saw this and startled them by bursting out laughing.

"You are as bad as Isaac," she declared in fluent Dutch.

At which, Jannie went bright red and Henri laughed.

"That'll teach you to swear in a lady's house."

Jannie stopped himself from swearing again. "You knew all the time."

"Ja," replied Henri, "And so would you have if you had been paying attention."

"Mevrouw, my sincere apologies," Jannie began, only to have his words brushed aside by Miriam's cheerful, "I haven't had such fun in years."

*

"It is many years since I cried for my children," Miriam said quietly. "It was a dreadful time, with Ike in hospital and his parents dying a few days later."

Henri, sitting opposite, noticed how tightly she gripped the arms of her chair. Jannie reached out and put his hand on hers.

"You don't have to tell us, mevrouw. It is too distressing."

"No Jannie, not so much now."

She thought for a minute before continuing. "Ike did not catch the 'flu in hospital, and nor did I at home" She stopped again. "Though it stopped being home the day our children died. I stayed there to look after Ike's parents. He was still in hospital when they died."

She looked at Henri and then Jannie. "Ike was an only child. Imagine what they felt when he joined the army. He enlisted straight away. My dear husband was a romantic, a dreamer. He fought for a noble cause." She sighed. "Such a foolish notion."

"Perhaps not," murmured Henri. "Some wars have to be fought."

"Always by young men," Miriam replied, to which both Henri and Jannie shrugged.

Miriam gasped, "Oh, you must think I am so rude. Forgive me, please?"

"There is nothing to forgive," replied Henri. "We did not fight, it is true. We escaped. No-one stopped us." Neither he nor Jannie thought of mentioning their passengers.

Miriam passed round her cigarettes.

"Isaac came out of hospital in March. He was not badly wounded this time. There were too many ghosts in his parents' house for us to stay there. Besides which, Isaac was now a wealthy man. What with inheriting his father's investments and selling that house, we could have moved anywhere in the world. But Ike wanted to live here, among what he called 'real' people." She smiled. "We came to live here because his sergeant told him

149

stories about the lace weavers; and about the Jewish migrants who followed them. How hard their lives were, yet how strong their sense of community. He sowed an idea in Ike's mind over the course of those long years in the trenches and behind the lines, the idea of helping the young men who never moved from these slums, who became degraded as they lost hope. They talked for hours about attracting them to another way to live, another way to bring up children, about how they would start some sort of school where young men could learn much more than just a trade." She sighed. "We changed direction after the children died. It would have been too painful to have our school without them in it." She went quiet and sat for a moment to compose herself. "You must forgive me," she whispered, "I have not spoken about this since Ike died."

"There is nothing to forgive, mevrouw. Sometimes it is easier to talk to strangers" Jannie said.

"It was easier for Ike and I not to talk to anyone. That is why we came here, to live among strangers and help them in little ways, ways that only those we helped knew about. That is what we did."

Miriam looked at her guests. "Ike was a good man. We made new friends here. He was helping people, our neighbours, when the Blackshirts tried to march through the heart of the Jewish community. They wanted to start a fight and they did. Thousands of people took to the streets to stop them, mostly Jews and Irish. The Government sent the police. Not to stop the march but to stop the people."

She shook her head. "None of it made any sense. Ike went to help a child who had been knocked down by a police horse. A policeman on another horse beat Ike to the ground. He was unconscious when some men brought him home. He was very ill for weeks." Her voice faltered. "And then he died."

She glanced up. "Christmas Eve, 1936. He was not a brave man, not then and not ever. He died as he lived, a good man helping a neighbour."

Miriam stood and straightened her back. "I have talked too much and now I want a drink. Not one of your little measures either, meneer," she said to Henri, laughing, her voice firm, much to his amazement.

She stopped, and looked at him, "Why are you surprised? This has happened and I cannot change it. You are here and you give me small measures and make me talk too much. Make me cry. And land me with a boy I would never have heard of if Ike had not died."

She brought the bottle over, poured herself a healthy tot before passing it to Jannie. She said "Sam tells me he is fifteen. Is that true?"

"Nee, mevrouw. He is thirteen. He will be fourteen next month. His papers also say he is South African."

"Why?" asked Miriam.

"Simon thinks it will be easier for an older boy from the Empire to go to Canada than a Dutch kid."

"His papers are good, mevrouw." Henri added. "Simon got them from his cousin in the South African Embassy."

"Simon and his cousins," said Miriam. "Ike never talked about Simon. I never knew he existed until he wrote to me. I have no idea how he found my address, how he knew Ike had died."

Henri shrugged. "I think Simon must have heard about your work here. He was a sailor before he took over his father's café, one of those men who has met many people and keeps in touch with them. He was always writing and receiving letters."

Miriam looked at the two men and raised her hands in a small gesture of helplessness. "What am I supposed to do now?"

It was Jannie who answered. "Only you can answer that question. We promised our Kapitein we would bring Sam to England. We have done so. If it is not convenient for him to stay here, we will go elsewhere. Sam is our responsibility, not yours. We will look after him until we can take him home again."

Eventually Miriam replied, speaking softly and carefully. "Sam is welcome to stay here as long as he wants. But I cannot look after him on my own." With a slight catch in her voice she said, "I know nothing about boys. The schools have closed and gone to the countryside. We may be bombed any day."

She stopped to look at Jannie and Henri before asking them, "Would you stay here? Please. Help me look after Sam."

They were all standing. The room was filled with shadows from the table lamps. It was very quiet.

"I would be honoured," answered Jannie with a slight bow.

"As would I," said Henri.

"Thank you," Miriam said, smiling at her new house-guests. "It will be interesting to hear what Sam has to say about this when he wakes up."

*

Miriam woke early, as she did every day, drew her blackout curtains and opened the shutters onto the Monday morning bustle of Wilkes Street. She stood in her silk house coat, arms crossed tightly, wondering how she was going to look after Sam, even with the help of those sailors. She walked back to her bed and sat down. She rested her head in her hands, elbows on her knees and sighed deeply.

When she heard Sam knock into his bedside table she waited, expecting to hear him walk across the floor and open the door. Nothing. His bed creaked. She heard muffled sobs. Closing her eyes, she listened for another moment, every instinct telling her to go to him, even as her mind recoiled from the pain of her two babies sobbing and coughing as their lives ebbed away.

Miriam paused briefly before striding across the floor and into Sam's room. She left the door open to give her enough light to make her way to the side of his bed. Sam did not hear her and jumped when she sat beside him. Miriam stretched out her arm and rested her hand on his back. Stroking it lightly, she whispered, "Shall I open the window, Sam?"

Sam nodded, the sobs diminishing. Drawing the black-out curtains, opening the shutters and then raising the bottom sash window took enough time for Sam to turn over, sit up and dry his eyes. He gazed at the slender form of Tante Miriam wrapped in a full-length, tightly belted, yellowy golden gown, wondering if she was an angel. She sat on the bed again and said, "I expect you'd like to wash and clean your teeth." Sam nodded. "When you've done that, come down to the kitchen and help me get breakfast ready." Sam looked at her, silent and uncertain. "You like a cooked breakfast, don't you?" Miriam asked, ruffling his tousled hair.

Sam smiled at her, "Oh yes, Tante Miriam. I am a very good cook." He then told her what he would need and once he was up, she put on her hat and coat and walked with him to Spitalfields Market.

Sam was soon tugging Tante Miriam to a stall piled with vegetables and then to a bakery for a loaf of freshly baked bread. They walked home, Sam chattering away about the stoomboot and how Jannie had taught him to cook. An admiral appeared in the conversation, as did something called 'engineer's tea'. Samuel was skipping along the pavement, his eyes bright and the night-time terrors forgotten. Tante Miriam, caught up in the joy of

152

the morning, even skipped a few paces herself before she remembered her dignity.

Henri and Jannie had heard Miriam go into Sam's room; heard them go downstairs and, a short while later, the front door closing behind them.

Washed, shaved and wearing clean shirts, they went into the garden for a smoke while they talked about what they had to do. Registering with the Dutch and South African Embassies was first, before finding a bank, opening an account and depositing their guilders. They needed to change some into pounds to give Tante Miriam for housekeeping.

"Don't forget flags," reminded Jannie. "South African for Sam and Dutch for us. We had better sew them on our jackets."

"And a bookshop," said Henri. "For a phrase book," he added, seeing Jannie's frown.

They had just put the kettle on when Miriam and Sam returned. "Good morning, mevrouw, good morning, Sam." Slight bows and broad smiles greeted the shoppers.

Sam turned to Miriam and said earnestly, "Tante Miriam, Jannie and I will cook breakfast. Perhaps you would like to take Henri for a walk?"

Miriam raised an eyebrow in Henri's direction. He nodded slightly and smiled at Jannie. "It would be a pleasure, Sam. About half an hour?"

"Ja, Tante Miriam, half an hour. That is good."

Henri coughed. "Perhaps Tante Miriam would like coffee, Sam. Did you ask her?"

Miriam took the hint. "Coffee? Yes please."

As they went out, she asked Henri, "What was that about?"

Henri laughed, "Sam has discovered what he calls 'Engineers Tea'. It is best drunk in a roasting engine-room, or in the middle watch in filthy weather. It puts hairs on your…" Henri stopped and went bright red.

"Excuse me, mevrouw."

Miriam was shaking with laughter as Henri stumbled to a halt.

"Not at all," she said. "Thank you for saving me."

They strolled along the side of a church and paused in front of the elegant, smoke-stained building where Miriam asked, "I don't suppose he'll have to go to services here?"

"Nee, unless you want him to," replied Henri.

Miriam shook her head as they turned back to see what there was for breakfast.

On their return, Sam gave them a happy smile before turning back to the unfamiliar galley. "Tante, Henri. Sit please."

Miriam was delighted to see the change in Sam. She leant across the table to whisper to Henri "He needs to be kept busy."

"Ja, mevrouw."

Breakfast was a cheerful meal.

Miriam watched the easy way her guests talked together and how the two men nurtured Sam without him noticing.

They shared their plans with her as they washed up. Miriam enjoyed the rare luxury of sitting in her own kitchen with coffee and a cigarette and nothing to do but talk.

Later, she rang the Dutch Embassy and was told Henri and Jannie should come before 10 o'clock. Then it was the South African Embassy. The official was happy to take Sam's details over the telephone; passport number, clearance at Chatham and address in London.

Miriam was told Sam would be called up when he was eighteen and that he should notify the Embassy of any change of address.

*

Her home felt surprisingly empty after the men had left for the Embassy. Miriam made herself a fresh pot of coffee and went upstairs to her drawing room to think.

She knew that London was no place for Sam. Nor was her house the right place. She was too old. She had deliberately cut herself off from her friends and she did not know anyone with children of his age. And all the schools were closed. And Henri and Jannie. What were they going to do? Her face softened as she remembered how she felt when Jannie had laid his hand on hers.; a comfort unknown since Isaac died.

Lighting another cigarette, she stood and began to pace up and down, occasionally looking out of the windows with their criss-crossings of brown sticky paper. It reminded her how frightened she had been at the beginning of the war: the mass evacuation of children, air-raid sirens, shelters, trenches, guns and balloons in parks and open spaces.

And now she had other people to worry about. Not any other people, but Simon's little boy and the two sailors.

She went down to the kitchen to listen to the news.

154

In slow, measured tones, the announcer filled her with dread as he explained how Hitler was trampling through Holland, Belgium and France. For all his talk of counter-attacks and holding some river, it was obvious the Allies were in retreat. 'Blitzkrieg' was a new and frightening word.

Miriam turned the wireless off and sat, deep in thought.

London, especially the East End, was an obvious target, with its close-packed, crowded houses and narrow streets abutting factories, docks and warehouses. Like most people, she was surprised it had not already been bombed.

*

Sam couldn't stay in London. That was obvious. But where could he go, and who would look after him?

The only person she knew who might have an answer was her accountant.

Miriam had been surprised when Isaac engaged the firm when he came out of the army. He had served under Harold in France so she supposed that was a good enough reason.

She would write to him today.

First, she must tell the Warden there were three more people here. That, she knew, would set tongues wagging. When they returned, she would have to take them to the police station to register and the Town Hall to get issued with gas masks and ration cards.

Picking up her cigarettes and lighter, she went out of the back door and into her synagogue to smoke and think. Isaac had been amused to find a house with a synagogue when they were looking for somewhere to live. Though he retained many of the customs and habits of his religion, he had left his faith in the mud of Flanders. However, he drew comfort from the sanctity of this little rectangular building.

Miriam sat in his large leather armchair, as she had done every day since he died. It was where she went to wrestle with problems, as well as to reflect on their life together. She looked around her, wondering what Henri and Jannie would make of the way Isaac had turned this holy place into his library. Stubbing out her cigarette, she stood and walked along the built-in book-shelves on the south wall, idly running her fingers along the spines until she reached Isaac's knee-hole desk. She sat down, opened a drawer, took out writing paper, her fountain pen and blotting paper and started her letter to Harold.

When she had finished, she picked up Isaac's address book. London or Cornwall? She decided on London. If he was still in the country, his office would forward it.

Miriam saw the A.R.P. warden on her way to the letter box and called "Oh, Mr Wilkins." He turned, saw who it was and smiled warmly.

"Good morning, Mrs Cohen, what can I do for you today?"

"Well," Miriam found herself surprisingly shy, "Er, I thought you ought to know some unexpected guests arrived yesterday." She saw she had piqued his interest and hurried on, "They are from Holland."

"Oh, I say," Mr Wilkins looked concerned, "The news ain't too good, not from over there it ain't."

"Yes," replied Miriam, "They managed to get out just in time." She paused, wondering how much to tell him. Knowing he would find out soon enough, she added, "On a boat. One of them is a relative, that's why they came here."

"Blimey, missus. How many have you got?"

"Just the boy," she replied, "And two sailors. They came with him to make sure he got here safely." Miriam was aware she was hurrying her words. "I don't know how long they'll be staying."

She paused, looked at Mr Wilkins and said firmly, "They have been very kind to the boy, Mr Wilkins, and are welcome to stay as long as they like."

"Thank you for letting me know, Mrs Cohen." Mr Wilkins knew that look. "I'll add them to the book now and come round to get their names later on, if that is convenient."

"I'm sure it will be. Thank you." Miriam continued, "I'll take them to the police station this afternoon and then on to collect ration books and gas masks."

"You've got a busy day ahead, Missus. I'll see you this evening." With a cheery wave, Mr Wilkins went on his way.

Miriam turned back after she had posted her letter. She still found it odd that their red letter boxes had been painted yellow last year. Her heart sank when she recalled they would change colour if poison gas was dropped nearby.

It was another beautiful day.

Miriam walked slowly home, remembering to buy more bread as she passed the bakers. She thought she had enough vegetables to make a thick soup for supper. They could fill up with some of that lovely cheese the boys had brought with them.

It was the first time since Ike died that Miriam had to think about what was in her larder.

∗

After Henri and Jannie had finished in the Dutch Embassy, they went to a bank to open accounts and pay in their guilders.

Sam was surprised when Henri said, "We'd better open an account for you."

"But I haven't got any money," he protested.

"Of course you have," laughed Jannie. "You haven't been working for nothing for the past three weeks." He dug his elbow into Sam's side. "You'll be able to buy us a beer later."

Neither Henri nor Jannie thought it wise to tell the boy they were also paying in the money his father had given them. Simon's comment as he handed it over, "In case we don't make it," was best kept to themselves.

Fortunately, Sam was not paying attention when they paid over £200 into the deposit account he had just opened.

It was nearly lunch-time before they finished their business and Sam needed feeding.

Miriam had lent them her street map, suggested some sights they might see, and told them to look out for a Lyons Corner House. "But don't order coffee." She pulled a face. "Tea is better."

After their introduction to the London Underground in the morning, they had spent a happy afternoon walking slowly through parks and along roads to join the river at Westminster Bridge. Once there, they drifted eastwards along the Embankment. Henri and Jannie kept stopping to look at the traffic on the water, commenting on finer points of seamanship as much for Sam's education as for their own enjoyment. Henri was impressed by the way the tug skippers worked their strings of lighters through the bridges in the fast-running tide.

The guns and trenches in the parks, barrage balloons floating above the city, piles of sandbags around memorials and buildings and the number of men and women in uniform muted their pleasure. So did the looks their uniforms attracted, reminding them to buy or make flags to sew on.

It was late afternoon when Sam pointed to an old man selling newspapers outside the entrance to Temple underground station.

'DUTCH QUEEN HERE.'

"Christ," Henri felt as if all the air had been punched out of him. Sam stumbled and clutched hold of Jannie's arm, his face white.

Jannie gripped Sam's shoulder tightly and said, "Let's go back to Tante Miriam. Maybe there is more on the wireless."

Negotiating the Underground took their minds off the dread that filled their hearts. It roared back, threatening to overwhelm them, when they saw the fear in Miriam's eyes.

Jannie stepped forward and took her hands in his. "You have heard, Mimi?" He spoke softly, as if to calm her, and was surprised when she smiled up at him and replied, "Where did that name come from?"

Jannie let go of her, his face turning bright red. Stuttering in his confusion, he muttered, "My apologies, meevrou."

"Shh, Jannie." She picked up his hands and squeezed them lightly. "It is a lovely name."

Henri looked down at Sam and smiled. "Hey Sam, stop staring and put the kettle on."

Miriam followed Sam into her kitchen and gave him a hug. "Let's make the tea together. We will listen to the wireless later."

"Jannie must like you, Tante Miriam."

Miriam smiled. "And what makes you say that, Sam?"

"To call you Mimi. Please don't be cross with him. He has only got us."

Miriam put her hand under Sam's chin and tipped his head up. She gazed at the boy for a moment before saying, "I am not cross with him, Sam. Jannie is a fine man." She smiled into Sam's eyes, "And you are a good man to stand up for him."

She turned away and picked the kettle up.

"Now, let's get that tea made."

As they were leaving the kitchen Miriam whispered. "Can you keep a secret?"

Sam nodded.

"I haven't been called Mimi since I was a little girl."

Sam gasped, "You don't mind do you, Tante Miriam? You're not cross?"

"No Sam, quite the opposite. I like it. And that is a secret you must keep."

*

"I forgot to tell you the good news."

Sam was curled up next to Tante Miriam on the sofa, fast asleep. He did not stir as Henri went on, "I was able to send a telegram to the River Lek Stoomboot office."

"What did you say?" Miriam looked down at Sam to make sure he was still asleep.

Henri grunted. "'Stoomboot *De Ruyter* commandeered by British Navy 10 May. Sailed at gunpoint to England. Arrived 12 May. All hands safe. Please inform families.' By now they should all have been told. Paul will tell Simon and Judith."

Smiling, Henri added, "It's near enough the truth to keep Paul out of trouble."

Miriam looked puzzled, "Why do you say 'near enough the truth'? Isn't that what happened."

"Yes, but not at gunpoint. We invited them onboard."

Jannie stood up and said, "Let's get Sam to bed. The poor boy is exhausted and the story sounds better over a drink."

He bent over, lifted Sam effortlessly and carried him up the stairs. "Hey, jonge," he whispered as he turned down Sam's bed with one hand before laying him on the sheet. "Let's get these clothes off you." Jannie slipped Sam out of his shirt, trousers and socks without waking him, and tucked him up in his underclothes. He looked up as Miriam came in, carrying a glass of water. "Thank you, Mimi, er, mevrouw…" He stood beside Sam's bed, looking down at the boy, not knowing what to say.

A sleep-filled voice came from the bed. "It's alright Jannie, she likes…" Sam stopped abruptly, eyes wide open.

Miriam laughed, "Go back to sleep Sam." She touched Jannie lightly on his arm. "I'll settle him. Why don't you go downstairs and find the brandy?"

Miriam sat on the side of Sam's bed and stroked his hair. "I'll leave the light on outside. We're all a bit shaken by the news. Call if you need me."

As she leaned over to kiss him goodnight, she said softly, "Thank you for keeping our secret."

Sam smiled and went back to sleep.

*

Miriam woke early and slipped out to buy milk, bread and a newspaper. Conversation was muted by the headlines, the same as those on yesterday's bill-board. "Dutch Queen Here." Stories of desperate fighting dominated the front page.

Sam was so frightened he felt sick. He nursed his cup of tea, unable to face any food.

"Cheer up," said Henri, putting the paper down. "We had a better time in Chatham than the Queen did in Buckingham Palace."

"Yes, Henri, you did." Sam joined in,

Jannie was quick to ask "What are you talking about?"

Sam grinned. "I saw him kissing milady." He stood up and walked over to Henri. "Like this" He bowed, lifted one of Henri's great hands, planted a smacking kiss on the back, and skipped smartly out of reach.

"See, Tante Mimi, and milady was ever so pleased."

"Well," blustered Henri, "It is good manners and, um…"

"Charm," added Jannie helpfully.

Sam said, "I'm going to make my bed," and disappeared upstairs.

They were silenced by the wireless.

Miriam turned up the volume and looked around the table. Jannie and Henri were sitting stock still, hands clasped in front of them as if in prayer. Their lined, weather-beaten faces were sombre as the announcement came through: 'All owners of self-propelled pleasure craft between thirty and one hundred feet to register them with the Admiralty within fourteen days.'

"Christ Almighty," breathed Henri, looking across at Jannie. "Why do you think they want those boats?"

Jannie shrugged, a resigned and helpless shrug. "I am only guessing. But it can only be to bring an army home." He stood to put the kettle on and took a cigarette from the packet on the table. "If that happens, we should take *De Ruyter* over."

"No," said Miriam, "You must not go back."

"Listen, Mimi," she thought Jannie had the most startling blue eyes she had ever seen, "our Queen may have run away but we won't." His hand closed a little tighter around Miriam's.

Henri slowly got to his feet. "I must telephone the Admiral."

"Admiral. You may need *De Ruyter* very soon. She is an old lady with an old engine. We will sail her for you." Henri listened. "Ja, my crew will sail her." There was another pause while the Admiral spoke. "Ja, we know. Perhaps you put some machine guns on her?" He paused, nodding once more. "And sailors to shoot them?" Another pause, "Danke Admiral. We will stand by. Please give regards to Milady Teagle. Danke. Goodbye."

Henri took a deep breath as he hung up, blew out his cheeks and exhaled noisily. "We stand by."

Miriam's eyes troubled. "What about you, Sam?" She reached out for the boy but he stepped back.

"I go, Tante Mimi."

He looked so stern, so grown up. Her heart felt as if it would break when he continued, "It is my duty. I am the ship's fireman."

Jannie nodded. "It is true, mevrouw." He smiled. "They may not call us, Mimi. We are standing by, that is all."

Henri broke the silence. "Let us get some lunch. A walk will do us good. Bloom's, is it?"

"Yes, Henri, Bloom's."

Lunch was long and merry, with Jannie and Henri vying with each other to tell increasingly unlikely tales of tall ships in wild oceans, exotic ports in the Far East, South America and the Caribbean, and to describe the scents and sights of the tropics.

Miriam egged them on with her questions, eyes sparkling as they took her aloft in a gale or down in a sweltering hold, unloading copra off some fly-blown island. Coaling ship in Aden struck her as the worst job in the world.

Sam sat there, entranced, steadily eating his way through all that the busy waiters placed before him.

Back at Wilkes Street, they settled into the comfort of the chairs and sofa, kicked off their shoes and happily slept through the remains of the afternoon and into the evening.

Since Sam had bagged the most comfortable of the two armchairs, it was only natural for Jannie to join Miriam on the sofa. As Jannie dozed off, Miriam curled up beside him and rested her head against his chest.

Sam soon woke and tiptoed out to go to the heads. The creaking of a floor-board woke Mimi. Her contented sigh woke Jannie. He stayed still, rejoicing in her warmth and scent, the feel of her against him.

It was the wireless that shattered the peace. Rotterdam was burning, bombed by waves of German aircraft until it was ablaze, thousands reported dead, their city destroyed.

Henri put a bottle of brandy and four glasses on the table. He handed each of them a full glass and drank silently. Jannie put a glass in Sam's hands and said, "Sip it, jonge." They sat back, silent, glasses cradled in both hands, staring into space.

It was Henri who spoke first, softly, urgently. "Listen to me Sam." He had to repeat himself, more sharply. "Listen jonge. Your family is safe. We know that."

"How do you know that?"

"Because they are with Oom Paul and Christina. They went to the farm before we sailed. That is where they will stay." Henri smiled. "Rachel will learn to milk a cow."

"And ride a horse," Sam whispered. "She will like that."

Miriam stood and tousled Sam's hair as she passed, "Will you help me with the blackout?"

"Of course," Sam got up. He stood there, looking down at Henri, his eyes searching his face. Henri sat very still, calmly returning Sam's gaze. Eventually the boy nodded to himself and said "Thank you, meneer". He pushed his almost full glass towards Henri and smiled. "You finish this."

*

The street beyond the black out curtains was silent when Sam woke and struggled out of the tight cocoon of sheet and blankets. He lay still for a moment as he remembered Tante Mimi tucking him in, then bending over to kiss him goodnight. She had smelt faintly of flowers.

Sam could hear voices and crept downstairs, looking for Jannie and Henri. Putting his ear to the drawing room door he heard the grown-ups talking about the concert onboard *De Ruyter*.

He opened the door and was glad when Tante Mimi told him to sit between her and Jannie.

"What were you talking about, Tante Mimi," he said brightly, sensing the gloomy atmosphere in the room. "Was it about Jannie's cooking?"

162

"Nee, jonge," said Jannie slowly. "We were talking about meeting meneer Hartley tomorrow. Mimi thinks he can help us to leave London soon."

"Before they bomb it?" asked Sam, quieter and more serious now.

"Ja, before they bomb it."

"Will you be coming too?" Sam asked Jannie.

"Of course," Jannie said, then hesitated before turning to Miriam. "If you would like me to?"

She did not answer him but leant forward to Sam. "Do you think I should ask Jannie?" She smiled mischievously at the boy, "After all, we have only just met and were never properly introduced."

Henri rose from his chair and came to the sofa. With an elaborate bow, he announced, "Mevrouw Cohen, may I have the pleasure of introducing Engineer Officer Jantzen? Jantzen, arise and meet Mevrouw Cohen."

Miriam rose and curtseyed gracefully to the blushing Dutchman.

"And now we have been introduced," Henri said, "let us consider what lies ahead." He pulled up one of a matching pair of elegant wooden chairs and sat close to the sofa.

"We could stay here," said Sam. "It is a very nice house and we could build a bomb shelter."

"It is a very nice house," answered Miriam, "But it is very old and any bomb shelter would be very small."

"And it is in the middle of London," added Jannie.

"And we know what the Germans do to cities," Henri said.

"Yes," replied Sam, "But they are far away."

"No, Sam," said Jannie, putting an arm round the boy. "Not now they are in the Low Countries."

"Fuck them!" Sam said.

Miriam burst out laughing, setting off Henri. Jannie smiled and shook his head. "It is not polite to use bad language in front of ladies, Sam. You know that."

Sam turned to his great aunt, "Sorry, Tante Mimi." She hugged the boy and murmured over his head, "That's alright. You just took us by surprise."

By the time they had made a pot of tea and decided they did not need toast as well and drunk their tea and persuaded Sam that it would be better not to swear but if he really must, perhaps he should swear in Dutch, "Or

163

Yiddish," added Miriam helpfully, it was nearly midnight and their eyes were drooping.

"Don't lie in bed in the morning, boys," Miriam called after them as they went upstairs. "Mrs C will be here at nine."

"Who," asked Sam.

"Mrs Coward. She helps me round the house."

Henri grinned. "She will be surprised to find your strange men here."

"She has seen stranger," said Miriam, laughing to cover her blushes.

'She really is very beautiful when she does that,' thought Jannie as he went upstairs.

*

Mr Hartley regarded Miriam over the top of his glasses.

"Do you want them to go with you?"

Miram nodded. "Yes. The two men are great friends and Sam trusts them. He was working on the boat for three weeks before they escaped."

"Ah," said Harold, "I had not realised that."

He stood up and patted Miriam's shoulder. "They are also good for you, my dear."

She smiled. "So you agree that we should leave London?"

"I do." Harold replied. "Do you have any idea where you want to go?"

"Nothing definite." Miriam smiled again, "You have always said how peaceful it is in Cornwall."

"It is, Miriam, it really is." He picked up his briefcase and turned to leave. "I'll ask Sam to see me out."

Miriam took his hand. "He has only been here a few days and yet..." She hesitated, searching for the right words, "And yet..."

"And yet he completes you."

"Yes, dear Harold, he really does complete me."

Miriam kissed Harold on the cheek and walked him to the door of the drawing room.

"I will write very soon, once I have thought about where you might go, you and your Dutch pirates."

Harold walked downstairs to find Sam. "Would you show me to the door please?" he asked.

"Ja meneer, of course."

164

Sam sprung up and walked along the small hall to open the front door. Mr Hartley stopped. "Will you walk to the end of the road with me?"

A bit surprised, Sam agreed and fell in beside the smartly dressed businessman.

"I am very sorry that you are here, Sam." He held up his hand as Sam started to speak. "That you have had to leave your family and your homeland. Tell me this, please, do you really want to go to the country with Mrs Cohen?" Seeing Sam's confusion, he added, "Tante Miriam."

"Oh yes, meneer. Please. I am safe with her."

"And with the two men?"

"Oh yes," said Sam. "They are my shipmates."

"Of course, Sam. We shall see each other again soon. Thank you for your company."

They shook hands and Mr Hartley walked slowly towards Liverpool Street Station. He began to whistle as he thought about the morning.

"I wonder if it's only young Sam who completes you," he said aloud as he crossed Commercial Street.

*

Sam skipped up Wilkes Street, banged the door noisily behind him, bounded into the kitchen, slapped Jannie on the back and gave Tante Mimi a noisy kiss on the cheek. Henri's fierce scowl was enough to save him from a similar fate.

"What in heaven's name did Mr Hartley give you?" he said.

"Nothing." Sam smiled innocently, "We just talked."

He picked up an old newspaper and started looking at the pictures. A headline caught his eye. He read out, haltingly, "It say here Dutch Queen made flaming protest when Germans invade."

He harrumphed as he had heard Jannie harrumph. "Is that why those klootzakken burn Rotterdam?"

"Language, Sam," said Jannie.

"Sorry." Sam did not look sorry.

He put the paper down. "Is that why we are leaving London?"

"Yes," replied Miriam. "We agreed this morning. Mr Hartley is going to enquire about places we might move to."

"All of us?"

"All of us." Saying that made Miriam unexpectedly happy. She turned to Jannie and Henri, "Will you help me pack a few things we might need?"

"Of course, though Jannie and I won't be going anywhere until the admiral says we can." Seeing her frown, Henri went on, "Don't forget we may be needed onboard *De Ruyter*."

"And me." Sam said emphatically.

"And you," Henri said. He had no wish to take the boy if they were called up but knew he had no choice. He felt Miriam's eyes on him and shrugged helplessly.

Sam poked Jannie, "We will see milady again."

"Yes," Jannie said, "And Queenie will give you another scrub in the bath."

Seeing the boy wriggle, Miriam said, "Perhaps I should be scrubbing you, Sam?"

"Nee, Tante Mimi, never, danke."

Henri stood. "We need fresh air. Shall we walk to the river?"

At a chandlers' on Wapping Wall they were able to buy some small Dutch and South African flags. On the Embankment they stared at the heavily sand-bagged Cleopatra's Needle and discussed the long tow from Egypt and across the Bay of Biscay. There was little traffic in Trafalgar Square or anywhere else but many more people outside the embassies. They stopped a bright red London Bus and sat upstairs, staring out of the front windows at the streets below.

A café in Hyde Park was open. They sat on benches by the Serpentine eating meat pies of dubious quality. Sam ate his with a relish shared only by the ducks at Miriam's feet. He was not so busy eating that he missed Jannie asking "Would you like something else, Mimi?"

Sam gave Henri a nudge to make sure he did not miss it either.

Henri got to his feet, "Come, Sam. We get the tea." To Jannie and Miriam he said, "We won't be long."

Somehow it took them much longer than expected to buy four mugs of tea. Perhaps it was because Sam spotted some iced cakes and thought they should be tasted. Or maybe it was because Henri decided to have a cigar sitting in the sun after they had tried the cakes.

Neither Miriam nor Jannie noticed or cared how long they had taken. Miriam talked about growing up in North London and Jannie talked about going to sea. They talked about their families, falling silent at sad memories, but not for long. The sun was shining, the water sparkling and fresh green leaves were dancing in the breeze. The ducks had moved a little way off. Sparrows were hopping busily at their feet looking for crumbs. There was much to talk about.

"Gosh, that didn't take long," said Miriam when Henri and Sam returned carrying a cheap tin tray laden with mugs of tea and a plate of iced buns.

"Why are you laughing?" she asked.

"Oh Tante Mimi, we have been hours." Sam and Henri sat down, broad grins on their faces, stretched their legs out and sighed happily.

Jannie smiled at Miriam. "I think they are right."

"Who cares?"

Passers-by were surprised and heartened by the gaiety of the four people sitting on the bench. There was little to laugh about in the newspapers and on the wireless.

*

The following Sunday morning, Jannie opened the door, tea in hand, to find a uniformed boy with his bicycle propped against the wall. Jannie took in the pill box hat, polished buttons on his smart blue tunic and pouch on his gleaming leather belt.

The boy came to attention and handed Jannie a brown envelope.

"Telegram for Mr… er… Cooper," he announced.

Jannie looked at the name, "Ah, Meneer Kuiper," and shouted over his shoulder, "Henri. Telegram for you."

Henri bustled into the hall and took the envelope from Jannie. The boy looked at him and asked, "Will there be a reply?"

"Wait a moment." Henri opened the telegram, read the message and passed it to Jannie. Miriam and Sam joined them in the hall.

"The Admiral asks me to return on Tuesday."

Miriam's heart thumped. She put a hand on Sam's shoulder to steady herself.

"And us?" asked Jannie.

"Just me," Henri said, "For now."

He turned to the boy, "Please tell the Admiral I will come."

"You have to write the reply, sir." He opened his pouch again and took out a pad and pencil. "You write on here, sir."

After Henri had signed and the boy had departed, they went back to the kitchen. Henri passed round his cigarettes and they lit up.

He looked at Jannie and Miriam and saw the strain on their faces.

It was Sam who stopped them dwelling on the telegram.

"It is my birthday tomorrow," he announced, and helped himself to his second tea of the morning.

*

"How old will you be, Sam?"

"Sixteen."

"Oh". Miriam smiled sweetly at him. "Then you are much too old for a birthday cake."

Sam's mouth dropped open. "We always have birthday cakes at home."

"Well," she said tartly, "You are not at home and fibbers never have cakes in my house."

Sam's eyes widened.

Miriam sat down beside him. "Listen, Sam. You must never lie to your family." She took his hand. "This war is doing terrible things to people and sometimes you may have to lie. But not to family, not here."

"I know Tante Mimi. I'm sorry. But my papers say I will be sixteen," Sam whispered.

"And they say you are South African," Tante Mimi was speaking slowly and softly. "And when you are asked for your papers, you say you are fifteen and you are South African." She squeezed his hand. "Your Papa has done this for you. He is a wise man and has done what is right to keep you safe."

She looked at him, "Sam." He looked up. "Your Papa may not be able to escape now." She saw his eyes flicker. "You know that, don't you?"

Sam hesitated, took a deep breath and sat a little straighter. "Yes, Tante Mimi. I know that." He looked at her solemnly. "With you, I am thirteen, Tante Mimi. Outside I am fifteen."

Which is why they had to pay the gatekeeper one shilling each to get into London Zoo.

*

Their Tube journey to Regent's Park was filled with noisy speculation about their destination, loud groans and laughter greeting each wrong station.

168

Miriam took Jannie's arm as they walked to the Zoo while Henri and Sam walked on ahead. But not before Henri had said, "What an inspired choice mevrouw." And bowed slightly to her.

And so it proved to be. There was wonder in Samuel's eyes as he gazed at creatures he had only ever seen in books. Tales of sea monsters and whales, icebergs, steamy rivers and tropical islands filled their minds and lifted their hearts. It was a quiet, sleepy group which dozed on the top deck of the bus on their homeward journey.

Mrs Coward had fetched the cake and left it in the middle of the kitchen table with fourteen wooden spills stuck in a circle in the icing. Next to it were three parcels, neatly wrapped in brown paper and tied up with string. There were also three envelopes with Sam's name written on each. She had even put a blue and white checked tablecloth on the table with Miriam's best tea service neatly laid out.

Jannie made the tea while the others sat round the table. Henri lit the spills and said to Sam, "You have to blow hard." He laughed. "Don't leave it too long or you'll burn your eyebrows off."

Sam stood up, took a deep breath, blew hard and put them all out.

Miriam handed him a sharp knife and said, "Don't forget to make a wish."

Sam did not forget. Closing his eyes, he pictured his mother, father and sister, wishing with his whole being that they were here with him.

Henri laid his hand gently on Sam's and said, "We all wish the same thing, Sam."

Sam shivered. "Ja, danke Henri. I know."

"Now I cut the cake."

Miriam's baker had excelled himself. She never asked him how and where he had found the ingredients. They all agreed it was the finest fruit cake they have ever tasted.

"Open your presents, Sam," Jannie pushed them towards him. "We want to know what you've got."

"Oh," said Sam as he stroked the brown leather writing case Miriam had given him. He found a fountain pen, notepaper and envelopes when he opened it.

"Oh danke, Tante Mimi," he breathed. "It is beautiful."

"And thank you, Henri," he said, holding the little brass pocket compass that Henri had found in the chandlers, "It will guide us home." He skipped round to give Henri a hug.

He was amazed when he opened the present from Jannie. "How did you know?" he said.

Jannie beamed at him. "I saw you staring at the belt that telegram boy was wearing."

"It is perfect,"

It was indeed perfect; a fine, polished leather belt with a gleaming brass buckle, "And plenty of room for when you get fat," laughed Henri.

It was a good birthday. They never turned the wireless on once.

*

"Why do you think the Admiral wants you back?" Jannie and Henri were sitting on their beds, early morning sunlight pouring into the room.

Henri sighed. "There is no good news from France. I think we will be needed there."

Jannie nodded. "But why not all of us?"

Henri smiled. "Don't worry, Jannie, I won't go without you."

"Or Sam."

Henri shook his head, "Why does he insist?"

"You know why?" Jannie stood up and moved to the window. "We are all he has, Henri. You and I. We are his family now."

"What about Miriam? She is family."

"I don't know, old friend." Jannie looked down for a moment. "She is growing very fond of him."

Henri looked at Jannie for a long time before asking. "What will you do when we come back?"

"What do you mean?"

"You know perfectly well what I mean." Henri laughed. "I am not blind."

"Is it that obvious?" Jannie's worried expression made Henri laugh louder.

"Yes." he said. "It is. And it has not gone unnoticed by Miriam." He smiled, "You are a lucky man, Jannie. I think she will grow very fond of you."

Henri stood and joined Jannie at the window. He put his hand on his shoulder and shook him slightly. "I think you and she should look after Sam together."

Jannie nodded. "When we come back, we will go far away together, you Mimi and me. We will all look after the boy."

Henri smiled. "That is something to hold on to when it gets rough." He took Jannie's hand and squeezed it, "A lifeline."

*

Breakfast was lively. Sam knew Tante Mimi was sad Henri was leaving and sensed she was worrying about him.

"Come," he said, "We are walking to the station with you Henri." He looked at his aunt. "You come too, Tante Mimi, to stop us getting lost."

Sam used his compass to navigate them down to the river, with judicious alterations of course from Miriam. His trousers were held up by his new belt. Henri told him not to bring his writing case as he needed help with his bags.

Safely onboard the Gillingham train, Henri lowered his window and leant out. "I will let you know what is happening, mevrouw. Look after these boys for me."

To Sam he said, "Make a lanyard for your compass. Jannie will help you."

Jannie nodded. They shook hands as the train started to move.

Miriam saw Jannie sigh and tucked her arm in his. With a brightness she did not feel she said, "Coffee!"

They entered a dark, wood panelled coffee house serving small pieces of exquisite almond cake and tiny cups of Turkish coffee.

"My father makes much better coffee," Sam whispered to Tante Mimi. He turned to Jannie. "Doesn't he?"

"Indeed he does," agreed Jannie. "And your mother makes the best cakes in the Netherlands."

Sam tugged her sleeve. "You will come and stay with us when I go home, won't you?"

"Of course I will." Miriam smiled at the boy and picked up her coffee cup.

She was glad Sam had not seen the photographs of Rotterdam after it had been bombed. Henri had shown her where Sam's home had been before he put the newspaper in the bin.

"Take us east, jonge, this side of the river," said.

"I wonder if we will see Tower Bridge open," Miriam added as they made their way through the streets of Bermondsey.

"Oh my," Sam said, wide-eyed at the magnificent structure. "I wish Papa could see this."

"One day," said Jannie.

Sam nodded, distracted by a ship sounding her siren as she approached. At that, a bell started ringing and the barriers came down.

"Quick!" Miriam took Sam's hand and ran up to the bascule nearest the barrier. The bridge opened silently and smoothly. The ship passed through and it closed again.

"Hydraulics," Jannie observed, "There's a steam pump somewhere." He had seen smoke coming out of a chimney in the nearest tower.

When they walked across, Sam stood with one foot either side of the slight gap in the middle, peering at the river beneath his feet. He jumped when a lorry crossed and the two halves moved.

By the time they reached Whitechapel Road they were tired and hungry. The smell of frying fish was irresistible. Jannie handed the others their fish and chips, liberally doused in vinegar, well-salted and wrapped in newspapers.

They ambled home, mouths full and fingers greasy as they ate their lunch on the hoof. Miriam had never eaten anything so delicious and wondered if that was because eating in the street was so unladylike.

*

Admiral Teagle rose to greet the Dutchman. He walked around his desk and led Henri to a small table where a pot of coffee and two cups had been set out.

"Black, no sugar?" Henri was surprised he remembered. He reached into his coat pocket and laid a box of cigars on the table. "For you, milord."

They sat in silence for a moment, savouring the freshly ground coffee and rich tobacco.

Admiral Teagle put his cup down and looked at Henri. "We may have to bring our army home."

Henri placed his own cup carefully on the table and took a long pull at his cigar.

"We will go," he said.

*

"Dear Mrs Cohen," Miriam read to Jannie and Sam. "I have found somewhere for you and your guests. It is a small cottage in the west of Cornwall, not far from Penzance. It has three bedrooms, a parlour and kitchen., together with a bathroom and w.c. under the same roof. The house has running water but no electricity." She raised her eyebrows. "Hmm. Trimming the lamps with be your job, Sam." She turned back to the letter, "The house is simply furnished and provided with adequate bedding, cutlery and crockery."

"I wonder what 'adequate' means." She looked at Jannie and answered her own question, "Much more than your passengers brought with them. Much more than my grandmother had when she came to England."

They sat down either side of the desk. Miriam pushed the cigarette box across. They lit up and smoked in silence for a while.

"What will you do if we have to go to sea?"

Miriam stared at him. It was a long time before she answered. "Wait for you to come back, I suppose."

Jannie felt curiously breathless.

"You will come back, won't you?" she said.

"God willing."

Miriam regarded him steadily before flicking Harold's letter. "What do you think about this cottage?"

He stubbed out his cigarette. "I think we should go."

"You do?"

He nodded. "If the war comes closer. It will be a good place for Sam, though it will be very quiet after the city life he's used to. We will have to find him some work."

*

De Ruyter was tucked away in the corner of a dockyard basin. Lieutenant Bell showed Henri where she was berthed and left him, saying, "Have a look round and tell me what you need to get her ready for sea. The Admiral

173

said you want some guns. We should have one or two spare machine guns. Let me know where you want them."

"Danke, meneer, ja, I do that."

He wished Lieutenant Gale was here.

As he was leaving, Bell called, "Oh, er, Lady Teagle has invited you for supper. Seven o'clock. No need to change, old chap."

Bell shook his head as he walked away. He doubted the old boy had a clean shirt to his name.

Henri walked slowly along the dock-side, looking over his ship. He was surprised to see a wisp of smoke curling from the cuddy stove-pipe and hurried to the gangway. Henri guessed who was onboard and was not surprised when Dirk and Willem appeared.

He shook them warmly by their hands and followed them to the after cabin.

"All well," he asked.

"All very well," they replied as they offered him a choice of drinks.

"Coffee, please. I have to see Milady at seven."

Settling down, Henri asked, "Have you been here all the time?"

"Ja," Willem replied, "We had nowhere to go and the Commander asked us to stay as ship-keepers."

Dirk joined it, "It has been good. We sleep here and eat in the canteen or cook for ourselves."

Willem laughed, "We will get fat."

"How is the ship?" Henri asked. "Any problems?"

"Nee, Baas. The boiler is out so we pump out by hand. She's not making any more than she did at home."

"Good boys, and you've been painting and polishing." Henri beamed at them, "Paul would be pleased."

They walked through the saloons together before Henri led the way up to the bridge and looked around. All was well.

He looked closely at the two young men and asked them, "Would you boys sail with me again?"

"Of course. Where?"

"I don't know. But we might be asked to go to sea." He looked carefully at them, "You must not say anything about this to anyone."

"Ja Baas."

"Good."

His ship was in good order. His crew was steady.

∗

Jannie and Sam took themselves off to Wapping after breakfast to buy some line and a book about knots and splices. They entered another world just a few paces off the busy Ratcliffe Highway, a world dominated by towering, soot-blackened red-brick walls, warehouses on one side and six metre high dock walls on the other. It was also dominated by noise: steam whistles, sirens, iron-bound cart wheels trundling over cobbled streets, lorries hooting, stevedores shouting, the creak of tackles swaying aloft or lowering bales and boxes on or off stationary wagons. It looked chaotic but every movement, each noise had a purpose that gradually made sense to the onlooker. Sam was mesmerised and Jannie had to make sure he did not lose the boy.

Jannie spotted the sign they were looking for. Lilley and Reynolds, and, taking Sam's arm, made it safely across the road.

A few minutes later, with Sam clutching a copy of Brown's Knots and Splices, they were on their way to the sail loft recommended by the shop assistant. "Ask for Nobby. He'll sort you out." He had told them. "And get a few off-cuts for the boy."

And so, when Miriam got home, she found Jannie and Sam in the kitchen pouring over a small light-blue book with lengths of rope spilling out of a brown paper bag. She sniffed. "What's that smell?"

Jannie straightened and smiled at her, "That's Stockholm Tar. The smell of sailing ships. They put it on ropes to stop them rotting."

"It is a good smell," Mimi put her hand on Sam's back, "Better than coal and oil?"

"On no, Tante Mimi," Sam said earnestly, "Nothing is better than that." He looked at Jannie, "Is it?"

Jannie shrugged at Mimi, "I am an engineer, Mimi, so is Sam. We…"

"Yes, Jannie." Mimi laughed, "I will have to get used to it."

Jannie gazed at her, wondering what she meant by that. So did Mimi.

∗

Henri had a quiet supper with Lady Teagle and returned onboard. He was conscious that the enormous pressure on her husband was weighing heavily on her which made her hospitality doubly welcome. She was fascinated by

175

his description of their reception by Tante Miriam and of the old lace-maker's house, and delighted to hear how well Sam seemed to be settling in. For a moment she forgot about the war when Henri told her about the spark between Jannie and Miriam, clapping her hands and saying, "I shall have to meet her."

When they parted, Lady Teagle said, "One of these days you must take me up to London to meet Miriam."

"I look forward to that, milady," Henri replied, bowing and lifting her right hand to his lips.

*

Lieutenant Bell and a grizzled older lieutenant he introduced as Bill Smith were onboard early.

"Lieutenant Smith will see what you want and if we can help you," he said. "Must go."

He seemed anxious to get away and hurried up the gangway.

"Doesn't want to get his uniform dirty," grunted Dirk, and spat over the side.

"Don't mind him, lad," Bill Smith said quietly.

Dirk made a pot of tea for Bill and coffee for them as they got down to talking about what the ship might be asked to do.

"Nothing official," Bill said, "No orders, but we'll need to make a few changes to make it easier for people to get on and off." He looked at the studied calm of the three Dutchmen. "Why did you ask the Admiral for machine guns?"

"We were nearly spotted leaving Rotterdam," Henri said. "All we could do was pray." He shook his head. "I don't want to be in that position again."

"Understood." Bill looked at them. "And you've asked for gunners to man them?"

"Jan, meneer. We don't know about fighting."

Bill sucked his teeth. "Well, we can give you some sailors" he said, "Though they won't know about fighting either" He smiled ruefully, "I think they will learn soon enough." He took a cigarette from the tin Willem had put on the table, and added, "They know how to shoot machine guns. Old Lewis guns. All we have. We can spare four of them."

"Thank you," Henri said, grave faced, "And a White Ensign please."

Bill looked puzzled.

"We gave our ship to the British Navy. We go to war under your flag." Henri did not care to explain the deep sense of shame he felt about his Queen or how the Dutch surrender left him feeling he had lost his country.

"I'll get you one," Bill smiled. "A big one."

"Good. Now let us see what must be done."

It did not take the Gunner long as there were only four guns to place. He explained why they would need to remove all uprights, including the davits in the port and starboard bridge wings, tape every window and remove the upper deck house.

"You don't want all that top hamper," he explained, "Not if someone starts shooting at you. There'd be splinters and glass everywhere."

When they got to the bridge he looked at the wheel-house. "If I was in your shoes, sir, I would want that down."

He moved inside and stood behind the wheel. "This is where you will be, Henri. Your best defence is seeing aircraft in time to get out of their way."

Henri exhaled very softly. "Ja, Bill, this is where I will be." He nodded at the bridge wings. "A machine gun each side?"

"Yes. You will have a good all-round view, so will the gunners." He pointed forward and aft. "We put a gun at each end." He paused, "I wish we could do more."

Henri shrugged. "It will have to do."

"We'll bring tin hats for your crew. Six isn't it."

"Ja," said Henri, "Though two are in the engine room." He stopped. "That reminds me, will you be able to spare a hand, anyone, to help with the stoking?"

"Why's that?" asked Bill. Bell had not mentioned this.

"Our fireman is only a boy."

"I'll see what I can do." Bill had his notebook out and added that to his list. "We'll move you to the coaling wharf this afternoon to top up your bunkers. I'll send you some spare floats, a couple of long grass warps, fenders." He paused. "Anything else?"

Willem said, "Our first aid kit isn't much use."

'So much for not knowing where they're going,' thought Bill grimly, adding them to his list.

"Right, I'd better go. Ring the Gunner's Office if you need me. They'll know where I am. I'll send a couple of Chippies over with a working party. And the tape." He looked at his watch. "The tug will be alongside at 1500."

Henri walked with him to the gangway. "How long have we got?" he said quietly.

Bill looked at him. He shook his head. "I don't know. A few more days. Maybe you won't be needed."

His eyes swept fore and aft, "But if you are, this ship will be a God-send. You could easily take fifteen-hundred men onboard."

"More like two thousand." Henri smiled, "Let us hope it never comes to that."

*

Henri had not expected to be closely questioned by the Admiral about the fighting qualities of the Germans.

"They are just men," Henri said. "Without armour, artillery and aircraft they are nothing special." Sir William was listening carefully. "They underestimated the Dutch army. They had not expected to be opposed. A few men stopped them." The Admiral had to lean forward to hear what Henri said next. "They had to burn my city because they could not take it."

The Dutchman sat back in his chair and looked the Admiral in the eye. "But they are ruthless, Sir William. That is all I can tell you."

'And yet you will take your old paddle-boat back if I ask you,' thought the Admiral. All he said was, "I wish I had more time, Henri."

Henri wondered what he had told the Admiral that he did not already know. He would have been surprised to learn that Sir William drew strength from his resolve and calm professionalism. Perhaps it was because they were much the same age and unencumbered by barriers of rank or society, perhaps it was because the admiral had those same qualities and found that talking to this quiet Dutchman helped him shrug off fatigue and think more clearly.

He was about to send four hundred marines and two hundred young sailors to France. Before he gave the order, he needed to know what sort of men they might have to fight. God forbid it came to that. Henri's quiet assertion they were "Just men," told him more about the enemy than he had heard all day.

When Lady Teagle came into the room, she was pleased to see William looking more relaxed than he had been for days, and silently thanked Providence for the arrival of the Dutchman.

"We'll be eating at eight tonight." She caught William's nod and asked, "Would you like to join us?"

"Danke, milady. If it pleases you, Sir William?"

"It certainly does, Henri." He smiled and went back to war.

*

The sight of *De Ruyter* with no wheel-house surprised Henri. She reminded him of an old lady in church without a hat.

Willem and Dirk had worked neatly and efficiently, the dismantled structure was ready to be taken ashore and stored. "No broken glass, Henri, and the frames unbolted without damage."

"Good work, boys." Henri stood behind the wheel and looked around him. He felt horribly exposed and shivered at the thought of an aircraft swooping down on the ship. 'Schijt,' he thought. 'We won't stand a chance.'

Moving out to the bridge-wing to clear his mind, he said, "That is much better. No-one can sneak up on us."

Willem and Dirk looked pleased. "No umbrellas, Henri," Dirk laughed.

"No wheelbarrows either," Henri replied.

"Nor Naval officers," added Jimmy, as he climbed up the companion way. "The three most useless things in a ship."

"Christus, Kapitein," Willem exclaimed. "You made us jump."

Smiles and handshakes were evidence of their delight at this unexpected reunion.

"Very good to see you, Kapitein." Henri kept hold of Jimmy's hand to tow him onto the bridge. "Come and see my fighting platform," he said with a wry smile. "We have guns coming, gunners too."

Jimmy looked at Henri and murmured, "I hope you won't need them."

Henri looked over to the boys and called, "Hey. How about some coffee?" and watched them disappear below.

Jimmy looked at the stern-faced Dutchman. "Why are you here, Henri?"

Henri took a deep drag on his cigarette. "I thought they might want *De Ruyter* and it seems they do."

Jimmy nodded.

"And what about you, Jimmy," Henri's blue eyes gazed at the smart young lieutenant. "What are you up to?"

Glancing around and moving away from the voice-pipe, Jimmy drew Henri close to him. "Guarding the coast." He gave a short laugh, "With boys armed with rifles and ten rounds of ammunition." He laughed again, "That may change." He looked at Henri. "It all depends on Hitler and Lieutenant Bell."

"Why Lieutenant Bell?"

"Ah," said Jimmy, "Lieutenant Nicholas John Bell is the distinguished senior Gunnery Lieutenant at *HMS Pembroke*. He is my superior officer, superior in every way. Breeding, education, sword of honour at Dartmouth, connections. Daddy is an admiral. He's got the lot." He paused. "He is also a complete shit."

Henri nodded. "I met him."

"Unfortunately, he will be commanding the sailors I have trained, little more than boys. Heaven help them if they go to France with him in charge."

"Why?"

"He is yellow."

"Does the admiral know, Sir Teagle?"

"I am sure he does," Jimmy said slowly, "He is a wise old bird." He smiled at Henri. "Unfortunately, Bell's daddy kicked up a stink when I was sent to Rotterdam. Thinks his son should have gone." Jimmy laughed again. "He is quite right. Bell should have gone, but the Old Man wanted me to go." He smiled. "I definitely do not want to go anywhere near France, so he's welcome to it. I've just had my appointment through. That's why I've come onboard. To ask you for a drink tonight. To celebrate."

Henri held out his hand and shook Jimmy's vigorously. "My congratulations. I would love to."

*

Jimmy was quiet that evening, though brightened when the Wardroom Mess Attendant told him Henri had arrived. He hurried to the door and took him into the bar. They took their beers to a table in the window and soon were lost in the life of a gunnery officer onboard a light cruiser. "I have dreamed of this for years," Jimmy said.

"I drink to your health, Jimmy." Henri touched the gold braid on Jimmy's sleeve. "You have earned these."

They had another half, talking quietly about their short voyage in the old paddle-boat. "We'll have to sail her home together," said Jimmy. "That is something to look forward to."

"I'll keep you to that." Henry raised his mug. "The return voyage."

They sat in silence for a while before Henri said, "And France?"

Jimmy stared at his beer. "Not good, Henri. Not good at all."

The mood lightened as they started discussing 17 Wilkes Street and Jannie, Tante Miriam and Sam, all of which was news to Jimmy.

"And Henk?" said Henri. "You must remember Henk?"

When Jimmy agreed he did indeed remember Henk, Henri told him what Henk would be up to in Hampshire and how he and Sarah would be looking after Ruth.

Jimmy nodded slowly. "That's good, Henri. Very good."

They drank up and then Jimmy walked with Henri to the mess door. "Enjoy your evening. I'll come round tomorrow to take you all to the pub."

He was surprised to find Nicholas Bell waiting for him when he returned to the bar. He seemed agitated. "Beer Jimmy?"

"No thanks, Dinger, I've had enough." His face was impassive as Bell winced at his lower-deck nickname.

"Look, Jimmy," Bell lowered his voice. "Can we talk?"

"Of course."

Bell's voice dropped to a whisper. "I'm standing by to go with Force Buttercup to Boulogne."

The news shocked Jimmy but he remained silent.

"The major's taking the marines. I've got the seamen."

Jimmy nodded. Bell should not be talking to him about this. He was sure of that. It was a serious breach of security, even here in the mess.

"You're on stand-by?"

Bell nodded. "Yes, though it's pretty obvious we'll be going tonight or tomorrow." There was a brief silence before Bell addressed himself to his hands. "Did you know I've just got engaged, Jimmy?"

"No. I've not been here much."

"Oh, of course." Bell gave him a brief smile, "We're getting married in June."

"Congratulations Nicholas, we'll have a drink another time." Jimmy started to move away. He was not expecting an invitation.

Bell caught hold of his arm. Jimmy stood still and looked at him until he let go.

"What is it?"

Bell gave a nervous laugh, "Oh come on Jimmy. I'm getting married." He laughed again. "You know this is a one-way ticket."

Jimmy face was set, granite in his eyes. He looked hard at Bell.

Bell could not meet his eyes. Looking at the floor, he said, "This is a job for a single man."

He raised his head and stared defiantly at Jimmy. Taking a shallow breath, he said quickly, "You should go."

"Why?" Jimmy spat the word out. "Why should I go?"

It was as if he had slapped the man.

Bell shrank from him, his face pale. On the verge of tears, he pleaded, "Please, Jimmy. There's no-one else."

Jimmy sighed. What choice did he have? If he refused, Bell would put it about he was a coward and that would be the end of his career. He almost laughed at the thought. He had never seen anyone in such a funk.

"I'll go." He grated the words out. Then swung a sucker punch. "You tell the Admiral."

Relief flooded across Bell's face. He made to shake Jimmy's hand but Jimmy stood back.

"Thank you, Jimmy." He gushed, and started to say more.

Jimmy cut him short. "Just leave. Tell the Admiral why you can't go."

He saw Bell hesitate and growled, "Do it, or I will."

*

Osborne gave a disapproving sniff when Lady Teagle asked him to lay an extra place for supper.

"It's all right, Osborne," she scolded him, "He has asked a friend round. That's all."

She wondered why she found it necessary to justify herself.

William was worried about the war in France. They all were. The Germans seemed unstoppable. Even the normally unflappable Osborne was subdued, going about his work without his usual monotonous and occasionally hilarious grumbling.

"Is your mother still in Portsmouth?"

Her question took him by surprise. "Yes, Milady. Nowhere else to go." He sniffed quietly. "Not that she'd move on account of that 'itler."

He looked at her, saw anxiety shrouding her and walked over to the sideboard. Pouring her a glass of sherry he took it to her on his silver tray. "No point in worrying, ma'am. Never 'elped anyone."

There was a knock on the dining room door and the messenger showed Henri in.

They both stood to greet him.

Henri showed no surprise at the sight of Lady Teagle sitting and drinking sherry with the Admiral's servant. He bowed.

"Goodness," she laughed, "I had no idea it was eight o'clock already." She took him by the arm and led him to the window seat she had just left. "We are having a sherry," she said as he sat down. "Would you like one?"

"Danke, Milady. A small one please."

It was Henri who noticed the Admiral standing by the door. He quickly got to his feet. Osborne turned to him. "May I fetch you a whisky, sir?"

Before he could answer, the Flag Lieutenant knocked on the door and came in to whisper to Sir William.

"Lieutenant Bell to see you, sir. Says it's urgent."

"Right. Five minutes then show him in." He turned to Emma, "I'm so sorry my dear."

As Emma moved to the door, Henri rose to follow her.

"Stay here Henri." Sir William looked at him. "I shan't say anything I regret if you are here." He smiled wryly, stood and moved to the fireplace.

"Lieutenant Bell, sir." Flags glanced at the seated Dutchman, raised an eyebrow and left.

Bell entered, saw Henri and stopped. "I… I was hoping for a word in private, Sir William.,"

"Anything you have to say to me, Bell, you can say in front of Captain de Kuiper."

"Sir, it's a personal matter." Bell looked flustered.

"Say it or leave."

Bell straightened up and, looking just above the Admiral's head, said in a rushed monotone, "Lieutenant Gale has volunteered to go in my place sir. Said it was a one-way ticket, sir."

"When?"

"Sir?"

"When did he say this?"

"Just now sir. When I told him I was getting married."

"You told him *what?*"

"I told him I was getting married, sir."

Sir William was about to erupt when he caught a movement from Henri out of the corner of his eye.

He took a breath and looked at Bell, eyes glacial. "I take it you have accepted Lieutenant Gale's offer?"

"Yessir," Bell whispered.

The Admiral nodded.

"Sir, I…"

"Get out," Sir William said quietly.

The lieutenant spun round and fled.

The Admiral lit a cigarette and glanced at the impassive old Dutchman. "I am sorry you had to hear that Henri." He went on, "And thank you."

Henri took a sip of coffee. "Why do you thank me?"

Sir William smiled, "You moved."

"Ja, milord, I moved." He stood up. "And you saw it."

He moved across to the fireplace and said quietly "You know Jimmy Gale better than me. He is a good man. Your sailors will be in safe hands."

"Do you really think he volunteered, Henri?"

"Perhaps," Henri shrugged, "Perhaps he had no choice." He gazed at the Admiral. "It is not a question I should like to ask him."

Sir William nodded. "It is not a question I shall ask him." He put his hand on Henri's shoulder. "Thank you, my friend."

Henri was asleep onboard *De Ruyter* when the sailors and marines of Force Buttercup were mustered in the Drill Shed in the early hours of Wednesday 23rd May. They embussed and departed for Dover at speed.

*

"Is this any good?" Sam held up his third attempt at making a lanyard for Jannie's inspection.

"It looks alright to me," said Jannie. He took it from Sam and tugged the eye-splices at each end.

"Now make one for your knife."

Life at Wilkes Street had settled into a comfortable routine while they awaited a summons to join their ship, though Sam thought there was too

184

much school work. Miriam had decided to help him improve his English. She picked 'Captains' Courageous' as a suitable book and made him read aloud while she listened, making him look up the meaning of words in the dictionary and correcting his pronunciation. Their attempts at different accents enjoyed variable success.

Jannie was pleased when Miriam suggested he might find out how good Sam was at mathematics. Though it had been decades since he had been at school, Jannie used basic maths every day in the engine room. He thought he would include how a steam engine worked, and a little technical drawing.

It was the practical lessons that Sam liked best, even learning how to darn his socks. The sight of his darning kit, carefully packed by his mother in another lifetime, brought tears to his eyes. He picked up one of the neatly folded kerchiefs his mother had ironed and pressed it against his cheek. He could smell lavender and remembered how she sprayed lavender water on her neck in the morning.

Miriam made him sew the South African flags onto his uniform jacket, one at the top of each arm. He did such a good job that Jannie asked him to sew on his Dutch flags. Though he protested noisily, Sam was secretly pleased.

"You can do my mending when you have finished," Miriam teased. He rolled his eyes and squeaked, "Nee, Tante Mimi, please." though he did make her a small canvas bag, a ditty bag he called it, and "a jolly useful size," he said.

One day they made sandwiches and a flask of tea and set off to have a picnic lunch at Tower Pier.

Miriam was surprised how quiet London had become. There were few cars about and the streets seemed emptier of people. A tall policeman wished them good morning, touching his helmet to Tante Mimi as he strolled past. Barrage balloons swayed and glinted against an azure sky. There was not a cloud in sight.

Sam had been silent for a while. Once settled on an empty bench by the river he asked, "Are these the same policemen who hit Oom Isaac?" He looked puzzled. "They are very kind to us."

Miriam sighed. "Yes, and they are very kind to us." She looked across Sam's head at Jannie. "Most policemen are the same as us. Most are good. A few are bad and fewer still are wicked."

Sam frowned. "But why were the police told to clear a way for the fascists?"

"That," said Miriam," is a question that was never answered. All I can tell you is there are powerful people in this country who support Hitler. They are friends of those Blackshirts. Sadly, a few are also policemen." She stopped and stood up. "Does that answer your question?"

"Ja, danke."

"Then let us enjoy this beautiful day and thank G-d we are alive."

She held out her hand and drew Jannie to his feet. They strolled away, arm in arm.

Sam scrambled after them, picking up the picnic bag as he went.

*

"I would like our guns placed today please. The forecastle and bridge are clear, ja?"

"Ja, all clear," said Willem. "It is just the top deck-house aft. The stanchions for all the canopies have been landed."

"Good," said Henri. "Get that down today." He looked at Bill. "Could we have the guns this afternoon please?"

"Yes. I'll get the Gunner's party to bring them over. They'll have to secure the mountings to the deck."

"Of course," replied Henri. "Put the ammunition in the cuddy. We can lock that. Also, another engine telegraph by the wheel, a ship's compass on a binnacle and a chart-table with the relevant charts, please."

Bill stood up. "I'll get going."

Henri went up to the gangway with hm. "Thank you Bill."

As they shook hands, he said, "Jimmy Gale is a steady young man. He will look after his sailors."

Bill nodded, saluted and went ashore.

*

"To Jannie and Sam stop return onboard A stop M stop 24 May stop acknowledge stop Henri"

Jannie stood beside Miriam's chair as she read the telegram and then put his hand on her shoulder. He felt her shiver.

"We have to go, Mimi," he said gently. "I am surprised he did not want us sooner."

186

"I know, Jannie, I know," Mimi whispered. She put her hand on Jannie's and squeezed his fingers. "But Sam is so young." Jannie knelt beside her.

"Listen, Mimi, he needs to go. We have talked about this. You know he needs to go." Jannie stroked the hair away from Mimi's face and kissed her lightly on the cheek. "We will come back to you, I promise."

Twisting in her chair to face him, Mimi asked, "How can you promise?"

Jannie leant forward and whispered in her ear, "Because I know we will come back." He held her for a moment and then stood up.

He laughed. "My knees are killing me."

Mimi shook her head and gazed fondly at this tough, tender man who had come to mean so much to her. "This bloody war."

She took his hand as she stood and then glanced at the telegram discarded between them.

"You had better answer that," she said.

*

"What about packing?"

Miriam sighed. She wished the boy had not spoken.

Jannie glanced at her and answered. "We won't need much, Sam. Dungarees, vests and socks." He thought for a while. "And underpants."

Sam laughed. "Is that all?"

Jannie looked hard at the boy. "That is all." He stood up to fetch a packet of cigarettes, passed one to Miriam and lit up. Inhaling deeply, he held the smoke for a moment before blowing a plume towards the ceiling.

"Listen, Sam. We take only what we need. Whatever our orders are, you and I will be busy." His face relaxed. "Bring you knife and your compass as well."

"I need the heads." Sam suddenly stood and ran upstairs.

"Is he alright?" Miriam half-rose to follow him. She had seen Sam go white.

"He will be fine, Mimi. Leave him."

"And you, Jannie," Miriam picked up his hand. "Will you also be fine?"

Jannie smiled sadly. "Mimi, look at me," he said. She lifted her eyes and blinked away tears. "You are very beautiful, Miriam," he said quietly.

She shook her head, afraid to speak.

"We must thank this war, you and I."

Miriam stiffened, a frown creasing her brow. "Why on earth should we thank this rotten war?"

"It is simple. If there was no war, I would not be sitting here holding your hands."

Miriam laughed. "And I would not be sitting here crying my eyes out like a school-girl."

Freeing her hands, she stood and, to Jannie's surprise, leaned forward and kissed him gently on the lips. Blushing, she turned and ran upstairs, calling Sam's name.

Jannie tilted his chair back and stared at the ceiling. Without thinking, he brushed the first two fingers of his right hand to and fro across his lips, a look of wonder on his face.

"Christ," he whispered.

Jannie and Sam left Wilkes Street early on that fine May morning. They paused before turning the corner and waved to Miriam one last time. She stood in the street long after the two figures had gone, before walking slowly back inside.

7.

Back on board

"What have they done to her?" Jannie stared in horror at *De Ruyter*.

"Look at the guns." Sam had been just as surprised to see how odd she looked, her tall funnel towering above the stripped-down top deck. But it was the guns that interested him, their fat barrels pointing to the sky. "Only four?"

Jannie laughed. "You are a bloodthirsty little tyke, Sam."

"Do you think I can fire one?"

Jannie blew out his cheeks. "The only thing you will be firing today is the boiler."

Sam laughed and ran down the gangway.

Willem stuck his head out of the cuddy to see what all the noise was about. "Hey, Henri! Dirk! Look whose here," he shouted, going on deck to pick Sam up and swing him round. "The ship's monkey is back!"

He put Sam down to shake Jannie's hand. "Good to see you, meneer."

He stood back and looked the engineer up and down. "You have changed."

"What do you mean?"

"I don't know." Willem shook his head. "You just look different."

Henri appeared on deck, gripped Jannie's hand and put out an arm to grab Sam. "It is good to have you back."

Jannie thought he looked tired and strained. He said quietly, "It is good to be here," He looked around at the changes. "You should have called for us sooner. This has been hard for you."

"Nee, Jannie. The Navy has done most of it." He looked down at Sam who was fidgeting and hopping from one foot to the other. "Go on, jonge. Just don't shoot anyone."

He stared at the boy swinging the Lewis gun around as if he was firing it. "Boys and guns," he muttered before shrugging. "Coffee, a jenever and you will tell me about London."

"You were going to find a kindly widow, Jannie." Willem was grinning. "Did you?"

Henri smiled to himself when he saw Jannie go pink. "Leave him," he laughed, "We cannot sail without him."

"Klootzakken," Jannie tried to look fierce, failed and raised his hands in surrender, "I may have."

He looked at Henri, "Now tell me what has happened to my ship."

Henri had scrounged a wireless which was playing music in the background as he began to brief Jannie on the alterations to *De Ruyter*.

The clear-cut voice of the BBC announcer was drowned by Sam's excited cry, "Listen." They fell silent as the announcer said, "Her Majesty Queen Wilhelmina of the Netherlands."

They listened in silence to her message of defiance. Though addressed to the nation she had left, it gave fresh heart to a small Dutch boy and his friends onboard an old paddle-boat exiled to a corner of this foreign dockyard.

"Well," Henri broke the silence as he turned off the wireless. "Now we know why she left."

"Thank goodness she did," said Jannie. He turned to Sam, "Did you understand what she said?"

Sam shrugged.

"She escaped those German klootzaken so she could fight on. She never surrendered," He looked across the saloon at Henri. "She has more balls than we thought."

"Ja, you are right. Thank goodness she does." He frowned at Sam, "But mind your language."

He put three small glasses on the table and filled them with jenever. "We should drink to her."

Jannie and Henri picked up a glass. So did Sam after a quick glance at Jannie and his approving nod.

"The Queen."

"Below!" The familiar voice of Bill Smith hailed them from the deck.

Henri went forward to meet him while Jannie got out another glass and Sam put the coffee on.

Bill looked gaunt and weary, deep lines etched either side of his unsmiling mouth, black bags beneath his eyes. He sat down with a sigh and folded his hands in front of him.

Henri gave him a lighted cigarette as Jannie placed a glass of jenever on the table in front of him. Bill thanked them with a nod. "Have you heard the news?"

His voice, slow, soft and sad, filled Sam with dread.

"Our Queen…" Henri started to say.

"Not your Queen." Bill sounded tense. There was silence before he spoke again. "It's Jimmy."

Sam went rigid. He gripped Jannie's hand, eyes prickling.

Henri put his cigar down and placed both hands face down on the table. Jannie freed his hand to put his arm around the trembling boy.

"You told us he sailed for Boulogne yesterday. With his sailors. That is all."

Bill grunted. "Well," he said in that same slow, sad voice, "He is back and so are all his men."

"That is wonderful," Sam cried out as he raised his fists in triumph. No-one else moved. Sam slumped against Jannie. "What happened?"

Bill looked at the boy. He had seen too many boys go off to war. He had not been much more than a boy at the start of the last one.

"Jimmy is badly wounded, Sam. He is on his way to hospital." Bill's voice caught in his throat, "He may not make it."

Jannie held Sam to his chest. He looked at the old Lieutenant and asked, "What about his men?"

"His men." Bill was sitting straighter, his voice firm. "The remarkable thing is that they all came back. All two hundred. They were boys, not men, not until they returned. Dusty and Sharky Ward were also wounded." He held up his hand to stop questions, "Flesh wounds, I think, though I can't be sure."

He looked at Henri and Jannie. "Have you ever been to Boulogne?"

Sam put the coffee on the table and sat, enthralled, as Bill described the fierce fighting between British destroyers and the German army and air force. He told of the Irish and Welsh Guards' fighting withdrawal, of Force

Buttercup's street battles behind hastily erected barricades, of German tanks and dive-bombers, machine guns, mortar bombs and Fifth Columnists sniping at the ships tied up alongside, and as they entered and left harbour.

"The boys can't tell me much," he said. "It was hard. They never thought they'd get home."

"And no-one knows if Kapitein Jimmy is alive or dead?" said Sam quietly.

"No-one knows, Sam. But Jimmy is very strong," he went on in the same soft voice he had used before. "He is also a fighter." He sighed, "From what Dusty told me, he will need all his strength if he is to make it."

The men were silent, staring at the table. Sam got quietly to his feet and went to stand next to the old Lieutenant. Cautiously he put his right hand on Bill's shoulder. "Please, meneer, will you tell Jimmy we pray for him?"

Bill blinked to clear his eyes and took a deep breath before replying, "Of course I will, Sam. And if I cannot see him myself, I shall ask the Admiral if he could tell him."

He smiled when Sam said, "Ask milady, meneer. She will tell our Kapitein."

Bill, nodded. "I will ask her," he replied, thinking 'how well this kid understands what goes on in the Admiral's household'.

*

"I think they will need us soon, Jannie."

It was well past midnight. The two old men had packed the youngsters off to bed and were sitting at the table, talking desultorily.

Jannie sighed and looked at Henri. "We are very vulnerable."

Henri gave a short laugh "We have our guns. And smoke." He filled their glasses and gazed at Jannie for a moment before asking, "Is your kindly widow who I think she is?"

Jannie choked on his cigar. "What was that, Henri?" he asked, with a quick glance at him.

"You heard," Henri replied. "I think you have grown fond of Miriam."

Jannie looked at him for a long time before saying, "I think I have." He shook his head in wonder, "What is surprising is that she may be fond of me."

He shrugged and gave Henri a smile. "I hope so. I really do hope so."

Henri smiled back, "So do I, Jannie."

He leant across the table and gripped his forearm. "You must tell her when we come back."

He drew on his cigar before continuing, "Our world is changing so quickly. I do not think this is the time to be shy." He gave a sigh. "You are a lucky man."

Jannie put his free hand on top of Henri's. "I am."

He looked at Henri and saw sadness mingled with fatigue in his lined and weather-beaten face.

Henri blinked when Jannie asked, "Have you seen much of milady?"

He paused slightly too long before answering, "No, not really."

He looked at Jannie and said, "Why do you ask?"

Jannie shrugged. "Just wondered. She is a very kind lady."

Henri pulled his hands away, folded them and sat up straight. "Yes. She is."

He paused. "Very kind and very married."

"More's the pity," murmured Jannie.

Henri stood up. "The Admiral is a good man, a kind and thoughtful husband. He is most fortunate to have such a good wife. I am most fortunate to have him and milady as my friends."

"We all are," agreed Jannie. "It is comforting to know there will be friends waiting for us when we return, even though we have only been here a few days."

It took Henri a while to get to sleep that night. Tired as he was, he could not stop thinking.

*

It was no surprise to see Lady Teagle walk onboard with Bill Smith while they were getting ready to swing the compass. With twin Lewis Guns fitted, the new engine telegraph and binnacle installed, the bridge wanted only the chart table to be ready for sea.

Dirk and Willem were lowering the foremast when Bill hailed them. "Permission to come onboard?"

"Aye aye Baas," came Dirk's cheerful reply. "Keep away from the fo'c'stle for a few minutes."

"They're in the engine room," added Willem.

Both men stared, none too subtly, when they realised milady was wearing riding britches. Dirk started to say something until Willem growled "Let's get this mast down."

Bill went down the ladder first, as Lady Teagle expected. He led the way to the engine room hatch from whence they heard voices over the clanking of shovels. Lady Teagle put her finger to her lips, whispering "Shhh" as she pushed Bill gently out of the way and climbed down the ladder as if it was something she did every day.

Sam spotted a boot feeling for the rungs and nudged Jannie. "Who's that?"

Henri and Jannie stared as Lady Teagle came down the ladder and jumped lightly onto the deck plates. She smiled at them and raised her head to call, "Come down, Bill."

She realised at once that her friends were tired and on edge. The news from France was of desperate fighting as the Germans drove the British and French armies back to the sea. These old Dutch men and boys, far from their homes and families, were going to take this elderly river boat across the sea to help bring them home. She sensed they knew what was awaiting them, all except Sam. She had seen that same look in the eyes of the Polish airmen who had passed through London on their way to join the R.A.F. It was a mixture of anger, hurt and determination.

"Milady," Sam was squeaking. "Come." He took her hand and brought her into the middle of the small space between the boiler and the engine.

"Oh," he gasped when he let go and saw how much oily coal-dust he had transferred. "Sorry." He grabbed a handful of cotton waste and tried to wipe it off.

Laughing, she took it away from him, cleaned herself and turned to the men.

"Good morning," she said brightly, "I thought you might have the kettle on."

In no time at all Jannie and Sam had a brew of Engineer's Tea on the go. Sam was sent to lay the table in the saloon and tell the others.

"Bill has some news about Jimmy," Lady Teagle said, once Sam had left.

"Jannie's shoulders sagged. "We've been told it's touch and go."

Lady Teagle nodded, "His father is with him. He won't leave Jimmy's side."

"He brought us here, and all those Jewish families," Henri whispered, "Right under the noses of the Germans."

"He did the same for his sailors," Bill said quietly. "I told you, led them ashore. All two hundred of them. Right under their guns. And they all came back." He paused. "With only three wounded."

"All we can do is pray, as young Sam asked us to." Lady Teagle smiled, "I don't know about you, but I need that tea." She patted Jannie on the arm. "Can you leave this long enough to join us?"

"Five minutes, milady. You go." He smiled at her. "I'll bring the tea."

Henri went up the ladder first and gave Lady Teagle his hand to help her over the coaming.

"Thank you, Henri," she said, giving it a gentle squeeze before letting go. "Are you ready?"

"Ja, milady. We'll swing the compass in the basin as soon as we have steam up, then top up with coal, come back here, clean ship and wait for orders."

They were walking slowly towards the saloon. Henri stopped, turned to face her and asked, "How is the Admiral?"

Emma was not expecting this softly-spoken man to be thinking about her husband. "Bless you for asking, Henri." She thought for a moment. "He is worried, very worried." She looked up into Henri's eyes. "You must know that." She lowered her voice. "You are the only person he talks to so freely." She gave a little laugh, "Apart from me, and I can't help him."

Henri shook his head, "Nee, milady, you help him more than ever he could tell you."

As he turned to open the door to the saloon, Emma put her hand on his arm to stop him. "How do you know this, Henri" she asked in a whisper.

"He has you to live for," he replied quietly.

"And you, Henri, who do you have to live for?" she whispered to herself as she watched him walk into the saloon.

*

"Tante Miriam?" The gravelly voice rumbled through the hall.

"Yes," Miriam replied, "But I do not believe I am your aunt."

The huge man smiled with relief. "Nee, mevrouw, but that is the only name I have."

He took off his cap and bowed to her, "Henk, mevrouw, seaman, from *De Ruyter*. I have come to speak to Henri."

"You had better come in," said Miriam, standing aside. She looked up and down the street to see if there were any more sailors making their way to her door before joining him in the kitchen.

Miriam invited Henk to sit down before giving him a mug of fresh coffee. He declined the proffered biscuits with a smile.

"Henri and Jannie have told me about you, Henk," Miriam said, smiling back. "And about Ruth and Sarah. How are they?"

"Ach, mevrouw, they are well, but not happy I left them." Henk closed his eyes. "I could not bring them to London. You understand?"

He looked anxiously at Miriam. "If Henri goes to sea, I have to go with him."

Miriam stretched out a hand to Henk. "I understand." The man looked lost. Henri and Jannie had told her how he had found the little girl. "Are Colonel and Mrs Benson looking after Ruth and Sarah?"

"Ja." Henk's face lit up. "They are very good people. They take strangers into their home. Two Jews and a Dutchman brought together by the war. Little Ruth seems already one of their family. Sarah is very happy there." He looked at Miriam. "So am I."

"Then why must you go back to sea?" whispered Miriam.

Henk shrugged. "I heard the news on the wireless. I know Henri. He will take *De Ruyter* to France."

"But why must you go with him?"

"For honour, mevrouw."

Miriam shook her head. "But what about your duty to Sarah and Ruth? Isn't that also a matter of honour?"

Henk's eyes dropped and his face tightened. "Mevrouw, Sarah wanted to come with me." He looked up at her. "You understand?"

Miriam nodded, her grip on his hand tightening.

"I had to tell Sarah that Henri would not take her." Henk sighed. "She is angry."

"But will he take you, Henk?" Miriam said quietly. "He did not send you a telegram; he said you should stay with Sarah and Ruth."

"Henri is an old man," Henk said sternly. "He will need me if he takes that ship to sea."

Miriam let go of Henk's hand and stood up. "I understand," she said. "You have to get to Chatham today?"

Henk nodded. "Ja. The news is bad. I think they go to sea very soon."

A few minutes later she handed him a packet wrapped in greaseproof paper and tied up with string, together with a thermos flask.

The big man looked uncertain. "Where is London Bridge?"

"Oh, that's easy," Miriam said, "I'll come with you."

The streets were quiet, so was Liverpool Street Station. Miriam brought their tickets for the Underground and travelled with Henk to London Bridge.

As the train approached, Miriam took his arm and told him, "Sarah will not be angry with you when you return. I was angry with my husband when he went to war last time. Angry and afraid. But only because I loved him and did not want to lose him." She put her other arm around Henk, held him for a moment and whispered, "Please give my love to Jannie."

When Henk nodded, she said, "I will write to Sarah."

The guard blew his whistle and Henk hurried aboard.

As it started to move, he leant out of the window and called, "Thank you. Tell Sarah and Ruth I love them."

He could not hear Miriam say, "They know." But he saw her lips move as she waved in acknowledgement and farewell.

*

It was on her third voyage out of the cauldron of shells, bombs and machine-guns that was Dunkirk, that *De Ruyter's* luck finally expired. No-one saw the aircraft come out of the early morning sun until it was too late to manoeuvre.

The bomb fell short, though close enough for the explosion to throw the ship around, damaging the hull and starboard paddles. It was when it came back that men were killed.

Undeterred by the volume of machine-gun and rifle fire from *De Ruyter*, the Stuka steadied and opened fire, swerving slightly from side to side to rake the decks before flying straight at the bridge.

Gary Faulkner, starboard Lewis gunner held his fire as bullets whipped past him, held it until he could not miss, then emptied the magazines into the aircraft. He saw his bullets striking home but never saw the aircraft rear up, stall and plunge into the sea half a cable to port. Neither did Henri who was badly wounded when bullets shattered the binnacle, sending a shower of red-hot shards of brass and iron into his face and body.

Dirk was thrown across the bridge when the final burst caught him. He was dead before he hit the railings.

Only Geordy Evans, port gunner, was left untouched on the bridge.

On deck and in the deck-house there were dead, dying and wounded soldiers lying where they fell.

*

Sam opened his eyes. He was lying where he had been thrown, aching and bruised, saved from injury by landing flat against the port bunker.

"Jannie," he called, "Jannie," his faint voice desperate and his heart racing.

"Here jonge." Jannie's calm response quietened the boy. "I'm here." Sam heard him cough. "It's a good job you didn't squash me."

Jannie struggled to his feet, groaning with the effort and muttering, "I'm too old for this."

"So am I," growled Fred Firth, the on-watch stoker.

"Are you hurt?" Jannie called.

Fred stuck his head round the corner of the work bench. "Felt better, mate," he replied, staggering to his feet. He winced, holding his head with one bloodied hand. "I'll survive."

Jannie rose unsteadily, shaking his limbs and body as he checked for broken bones. He stumbled over to Fred.

"Sit down," he ordered, pointing to the space next to Sam. He grabbed a handful of clean cotton waste and handed it to Fred. "I'll clean you up in a moment."

Jannie cranked the sound-powered telephone and waited.

There was no reply.

He tried again.

Silence.

"Shit," he muttered, looking around the engine room.

The last order from the bridge had been "Stop Engine."

"What the hell's going on?" They were stopped, sitting ducks and there was no-one on the bridge. He cranked the handle for about half a minute, muttering, "Come on, come one."

"Bridge." The deep bass voice of Henk rumbled in his ear.

"Why are we stopped?" Jannie asked, urgency sharpening his voice.

"The bridge has been hit, Jannie. Dirk and the starboard gunner are dead. Henri is unconscious."

Jannie flicked a quick glance at Sam, then said quietly. "Get us underway, Henk. Steer North West."

"Ja, North West." Henk breathed deeply. He sounded as if he was moving something heavy. "OK, Jannie. Half ahead please. I can't use the telegraph at the moment."

"Half ahead. I'll be as quick as I can," Jannie hung up, saw the steam pressure was dangerously high and slowly opened the valve. Steam leaked from pipes that had been shaken loose by the explosion but the engine turned. The starboard paddle wheel clanged and groaned as it began to rotate. Jannie knew that at least one bucket was bent, probably loose as well. He exhaled loudly when the wheel had completed a full turn, relieved the shaft was not buckled.

Opening the valve a little wider, the steam pressure began dropping and the paddles continued to turn. The loud, discordant clattering from starboard was joined by the hissing and wheezing of steam escaping under pressure and the slop of water beneath the deck plates.

Jannie rang the bridge. Sub Lieutenant Coombes answered. "We're taking water. I'll start the pump. Get the men to check the hull? Tell them to use their eyes and ears."

Pip rang off.

Jannie opened the valve a little more and went to check the fires.

Somehow Sam had fastened the cotton waste to Fred's head with a makeshift bandage and was trying to pass him a mug of water, though spilling most of it. He saw what Jannie was doing and pulled himself to his feet.

Fred followed and took the shovel from Jannie's hand. "Get the rake, Sam" he ordered, "The fires are all over the place."

Between them they riddled and levelled the coals and filled the fires. Fred saw the steam pressure had settled and told Sam to help Jannie, by then head down in the bilge. He had switched the inlet valve to pump out the bilge and was checking the elephant's foot was clear of debris.

Jannie looked up at Sam, "Get the pump going, quick as you can."

Levering himself back to his feet, he glanced at the bulkhead clock. To his surprise only five minutes had passed since the bomb exploded. He moved back to the controls and gave the engine more steam. The cacophony from the starboard paddle had not got any worse, so he brought the revolutions up to half ahead. Jannie rang the bridge and Pip answered immediately. "We're running at half ahead." Jannie told him. "We'll start pumping in a minute or two." He looked across at Sam and saw he was completing his checks methodically and without rushing them.

"We'll restart the generator next."

"Thanks, Jannie," Pip replied. "We're steering North West, making about 6 knots and a destroyer is keeping us company."

"Good," Jannie was pleased to know that. "Let me know when you've checked the hull," he told Pip, "We must know where this water's coming from."

Janie rang off, saw that Fred was able to carry on and joined Sam.

"Ready, Baas," Sam reported, his voice firmer.

Jannie nodded. "Start her up."

Sam cracked the steam valve, watched the pressure mounting, waited until it reached its mark and opened the suction pump. There were a few minor steam leaks which the boy stopped by tightening the glands with his adjustable spanner before checking the water pressure. He gave Jannie a shaky thumbs up and a quick smile.

"Well done." Jannie had to shout to make sure the boy heard. "Now work your way round the port piston. Don't overtighten the glands but see if you can stop those leaks." Sam nodded and set to work. Jannie did the same on the starboard piston. There were two very loose glands. He inspected them, tightened them as much as he dared then went to the work bench. He tore lengths of cloth into makeshift bandages to hold pads of cotton waste in place. It might stop them getting scalded if a joint burst.

The howl of the telephone cut through heat. "Pip here, Jannie. Come to the bridge please."

Jannie's eyes widened in surprise though his expression did not change. "Aye aye sir"

It was the only time that Jannie had left the engine room while at sea since they first sailed from Ramsgate a lifetime ago. He was shocked by how many soldiers were crammed below decks. He picked his way over the legs and guns of wet, filthy men, their faces grey with exhaustion.

On deck were the dead, the wounded next to them. Jannie had not heard the screams of the men when they were hit, nor seen their agony as they fell. Nor had had he heard the bullets striking the ship, had not realised they'd been strafed and dreaded what he would find on the bridge.

Pip Coombes saw him and came aft to stop him. Jannie put his mouth to Pip's ear so he did not have to shout. "Tell me, Pip." He saw the boy's eyes fill with tears and asked, "Is he dead?"

Pip shook his head. "No Jannie, he's blind."

"Is he conscious."

Pip shook his head again.

"Who else was hit?"

Pip took a deep breath. Only his training was holding him together. "Faulkner, starboard Lewis gunner and Dirk are dead. Henri is badly wounded." He whispered. "It was the binnacle." He stared at Jannie. "Henri was at the wheel. The bullets missed him. Hit the binnacle. Henri's been blinded by splinters."

"Who else was on the bridge?"

"Willem. He's unconscious, and Evans, he was on the port gun. I was behind Henri, putting our position on the chart. If I hadn't…"

"Look at me," Jannie said softly and waited until Pip raised his eyes. "There was nothing you could do to stop it." He shook him again before dropping his arms. "Understand?"

"Yes, sir." Pip whispered, close to tears again.

"Good," Jannie looked at him, saw him struggle for control and said, "I would like to see Henri now."

＊

Henk had raced up to the bridge as the water was cascading down. He could see young Geordy Evans standing at his gun, He did not expect to find any other bridge watchkeepers alive.

Gary Faulkner and Dirk were dead. The young seaman still held the Lewis gun with one hand even though most of his head was missing. Dirk had been shot in the chest. The bullets had flung him across the bridge, killing him instantly. If there had been any doubt, he had obviously broken his neck when he hit the screen.

Henri was bent over the wheel, his head resting on the shattered compass, blood pouring down his face. He tried to **raise it** when he heard Henk's footsteps. His "Wie da?" was a faint whisper that Henk only heard because he was lifting him carefully and cradling him to his chest.

"It is Henk," he replied. "I'll just make you comfortable."

The howl of the engine room telegraph cut through the din of escaping steam. He ignored it. Henri lifted his head a few inches and tried to sit up. "Nee," said Henk quietly, "Stay there." He pulled out his cleanest handkerchief to stop the bleeding from the jagged gash in Henri's forehead. When the telephone howled again and did not stop howling, Henk scrambled to his feet and picked it up, at the same time dragging a semi-conscious Willem out of the way.

"Get moving, Henk. Steer North West," ordered Jannie, realising Henri was out of action.

As the smoke thickened and the paddles began to turn, Henk looked for the sun, noting that the mist was clearing and a warship was rapidly approaching from astern. He brought the bows round to port until the sun was two points abaft the starboard beam. "Course North West." He reported to himself as the destroyer came up about half a cable to port, slowing down as she did.

Her captain called on the tannoy, "Do you need assistance?"

Henri found the speaking trumpet and answered, "A doctor. We have many injured."

"Stand by."

The destroyer's decks were crowded with soldiers staring at the bizarre sight of an old paddle-boat waddling along with her chimney on fire.

"Sorry, *De Ruyter*, the doctor's busy. He's putting together what supplies he can spare."

Henk acknowledged, his shoulders slumping.

They must be about five hours from Ramsgate at this speed.

Pip Coombes appeared, dishevelled and groggy, clambering over the wreckage of the chart table.

Henk had forgotten he had been on the bridge. "Are you hurt?"

"No," muttered Pip, aghast at the carnage around him. "I must have knocked myself out when…" He stopped, seeing Henri for the first time, "Oh God," he whispered.

"He is alive," Henk said quietly. "I think Jannie should come up." Pip turned his head quickly, stared at Henk and nodded.

"What is your best speed?"

The tannoy made Pip jump. He had not been aware of the ship just half a cable away. He shook his head to clear the fog in his brain. Henk patted his shoulder. "Get Jannie."

"Six knots," he replied to the destroyer.

"Roger." There was a pause. Henk could see the captain talking to his officers. "Stand by for a heaving line transfer."

Henk raised his speaking trumpet, "Thank you, meneer. To our bridge please."

"Will do." The destroyer captain could see there was no space on deck.

Henk looked across at Geordy Evans. "Will you deal with this?"

"Aye aye sir."

The destroyer closed to about twenty metres from the paddle-boat. A heaving line was thrown to *De Ruyter*'s bridge, caught, a bag swung over, detached and the line returned.

Engine telegraphs clanged onboard *HMS Vixen* as her captain leant over the bridge wing and called, "Good luck, *De Ruyter*. We'll hang around until we're relieved."

"Thank you," replied Henk from the wheel. "Good luck to you."

The sea boiled at the stern of *Vixen* as her screws bit. She surged ahead with a "whoop whoop" from her siren and cheers from her soldiers and crew.

Pip opened the bag of medical supplies, took out morphine, a syringe and a couple of dressings for Henri before telling Geordy to take the rest to the deck saloon.

There Geordy found a sergeant and handed the bag over. "Sorry, it's all they could spare."

The sergeant looked at the weary kid. "Don't apologise, mate. We glad to be ere'."

He thought for a minute before asking, "Was you on the bridge?"

Geordy nodded.

"Fuck me!"

The sergeant clapped him on the back. "That was fuckin' good shootin'! Was that you?"

Geordy shook his head, tears welling up. "No sir," he replied in a small voice, "That was my oppo." He stifled a sob. "He's dead."

"I am sorry." The sergeant put a grimy hand under Geordie's chin and lifted his head so he could look him in the eyes. " 'e saved us, your oppo did." The sergeant thought for a moment, "'oo's on the guns nah?"

"No-one sir. Not on the bridge. I'd better go, sir."

" 'ang on a sec," the sergeant ordered as he turned, raised his voice and barked, "Toft! Goodwin! Come 'ere."

Two corporals threaded their way over and around the men lying on the deck. They had picked up their rifles and packs, and attempted to straighten their soaking battle-dress as they approached their sergeant.

"Right lads?"

"Sarge" they answered.

"Good. You'll go with this lad and man the Lewis guns."

"Sarge." They looked at each other before Toft asked, "What's happened, Sarge?"

"This lad's knackered, that's what's 'appened, and the other one's dead. Any more questions?" He glared at them and then smiled, " I 'opes you bastards can shoot straight. This lad's mate, the one 'oo copped it, 'e shot that bleeder dahn." He smiled again. "Now 'oppit!"

They wheeled away and clattered after Geordie and onto the bridge.

The sergeant handed the bag to a struggling medical orderly and looked around for another corporal. Spotting Thurstan sleeping on the deck, he nudged him awake with his boot. "Job for you, George."

Thurstan blinked, rubbed his grimy face with both filthy hands and struggled to his feet.

"Sarge."

"Grab a couple of men and get all the ammo you can off this lot. Fill a couple of packs. Then go round them Lewis guns and refill their mags."

The sergeant was fed-up with being bombed and shot at. He thought he would see what else he could do.

*

Jannie knelt beside Henri, picked up his left arm and felt the feeble fluttering of his pulse. Henk's kerchief had slowed the flow of blood to a trickle. Jannie opened one of the dressings and used it to wipe the blood from Henri's eyes and cheeks. His face had been peppered by tiny bronze and iron splinters. Jannie raised each eye-lid in turn, breathing a sigh of relief when he saw that Henri's eyes had escaped injury.

Jannie moved slightly and saw fresh blood coming from the righthand side of Henri's chest. "Shit," he whispered as he undid his jacket. Henri groaned when Jannie moved him gently to see the wound. Looking up, Jannie was disconcerted to find Henri staring at him and trying to say something. Jannie moved so that his head was next to Henri's. "Hello Henri," he whispered. "This is a fine way to spend the morning."

Henri coughed, blinked the blood out of his eyes and took a shallow breath. Gazing at Jannie, his brilliant blue eyes steady, Henri whispered, "I'm going west, my friend." He coughed again, flecks of blood spattering Jannie's face. His clear eyes locked onto Jannie's as he struggled to take another breath. "Tell Emma," he gasped, his voice faint and fading, "Tell her…" He stopped to take another breath and closed his eyes.

Jannie knew he was slipping away. He was gazing at Henri's face when his eyes flicked open.

It took Henri a few seconds to focus on Jannie before he whispered so faintly that Jannie had to bend his head until his ear was almost touching Henri's lips, "We did our duty, Jannie."

"Ja, my friend we did our duty," Jannie whispered back.

Henri's eyes closed again. His breathing became laboured, seven or eight quick, shallow gasps, the last inhalation followed by a long pause. Each pause so long that Jannie thought he had died until Henri exhaled loudly, and the panting started anew. He slowly turned his head into Jannie's shoulder. Jannie sat very still as Henri took a few more shallow breaths. Then his heart stopped.

Henri died as he had lived, quietly and without fuss.

*

Jannie sat very still, cradling Henri's head and shoulders against his chest. Silence ballooned about him. Sounds were smothered by disbelief and loss. Jannie was conscious of nothing, not even the clear, blue sky, as he leant back against the screen.

Henk glanced down at his two friends and quickly looked away. The ship needed Jannie to get them home, but a few more minutes would not sink them.

The clattering of hob-nailed boots and the "Fuck me!" of Corporal Toft as he saw Gary Faulkner's body broke the spell.

Jannie blinked and gently laid Henri's head on the deck. He looked up at Henk and asked, "Can he stay here?" his voice soft.

"Ja, of course," Henk replied. "I'll put Dirk beside him." He looked at Jannie and added, "They will keep each other company."

Jannie got to his feet slowly, stretched and looked down at Henri and across to Dirk. "They would like that."

He turned to Henk and asked, "Have they found the leak?"

"Ja, Baas." Henk growled. "Rivets popped and some plates started, all in the same area forward of the starboard paddle."

When Jannie nodded, Henk continued, "The Navy's breaking out a tarpaulin. The officer told me they will pull it under the ship until it covers the plates, then lash it in place. It gets sucked into the holes and slows the leaks."

Jannie heard Henk's voice from a great distance. He patted his shoulder and, looking at the shattered compass, said, "Sam has a compass. Henri gave it to him. Send Willem to fetch it. Henri will take us home."

He looked at Henk again before adding, "Then tell Willem to set up the forrard and after deck pumps and get the soldiers pumping."

He returned to the engine room in a trance, never seeing the soldiers pressing back or rolling out of his way. He was a grim sight, blackened by coal dust and oil, his face, hands, arms and filthy white singlet smudged and stained with blood, as were his faded blue trousers.

Sam was too busy to notice Jannie coming down the ladder. The noise of the damaged paddle drowned all sound except the high-pitched hissing of escaping steam. Fred had been joined on the plates by Steve Buckland. Neither noticed him. Two boys and a man, thought Jannie as he stared about him. His grim expression softened as he thought how proud Henri would be if he could see Sam now. That thought almost unmanned him. He sighed deeply and walked over to Sam. Standing beside him, Jannie shouted above the din, "Well done, jonge."

Sam jumped and spun round. Horror chased relief from his eyes. "What's happened, Jannie? Are you hurt?" He put a hand out to Jannie. "You're covered in blood."

Jannie took Sam's hand and held it tightly. "I'm fine, Sam."

He took a deep breath and said, "Henri is dead."

Sam buckled. He clung to Jannie with both hands, staring at him, shaking his head. Jannie had to lean forward to hear what he was muttering.

"No, no no," over and over again, his voice getting louder and louder.

Jannie pulled Sam upright and shook him.

"Yes, Sam. Yes." He barked, "Henri is dead." He saw his words hit the boy like punches. "He is dead. And so will we be if we don't keep this ship moving."

He shook Sam roughly. "Get a grip, jonge. I have to check the hull and paddle."

Sam looked at Jannie as if he was a stranger. He had never seen anyone looking so fierce. He stepped back, gulped for air and clenched his jaw to stop it trembling. "What do you..?"

Jannie cut him short. "Speak up," he shouted, "I can't hear you."

Taking another breath, steadier now, Sam stood straight and asked in a loud, clear voice, "What do you want me to do?"

Jannie nodded at him, his grim face softening slightly as he gave his orders.

"Check both pistons. Keep an eye on the pump. Got that?"

"Yes Baas," Sam shouted.

Jannie tapped his shoulder and went over to the stokers. He nodded at Buckland, told Fred to keep an eye on Sam and grabbed a handful of cotton waste.

He damped it and wiped his face, hands and arms before leaving the engine room and pushing through the crowded 'tween decks into the forward saloon. The boards had been lifted, exposing the leaking plates. He could make out the clanking of the forward chain pump above the noise of the damaged paddles.

Jannie felt and heard the beat of the paddles slowing. He craned his neck to look forward and saw through the ports the tarpaulin being lowered over the side. He concentrated on its the slow progress, willing it aft. The noise of rushing water was plain for all to hear, so was the sound of men on the verge of panic.

Jannie raised himself onto a box, put two fingers in his mouth and gave a piercing whistle. There was a sudden silence, except for the splash of wavelets against the hull, the suck and clank of the pump – and the sound of running water.

Hundreds of tired, fearful faces turned to look at him. Raising his voice, Jannie called out, "I am Jannie. The engineer. We have stopped to secure canvas over the leaking plates. It will slow the leak enough to get home. We'll be off as soon as it does – and this time the Navy is escorting us."

There was a muted cheer. Jannie looked around the saloon and saw the canvas reach the ports above the leaks.

The rushing sound quietened slightly, then suddenly stopped. There was a moment of disbelief, followed by waves of cheering throughout the ship.

Jannie pushed his way through the relieved, excited men to the engine room, ran to the telephone and called the bridge.

"Ja," Henk, calm, answered.

"Tell Pip it works. Have someone watching in the saloon and a runner. It might wash off once we get underway. And he'll need to keep an eye on the ropes as they'll be chafing. Tell him to get another tarp ready."

"Ja, got that. What about the paddle?"

Jannie smacked his hand against the bulkhead. It was not like him to forget something as important as that. "I'll check that now. We'll turn the engine slowly for a couple of revolutions."

Jannie told Sam what to do when he banged on the hull with a spanner, climbed back up the ladder and out onto the starboard paddle box. He undid the inspection plate and hit the hull twice.

As the paddle-wheel slowly turned, Jannie saw that three of the buckets were bent out of true. None appeared to be loose. He saw that the buckled paddles smacked against the hull. There was nothing he could do about that. He hit the hull twice more and, as the paddle stopped, secured the inspection plate.

Jannie waved his right forefinger at Sam in a circular motion and watched as he restarted the engine. He mouthed "Half ahead," saw Sam nod and rang the bridge.

"Coming to half ahead now, Henk. Any chance of using the telegraph?"

"Ja," rumbled Henk, "Willem's back with us. A bit groggy so I'm keeping him here."

"Good. Ring on half ahead and give all orders on the telegraph. And send Willem down for Sam's compass.'

"Ja Baas." Henk rang off and the telegraph bell clanged as the pointer moved to Half Ahead.

"Orders by telegraph, Sam." Jannie told the boy.

He watched Sam closely as he repeated the order. He was very pale beneath the grime.

Moving over to Buckland he asked, "What are you doing here, Steve?"

Steve straightened his back before replying, "I thought you might need a hand."

Jannie grunted, gave Steve a piercing look and replied. "Thank you," then snapped. "D'you remember where the tea is kept?"

*

"Bridge," Pip Coombes answered.

"We could try little more speed," Jannie said. "Maybe another knot, if you think the canvas will hold."

"It would help," Pip's reply made Jannie smile.

"We will give it a go," Jannie said in the same laconic tone, and rang off.

"Sam," he called, "Five more revolutions."

Sam moved to the engine controls and eased the valves open. The noise was painful. High pitched steam was jetting out of one of the loose flanges on the port piston.

"Down five," Jannie shouted in Sam's ear.

He rang the bridge. "Sorry, Pip," he reported, "It will have to be slow and steady."

Slow and steady it was, creeping towards the coast of Kent for hour after weary hour. *Vixen* had been relieved by *Viper*. Two hours later she closed to hail them, "The RAF will look after you now. Only eighteen miles to go." She gave their position and sheered off, heeling as she increased speed and altered course for Dunkirk.

No-one cheered.

There were ships and boats of all shapes and sizes making their way to and from France on that calm blue sea, but there was no comfort in that remarkable sight. A tall plume of black smoke trailed from *De Ruyter*'s funnel, a signpost for every German aircraft. Soldiers relieved sailors on the Lewis guns. Every man on deck scoured the sky with tired, strained eyes except those sweating at the chain pumps.

Down below, men toiled in the little galley to turn out endless fannies of tea, soup, wads of bread and bully beef sandwiches from the stores dumped onboard in Ramsgate. The wounded lay quietly in the deck saloon, nursed tenderly by exhausted comrades. The dead had been moved to the foredeck and lay in lines, covered by greatcoats, their helmets, packs and rifles on top. There were twenty-six of them. That was not all the dead.

Gary Faulkner, Dirk and Henri lay side by side next to the wheel and shattered binnacle. Henk refused to let Pip move them.

"They stay with me," he growled at the young officer. "Fetch hammocks please."

He covered each man with a hammock, tucking the sides and lashings beneath them before taking the wheel again.

*

Sam was too tired to think of anything but obeying the relentless flow of orders barked out by Jannie. The endless crashing of metal on metal from the starboard paddle wheel and the high-pitched hissing of escaping steam never stopped. Nor did the tension and dread, the instinctive flinching from every unexpected sound. A rifle dropped overhead sounded like a bomb, boots thudding along the passage like bullets hammering home.

Sam jumped when the telephone howled, jumped again and Jannie shouted at him, "Pick it up."

He took a breath, calmed himself and answered, "Engine Room."

"That you, Sam?" Henk's rumble was gentle. Sam thought he was smiling.

"Ja, it's me."

"Tell Jannie to stand by to enter harbour." Henk was definitely smiling now. "We are one mile off."

"Thank you, Henk." Sam felt the tiredness slip away. "Standing by."

He looked around, caught Jannie's eye and beckoned him over, a great smile splitting his coal-black face.

Jannie looked down at the boy and rumpled his greasy hair. "Are we there?"

Sam nodded, his spirits soaring. "Stand by to enter harbour."

He suddenly laughed and yelled at Steve and Fred, "Stand by to enter harbour!"

He danced across the engine room plates, seized Steve, shook him and shouted, "We did it!"

Steve grabbed Sam and spun him round, laughing with him. Fred stood back and looked across at Jannie. He was shocked how gaunt he looked. Weariness and grief were etched deep into his coal-blackened face.

The engine telegraph clanged, ringing down "Slow Ahead" and bringing the boys back to their senses. Sam skipped to ring the acknowledgment and turned to close the steam valve.

The clanging slowed; the amount of steam leaking from the engines also slowed. They could speak in normal voices again.

They were busy for a few more manoeuvres before feeling *De Ruyter* bump hard against a pier. Sam heard Jannie grunt and put his hand on the old man's arm. Jannie looked down at him and said quietly, "Henk has to learn."

"Ring Off" was followed by the howl of the telephone. Jannie answered this time. He nodded, said "Ja," and put the phone down.

Jannie called Fred and Steve over. "I have to go to the bridge." He looked at Fred and asked him, "Can you keep the pump going?"

"Yes boss."

Jannie nodded. "Check the elephant's foot. It's been a while since I cleared it."

"Aye aye chief." He paused then asked, "Keep steam up?"

"Yes, keep steam up." Jannie replied. "We won't be staying here."

He glanced at the two Navy men and told them, "I'll take Sam with me."

Jannie took his time about leaving, checking the loose flanges on the engines and inspecting others for signs of weakness. He did not want to be caught out if they had to sail in a hurry.

Satisfied, he called Sam over and told Fred, "We'll be on the bridge."

Fred sketched him a salute and began to check the steam pump with Buckland.

∗

Sam thought soldiers must spend their life queuing. He had seen lines of them on the sands and in the sea a few hours ago, patiently waiting for boats to pick them up. And here they were, patiently queuing to disembark. No pushing and shoving, no shouting, no arguing. A few quiet conversations. No laughter.

They made way for Jannie and Sam as though they had not yet realised they were safe. Dull-eyed with exhaustion, they seemed to be listening, heads cocked, as if expecting to hear… what, Sam wondered. Gunfire? Bombs? A dive bomber? Tension crackled in the air, easing as they shuffled onto the upper deck. Vanishing, at least for now, when they saw the crowds

211

on the quay, buses and trucks waiting for them and rows of smiling, aproned women behind tables, handing out mugs of tea, cigarettes and packets of sandwiches.

Jannie led Sam onto the companion way to the bridge and stopped, waiting until he was beside him.

He put a hand on Sam's shoulder and said, "We are taking Gary back to Chatham." He looked carefully at Sam as he told him, "We will bury Henri and Dirk at sea."

Sam winced and closed his eyes for a moment. He took a long, slow breath and held it for a while. He opened his eyes as he blew it out. "Right," he said, staring through the harbour entrance. "Out there?"

"Ja, Sam. Out there." Jannie went on, his voice soft and sad, "It is as close as they will get to home."

Sam looked up and gave him a faint smile. "Ja, it is not so far." He thought for a moment before asking, "Can I see Henri?"

"Ja." Jannie glanced at Sam and added, "He was wounded in the face."

Sam squeezed his eyes shut. His head rocked back as he took a sharp breath. "Schijt." He exhaled and shook his head.

"Come, jonge." Jannie took his arm and led him up onto the bridge.

Pip and Henk were on the port wing, watching the khaki stream flowing ashore. Geordy and Willem stood close by. Sam noticed the unmanned guns pointing skywards, steam and smoke escaping from the pock-marked funnel, the splintered bridge and shattered binnacle. He staggered slightly when he saw three bodies lying beneath white hammocks on the other side of the wheel. Jannie's grip on his arm tightened.

The four men on the bridge walked over to them.

"Well," said Pip, "We won't be going back." He gave a tight smile. "We've been ordered to anchor off as soon as we've disembarked our passengers." He grimaced. "We sail for Chatham at first light."

"Another anchor watch," groaned Willem.

Henk looked at Pip and asked "You are staying onboard?"

"Yes," Pip smiled, "We sail with you."

"Good," Henk and Jannie spoke simultaneously.

They heard shouting on the quay and went back to the port wing.

The burly sergeant whom Geordy had met in the deck house, and who had taken charge of the Lewis guns, was shouting at his platoon as they came over the gangway. They watched them form up in three lines, shuffling about with their left arms stretched out until they were evenly spaced and perfectly aligned. Another shout. Their heads snapped to the front and arms to their sides.

"I say," Sam heard Pip mutter, "They're awfully smart."

Every man was properly dressed, packs on their backs, helmets on their heads, rifles at their sides and facing the battered old paddle steamer.

The sergeant marched to the front of them, stamped to a halt and wheeled to face *De Ruyter*. As he barked out a series of commands, thirty rifles were lifted as one and smacked firmly onto the men's left shoulders. More commands and they presented arms to the ship. The sergeant, crisp as a guardsman, saluted the bridge. Pip hurriedly adjusted his cap and returned the salute, the Dutch and Navy sailors beside him standing as smartly as they could.

Pip lowered his arm. The sergeant barked more orders and the platoon turned into columns and marched away.

The men on the bridge watched in silence. It was hard to equate the sodden, filthy, exhausted men who had climbed wearily onboard a few hours ago with those thirty-one soldiers marching off as if on parade.

Jannie broke the silence. He looked at Pip. "I wonder what Hitler would make of that."

Pip was about to reply when his eyes were drawn to a file of soldiers coming onboard carrying stretchers. Covered lorries were stopping alongside.

Pip sighed. The wounded had left the ship first, and that platoon was the last of the living.

"We'll come with you," Jannie said and led the men down to the foredeck. An Army captain was waiting for them with a sergeant who was talking quietly to Henk.

When Pip walked over to introduce himself, Jannie told Sam to ask Fred and Steve to come on deck. "Tell them to stop the pump. The ship won't sink in the next five minutes."

It was more than five minutes before the last body was lifted onto a stretcher and carried off the ship and into the final lorry. *De Ruyter*'s Dutch and English crew stood shoulder to shoulder throughout, paying their silent tribute to the dead.

The Army officer looked round the stained and empty deck before coming over to Pip. He saluted smartly. "Thank you," he said, raising his voice so all could hear. "We will take care of them now."

Pip saluted again as he walked over the gangway. The men stood for a moment longer, then Fred nudged Buckland, muttered "Come on lad," and led him below.

Jannie knew Pip was still in shock and went over to him. "If you get your men to clean up down below, we'll sort out the upper deck and deckhouse."

Pip looked blankly at Jannie. All he could see was body after body being carried feet first over that gangway, faces hidden beneath greatcoats, boots or bare feet sticking out and swaying from side to side.

"Pip!" Jannie's voice was sharp.

Pip blinked at him, his head twitched and his shoulders relaxed. "Sorry, Jannie." He looked close to tears. "What did you say?"

"Take your men below, Pip. Get the saloons cleared up. We'll sort out the deck."

"Right," Pip nodded, braced himself and looked across at his sailors. "You heard" and led the way below.

Leading Seaman Spencer came over to Jannie. "He's in a bad way." He said quietly.

"Ja." Jannie took him by the arm, away from the others and told him, "He's blaming himself." He shrugged. "There was nothing he or anyone could do. Only young Gary…" His voice tapered off as he closed his eyes briefly.

"And he shot that bastard down." Spencer finished the sentence.

"Ja, he shot him down."

Jannie looked at Spencer. "We will take him with us, back to Chatham." Spencer nodded.

Jannie spoke slowly, choosing his words with care. "We bury Henri and Dirk out there in the morning." Spencer nodded again and left to find his officer.

"What next?" Jannie looked around, thinking about all the details Henri would have dealt with; ammunition, supplies, water, bandages, any special orders. Not coal, they would not need that for a day or two. He was so tired he had forgotten *De Ruyter* had been badly damaged.

An elderly Commander was coming onboard. He looked surprised when Jannie walked over and asked, "Can I help you?"

"I'm looking for the captain."

"He's dead. I am the engineer. Jannie. I am in charge until we're back at sea."

"Commander Sands." The naval officer glanced around the ship. "*Vixen* reported you were bombed and shot up." He looked keenly at Jannie "And that you shot the aircraft down."

"So I was told," Jannie answered, "We were busy at the time."

A smile flickered across the Commander's face. "I daresay." He glanced at the damaged boat. "Can you make it back to Chatham?"

Jannie nodded, "Ja, half speed, no more. If the sea stays calm."

"Good. You have a naval officer onboard?" When Jannie nodded, he went on, "He and his men will stay with you. I'll send down more ammunition and supplies. Take on water as you need it." He looked at his watch. "Get underway as soon as you can. Anchor clear of the fairway and sail for Chatham at dawn."

Jannie smiled at him. "Ja, meneer. And if we start sinking, we'll drive her ashore."

Commander Sands smiled back. "Anything else?"

He was surprised by Jannie's answer. "We take your brave sailor to Chatham for his family. Henri and Dirk have no family here. We bury them at sea."

Commander Sands thought for a moment, then said, "The deepest water is about ten miles offshore. I'll let the guard-ship know."

"Thank you meneer."

"It is the least we can do," the Commander replied, before saluting and leaving.

*

It was a beautiful night, calm with a light breeze dying away as the land cooled. *De Ruyter* had anchored a mile offshore, clear of the myriad of craft entering and leaving Ramsgate. Some anchored, others headed straight back to Dunkirk, their passage marked by phosphorescent wakes curling away astern. The coast of England was a black undulating mass to the west with not a light to be seen.

Pip had been told where to anchor, plotting the position on the chart before showing Henk, who steered by Sam's compass.

Once anchored, Jannie ordered the crew to meet on the bridge. He checked round the engine room before following the others up the ladder.

"Listen," he started, "Bridge look-outs at all times, manning the guns. Pip, see to that."

"Aye aye," Pip answered and detailed two men off. "What about the other guns?"

"Make sure they are loaded. Ready to fire. Tell two of your men to stand by them."

"Aye aye."

"We sail at dawn for North Goodwin Light. We will bury Henri and Dirk about five miles east of it." Jannie heard Sam catch his breath. "Henk, you and Willem sew them into their hammocks." He could feel the silence deepening around him. "Pip, as soon as I've finished, you'll need all hands bar the look-outs to range and break a shackle of cable and feed it into the forward saloon. Fred, Sam, cut two separate fathoms of chain cable and give them to Henk. You can use the oxyacetylene torch below decks. Make sure the black-out is good."

"And make sure you don't set fire to the ship." Henk's gravelly voice broke the silence.

"Henri, Dirk and Gary must be moved to the foredeck," Jannie went on. "Henk. See to that. You'll need to fashion a stretcher."

"Ja, Baas."

"Any questions?" There were none. Jannie turned and went below.

Back in his old, familiar surroundings Jannie closed his eyes and took a long, shuddering breath. He held it for a while before exhaling slowly.

The bilge pump was chattering away, steam pressure was steady and he needed a cigar and a mug of tea. He hoped Henri would have approved of the arrangements. Probably not, Jannie snorted. Henri would have ranged the cable as soon as they left harbour and cut it on deck in daylight.

With a mug of strong tea in one hand and a cigar alight in the other, Jannie leaned against the port bunker, savouring the solitude. There would time enough to mourn Henri in the days and months to come. All he could think of now was burying him, burying young Dirk with him, and getting the crew of this tired and damaged ship to safety.

"Better check the bilges," he muttered, hanging his empty mug on its hook and tossing the cigar stub into the furnace.

Lying flat on the engine-room plates, he was feeling around the elephant's foot when he heard Sam's footsteps on the ladder.

"Hallo Sam," he said, his voice gentle and his eyes kind. "What can I do for you?"

Sam took a pace forwards and flung himself at Jannie. He clung to the old man. Jannie could feel him trembling and put an arm round his shoulders. "They are moving Henri," he whispered, "Henk told me to come down here and give you a hand."

"That is kind of Henk," replied Jannie. "I was just about to rake the fires and start filling the ash buckets. I could do with your help."

Jannie glanced at Sam, saw he was engrossed in raking the fires and headed up to the foredeck. He was relieved to see three of the long saloon tables had been placed there. Two had been put against the starboard gangway access, about half a meter apart. The third was on the centreline, a third of the way from the bows.

There was enough light from the stars to see Gary, lying on his back on a hammock on the single table. Henri and Dirk lay uncovered on deck while Henk and Willem heaved a fathom of chain onto each of the hammocks now lying open on planks on separate tables.

"No need for the stitch through their noses," Jannie said, conscious he was talking to a traditional sailorman.

"I suppose not," agreed Henk. "It would upset the boys."

"Thanks. You had better go through their pockets. Take everything out." He looked at Henk, "See if either of them had a money belt, rings, anything round their necks."

"We will, don't worry. I have a ditty bag for each of them." Henk was steadfast and reassuring, as if he did this every day.

"Thanks, Henk, and for sending Sam below." He looked at Willem and asked him, "Are you alright, jonge?"

Willem nodded.

Jannie patted him on the back and said as he left, "Let me know when you have finished."

He bumped into Pip in the passageway and asked him, "Would you like Henk and Willem to sew Gary into his hammock?"

It was too dark to see Pip's face but his voice was faint. "No thanks, Jannie, Spencer will do that."

"Tea's wet, Pip," he said, "Come and join us." He pushed Pip towards the ladder and followed him down.

*

The night passed quickly and peacefully. Watches changed, but no-one turned in. Though bone-weary, those off watch kept their dead ship-mates company, Henk once murmuring to Jannie, "It is a pity we cannot set fire to the ship and give them a proper funeral."

Jannie looked at the gentle, red-bearded sailor, wondering if a Beserker lurked within his barrel chest.

As the sky lightened to the east, they slipped the anchor and headed for the stubby tower of the North Goodwin Light Vessel.

Leaving it close to starboard, Henk turned the bows towards the sun, glanced at Sam's compass, pulled out his watch and said, "One hour." He then rang the engine room and told them.

Pip, looking less tense in the early morning light, asked, "Shall I get breakfast organised?"

"Ja, there is bacon, eggs and bread. Plenty of tea and coffee too."

They ate on deck, in the engine room and on the bridge, the starboard paddle clanking away, steam and smoke drifting to leeward, their broad wake gleaming on the calm sea. All four guns were manned. All hands scoured the sky for aircraft, peering through fingers in front of their eyes to look into the sun.

Fifty minutes after departing from the light-ship, Henk rang down "Slow Ahead". Five minutes later he rang "Stop".

When the ship was stopped in the water, he rang the engine room.

For five or six minutes the ship was as vulnerable as she had ever been.

Only the two bridge gunners kept their ceaseless vigil as Jannie stepped forward to stand before the bodies of Henri and Dirk. He bowed his head for a moment before turning to look at the assembled Dutch and English sailors and telling them, "The last words Henri said to me were, 'We did our duty.'" He paused to steady himself before carrying on. "Every man and boy onboard has done his duty. Henri brought us from Holland with over seven hundred Jewish refugees. He took us to France three times and brought back over five thousand men."

He stopped, looked at the body of his old friend and placed a hand on his shroud. "You did your duty, Henri. You gave us the courage to do ours. If young Gary Faulkner had flinched, I doubt we would be here today. He and Dirk took heart from you. We take heart from you."

He gazed at Pip and the English sailors standing with him and said to them, "It has been an honour to serve with you. If Henri was alive today, he would tell you that himself." He turned to face his two dead shipmates. "I am sorry, Henri, Dirk. I do not know any prayers. You did your duty. Now rest in peace."

He stood back and nodded to the burial party. They stepped forward, lifted the boards that Henri rested on and slid him over the side. Dirk followed a few seconds later.

Jannie stared down at the ripples as they spread away from the hull. Sam approached quietly, took his hand and led the old engineer away, "Come, Jannie, we have our duty below."

*

It was dark when Henk eased *De Ruyter* alongside *Thunderbolt*.

"Finished with engine."

Sam never heard the order, nor did he notice the silence. Jannie had told him to sit down before he collapsed. Sam had slumped onto the deck plates, propped his back against the work bench and dozed restlessly. Jannie watched him twitching and jerking, opening his eyes wide, unseeing, at every sudden noise. He wondered how long it would take the boy to recover.

"Keep steam up?" Fred asked.

"We'd better," Jannie answered, almost too tired to think, "Keep the pump running." He stretched and yawned. "Be a shame to sink now."

No-one saw any reason to go ashore.

The passage back to Chatham had been slow and nerve-wracking. Twice they saw German aircraft being intercepted by RAF fighters as they came swooping in from the east, looking for easy targets.

Only Jannie and his stokers were below. The others were on deck, struggling to stay awake and alert, the endless clanking of the damaged paddle-wheel and slow speed a dismal reminder of their vulnerability.

Faulkner's body had been taken into the deck saloon soon after Henri and Dirk had been buried. He lay alone on the scuffed and stained deck, neatly sewn into a hammock with his pack and helmet at his feet. Apart from Sam, he was the only member of the crew at rest.

*

No air raid sirens broke the night, no dockyard police came near *De Ruyter* on their patrols. The wake of a tug, hurrying to beat the ebb tide with three lighters in tow, made *De Ruyter* surge and grind against her fenders.

No-one slept.

Henk had a line over the side, more out of habit than with any hope of catching a fish. He stared at the changing patterns on the surface of the ink-black river as it flowed past. He had always sought solace on the banks of rivers and canals, even as a child. He thought of Ruth, standing where he now sat, her little hands holding the guard-rail as if her life depended on never letting go, staring across the wide river at the bombs exploding and fires raging. He remembered her face lighting up when he held his pocket watch to her ear to distract her and how she had promised to look after it when he left to go back to sea. He knew Sarah would wind it carefully each night before she placed it under Ruth's pillow and wondered if she would forgive him for leaving her.

Willem and Geordy Evans spent what was left of the night scrubbing and scouring in the galley, putting every gleaming cup, plate and pan back where it belonged. Spencer and Buckland hucked out the stern cabin, piling on deck the debris left behind by exhausted soldiers, before washing the brightwork and scrubbing the sole.

*

Pip had relieved the bow gunner and taken his place, watchful, wide awake and going over and over the moment he heard Henri ring down "Stop Engine" and had looked up from the chart table to see a Stuka diving straight at them.

They had all been so tired, blinded by the glare of the sun shining through the mist. But he had been staring at the chart, not keeping a sharp lookout.

Henri had seen the plane, had started his evasive manoeuvres. They had worked before. They would have worked again if they had seen that aircraft in time. Pip knew the bomb only missed because Henri had altered course at the very last minute, just as the ship was slowing.

220

Pip started to think more clearly as the sun rose. Henri's quick reactions had saved the starboard paddle-wheel from the full force of the explosion. Pip knew there was nothing he could have done to stop them from being shot up. He had weathered a storm, though sleepless nights and bad dreams would continue to haunt him until they were driven out by the strain and weariness of watch-keeping on endless Atlantic convoys.

*

In the engine room, Jannie had sent Firth up top, needing to be alone to mourn his friend. He stood, one hand on the closed steam valve, staring ahead without seeing, his ears tuned to the endless chatter of the pump. Occasionally he stirred to open a fire door and throw in more coal, scarcely noticing Sam, twitching and gurning on the engine room plates.

Jannie could not remember when Henri and he had first got into the habit of spending their evenings together at the end of another day's work on the river. They would sit in silence either side of the stove in the cuddy, the lamp swaying as they smoked their cigars and watched the smoke curl away. They would make a pot of coffee and have a cognac or two before one of them might speak.

Twenty years they had been friends. They had met onboard, when Jannie had had enough of deep-sea sailing and secured a job with the company, a year after Henri had done the same to get married.

They were good years, though not when Henri's wife was dying.

Jannie shied away from the thought that it was, perhaps, as well she was not alive today.

He looked at Sam and wondered if Simon and Judith were safe, and how long it would be before Sam would see them again.

He sighed and shook his head to keep awake, remembering the bubbles rising to the surface as Henri's body sank through the green water of the North Sea, and the vow Jannie had made to keep the boy safe.

*

Dawn came at the end of the Middle Watch, the gunners anxiously searching the lightening sky. Henk stood and coiled his fishing line. Pip handed the Lewis gun to his relief and went back to the bridge.

There was no need to order the crew to "Stand To." They were all on deck, looking aloft and listening hard. All, that is, save Jannie and Sam.

221

It was the howl of the telephone that broke Jannie's reverie and startled Sam into trembling, confused wakefulness. Jannie instinctively reached for the receiver while watching the boy stumble to his feet. "Engine Room," he answered.

"Pip, here. Morning Jannie." Jannie grunted.

"Could we have pressure on the fire main for an hour or so?" Jannie heard the tremble in Pip's voice. "We need to scrub decks." He paused, took a breath and said in a rush. "And the bridge. It's..."

Jannie cut in, brusquely. "Yes, straight away. There's bleach powder in the deck locker. Henk knows where it is."

He rang off and put out a hand to steady Sam.

"Morning watchmen, jonge, scrubbing decks." he explained with a smile, "Typical Navy." Sam smiled back as Jannie said "Close the bilge-pump valve and open the sea-water inlet. Let the bridge know when there's pressure on the fire main."

*

"It's Henri, isn't it?" Emma asked, her voice faint and cracking.

"I'm afraid so, my love." William felt her shoulders heave as she took a deep breath. He held her tightly as he went on. "Henri and Dirk. And young Faulkner."

Emma shook her head. "Such a waste," she sighed, "Such a bloody waste."

Sir William sat in silence, holding his wife and rocking her gently, as he had rocked their children when they were upset. Emma looked up at his kind, troubled face. William wiped her tears away and bent to kiss her brow.

"We'll go onboard when I've had my bath," he whispered, "It's the very least we can do."

"Thank you, I should like that," Emma whispered back, resting her head against his for a moment before pushing herself away.

"Go on, Osborne has run your bath."

"Osborne runs my life," he said and kissed her softly on the lips.

Bathed, shaved and in clean clothes, Sir William came out of his dressing room to find Emma had changed, washed her face and was discreetly made-up. He felt his heart lift, as it had done every day of their life together, whenever he saw her anew.

She tilted her chin at him as he took her hand and led her down the staircase.

His Flag Lieutenant and Lieutenant Smith were waiting for them in the foyer. So was Leading Steward Osborne.

"Morning Bill, Flags," Sir William said. "You've heard the news?"

"Yes, sir," they replied.

"And have you heard they brought back over three thousand soldiers?" Sir William asked.

"Could be more than five thousand, Sir William," Flags replied. "We won't know exactly how many for a few days."

Sir William returned the sentry's salute and led the way across to *Thunderbolt*.

He distinctly heard the loud, clear cry from the bridge of "Fuck me! There's an Admiral coming onboard," as he stepped onto the gangway down to the hulk. He also heard his two accompanying officers suppressed laughter.

He glanced at Emma and gave her a quick wink. To his relief, she smiled back.

Sub Lieutenant Coombes snapped a smart salute as the Admiral came onboard. His sailors and the Dutch crew were standing to attention in front of the deck-house. A body, neatly sewn into a hammock, lay on a table on the foredeck.

Sir William, saluting as he came over the side, said, "Thank you, Coombes. Fall out the men. I should like to talk to them below." Before Pip could give the order, Sir William asked, "Who is that?" nodding at the body.

"Ordinary Seaman Faulkner, sir," Pip replied.

"Thank you, carry on."

The Admiral walked into the deck house and went down to the after saloon with Lady Teagle following close behind.

The Flag Lieutenant called Pip over. "I'll stay on deck," he said. "Get your men below."

"What about the gunners, sir?" Pip asked.

"Them too." Flags replied. "They'll be up quick enough if there's an air raid warning."

Bill Smith sketched a salute to Flags and said, "Well done. They'll appreciate hearing what the Old Man has to say."

The Flag Lieutenant walked slowly up to the bridge to pay his respects to the men who had died there.

Down below, Sir William was paying his respects to the living.

"Sit down, gentlemen. Smoke if you wish." He took his cap off and put it on the bar before looking carefully at the tired, grimy men and boys before him.

"I wanted to tell you myself how very sad I am at the deaths of Henri, Dirk, Faulkner and all those soldiers." He paused for a moment, the saloon silent except for the indistinct chatter of the bilge pump and the steady splashing of the water it discharged.

"Judging from the amount of water being pumped out, it is remarkable you made it back to Ramsgate and another fifteen hundred men got home."

"In a few minutes," he said to Pip Coombes and the small group of Naval ratings sitting with him, "You will leave *De Ruyter* and return to barracks to await your ships." He turned to include the Dutch crew. "Whatever lies ahead of you, you must always remember that without you, and countless others like you, we would have lost tens of thousands of men. If Providence continues to favour us, we will bring home tens of thousands more."

Looking at the four remaining Dutch crew, he said, "No-one asked you to take your ship to sea. Thank you for doing so. Now you must leave her with us to repair and send back to sea with a Naval crew onboard."

Sir William glanced at his watch and said, "I've talked enough." He looked at Sam and asked, "Is it possible to have a mug of your engineer's tea before I leave?" adding, "Perhaps a cup of coffee for Lady Teagle and the others?"

Before Sam could move, Jannie stood up. "Milord, I must tell you."

The saloon went very quiet. He looked first at the Admiral and then at Lady Teagle, "Before he died, Henri said, 'Tell the Admiral we did our duty'. I have already told this to our crew. Henri was proud of them, proud to sail in your Navy. He did his duty, milord."

Quiet, shy Henk shuffled to his feet, twisting his stained cap in his hands. He blushed almost as red as his beard as he opened his mouth to ask hesitantly, "May I speak, milord?"

"Of course," replied the Admiral. "It is Henk, isn't it?"

"Ja, milord," he replied, surprised to be remembered.

He put his hat down. "Gary Faulkner was our gunner. He saved our lives. I just wanted you to know."

Henk sat down.

No-one stirred. Lady Teagle had turned away from the gaze of the sailors and was leaning against Osborne.

Sir William addressed the silent men before him. "Thank you, every one of you. As Henri said, you did your duty. I hope, if I am tested in battle, I will do my duty as well as you."

Jannie gave Sam a nudge, "Now make the Admiral his tea."

*

Lieutenant Smith had organised an ambulance to take Faulkner's body to the Naval hospital and a lorry to take Pip and his sailors back to the barracks. They arrived at 0630.

Faulkner was placed on a stretcher and carried past the assembled crew. Pip called the men to attention and saluted as the body left the ship, as did the Admiral and his officers.

Lady Teagle, standing next to Jannie, took his hand, squeezing his fingers hard. It took her two days to scrub the oil from her hand.

Sir William and Flags left soon after. Lieutenant Smith went with the Naval party, having told Jannie to hand over to the relief crew at 1000. Lady Teagle and Osborne remained onboard long enough to invite the four Dutchmen to have a bath and breakfast in Admiralty House.

*

Sir William went back to war leaving Lady Teagle to look after the four survivors of one amongst thousands of its brutal actions.

Osborne told them to put their kit bags in the hall and led them down the passage to the scullery. "Be easier to get the worst off in 'ere," he said. "There's plenty of 'ot water. Towels over there." He looked at Sam and said to Jannie, "We'll get 'im in the tub first." Jannie nodded.

Queenie took Sam up the stairs to the bathroom, carrying his kit bag for him. "Get them clothes off, Sam," she said, "And get in the tub."

"Meek as a lamb, he was," she told Lady Teagle later. "Just did as he was told. But his eyes are dead, ma'am."

It took a long time to get Sam clean. Jannie took longer. He scrubbed his hands until they were raw, as if they were still stained with Henri's blood. Henk was last.

"Blimey, ma'am," Queenie said to Lady Teagle while the men were toying with their breakfast, "He left that bathroom as clean as it's ever been."

"Lucky Sarah," replied Emma.

"Who is going to look after Sam?" Queenie gave Lady Teagle a searching look. "He is never sixteen. More like thirteen. Any road, he's far too young for what he's been through."

"His aunt, I suppose," replied Lady Teagle, "And Jannie."

"Hmm," Queenie sounded doubtful. "That man needs looking after himself." She sighed, "Henri died in his arms."

Lady Teagle's eyes filled with tears. For a moment Queenie wondered who the tears were for, before brushing the thought from her mind and saying, in the same gentle voice, "They have all lost more than we'll ever know, those Dutchies."

Lady Teagle dried her eyes. "Well," she said briskly, "We can't do much for them standing here. I think we should join the men, don't you?"

Scrubbed and in clean if crumpled clothes, Sam and the three men were sitting in silence around the dining room table.

"They 'ave 'ad their breakfast, ma'am," Osborne told Lady Teagle, "Didn't eat much. Didn't say nothing, neither. Reckon they're a bit shell-shocked, ma'am, especially the boy."

"Thank you, Osborne. Please could you put a fresh pot of coffee on the table?"

Lady Teagle sat down and looked at the four silent sailors. Only Henk met her eyes. He gave her a brief nod before looking away. Jannie was staring out of the window, a distant look on his face. She had seen that same expression when her brother came home on leave in the last war. She could not see Sam's face. He had not turned to greet her and she wondered if he even knew she had sat down beside him. Willem was leaning back in his chair, gazing into the empty cup he was cradling with both hands.

Osborne handed Lady Teagle a cup of coffee and put the pot on the table. "Could you pass the sugar please, Sam?" Emma asked.

Sam twitched, blinked once or twice and turned to her, "Sorry, milady," he said. "What was that?"

"Could you pass the sugar please." It was all she could think of to break his chain of thought.

As Sam stretched out a hand, picked up the silver sugar bowl and handed it to her, the spoon fell out, clattering onto a plate before landing in Lady Teagle's lap. She took the bowl off him, put it down and placed her hand over his, squeezing it gently as she did so.

"Hello Sam," Lady Teagle said quietly.

Sam slipped his hand into hers and held it tightly. He tried to speak, cleared his throat and swallowed, "Hello, milady." His voice was tremulous but there was a brief spark in his eyes.

"I am so pleased you are back, Sam" she said. "Did you get any sleep at all?"

Sam did not answer for a long time. He sat very still, head bowed, gripping Lady Teagle's hand so hard it hurt her.

"Nee, milady," he said in a quiet monotone, "Not much sleep."

"I'll see you later, Sam," she said, "I need to talk to Jannie."

Hearing his name, Jannie stood and joined Lady Teagle. "Will you come with me?" she asked him, "Just for a moment."

"Of course, milady." He followed her into the drawing room.

Emma stopped in front of the fireplace and, turned, holding her hands out to him. Jannie took them gently. He gazed for a long time at her tired, strained face before saying, "I am so sorry, milady, so very sorry."

Tears welled in her grey eyes before she blinked them away. "Thank you, Jannie," she said quietly, "He was a dear, brave man." She looked at him, "You all are."

"Milady, you know I was with Henri when he died?"

Emma nodded. "It must have been horrible over there. I have heard stories. William has told me a little." She shook her head, "The ship getting bombed and shot up. So many dead, dear Henri dead."

She suddenly asked, "Was he in much pain?"

"Nee, milady," Jannie's voice was soft. "He knew he was dying, but, thank God, he was not in pain." He closed his eyes, hearing again the stuttering breathing of his friend, the silence when it stopped. He put his hand into his breast pocket and removed a flat package which he handed to Lady Teagle. "He had it in his breast pocket. I wrapped it in the paper."

Emma felt the soft packet and knew it was her gift to him. "Is it covered in blood?" she whispered.

"Nee, milady," Jannie knelt beside her chair, "It was over his heart and…" He took a deep breath, "And that side of his body was untouched."

Emma put the packet down and looked at the bleak face of the old engineer. "Will you keep it, Jannie? Look after it for me until the war is over?"

He looked puzzled.

"Henri is very dear to me; but that does not explain why I gave this to him." She looked steadily at Jannie. "Perhaps it should have been buried with him" She folded the paper back, lifted the scarf out and shook it. The silk rippled like a flag until she placed it over the arm of her chair.

"I'm sorry, milady," Jannie said. "We thought you should have it."

Emma smiled at his serious face. "If Miriam is as beautiful as Sam says, the colour will suit her."

Jannie's face softened, "As you wish, milady." He folded the scarf with care and wrapped the paper around it.

*

Bill Smith found the four Dutch crew in the after cabin when he came onboard. Only Sam was awake, furiously polishing a gleaming brass lamp. He glanced up at the visitor without stopping.

Henk opened his eyes, nudged Jannie awake and stood up. "Time to go?" he asked quietly.

"Time to go," affirmed Bill as Jannie and Willem stretched and climbed slowly to their feet.

Jannie put his hand on Sam's shoulder to get his attention. "Come, Sam. Bring the lamp." He gazed around the cabin as he helped the boy to his feet.

"Got everything?"

Sam nodded and followed Jannie off the ship.

Sam's eyes brightened when they were shown into the admiral's office and he saw Sir William rising from his chair. Shyly he pushed past Jannie and held up the brass saloon lamp.

"What is this, Sam?" asked Sir William as he took the lamp off the boy.

"M-milord," Sam stuttered, "It is…" His voice trailed off.

Jannie wrapped an arm round Sam. "It is for you, Admiral, for you both. Sam would like you to look after it for him until he can take it home."

"Please, milord," Sam said quietly, in a steadier voice.

"Thank you, Sam. Of course we will." Sir William placed the lamp carefully on a small table before continuing. "We will hang it wherever we live and light it each night." He smiled at Sam. "It will remind us of you and your ship."

"Danke, milord." Sam's body relaxed against Jannie's side.

Sir William turned to Jannie. "I hope you will keep in touch with us, Jannie. Emma and I would like to know how you are and how Sam gets on." He smiled again. "It will be Emma who writes. I'm afraid I do not have much time these days."

"Yes, though I expect Sam will write more often than me," replied Jannie. He took Henri's bone-handled switch knife out of his pocket and handed it to the Admiral. "This is for you, Sir William," he said quietly. "Henri always carried it with him. I would like you to have it."

"Thank you, Jannie, I shall remember a good friend every time I use it."

He glanced at his wife who was watching the boy carefully. The only colours in Sam's white face were the dark shadows round his expressionless eyes.

"Hello, Sam," she said quietly when she reached his side.

Sam looked at her blankly for a long moment before his eyes cleared and he replied, "Milady."

"Will you write to me sometimes?" she asked him, "I should like that very much."

Sam gazed at her. He took a breath and held it, before exhaling quietly and replying, "I should be writing to my mother and father." His voice was as expressionless as his face had been. "I cannot write to them so I will write to you."

"Thank you, Sam," Lady Teagle stood very still, as if any movement would startle the boy into flight.

Sam stared at her, his eyes steady. To her surprise, he then repeated her words. "I should like that very much."

"Good." Lady Teagle nodded at the boy, "I have your address in London. I will give you my address before you go."

"Danke milady."

There was a flurry of movement and suddenly Willem was shaking hands with his shipmates and being led away by Bill Smith while the others piled their kit into the boot of the Admiral's car. They stood in a neat row, saluted Sir William and Lady Teagle, and were gone.

The Admiral was not surprised to see tears in Emma's eyes. He put his arm round her waist and took her into his study.

"Look at what Sam has left behind," he said, showing her the gleaming oil lamp. "He wants us to look after it until he can take it home."

"That poor boy," Emma whispered. She put out a hand to stroke the brass.

"I told him we'd light it every night," Sir William said, just as Osborne knocked and entered the room. "Though I suspect we won't be able to."

Osborne cleared his throat, caught the Admiral's eye and refrained from saying what he thought of cleaning all that brass.

"Would you like any more coffee, sir, ma'am?" he asked and left when they declined.

"Don't worry about him," smiled Emma. "He'll be happy to help me." She dried her eyes and said, "I shall be writing to Sam from time to time. It would be a shame to lose touch with him."

"And the others?" murmured William.

Emma looked at him. "I shall miss Henri, my dear." The Admiral nodded before putting both arms round Emma. Holding her close to him, he murmured, "We must go on to the end. Whatever it takes."

"Whatever it takes?" Emma asked softly, before answering her own question, "Yes, I suppose so. Whatever it takes."

She paused for a few seconds before whispering, "Just think what it has taken to get those men off the beaches, all the ships and boats, all those sailors and civilians." She hugged her husband fiercely, "I am proud of you, my love, and proud of all those men and boys who brought them home."

Sir William felt his wife's arms around him. "Now all we have to do is make sure those bastards can't follow," he said.

8.

Departure from London

"He hasn't said a word since he arrived," Miriam said quietly to Henk.

They were sitting in the kitchen while Jannie took Sam up to his room and put him to bed. Henk put his mug down.

"Sam is young. He must be kept busy. Henri and Jannie kept him busy onboard so he never had time to think about his family. He should stay with Jannie and you." Henk smiled at Miriam, "You are his family now."

Miriam lit a cigarette and stared at the smoke curling upwards before looking at Henk and smiling. "Yes," she agreed, "We are his family, and yes, it would be better for Sam to be busy in the country. There is nothing for him to do here."

Jannie came into the kitchen. "Nothing for who to do here?"

They told him.

Jannie sat down. He did not know what to say so he said nothing while he took a packet of cigarettes and a box of matches out of his trouser pocket. He placed them carefully side by side on the table, pulled his mug towards them and then looked up. "What do you think, Mimi?" he asked.

"I think Henk is right." She smiled at Jannie, "If I can arrange this, would you come with Sam and me?"

The answer was instant and unwavering.

"Yes."

*

Henk was up early, anxious to get home to Sarah and Ruth. Miriam found him in the kitchen waiting for the kettle to boil, his bags in the hall. "Good morning mevrouw." He greeted her with a smile, "Is Sam awake?"

231

"Not yet." Miriam shook her head, "He is worn out."

"Ja, mevrouw," replied Henk, "But he is young. He will soon catch up with his sleep. It is his mind that will take time."

He turned to Jannie who had come into the kitchen.

"I have to go, Jannie." He smiled. "The Colonel gave Ruth a puppy just before I left. I think you should find a puppy for Sam." He looked from Miriam to Jannie, "I think you should go to the countryside soon and find a puppy there." He smiled at Jannie. "It will be good for you as well, my friend."

Henk bowed to Miriam, lifted her hand and kissed it. He slapped Jannie on his back and said, "Tell Sam I will see him again."

Picking up his bags he called, "Go with God" as he closed the front door quietly behind him.

Jannie poured them both another coffee and offered Miriam a cigarette.

"He left quickly because it is hard to say good-by." Jannie was speaking softly, partly to himself. "We knew he had to go."

"Oh Jannie," Miriam took his hand in hers, "You have all had such a terrible time." She struggled for self-control before going on, "I rang Harold last night about going away. He will be here soon. He may be able to help us."

"Good," Jannie blew a smoke ring. "And then I must go to the Embassy," he sighed, "To report the deaths of Henri and Dirk." He looked at Miriam, "Will you come with me, please?"

Miriam nodded.

They had more coffee and smoked several cigarettes, sitting in silence with the door open and the sunlight streaming in. Eventually, Jannie stirred, stretched his legs and arched his back before getting slowly to his feet. "I will wake Sam." He looked down at Miriam. "Perhaps he will eat something this morning." He flicked his cigarette end away. "I hope so."

Miriam hoped so too. She got up slowly and went inside to make him breakfast.

*

Harold Hartley cleared his throat. He stood up and leant against the mantlepiece. "Miriam asked me if I knew anywhere in Cornwall where you could stay." He looked from Jannie to Sam. "Well, it happens I do. My wife and I bought a place a few years ago." He smiled at Miriam. "It is alright.

Nothing fancy, but it is furnished and has running water and there's a fireplace in every room. It is not far from Penzance, about as far west as you can go before you fall into the sea." He laughed. "It's a mile outside a little town and has a garden, and you can see the ocean," He paused. "It is a happy little house. That's why we bought it."

"It sounds very nice, meneer," Sam piped up. "But why can't we stay here?"

"It is better not to be here, Sam," said Jannie. "And we will find work in the country." He smiled. "Henk is very happy and we will be too."

Miriam looked across to Harold. "How soon can we go?"

*

Whistles blew, doors slammed and the crowded 10 o'clock train, The Cornish Riviera, pulled slowly out of Paddington Station. Steam and smoke swirled across Platform One and in through the open window of their compartment.

Jannie shut it, tugging the leather strap before securing it to a brass lug, shiny with constant use. Miriam had insisted her men had the window seats, asking the soldiers already sitting there if they would mind moving to let her Dutch friends see something of England. A little grousing soon quietened when she offered her cigarettes round and asked the Major for a light.

"Such a flirt," said Jannie to Sam in Dutch. Sam smiled briefly before turning away, his back straight and shoulders stiff. Miriam gave Jannie a swift look, smiled to herself and settled down.

It was only three days ago that Harold Hartley had told them he had somewhere for them to stay. Miriam asked him to find someone to live in and look after her home in return for free accommodation. She told the A.R.P Warden she was leaving and what was happening to the house before going to her bank to open an account in Penzance. Jannie and Sam helped as best they could but Miriam was so well organised they had little to do except pack all they owned in their kitbags and a suitcase. Taking her example from them, Miriam packed for the country with ruthless efficiency. Apart from clothes, toiletries and another pair of shoes, she only packed her photograph album, her letters from Ike and her favourite tea-pot.

She glanced at her two men, both staring out of the grimy window as the train gathered speed. Jannie, sitting opposite Sam, looked relaxed and

233

interested in the scenery. She could not see Sam's face, just the rigid set of his shoulders and the tension in his clasped hands. She closed her eyes and said a quick prayer for their safe journey.

Miriam had no regrets about leaving Wilkes Street. She knew Sam needed time, love and patient care to rebuild his life, and, of course, to be kept busy. Harold had spoken about a farmer he knew who might welcome a hand. He told them his daughter had gone down two days ago to air the house and get it ready. She would help them settle in and take Sam to meet the farmer.

She began to doze and it was the rustling of paper that woke her. She blinked hazily and saw Sam folding a letter he had received from Lady Teagle, tucking it back in its envelope and carefully putting it in his inside pocket before staring out of the window. Miriam wished she could put her arms round Sam and hold him to her; but not under the gaze of the soldiers.

The train steamed slowly across the sunlit glory of England in the early summer. Sam sat stiff and unbending when awake, his head turned to the window. His monosyllabic replies to the few questions from Jannie and Miriam discouraged conversation amongst the others.

As they approached Taunton the Major stood and shook the others. "We get off here, ma'am," he said to Miriam, "You'll probably have the compartment to yourself as far as Plymouth."

"Thank you, Major," she replied. She glanced at Sam and added, "I'm sorry we have not been good company. My sailors have had a bad time recently."

"Dunkirk?" he asked.

Miriam nodded.

"Ah," he sighed, "We were there." He looked down at Sam. "It is not something they will ever forget. Nor will we."

While there was considerable activity on the platforms, no-one got into their compartment, for which they were grateful.

"Take your boots off, Sam," Miriam said as she moved across to sit beside Jannie. "You can lie down if you want."

Sam did as she suggested and was soon asleep. Miriam and Jannie lit up. "Strange that you were all at Dunkirk," she said quietly.

"Ja, Mimi." He looked at her. "Maybe they sailed with us." He laughed, "Sam and I would not have known." He shook his head. "And they would not have seen us."

Miriam yawned and kicked her shoes off. "Budge up," she told Jannie as she swung her feet up onto the seat and leant back against his shoulder. "I am going to sleep."

Jannie settled into the corner, moved his arm onto the back of the seat and then said, "We'll both be more comfortable if you lie down properly with your head on my leg."

"Thank you," Miriam murmured, did as he suggested and was soon asleep.

The window was still open and the air warm. The occasional smut of soot came in, bringing with it the familiar and welcome smell of steam, hot oil and burnt coal. Jannie was happy. Someone else was doing all the work on the foot-plate, the sun was sparkling on the sea to their left, he had a full belly and a woman by his side. He looked down at her and was disconcerted to find her staring up at him. She smiled sleepily, reached for his hand, placed it on her stomach and held it in hers as her eyes closed again.

Jannie closed his eyes and concentrated on the sound of his heart bumping and his blood singing.

*

Sam was the first to wake as the train slowed on entering Plymouth. He turned onto his side and stared in wonder at Jannie and Tante Mimi. He looked at Jannie's hands, one held by his aunt on her stomach and the other holding her shoulder. 'I hope they are clean,' he thought, looking at his own stained hands. He looked harder at Jannie's face. He looked different.

There was no hold up and no-one got into their compartment when the train left Plymouth. The three of them gazed in wonder at the cranes, masts and funnels visible over the high dockyard walls. Occasionally they caught glimpses of ships lying alongside in the basins. Oxyacetylene torches flickered, sparks flew from grinders and welding rods, the jibs of cranes rose and fell; they could sense the urgency of the dockyard workers swarming over the battered destroyers. There were more ships moored between buoys in the river; launches cut busily through the water; tugs towing heavily laden lighters were coming downstream and others, with empty lighters, went upstream.

"They must have been there," muttered Jannie.

Sam stared at him. "Where will those ships go now?"

"To stop the Germans coming here," Jannie looked down at the boy. "That is what the Navy is doing now."

"That is what our Admiral is doing," said the boy. His voice held wonder.

"You can write and tell him what you've seen," suggested Tante Miriam as she sat down.

"I will," said Sam, "And tell him I join the Navy when I am old enough."

They were back at the window as the train trundled slowly across Brunel's mighty bridge, gazing at the rows of ships moored two or three abreast, before staring at a chain ferry clanking slowly across the river loaded with cars and people.

"You are now in Cornwall," announced Miriam as she held a jam sandwich in front of Sam until he took it. She poured three cups of lukewarm tea from her flask and settled back with a cigarette.

Sam soon sprawled on one side of the compartment, apparently asleep. Miriam glanced at Jannie who was gazing out of the window rather too studiously. She leaned sideways and rested her head on his shoulder, whispering, "I was very comfortable before."

Jannie relaxed, smiled and whispered back, "So was I."

Sam gazed through his eyelashes with great interest as Miriam lay down and Jannie took her hand once her head was resting on his leg. He went to sleep comforted by their happiness.

It was only when the guard slid their door open that they awoke. "Just leaving St Erth," he announced. "Penzance next stop."

By the time they had stretched and found their boots and shoes, the setting sun was lighting up a fairy-tale castle on an island and dancing on the calm turquoise sea.

Miriam put her arm round Sam and hugged him tightly. She felt him stiffen, take another deep breath, and suddenly relax.

"Here we are Sam," she whispered, "Isn't it beautiful."

*

Mimi saw Betty first. She was a smiling, bespectacled young woman with both hands outstretched.

"Welcome to Cornwall, Miriam." Betty looked at Sam and Jannie, "Hello, honey," she said to the boy, "You must be Sam."

"Ja, mevrouw," Sam replied politely as he bowed to her.

Miriam let go of Betty's hands, "Let me introduce Jannie, Sam's guardian."

Betty shook hands with Jannie, noticing his watchful reserve and the tension in his face and bearing.

"Is this your first visit to Cornwall?"

"Ja mevrouw," Jannie replied with a slight smile, surprised by her firm grip and the roughness of her hand. "I have sailed past many times."

Betty smiled back, "I hope you will like it." Turning to Sam she said, "I hope you will too." She smiled again, "We mustn't keep Jim waiting. His car is just outside."

"Oh my," breathed Sam as they approached the gleaming black limousine.

"Here we are, Jim," Betty announced gaily to the short, broad and weather-beaten man standing by the driver's door in his tweed suit. "And not much luggage either."

Jannie wondered at Miss Hartley's uniform of fawn twill britches, light brown woollen socks and a dark green V-necked pullover. She was obviously used to taking charge of people.

The journey from Penzance took them through countryside unlike any they had seen before, with a few scattered farms on either side of the narrow, windy road and wild-looking moorland on the hills rising behind them. "That is an engine house," explained Betty, pointing to a tall chimney stack next to a building nearly as tall, perched on top of a distant hill. "It's an old tin mine."

The road got narrower and windier as the car climbed up a hill between grassy banks topped with thorn bushes bent by the wind. There was a little chapel near the top with a small graveyard beside it.

Miriam shivered. Even in the warmth of the setting sun, they seemed to be entering a bleak, grey place with few signs of life.

Sam gasped when he saw the sea gleaming in the low sun and stretching from one side of the land to the other. It looked higher than the road, higher than the land in front of them. Above it rose a great arc of clear azure sky, bigger and bluer than any sky he had seen before.

Jim glanced at Sam's wide eyes and open mouth and pulled into the side of the road. He looked in the mirror as he asked, "Would you like to step out for a moment, Miss Hartley?"

Jannie lifted his face to the sun and closed his eyes as he breathed in deeply, absorbing the warm, honeysuckled scent of early summer. Sam held Miriam's hand as he whispered, "Rachel would love this."

Miriam put her arm round his shoulder as she whispered back, "Yes, and so would your mother and father. You have to bring them here one day."

"I will, Tante Mimi, I will," Sam said fiercely. He took a pace towards Jim and asked, "Are those islands?" pointing to the horizon.

"They are," replied Jim, "The Scillies. Twenty-eight miles away, they be."

"And what is that?" asked Sam, pointing to some rocks sticking out of the sea with a tower on them. "Rocks." Jim told him. "The Longships we call them. And that there tower is the Longships light house."

"Let's get you home." Betty said before Sam could ask any more questions, "You can have a closer look from there."

As they entered a small town, Sam asked "Does anyone live here?"

Jim was driving slowly along a narrow road lined with grey stone houses. They and a few closed shops were separated from the road by a narrow pavement. The town looked grim and forbidding, even in the bright evening sun. The car crossed a small square lined with bars and shops; the square tower of an old church rose out of one corner. Not a soul was to be seen.

"Lord yes," answered Miss Hartley, "Quite a lot, actually." She gave a short laugh, "I expect they are listening to the wireless."

The sun was in their eyes as they drove out of the town. The road wriggled between tall grey stone walls, descending all the while. Jim said quietly, "That's my farm," pointing to a small house with a barn and two smaller buildings nearby. "Seventeen acres I've got."

Jim drove slowly down a rough track before parking on a grassy slope beside a house.

"'Ere we be," he announced as he climbed out to open the back door. Sam hopped out to do the same but suddenly stopped. He cocked his head to one side and seemed to be straining to hear something.

"Listen," he whispered, "Listen to that sound," He turned to ask Miss Hartley, "What is it?"

She listened carefully, hearing only the familiar distant chattering of the stream running through the valley below and the occasional crunch of a wave breaking against the cliffs. It took her a moment to realise it was this gentle, ever-present sound that Sam was hearing for the first time.

While Jim took their bags to the back door and put them on the kitchen floor, Betty Hartley led her guests onto the road and a little way down the lane to a gate at the seaward end. She watched them standing and staring out to sea.

Eventually Miriam turned away, shaking her head in wonder. Jannie looked down at Sam, nudged him gently and murmured, "It's not always like this."

Sam laughed, "But today it is," and skipped up the path. He waited for Jannie by the open front door. "Look, Jannie," he said, pointing at the door knocker, "Like the lions at Westminster Bridge."

"Come on you two," Miriam called, "Let's get you settled in."

Jannie and Sam unlaced their boots and entered in their stockinged feet. They walked past the W.C. and separate bathroom into a small hall. Miss Hartley called them from a room to their right where she and Miriam were standing in a big bow window. "Come, boys." She beckoned them over and stood aside so they could stand beside Miriam.

"This is the Count House window," she smiled, "It is very special in our family."

"I can see why," replied Miriam, "What a wonderful view."

And it was, for there, on the horizon, were the Isles of Scilly, silhouetted by the setting sun.

Miss Hartley moved away down a dark corridor. The wooden floor echoed beneath her shoes. "This is my room," she said, pointing to the first door on their right.

She opened the next door and said, "Jannie, you and Sam are in the Pink Room." They peered in. Jannie quickly told Sam, "You have the bed by the window."

He had seen the sash window and knew it would be draughty. Sam thought he was being kind, giving him the bed with a view across the valley.

Opening the door at the end of the corridor, Miss Hartley ushered Miriam ahead of her. "This is your room. The Green Room."

"Oh my word," breathed Miriam, "It's lovely."

Light flooded through the two windows, a vase of wild flowers on the chest of drawers filled the room with their scent and the big twin beds were covered by yellow candlewick bedspreads.

Betty left Miriam to explore her room and opened a door into the kitchen at the back of the house, telling Jannie and Sam, "Jim's dropped your bags here. Put your things away while I make a pot of tea."

"Look Sam," laughed Jannie, pointing at the cast iron grate set in the wall of their room. "We even have our own fire."

Sam smiled as he bounced on the iron-framed bed, setting the springs jangling. "You can have first watch, Jannie, though there isn't any coal."

"Huh." Jannie thought for a moment, "Maybe it is rationed?"

"Miss Hartley will know." Sam had stopped bouncing and had got off the bed to put his clothes away.

Miriam called, "Hurry up! We are going for a walk before the sun goes."

They went to what Miss Hartley called, 'The White Gate'. The clear blue sky was fading, changing to a faint apricot that deepened to orange as it neared the sea. The sun became a fiery ball as it slipped below the horizon.

Miss Hartley walked briskly ahead, stopping at a large granite style beside a gateway a few yards back from the edge of the cliff. Two jagged rocks stuck out of the calm sea about a mile offshore.

"Look Jannie," Sam called excitedly, "Destroyers." He had eyes only for the three ancient V & W destroyers steaming at high speed around a convoy of merchant ships. Jannie saw Sam suddenly go very still, seeming to shrink within his clothes. He moved quickly to the side of the boy and put his arm around him. They had seen destroyers like these when they buried Henri and Dirk.

Sam shivered and looked up at the old man, his eyes full of tears. "Oh Jannie," he sighed, "I miss him."

"So do I, Sam," Jannie shook him lightly. "But he would not like to see us moping about, would he?"

"Nee, Baas." Sam smiled, wiped his eyes and straightened up. "Let's go home."

Tante Mimi turned to Betty, "We have to keep him busy," she whispered. Betty took her arm as they turned to walk home. "The farm is there," she said, pointing to some buildings nestling into the side of the valley to the north of them. "We will go tomorrow morning, when they have finished milking." She smiled at Miriam. "If they like Sam he will be kept very busy."

They walked faster to catch Jannie and Sam and point out the farm to them. Sam glanced at it without pausing. He was a stoker, not a farm labourer. Jannie tugged his arm to stop him.

"Listen Sam," he said quietly, "We all have to make changes. Big changes. We will keep ourselves busy, keep strong and stay calm. One day we will be ready."

"Ready for what?"

Jannie gazed at the small face turned up to him. When he spoke, his voice was almost gentle.

"Ready to fight back, Sam."

9.

Mediterranean Sea. January 1943

Jimmy groaned as the boy stirred, jarring his leg. The force of the explosion had broken the same leg that had been smashed in Boulogne. He had been lucky to escape when the ship started to list. Ward, now a Chief Petty Officer, had pulled him out and helped him overboard when the Old Man ordered "Abandon Ship".

The sea was very cold but it was the biting north easter that was deadly. Sweeping down from the snow-clad Apennines, it cut through their wet clothes and pierced their bones.

There were men on the raft and others in the water, clinging to the lifelines around the edge. Jimmy was the only officer and had done his best to keep them awake and their spirits up, even though every little movement of the raft made his broken bones grate and sent flares of pain through him.

Gradually the cries and groans had stopped. Numb hands lost their ability to hold on to the lifelines. Some slipped away in the darkness to die on their own. Other panicked, thrashing and flailing to climb onboard, their voices weakening as their strength ebbed away.

Those left on the raft died quietly.

Jimmy had slipped into unconsciousness after striving to keep his shipmates alive. Now he was being dragged back by an annoying, insistent tugging at his arm.

The sudden shock of being struck on the cheek brought him fully awake.

A kid's face hung above him, white against the night. Jimmy shook his head. "Did you just slap me?".

"Yes, sir." Came the stuttering reply. "Sorry sir. You have to stay awake."

"Do I?" grunted Jimmy through the white, bright arc of pain that flooded through him.

"Yes sir," whispered the shivering boy. "There is no-one else."

"Christ." Jimmy tried to heave himself up. "No-one?"

"No sir. Just you and me."

Jimmy shook his head to clear the fuzziness from his mind and looked more closely at the boy.

"What is your name?" he asked.

"Sam." The boy stopped, "Da Souza, Sir, Ordinary Seaman." He paused, "Oerlikon gunner, sir."

"Well, Sam, then I must know you." Jimmy smiled. "I'm afraid my mind's gone blank."

Sam looked up shyly. "*De Ruyter?*"

Sam felt Jimmy's shock.

"Christ!" Jimmy looked more closely at the boy. "Were you the stoker?"

"Second engineer, sir," whispered Sam.

Jimmy looked down at the boy. "How old are you, Sam?"

"Sixteen."

Knowing they must keep talking, keep awake, if they were to have any chance of living, he asked, "Tell me Sam, did you keep on being an engineer before you joined the Navy?"

"Oh no, Kapitein, "Sam laughed, "I worked on a farm."

He suddenly stopped, tense and still.

"What happened, Sam?"

"The Germans happened. They follow me."

"Why do you say that?"

But Sam was sliding into sleep.

Jimmy shook him awake and made him as comfortable as possible. His leg throbbed but the cold had numbed the worst of the pain. He had no idea how long it was till dawn, or if there were still ships searching for survivors.

"Where is your farm, Sam?"

"Cornwall," replied Sam softly.

"My word," said Jimmy, "That is a long way from London."

"As far as can be." Sam replied dreamily. "There is the farm and then the ocean." He gave a great sigh and started coughing.

Jimmy patted his back until the coughing subsided. "Go on," he said.

"There is also Annie."

"Who is Annie?"

Sam stirred and tried to raise himself. Jimmy bent his head to hear the whispered answer.

"She is the warm west wind," Sam said. "The gentlest evening breeze."

There was a long silence. Jimmy carefully shook Sam awake. "Where did you meet her?"

Sam took a shallow breath. "On the farm. Jannie told me to stop staring."

Jimmy smiled. "Why was Jannie there?"

Sam shook his head a little. "Jannie and Tante Mimi" He whispered. "They took me to the farm." He paused to take a shallow breath "They said it would be safer. That was before the Germans came. I work there for two years. It was hard at first, to be a farm boy. Horses, cows, pigs, hens all make so much shit. Every day I shovel shit." He laughed quietly. "I was very good. Mr T say he never had a better farm hand. I learn many new things, meneer. Milking. I love milking."

Sam was silent. Jimmy squeezed his shoulder. "Go on, lad. Keep talking."

Sam lifted his head. "Baby pigs are very naughty. They keep running away." Jimmy could hear the smile in his voice. "I catch them and carry them to their pen. They were happy." He coughed and spat over the side.

"Sorry, Kapitein, I swallow some oil."

"So did I, Sam," replied Jimmy. "Filthy stuff."

"Ja, meneer. Coal is better." Sam was smiling again as his head sank onto his chest.

He woke when Jimmy shifted and looked at his Kapitein, "Jannie and Tante Mimi went back to London." Sam shook himself slightly. "It was when the bombing started, Tante Mimi had to help her friends. Jannie went to help her. I was very sad."

The silences were growing longer. "Sam!" Jimmy's voice was sharp. "Sam!" He shook him awake. "Tell me about Annie."

Sam raised his head, staring out into the blackness, "I tell my cows many stories, how it was at home, escape, everything His head drooped as his voice sank to a faint whisper "They know my Mutti and Papa. They know Rachel and Jannie and Tante Mimi."

He turned to Jimmy. "One day I tell them about Piet." Tears filled his eyes. "Annie hear me. She was angry with him." He tried to sit up straighter. "I shout at her. Then I cry and she is sad."

There was a long silence. "We were friends after that. Annie tried to teach me to ride. I was never good. I try to teach her to be a fireman when the engine came. She was never good."

"What engine was that?" Jimmy said.

"Steam engine with the threshing machine. It was a good time. Except..."

"Except what, Sam?"

Sam took a shuddering breath, "Except last time the threshing machine came. That's when the Germans shot us. They fly over, bomb cities, then shoot us on their way back. Everywhere I go Germans follow. They shoot Henri, Dirk, Gary, all those soldiers. I go to the farm. They find me and shoot Annie's mum. That is why I join the Navy. To fight them."

He looked up at Jimmy, searching for his eyes in the dark. "They find me again tonight."

There was a long silence before Sam continued. "I am going to live on the farm with Annie. She is my wife."

"Your wife, Sam? You're far too young to be married."

"Nee, Kapitain," Sam smiled in the darkness. "Not too young. I went back to the farm before joining the ship. We made a baby. It will be born in May."

He grasped Jimmy's arm to pull himself up, panting with effort. Jimmy helped him settle and wrapped the sodden jacket closer around him.

"Listen Kapitein," Sam fumbled inside the top of his clothes to reach the cord around his neck. "Take this, please." He took Jimmy's hand and placed it on the cord. "You must take this. Put it round your neck."

Jimmy tugged gently, lifting the cord over Sam's head. He felt a ring hanging from it and asked, "Is this Annie's?"

"Nee," Sam stuttered, "Not Annie's. She gave it to me. It was her mother's. You must give it to Annie."

"You should give it to her yourself, Sam." Jimmy's voice was gentle.

"I will, Kapitein, when we get properly married, but you look after it please."

"I promise."

"Danke." Sam leaned against Jimmy's shoulder.

*

That was how they were found, shortly after dawn. The coxswain of the whaler thought they were both dead when they bumped alongside the liferaft. Then the older man's eyes flickered open.

"Take the boy first," he whispered. "He's only just gone to sleep."

He watched as the men lifted the boy. They were gentle, almost as if afraid of waking him.

Epilogue

During my research I learnt what happened to many of the people mentioned in this account.

Admiral Sir William Teagle had no hesitation in recommending Henri and Faulkner for posthumous gallantry awards. Henri De Kuiper was awarded the Distinguished Service Cross and Gary Faulkner the Distinguished Service Medal.

Before Annie gave birth, she changed her name by deed poll to Da Souza. Her daughter was christened Martha Rachel. Her daughter, also christened Martha, kept her maiden name when she married and continues to farm in West Cornwall.

Miriam and Jannie lived together in her home throughout the war, devoting their time to helping families, especially, but not only, Jewish families in the area.

After the war they travelled to Holland to stay with Paul and Christina. That first visit was full of sorrow, for they learnt the dreadful fate that befell Simon, Judith and Rachel. They were walking in the countryside when Piet de Vink, Sam's boyhood friend, cycled past. Rachel recognised him and called out. Piet glanced across without stopping.

Simon, understanding they were now in great danger, hurried his family into a nearby copse.

Later realising it was Rachel who had called to him, Piet told his father, not knowing he was one of Holland's most notorious Jew-hunters.

De Vink raced to the copse and soon found them. Rachel screamed when he grabbed her, prompting Simon to hit him. De Vink drew his pistol and killed Simon.

De Vink was seen leading Judith and Rachel away at gunpoint. Discreet enquiries revealed they had been shipped to Auschwitz where they were murdered. Overcome by grief and guilt, Piet hanged himself.

Jannie and Miriam returned several times to stay with Paul and Christina. De Vink was found shot dead in his flat after one of their visits. His killer was never caught.

Henk and Sarah married and continued to work on the Colonel's estate. They had two children of their own and adopted Ruth when they learnt her parents had perished at Auschwitz.

Willem joined the Royal Navy, retiring as a seaman Petty Officer. He and his wife ran a guest house near Ramsgate, from where he could see the North Goodwin Light Vessel. Every year at the end of May he hired a fishing boat to take him out to cast a wreath upon the waters where Henri and Dirk were buried. Henk and Sarah often joined him.

Sir William and Emma Teagle moved to the Meon Valley in Hampshire when he retired. He drank his afternoon 'engineer's tea' from Sam's battered and stained tin mug. Osborne moved his mother from Portsmouth to a nearby cottage. He continued to help the Teagles and never had to polish the old oil lamp. Lady Teagle did that once a week.

Sam was buried at sea. He had given his knife and compass to Annie when he joined the Navy.

My father was landed in Malta where his leg was set before he was flown to England. He remembered nothing of what passed on the night of Sam's death until that afternoon before he died.

He was awarded the Distinguished Service Cross for gallantry in the withdrawal from Boulogne and never talked about that brief, violent action.

Philip Gale
Cornwall
2024

Acknowledgements

With the author's grateful thanks to:

My editor, Andrew Bridgmont, for his gentle guidance and support. Jo Fitzgerald for inspiring and encouraging me to write this book and Esther Kieboom for her insights into aspect of life in Holland during the war. Vanda Jeffrey of Essex Record Office for sending me details of the escape of *Malines*, including a letter by Captain Mallory to his wife.

Stuart Wood for reading and validating scenes in the engine room. Emma Ellis for all her help but especially for introducing me to Ian Hooper. Brittany Wilson for her dramatic cover design. Ian Hooper and all at Leschenault Press

And finally, to my dear wife, Philippa, for patiently listening to the story as it unfolded.

Why I wrote this story

My book is inspired by a woman I scarcely knew who gave me an unexpected hug while I was talking to her daughter after a concert in the local chapel.

We became friends and one day she told me what happened to her distant Dutch Jewish cousin, the composer Sim Gokkes, who had been arrested and sent to Auschwitz with his wife and daughter after a confrontation with a German. They were murdered in 1943.

Believing no one knew what had happened to their fourteen-year-old son, David, led me to write about how a young Jewish boy escaped from Holland.

During her research into the life of Sim, my friend and her partner stayed in Amsterdam onboard one of the old Dutch paddle-boats, now converted to a hotel.

Curiosity led me to find out more about those paddle-boats, and about Holland before and during the German invasion. My friend suggested I write a story. Covid gave me a wonderful opportunity to read widely, research deeply and start writing

And so, Samuel Da Souza, a 13 year-old Sephardic Jewish boy, came into my life and onto these pages. His adventures dominate my life to this day.

The themes of love, duty and service are explored in Rotterdam, at sea, in the East End of London and on a Cornish farm. Underlying the story is the love of an old man for the boy he unexpectedly has to care for. That love is like *a flower in winter.*

In writing this book, I drew on my own background, having been at sea, and working with people of all ages, backgrounds and nationalities as a Naval officer, a seafarer under sail and the director of three national youth charities, as well as having recently owned and run a café-bookshop with my wife.

As this is a story of another age and a different culture from mine, it has taken extensive research to present it according to historical facts and the perspective, language and geo-politics of the time.

I apologise to the people of Rotterdam and Chatham for the geographical liberties I have taken with their port and dockyard for the sake of the story.

In June 2024 I learnt that David Gokkes had not escaped. He was murdered with his family on 5th February 1943 in Auschwitz. This book is dedicated to his memory.

David James
28 October 2024

About the Author

While a student at Portsmouth Technical College, David was tempted to follow his heart and become a writer. Instead, having been brought up in a service family, duty called and he joined the Royal Navy as a seaman officer.

In 1971 he left the Senior Service to pursue his other dream - of becoming a professional civilian sailor.

Hard years followed before he was sufficiently experienced and qualified to captain groups of young Londoners on adventurous sailing voyages in a traditional old Norwegian sailing rescue ship.

In 1977 David was recruited to run Ocean Youth Club, Britain's largest sail training fleet. In 1985 he was head-hunted by the Drake Fellowship which he soon merged with Fairbridge to create Fairbridge-Drake. This became the UK's most effective motivational training charity for unemployed young people in inner cities.

David eventually left London for West Cornwall, where, at the age when most people retire, his wife suggested opening a bookshop. They transformed a local tea-room into a much-loved café and second-hand bookshop where David started writing poetry again, publishing *Any Cornish Beach* in 2009.

David relished the solitude imposed by the Covid lockdown and began to write his first novel, *A Flower in Winter*

www.ingramcontent.com/pod-product-compliance
Ingram Content Group UK Ltd.
Pitfield, Milton Keynes, MK11 3LW, UK
UKHW032238030225
4429UKWH00002B/400

9 781923 020894